THE BOOK OF SWORDS
PART II

THE BOOK OF SWORDS PART II

EDITED BY

GARDNER DOZOIS

HARPER
Voyager

Harper*Voyager*
An imprint of HarperCollins*Publishers* Ltd
1 London Bridge Street
London SE1 9GF

www.harpercollins.co.uk

This paperback edition 2018
1

First published by HarperCollins*Publishers* 2017

A catalogue record for this book is available from the British Library

ISBN: 978-0-00-827470-2

Set in Adobe Caslon Pro by Palimpsest Book Production Limited,
Falkirk, Stirlingshire

Printed and bound in the UK by CPI Group (UK) Ltd, Croydon CR0 4YY

MIX
Paper from
responsible sources
FSC
www.fsc.org FSC™ C007454

Copyright Acknowledgements

For George R.R. Martin, Fritz Leiber, Jack Vance,
Robert E. Howard, C. L. Moore, Leigh Brackett, L. Sprague de Camp,
Roger Zelazny, and all the other authors who ever wielded an
imaginary sword, and for Kay McCauley, Anne Groell, and
Sean Swanwick, for helping me bring this to you.

Contents

Introduction by Gardner Dozois	xi
When I Was a Highwayman by Ellen Kushner	3
The Smoke of Gold Is Glory by Scott Lynch	25
The Colgrid Conundrum by Rich Larson	69
The King's Evil by Elizabeth Bear	103
Waterfalling by Lavie Tidhar	135
The Sword Tyraste by Cecelia Holland	169
The Sons of the Dragon by George R.R. Martin	195

Introduction by Gardner Dozois

One day in 1963, I stopped in a drugstore on the way home from high school (at that point in time, spinner racks full of mass-market paperbacks in drugstores were one of the few places in our town where books were available; there was no actual bookstore), and spotted on the rack an anthology called *The Unknown*, edited by D. R. Bensen. I picked it up, bought it, and was immediately enthralled by it; it was the first anthology I ever bought, and a purchase that would have a long-term effect on my future career although I didn't know that at the time. What it was was a collection of stories that Bensen had culled from the legendary (if short-lived) fantasy magazine *Unknown*, edited by equally legendary editor John W. Campbell, Jr., who at about the same time as he was revolutionizing science fiction as the editor of *Astounding* was revolutionizing fantasy in the pages of *Astounding*'s sister magazine *Unknown* from 1939 to 1943, when the magazine was killed by wartime paper shortages. In the early sixties, in a decade when the publishing industry was still coming out from under the shadow of postwar grim social realism, there was very little fantasy being published in a format affordable to purchase by a short-of-funds high-school student (except for the stories in genre magazines such as *The Magazine of Fantasy & Science Fiction*, which I didn't know about at the time), and the rich harvest of different types of fantasy story available in *Unknown* was a revelation to me.

The story that had the biggest effect on me, though, was a bizarre, richly atmospheric story called "The Bleak Shore," by Fritz Leiber, in which two seemingly mismatched adventurers, a giant swordsman from the icy North named Fafhrd and a sly, clever, nimble little man from the Southern climes called the Gray Mouser, are compelled to go on a doomed mission which seems destined to send them to their death (which fate, however, they cleverly avoid). It was a story unlike anything I'd ever read before, and I immediately wanted to read more stories like that.

Fortunately, it wasn't long before I discovered another anthology on the drugstore spinner racks, *Swords & Sorcery*, edited by L. Sprague de Camp, this one not only containing another Fafhrd and the Gray Mouser story, but dedicated entirely to the same kind of fantasy story, which I learned was called "Sword & Sorcery," a name for the subgenre coined by Leiber himself; in the pages of this anthology, I read for the first time one of the adventures of Robert E. Howard's Conan the Barbarian and C. L. Moore's Jirel of Joiry, as well as stories by Poul Anderson, Lord Dunsany, Clark Ashton Smith, and others. And I was hooked, becoming a lifelong fan of Sword & Sorcery, soon haunting used-book stores in what was then Scollay Square in Boston (now buried under the grim mass of Government Center), hunting through piles of moldering old pulp magazines for back issues of *Unknown* and *Weird Tales* that featured stories of Conan the Barbarian and Fafhrd and the Gray Mouser and other swashbuckling heroes.

What I had blundered into was the first great revival of interest in Sword & Sorcery, a subgenre of fantasy that had at that point lain fallow for decades, with almost all of the material in those anthologies and those old pulp magazines having been published in the thirties or forties or even earlier, about the time that stories that took place in distinct fantasy worlds instead of seventeenth-century France or imaginary Central European countries began to precipitate out from the larger and older body of work about swashbuckling, sword-swinging adventurers written by authors such as Alexandre Dumas, Rafael Sabatini, Talbot Mundy, and Harold Lamb. After Edgar Rice Burroughs in *A Princess of Mars* and its many sequels sent adventurer John Carter to his own version of Mars, called Barsoom, to rescue princesses and have sword fights with giant four-armed Tharks, a closely parallel form to Sword & Sorcery sometimes called "Planetary Romance" or "Sword & Planet" stories developed, most prominently in the pages of pulp magazine *Planet Stories* between 1939 and 1955, with the two subgenres exchanging influences, and even many of the same authors, including authors such as C. L. Moore and Leigh Brackett, who were highly influential in both forms. The richly colored tales that made up Jack Vance's classic *The Dying Earth*, also published about then, were also technically science fiction, but with their inter-dimensional intrusions, strange creatures, and mages who wielded what could either be looked at as magic or the highest of high technology, they could also function as fantasy as well.

Probably not coincidentally, interest in Sword & Sorcery, which had faded over the wartime years and throughout the fifties, began to revive in the sixties, after the Mariner and Venera and other space probes were making it increasingly obvious that the rest of the solar system was incapable of supporting life as we knew it—no ferocious warriors to have sword fights with or beautiful princesses in diaphanous gowns to romance. Nothing but airless balls of barren rock.

From now on, if you wanted to tell those kinds of stories, you were going to have to do it in fantasy.

Throughout the early sixties, Sword & Sorcery boomed, with D. R. Bensen, L. Sprague de Camp, and Leo Margulies mining the rich lodes of *Unknown* and *Weird Tales* magazines for other anthologies (Bensen—an important figure in the development of modern fantasy, now, sadly, mostly forgotten—was the editor of Pyramid Books, and also mined the pages of *Unknown* for classic fantasy novels such as de Camp and Fletcher Pratt's *The Incomplete Enchanter* and *The Castle of Iron* to reprint), collections of the original Conan stories being reissued, new Conan stories and novels being produced by other hands, Michael Moorcock producing his hugely popular stories and novels about Elric of Melniboné (which have continued to the present day), and obvious imitations of Conan such as John Jakes's "Brak the Barbarian" stories being turned out. (At about this time, Cele Goldsmith, the editor of *Amazing* and *Fantastic* magazines, began to coax Fritz Leiber out of semiretirement and got him to write new Fafhrd and the Gray Mouser stories for *Fantastic*, which, once I noticed that, induced me to begin regularly picking a genre magazine up off the newsstands for the first time, which in turn induced me to begin buying science-fiction magazines such as *Amazing*, *Galaxy*, and *Worlds of If*—which means that, ironically, although I'd later become associated with science fiction, and would edit a science-fiction magazine myself, I came to them first because I was looking for more Fafhrd and the Gray Mouser stories in the pages of a fantasy magazine ... although to be fair I was at the same time reading SF such as the Robert A. Heinlein and Andre Norton "juveniles," and stuff such as Hal Clement's *Cycle of Fire* and—also published by Pyramid Books—*Mission of Gravity*.)

Then came J.R.R. Tolkien.

J.R.R. Tolkien's The Lord of the Rings trilogy is often cited these days as having single-handedly created the modern fantasy genre, but, while it is certainly hard to overestimate Tolkien's influence—almost every subsequent fantasist was hugely influenced by Tolkien, even, haplessly, those who didn't like him and reacted against him—what is sometimes forgotten these days is that Don Wollheim published the infamous "pirated" edition of *The Fellowship of the Ring* (the opening book of the trilogy) as an Ace paperback in the first place because he was casting desperately around for something—anything!—with which to feed the hunger of the swelling audience for Sword & Sorcery. The cover art of the Ace edition of *The Fellowship of the Ring* (by Jack Gaughn, of a wizard waving a sword and a staff aloft on top of a mountain) makes it clear that Wollheim thought of it as a "sword & sorcery" book, and his signed interior copy makes that explicit by touting the Tolkien volume as "a book of sword-and-sorcery that anyone can read with delight and pleasure." In other words, in the United States at least, the genre audience for fantasy definitely predated Tolkien, rather than being created by him, as the modern myth would have it. Don Wollheim knew very well that there was a genre fantasy audience already out there, already in place, a hungry audience waiting to be fed—although I doubt if even he had the remotest idea just how tremendous a response there would be to the tidbit of "sword & sorcery" that he was about to feed them. The Tolkien novels had already appeared in expensive hardcover editions in Britain, but the Ace paperback editions—and the "authorized" paperback editions that followed from Ballantine Books—made them available for the first time in editions that kids like me and millions of others could afford to buy.

After Tolkien, everything changed. The audience for genre fantasy may have already existed, but there can be no doubt that Tolkien widened it tremendously. The immense commercial success of Tolkien's work also opened the eyes of other publishers to the fact that there was an intense hunger for fantasy in the reading audience—and they too began looking around for something to feed that hunger. On the strength of Tolkien's success, Lin Carter was able to create the first mass-market paperback fantasy line, the Ballantine Adult Fantasy line, which brought back into print long-forgotten and long-unavailable works by writers such as Clark Ashton Smith, E. R. Eddison, James Branch Cabell, Mervyn Peake, and Lord Dunsany. A few years later, Lester del Rey took over from Lin Carter and began to search for more commercial, less high-toned stuff that would appeal more directly to an audience still hungry for something as much like Tolkien as possible. In 1974, he brought out Terry Brooks's *The Sword of Shannara*, and although it was dismissed by many critics as a clumsy retread of Tolkien, it proved hugely successful commercially, as did its many sequels. In 1977, Del Rey also scored big with *Lord Foul's Bane*, the beginning of the somewhat quirkier and less derivative trilogy, The Chronicles of Thomas Covenant the Unbeliever, by Stephen R. Donaldson, and *its* many sequels.

Oddly, as fantasy books began to sell better by far than ever before, interest in Sword & Sorcery began to fade. Sword & Sorcery had always been a subgenre mostly driven by short fiction, but, inspired by Tolkien, the new fantasy novels began to get longer and longer and spawn more and more sequels, and now began to be largely thought of as a distinct subgenre, "Epic Fantasy." It's sometimes difficult for me to make a distinction between Epic Fantasy and Sword & Sorcery—both are set in invented fantasy worlds, both have thieves and sword-wielding adventurers, both take place in worlds in which magic exists and there are sorcerers of greater or lesser potency, both feature fantasy creatures such as dragons and giants and monsters—although some critics say they can distinguish one from the other by criteria other than length. Be that as it may, as books thought of as Epic Fantasy became more and more prominent, people talked less about Sword & Sorcery. It never disappeared entirely—Lin Carter edited five volumes of the *Flashing Swords!* anthology series between 1971 and 1981, Andrew J. Offutt, Jr. edited five volumes of the *Swords Against Darkness* anthology series between 1977 and 1979, Robert Lynn Asprin started the long-running series of *Thieves' World* shared-world anthologies in 1978, Robert Jordan produced a long sequence of Conan novels throughout the eighties before turning to his multivolume Wheel of Time Epic Fantasy series, Glen Cook produced recognizable Sword and Sorcery work (notably his tales about the Black Company) throughout the same period, as did C. J. Cherryh, Robin Hobb, Fred Saberhagen, Tanith Lee, Karl Edward Wagner, and others; Marion Zimmer Bradley edited a long sequence of *Sword and Sorceress* anthologies, with the emphasis on female adventurers, throughout the seventies, and Jessica Amanda Salmonson produced a similarly female-oriented set of anthologies, *Amazons* and *Amazons II*, in 1979 and 1982 respectively.

Nevertheless, as the eighties progressed into the nineties, Sword & Sorcery continued to fade as a subgenre, until it was rarely ever mentioned and was in danger of being altogether forgotten.

Then, at the end of the nineties, things began to turn around.

Why they did is difficult to pinpoint. Perhaps it was the enormous commercial success of George R.R. Martin's *A Game of Thrones*, published in 1996, and its sequels, which influenced newer writers by showing them a grittier, more realistic, harder-edged kind of Epic Fantasy, one with characters who were often so morally ambiguous that it was impossible to tell the good guys from the bad guys. Perhaps it was just time for a new generation of writers, who had been influenced by the classic work of writers like Leiber and Howard and Moorcock, to take the stage and produce their own new variations on the form.

Whatever the reason, the ice began to thaw. Soon people began to talk about "The New Sword and Sorcery," and in the last few years of the twentieth century and the early years of the twenty-first century, there were writers such as Joe Abercrombie, K. J. Parker, Scott Lynch, Elizabeth Bear, Steven Erikson, Garth Nix, Patrick Rothfuss, Kate Elliott, Daniel Abraham, Brandon Sanderson, and James Enge making names for themselves, there were new markets in addition to existing ones such as *F&SF* for Sword & Sorcery, such as the online magazine *Beneath Ceaseless Skies* and print magazine *Black Gate*, and new anthologies began to appear, such as my own *Modern Classics of Fantasy* in 1997, which featured classic Sword & Sorcery stories by Fritz Leiber and Jack Vance, *The Sword & Sorcery Anthology*, edited by David G. Hartwell and Jacob Weisman, a retrospective of some of the best old stories of the form, and *Epic: Legends of Fantasy*, edited by John Joseph Adams, an anthology reprinting newer work by newer authors. Most importantly, *new* short work began to appear, collected in anthologies such as *Legends* and *Legends II*, edited by Robert Silverberg, and later in *Fast Ships, Black Sails*, edited by Ann VanderMeer and Jeff VanderMeer, and *Swords & Dark Magic: The New Sword and Sorcery*, edited by Jonathan Strahan and Lou Anders, the first dedicated anthology of the New Sword and Sorcery.

All at once, we were in the middle of another great revival of interest in Sword & Sorcery, one which has so far not faded again as we progress deeper into the second decade of the twenty-first century. Already there's another generation of newer writers such as Ken Liu, Rich Larson, Carrie Vaughn, Aliette de Bodard, Lavie Tidhar, and others, taking up the challenges of the form, and sometimes evolving it in unexpected directions—and behind *them* are yet more new generations.

So, call it Sword & Sorcery, or call it Epic Fantasy, it looks like this kind of story is going to be around for a while for us to enjoy.

I've edited other anthologies with new Sword & Sorcery stories in them, such as the Jack Vance tribute anthology *Songs of the Dying Earth*, *Warriors*, *Dangerous Women*, and *Rogues* (all edited with that other big-time Sword & Sorcery fan, George R.R. Martin), but I've always wanted to edit an anthology of nothing but such stories, which is what I've done here with *The Book of Swords*, bringing you the best work of some of the best writers working in the form today, from across several different literary generations.

I hope that you enjoy it. And it's my hope that to some young kid out there, it will prove as enthralling and inspirational as *Unknown* and *Swords & Sorcery* did to me back in 1963—and so a new Sword & Sorcery fan will be born, to carry the love of this kind of swashbuckling fantasy tale on into the distant future.

Ellen Kushner

Ellen Kushner's first novel, *Swordspoint*, introduced readers to Riverside, home of the city to which she has since returned in *The Privilege of the Sword* (a Locus Award winner and Nebula nominee), *The Fall of the Kings* (written with Delia Sherman), a handful of related short stories, and, most recently, the collaborative Riverside prequel *Tremontaine* for SerialBox.com and Saga Press. The author herself recorded all three novels in audiobook form for Neil Gaiman Presents / Audible.com, winning a 2012 Audie Award for *Swordspoint*. With Holly Black, she coedited *Welcome to Bordertown*, a revival of the original urban-fantasy shared-world series created by Terri Windling. A popular performer and public speaker, Ellen Kushner created and hosted the long-running public radio show *Sound & Spirit*, which Bill Moyers called "the best thing on public radio." She has taught creative writing at the Clarion and Odyssey workshops, and is an instructor in Hollins University's Children's Literature M.F.A. program. She lives in New York City with Delia Sherman and no cats whatsoever, in an apartment full of theater and airplane ticket stubs.

Here she introduces us to a young man newly arrived in Riverside to seek his fortune, one who, like many young men come to the big city before him, finds that he's got a lot to learn to succeed—and that many of the lessons aren't pleasant.

WHEN I WAS A HIGHWAYMAN

"Do it," Jess said. "It'll be fun."

I had no wish to be a highwayman, even for a day, but we needed the money. So I considered it.

Since I had come to Riverside, I had learned that not everyone there gives a stranger from the country good advice. If Riversiders advise a new blade to challenge that guy over there by the fire to a duel—you can take him, no problem!—well, it's lucky that you do turn out to be better than he is. Of course, now he hates you and won't recommend you for any jobs uptown, which is where the glory and the money are. Bad advice.

But since Jessamyn and I had begun keeping company toward the end of winter, I'd learned she usually had my best interests at heart, especially when it came to advice about making money. She was expert at that herself: the cleverest con artist the city had to offer, according to her admirers, and the slyest shyster ever to pick a pocket, according to the others.

Jessamyn was pretty, too. A mane of moon-pale hair such as I'd never seen before, fun to get tangled in at night, fun to braid up tight in the morning so she looked like a middle-city girl, decent yet delectable. That was how she played her game.

We made a good pair. *Silver and smoke; ice and steel,* people said. I could go anywhere with her: suddenly, all the taverns of Riverside were open to me, even the Maiden's Fancy, where women like Flash Annie and Kathy Blount told one another their secrets. Everyone knew Jess, and if they didn't like her, at least they admired her skill—and the way she took marks in uptown. She knew the handkerchief trick, the Lost Baby trick, the Pigeon Drop, and the Lover's Dare.

I never went on jobs with her, though, because it was important for people to know my face if I was going to get work—and it was very, *very* important that no one remember hers.

Jessamyn had a wardrobe a duchess would envy, for quantity if not for quality: velvet with the nap rubbed away in back, raveled silk stockings, lace frontlets and silk shawls stained underneath, ribbons in every color imaginable to trim and retrim her many hats, feathers picked up on the street—

"It just has to *look* right, Richard," she'd explain. "No one's going to lift up my fine linen skirt to see the patched petticoats underneath. If I paint a thing gold, and wear it like it's gold, only a jeweler will know it's not." She arched her neck, laughing. "And I never get anywhere near a real jeweler, so that's no problem."

I stroked the nape of her smooth neck, where the soft hair grew in an arrow shape. "I'll get you near a real one. We're going to make money, Jessamyn—*I'm* going to make it. A swordsman can get rich in this town. Look at Rivers. And de Maris, before his last fight. I'm going to be better than them. And then we'll go up to Lassiter's Row and buy you gold earrings with jewels in them, the biggest they've got!"

I didn't know much about jewels, then; not their names, nor what they were worth, really. I just liked the way they sparkled, catching the sun with a rainbow's fire. I'd only seen my first diamond, at a merchant's wedding I was playing guard at. I'd thought it was a composite of all other jewels, compressed into one, till someone set me right.

Jess and I shared a couple of rooms upstairs in a crumbling old house on a narrow street full of them. Like its neighbors, it had been grand and glorious once, before the rich abandoned Riverside to move over the Bridge into the rest of the city. Our two rooms still had carvings and fancy molding clinging to the peeling walls. There was plenty of space for Jess's massive collection of costumes. The house's owner was a laundress who plied her trade in the courtyard's ancient stone well and rented out her upstairs rooms by the week, which suited us fine.

Whenever either of us got—or did—a job, we'd pay Marie her rent first, then go out and spend the rest on whatever pleased our fancy: dresses and hats and fine cloaks for Jessamyn (really just business, she explained), and whatever pretty flotsam had turned up in the Old Market at the heart of Riverside: stuff salvaged from crumbling houses, things no one could pawn, like cracked porcelain vases, a fragment of gilded picture frame, a carved boxwood figure with its arms missing.

The money for that, I got from working a wedding uptown: the most boring job in the world. I always felt ridiculous with my sword out and that stupid wreath on my head, marching behind the bridal party to the temple, then standing there on display while the priests read the same words over each couple. It's not as though anyone was ever coming to actually steal away the bride.

Jess said it was a way to get noticed, and I was lucky I looked good in a wreath. "You're, what, barely eighteen?" she'd ask, knowing perfectly well I wasn't even that yet. "There's time."

But I hadn't come to the city to stand around watching people get married. Everyone here in Riverside knew I was a serious duelist; sometimes I was able to prove it there, when another swordsman got fresh with Jess, or a new blade came down looking for trouble and decided to see if I was any good.

Still, it was from working a wedding that I finally got a chance to prove myself to the ones who counted. I'd gotten the job because Hugo Seville was already scheduled for a demonstration duel at some Hill noble's birthday party, lucky stiff, so he'd passed the wedding job on to me.

"I'm recommending you because I know you'll do your best," he said pompously, as though there was real effort involved in standing very still and not scratching your nose. "These people are important, Richard. Lord Hastings never comes to town, but he's here to marry off his seventh daughter to Condell's eldest."

I could never remember their names; I just put on my clean shirt and my blue doublet, polished my boots, and went over the Bridge.

It was a very fancy wedding. A whole band of musicians walked us to the temple, not just one or two flute players. Little girls tossed lavender and rosemary in the bride's path; when we stepped on the herbs, the scent made me suddenly homesick for my mother's garden.

I wasn't the only swordsman, either. Lord Hastings had a House Sword who walked beside me, a tall, quiet, older man who didn't want trouble; I could tell by the way he gave me enough space, and I appreciated that.

Lord Hastings' blade and I left the temple together, well after the musicians had played the wedding party and their guests away. Our part was done; I guess the bride belonged to her husband's family, now. Hastings' swordsman was no Riversider: maybe one of those men who learn from an academy, or even from their fathers, and make their way up in a nobleman's service, fighting exhibition duels, doing weddings, showing off grace and form, and standing ready in case anyone tries to challenge their noble masters. I'd never really gotten the chance to talk to one of them; the last wedding with two swords, the other wouldn't answer any questions, and when I challenged him after, he spat and called me Riverside guttertrash, the poser.

I was beginning to think about asking Lord Hastings' quiet swordsman how to get work as a duelist uptown, when suddenly he staggered and fell against the wall.

"Are you hurt?" I said. He was very pale.

A woman in a simple dress with bright starched cap and collar came running up. "Oh, George, George, I told you you were too ill for this today!"

"Marjorie." He grinned feebly at her. "How could I disappoint his lordship, after all this time? And little Amilette . . . Lucky Seventh, right? Didn't she look lovely?"

"You're going to disappoint him even more, now, for you're in no fit shape to duel for the guests at the party."

He'd started shivering; some kind of fever, I guessed. There were a lot of those in the city. "They've seen me fight before. Many times. They'll like seeing someone new. What's your name, boy?"

I let the "boy" go because he was so ill.

"Richard St. Vier."

"Of the banking St. Viers?" the woman asked.

"Do I look like a banker?" But I said it with a smile; I'd gotten used to that question here. (My mother had once been a daughter of that family—but that was no one's business but hers.) "I am a swordsman, madam, and I would be happy to take up this duel if you will tell me where to go."

"Come, George." She had her arms around him. "I'll take you home. And you, Master St. Vier, if you could just give me a hand with him— No, of course you don't need one, George, but I do!—I'll give you directions to Lord Condell's. You've got plenty of time; there's all the eating and drinking before the entertainment."

I'd never been up on the Hill before, where the nobles' fine houses were. They didn't want you there if you weren't working for them. But this time

I was, so I walked boldly along the wide, open streets lined with the walls and massive iron gates of great houses on either side. An occasional carriage passed me—one of theirs, flash with high-headed horses and glitzy harness—or a liveried servant, on foot, out on some errand I couldn't imagine.

At Lord Condell's house I gave my name, explained my business, and assured them that I was not there to challenge their master at his son's wedding feast. They reminded me that I was to use the *back* entrance, but that Cook might have something hot for me.

Lord Condell's servants were all madly busy with the feast and didn't have time for me. So I went out to the side yard to warm up and practice my moves until someone came out to tell me it was time.

The duel was to be held in the entry hall of the house. Very dressed-up people encircled the space, many of them on the landing to the main stairs, and more of them crowding the stairs themselves or leaning from the upstairs balcony. I walked slowly, trying to look like I knew what I was doing. The people didn't matter, but my opponent did.

He was a fair man of about my size and reach. I stood across the hall from him while a liveried man announced:

"For the honor and pleasure of the bride and groom, the duel will be to first blood, or until one man yields."

I knew about first blood. It could mean a scratch, a slash, or a deep puncture wound. I imagined duels at a wedding feast called for just a scratch, and took a long breath to remind myself to go no further in this bout.

After a few more formalities, it began.

My opponent and I moved slowly, testing, observing, as is right. We circled each other. The crowd was silent. In Riverside, they would have started shouting bets already. I made a feint to see what he'd do, and he did nothing but raise his eyebrows and cock up one corner of his mouth at me. Not easily drawn. This was going to be a longer fight than I'd expected.

We let the swords converse a little, back and forth, feeling each other's strength in the pressure of the blades, trying to hide our real abilities from each other. Suddenly his high wrist dropped and he struck low, like a swooping falcon; but I'd felt it coming and countered easily. He stepped back, surprised, to give himself time to assess, and to avoid me.

Once they start stepping back, you have them. I pressed forward, forward, forward, quickly, not giving him time to think, showing off a new move every time for those who could see fast enough, wanting to impress them all. He defended himself ably, but I never let him pick up an attack, just kept pushing him back.

He was a pleasure to fight because I knew it would be hard to make my touch on him but that he didn't stand a chance at hitting me. When we closed together with our *quillons* crossed, he hissed at me, "What are you doing? Fall back!"

I understood his words only well enough to gasp, "What? No!"

He turned his blade so that we half circled each other, still close together. "This is for their entertainment! They want to see some back-and-forth!"

I disengaged, sliding my blade back along his, until their tips alone touched. We messed around like that for a bit, like some kind of kiddie training exercise, circling each other, circling the blades ... The noble guests were enchanted. They seemed to think something was happening, and started shouting encouragement. I saw a woman's face, very white, her hands twisting a handkerchief as though there were real danger here. Were these the arbiters of skill, the people I was so eager to impress?

My opponent thought he held the match in his hand, that having acceded to his suggestion, I would let him control the finish. With a triumphant grin, he advanced ferociously.

I fell back just long enough to gauge my distance and leap in over his blade, touching him in the upper breast as gently as I could manage. It drew blood. The bout was over.

My opponent bowed, and was helped away by a footman. I stood there in the hallway with shouts of "Blood!" and "Bravo!" ringing in my ears, wondering what I should do next. A servant brought me a silver cup filled with a cool drink. When I'd emptied it, the nobles started crowding around me, congratulating me, asking my name, how long had I been in Lord Hastings' employ, did I take commissions, what was my next fight, where could they find me ... ?

To be honest, it was a little too much. Success was wonderful, new jobs were wonderful, but the people all moving in and out of my vision, arms and hands and heads, right after I'd been fighting—

"Richard St. Vier," I said. "My name is St. Vier, and you can find me in Riverside. At the, ah, the Maiden's Fancy. Thank you. Yes, thank you. I must—I have to go and clean my blade. Really. It's important. If you'd just let me through—"

"Absolutely."

A young man with soft, curling brown hair and one red jewel in his ear raised a hand where I could see it, and slowly put his arm around my shoulder. They fell back a little when he did that, and I was grateful. "You must go and refresh yourself, Master St. Vier. Allow me to assist you."

The crowds parted for us. He was in lace and velvet: one of them. "Have you been paid?" he murmured. I shook my head. "Well, never mind. Condell is busy now; you can come back tomorrow. "

Instead of away toward the kitchens, he led me out the big front door. The air on the steps was cooler. "Just a moment," he said. "Stay here while I send for my carriage."

The seats in the nobleman's carriage were soft as down. It smelt a little of leather, a little of horses, and a little of the man himself, a scent like roses and amber.

"My name is Thomas Berowne," he told me. He rested his gloved hand on my leg for a moment, and I let him. "Please allow me to take you wherever you wish to go." He ducked his head slightly. "This includes my own rooms if you would be so kind as to have it so."

I thought, Why not? Jess wouldn't mind; she was out some nights herself, keeping up contacts, solidifying friendships, forging alliances or just plain having fun. She might even be pleased to learn that I had been taken home by a lordling.

Lord Thomas Berowne was courtesy itself. When we came to his family town house, we took a side entrance, "so as not to alarm my parents," and went up one set of stairs then another, into a room all rosy with velvet and firelight, shadows playing on a glint of painting here, a fall of tapestry there.

He was beautiful without his clothes on, and he knew how to please me. My boyhood friend Crispin and I had had our little rituals, but Thomas Berowne was a grown man who clearly had a lot of practice. All that night, when I woke to the fall of the light on his skin, or the candles guttering, or a glass of wine being sleepily handed to me, I felt oddly safe, and oddly happy. He asked very few questions, but I found myself telling him about my hopes for work, my wish to challenge worthy opponents, to duel to my utmost strength and skill. Until I had come to the city, I hadn't realized I was that good. I thought everyone could do what I do, more or less, with the right training. My drunk old master, a wanderer my mother had taken in off the road out of pity, who had trained me mercilessly, always told me not to be too sure of myself. I took that to heart. But he had also taught me how to assess an opponent and how to take advantage of their every weakness. The men I'd fought so far in the confines of Riverside were no match for me; those who were steered clear of my sword. There were no demonstration bouts in Riverside.

Thomas Berowne was only a little older than me—not yet twenty, as he admitted, and so, though his father was rich, he wasn't, and he was also a second son. What funds he had went to collecting objects of art, and he hoped I didn't take offense if he said I was one of the finest, ". . . not that I could afford your true price."

I asked what he thought that was, wondering uneasily if he was planning to pay me. That would make me a nobleman's whore, which was far from my ambition. He kissed me, said this was an open exchange of willing hearts. He said that my skill with the sword might be for the marketplace, but when it came to . . . Well, I can't honestly remember what he said, but it was along those lines.

You couldn't exactly call it morning when we finally got out of bed to drink the chocolate his valet had brought in. It was amazing stuff; you couldn't get anything like that in Riverside. There were crisp white rolls, too, and butter so sweet it must have come from the country.

In the light of day, I admired the nobleman's treasures: the tapestry of lovers in a rose garden that covered half a wall; the ancient chest carved with deer and oak leaves, gleaming with beeswax . . . even the bed curtains were works of art, embroidered with moons and stars.

I picked up something small, an ivory statue of a boy king, with his many braids and naked chest, barely bigger than my palm. "I know you can't afford a swordsman," I told him lightly, trying not to want it too much. "But I'd fight a challenge for this."

Thomas Berowne's lips curved. His curly hair was tousled, and his mouth was the kissable color of certain roses. "You have good taste," he said. "You could fight a dozen challenges for that, and still not come near its worth."

I put it down carefully.

"Now then." Lord Thomas kissed my shoulder. "I am expected somewhere, and I imagine you are, too. It will, however, take me much longer to be made presentable to the outside world, so if you'd like me to call my carriage to carry you up to Lord Condell's—"

I shook my head. Their houses were so close I was amazed that he felt the need to ride between them.

"Well, then," Lord Thomas said; "let me assist you in dressing, to make up for being so eager to undress you last night."

As he slipped the linen shirt over my head, I realized that it was much finer than my own. I didn't say anything; he probably had chests full of them, and if this was the gift he wanted to give me, well, having a third shirt to my name was only to the good.

I found Jessamyn at the Maiden's Fancy, drinking with our friend Kathy Blount.

"Well, if it isn't the great St. Vier!" Jess tipped her chair back. "And here I thought you'd run off with the bride."

"She wouldn't have me," I said casually. "So I fought a duel instead."

"Yeah, at Lord Condell's; I heard." I'd been looking forward to telling her myself. "Nimble Willie was just up there, checking it out for Kathy's ma and her gang. He went as a delivery boy, and they were all bragging about your fight in the kitchens."

I spilled Lord Condell's coins on the table in front of her. Kathy, at least, had the grace to look impressed. Jess just grabbed one and held it up like a prize. "Rosalie! This is for the tab—and for another round. For the house! For luck! For Annie."

She was far from sober. "Where's Annie?" I said. "What happened?"

Kathy wiped her eyes with the back of her hand. "Annie got nabbed. Yesterday morning. They whipped her today, in Justice Place. Jessamyn went, and I went with her. So she knew we both was there in the crowd."

"*Were* there," Jess corrected savagely. "You'll never make it uptown if you talk like that, Kath. You'll end up just like Annie, rotten straw from the jail in your hair, your dress torn open for them to see your tits while they whip you for stealing what they wish they had—"

"Shut up!" Kathy pushed back from the table so fast her bench tipped over. "You just shut up, Jessamyn Fancypants! You think you're any better?

You may be able to pass uptown for an hour's grift, but you drink and you fuck down here in Riverside with the rest of us."

I knew Kath had a knife up her sleeve, but she made no move to use it, so I just watched as she knuckled her eyes with her fist, rose, and dashed out of the tavern.

Jess made a face.

"Cheapskate didn't even pay her tab," she said. She took another coin from my pile. "But that's all right. We've got plenty to spend, now, love, haven't we? Let's go see if Salamander still has that snake-headed dagger you liked."

I put my hand over hers. "Rent first," I said. "That's the rule. And while we're back there, maybe we should go upstairs." I put my hands behind her head, weaving my fingers in her moonlight hair, and I kissed her there in the tavern, I wanted her so much.

She slid her free hand down my thigh. "Rules are rules," she said. "Let's go pay the rent and have some fun."

The snake-headed dagger was gone, but Salamander had a plain one with a balance so perfect it could have been made for me. We got that, and a dagger made of glass because it was just so unbelievable, and bangles for Jess that Sal said came from Cham, and five silver forks that ended in nymph's heads. Then we went over to Maddie's to see what clothing she had in. Jessamyn carefully scrutinized all the servants' castoffs for the best, dresses made over from hand-me-downs of generous mistresses that could be tarted up to look new. She found a skirt and petticoat almost perfect, and a bundle of collars and neckerchiefs Mad let her have for cheap because they'd been scorched by a careless ironing maid. Jessamyn spent some time cooing over an old bodice of gold thread brocade, most of its tiny silk rosettes still intact, but then said she had no use for it. I bought it for her anyway, just for fun. We found plenty of use for it back home.

We went on spending freely because we knew there would be more. And, that spring, there was. Nobles started sending emissaries down to the Maiden, offering me jobs. Demonstration bouts, mostly, for parties and things—still no actual duels, but Jess and our friend Ginnie Vandall said to be patient, that was how you got noticed. Ginnie knew everything about swordsmen.

She didn't like it when I turned down Lord Condell's offer to spend a month on his summer estates. I told her I'd just come from the country, and I didn't want to turn around and go back there. I didn't say I didn't want to leave Jess for so long, but that was clear.

Then Jess got pregnant, despite all our care, and it was expensive to get rid of it. She was sick for a while after and couldn't go out on jobs. That was when the money started drying up for me, too. I went over all my recent paying duels, trying to figure out what I'd done wrong. Was I too predictable? Should I have let someone beat me, just the once?

"I could have told you," Ginnie said. "Take all the work while you can get it! Yeah, even the weddings, Richard. Because guess what? Summer's coming, and they all go to the country. Not just Lord Condell. No one needs a swordsman here in summer."

"Richard only takes the jobs he wants, now." Jess coiled around me on the settle like a big white cat. We both knew Ginnie fancied me like mad, but whatever I got up to on the Hill, I had only one love in Riverside. "He's sick of weddings. Everyone knows he's the best. We'll be just fine till their lordships come home in the fall and start having fun again."

First we had to pawn the nymph forks. And sell the brocade bodice, then pawn Jessamyn's winter clothes. "I'll get them back," she said with a shrug. "Soon as I'm better."

When that day came we braided her hair up tight again, and she went across the Bridge to find a mark and make some money with the Turned-Out Servant Girl trick.

"I'm thin enough now." She grinned at me. "It'll be a snap."

Jess came home with a kerchief full of apples, bread and new cheese, and we gorged ourselves on food and kisses. But when I lifted her skirts, I found her petticoats were gone.

"I'll get them back," she said fiercely. "It's my stuff, I can do what I want with it. I just wasn't ready, yet."

I sold the green glass, and the armless statue, because the Salamander wouldn't take them in pawn. Maddie bought back most of Jess's linen— "Your luck will turn," she said, and pressed one of the scorched collars back into Jessamyn's hands. "A girl's got to earn a living. Don't worry, love, I've seen it before. You'll come around."

If there were any wedding jobs, I would have taken them. But it seemed summer wasn't a good time for weddings, either.

That was when Marco and Ivan came up with their grand scheme.

We were drinking at Rosalie's, because her tavern is underground, in the cellar of an old town house. The cellar was god-awful damp in winter, but in summer it was a blessing. Even her beer was relatively cool—and Rosalie was one of the few who still let us eat on credit.

"Richard St. Vier!" They strolled on up to our table, feathers in their hats and a swagger in their stride. "Have you ever been on the highway?"

"Of course I've been on the highway. How do you think I got here?"

Ivan poked Marco in the ribs. "I like this kid. He's got a sense of humor."

Jess just sat there with a little smile at the corner of her lips, watching the show.

"Richard." Marco leaned into the table. He was unarmed, so I let him. "Where do you think this hat came from? Or these buckles? Or these shoes?" I waited. They were really ugly buckles. "From noblemen's coaches, that's where. Out on the highway. Where they pass to and fro without a care, just waiting for gentlemen like us to stop and relieve them of some of their gold."

"And personal effects," said Ivan, stroking the world's gaudiest hatpin.

Marco turned to Jessamyn. "There are ladies, too, you know. Miserable old hags wearing silks and jewels they shoulda left off long ago, to adorn some younger, sprightlier dame."

Jessamyn nodded. "Go on, Richard," she said brightly. "You should try it! You can get me some new petticoats."

I asked, "What would I have to do?"

"There's a carriage coming by," Marco said. "Tomorrow morning. Carrying all kinds of fancy stuff. I had it from Fat Tom, whose brother's wife's cousin works up on the Hill and knows the guy who's driving. All we have to do is lie in wait at a particular bend in the road we happen to be familiar with, well hid from any passersby. You step out and challenge the driver. The coach stops, and—"

Who did they think I was? "I'm not challenging any driver!" A sword fights only other swords.

Jess stroked my arm. "You don't challenge him, not really. Just get him to stop."

"Or we can do that," Ivan said hastily. "We can stop him, if you want. It just looks better when you do it. You know, with a sword."

"But there's a guard," Marco explained. "A footman, usually, not a blade, but trained with knives and stuff. Sometimes two of them. Plus the coachman. That's where you come in."

"Scare 'em off. They'll know what swords can do. They respect that. You just round 'em up and keep 'em still. Look menacing. Don't let 'em pull any tricks, while we rifle the coach, then we're off!"

"Off in the bushes, or off on a horse?" Jess asked.

Marco looked pious. "We always rent Brown Bess. She is most reliable, and has a very smooth trot."

"She's not going to carry three."

"They're not going to chase after a swordsman."

It sounded like hell to me. "I'd rather do weddings." But that wasn't entirely true. And Jess knew it.

"At least you'll get to fight, Richard," she said; "or pretend to, anyway. You can fix them with that awful stare you get when you're practicing. And I promise you won't be bored."

"Easy money," Marco said.

"Do it," Jess said. "It'll be fun!"

I was plenty bored.

Marco and Ivan appeared on Brown Bess at the white part of dawn, when many Riversiders were just coming home off jobs. They let me ride up behind them, and we plodded along the highway for a long time, until we came to their particular spot. Ivan tied up Bess in the woods, and we lay on a verge in the still-damp grass, watching the road.

And watching the road. And watching the road. I fell asleep for a little bit; then Ivan nudged me with a "Here they come!" but it was only a delivery cart, its two mules laboring slowly up the slope.

"Remember," Marco murmured when it had passed. "Don't kill anyone. It is very important that you don't kill anyone."

"Why?"

"For robbery, you get jailed and lashed. For murder, you swing. All of us."

I said nothing. "Yeah," said Ivan; "it's a funny old world. You kill a guy in a duel for them, it's right as rain, no questions asked. We kill someone by accident while trying to make a living, and it's up the gibbet to do the Solo Jig."

"Of course," Marco added, "if you do kill anyone—if we do, I mean—you'd better kill them all."

"Why?"

"So they don't tell. That way, we've got a chance."

I was very, very sorry I'd come. This was all I needed, to be marked out a common murderer, and with a true blade, yet. That would be the end of me as a swordsman, the end of everything my old master had taught me. All for nothing.

"Hey, now." Marco must have seen my frown. "Nobody's getting killed, here. The highway life is all gold and glory, don't let anyone tell you otherwise. They may even write a song about you! You know, like that one about Dapper Dan, or whatever his name is." He started singing: "Dapper Dan, Dapper Dan, steals your wife and bones your—"

"Shhh!" Ivan flapped his hand at us. "They're coming!"

This time, they truly were.

Matched white horses pulled a gorgeous carriage. It looked strangely familiar to me—and when Ivan and Marco had stopped it, pulled the coachman off his perch while I held the horses, then had me threaten the footman with my blade until he and the coachman were safely tied up together, I found out why.

Marco banged on the door of the carriage with the butt of his knife, scarring the painted coat of arms with a certain pleasure. The young nobleman who emerged was very familiar, indeed.

"Hello, Thomas," I said.

"Richard!" He looked almost pleased. "What are you doing here?"

"I'm afraid my associates and I are going to take all your money and jewels, now."

Lord Thomas Berowne was scared, I could tell—but he handled it well: Though his hand was shaking, he kept his voice even and his head high.

"If you must, you must," he said. "My father will be very upset, but when I explain how you outnumbered us, I'm sure he'll understand."

"This is messed up," Ivan said, craning around the horses to see what was going on. "Stop talking and knock him out."

I hesitated. It was messed up. Marco sighed gustily. "All right, we get it, Richard: the one noble in town you actually know, you've worked for him, you don't want to lose a patron. Just our luck. As usual. You should've come masked."

"Just so," said Lord Thomas, in that soft and friendly way of his. "It is unfortunate that we had to meet again like this, Master St. Vier. The Watch—and my father—will demand a full description of the criminals." He pointed his chin at Marco. "You gentlemen, of course, I do not know."

Both his hands were shaking badly now. I was surprised he was still standing, because usually the knees go first. "My father is hard to lie to, but I will try."

"How kind," Marco sneered. "What for?"

Berowne turned to me. "If I might ask, in return, that you would consent to visit me again? Soon?"

"Yes," I said, surprised. "I would like that."

"See, Richard," Marco crowed. "And you even got a job out of it! Now let's bash him on the head and get this over with."

Berowne paled, and Marco said with savage cheer, "Fathers like it when we bash you on the head."

"I'd rather you didn't," Thomas said desperately. "I have a very soft head—my father says so—"

"Shut up," snapped Marco, but I said:

"Wait."

"Richard, what the hell are you doing?"

"Knocking him out," I said.

I knew Thomas closed his eyes when he kissed, and kept them closed. So I sheathed my sword and put my arms around him, and my damp cloak, as well, hiding Ivan and Marco from his sight and he from theirs. It was sort of lovely, the way his whole body was shaking against me. I kissed him, and after a while he started kissing back, a thing he does very well.

Behind us, Marco and Ivan were looting the carriage. I murmured with pleasure, so Thomas wouldn't hear them, wouldn't think about it. He pressed in closer to me. His hands had stopped shaking, were moving against my back. I wasn't sure how long either of us was going to be able to remain standing. I wanted to shove him up against the side of the carriage, which would be foolish, or against one of those god-awful trees, which would be difficult. The more I thought about it, the more I wanted to—so it was a relief when I heard Marco say, "Let's go."

"What about his rings?" Ivan whined.

I unpeeled myself from Thomas Berowne. "Leave the goddamned rings," I said harshly, not quite master of my breath. "Get in the coach, Thomas, and keep your head down." Luggage was scattered across the road; shirts and stockings and waistcoats and broken-open boxes and books. "Leave it! Leave it and get in. No, don't, Marco—"

But this time, they didn't heed me. Marco elbowed him in the kidneys, then bound his hands with a neckcloth, stuffed a stocking in his mouth, and left Lord Thomas Berowne in his coach for the next traveler to find.

As arranged, we met up at the Four Horse Quarters, a tavern on a side road to Azay, about a mile outside of town. Marco and Ivan were in the back room, organizing their takings, which ranged from plentiful coins to jeweled neck pins. They were delighted to see me.

"So," Ivan said, practically bouncing on his toes; "we're gonna do that again, right?"

"Not really."

"Not really? But it was perfect! You're even more than a Gentleman Robber—you're the Robber Lover! There'll be songs out there in a week. Less!"

"Not just songs"—Marco leered—"they'll be lining up on the high road to get 'knocked out' by you!"

"Just watch you don't knock 'em *up*!" said Ivan, which was his idea of humor.

"No," I said again, taking the flagon from in front of him and drinking it straight down. "I spent hours in the grass getting bored and wet. I'm going to have to oil my sword again, and I didn't really use it. I had to walk all the way back here. And I missed a whole day's practice."

Marco sat back a little, his hands on the table. "And the money?"

"I'll take it."

Jess and I lived well for a few weeks. We got her linen back, and I bought her a dress, nearly new, white with bright flowers scattered all over it. She put it on to go uptown to do the Missing Pocket trick, her braids tidy, her skirts neat, looking for all the world like the pampered daughter of a country gentleman.

She came home late, red-faced and drunk, her hair in a half-knot, the rest straggling down her front. I hadn't realized how dark it had gotten: I'd been practicing, which is important whether you have work or not, and I don't really need to see if there's no one else there.

"Look!" she said. "Look what he gave me!"

She parted her hair to display a gold necklace, curlicued and jeweled. "Dipped," she said. "And fake. But it'll be real next time." Her kiss tasted of brandy. That was her favorite, when she could get it. "I'm coming up in the world!"

I didn't ask her what happened. Sometimes, things just did. I had to hear it from Nimble Willy, that Jess had nearly been nabbed up on Tilton Street. But the man with the necklace had stepped forward and vouched for her to the Watch, then he offered her a drink.

She sold the necklace, and bought more dresses. When she came back from her expeditions in town, she didn't boast of her sharp cons, the way she used to. Sometimes, she didn't want to talk at all.

That gave me more time to practice. It was a hot summer, and our rooms were stifling. Jess thought I should go drill out in the courtyard, but that was too public: the moves I practiced were mine. A winning fight is where they don't have any idea what you're likely to do next.

Jess said my endless practice was no fun, and she started spending more time out at Riverside taverns. That might not have been such a great idea. I could see for myself that her hands were shaky sometimes. Picking gentlemen's pockets would be out of the question. And yet she came home with all kinds of gauds and bangles. "Coming up in the world," she'd tell anyone who asked her. "Marks can be so stupid if you know how to manage them." And no one contradicted her. Maybe because she shared some of her trinkets out with her friends at the Maiden's Fancy, the ones she didn't keep, the ones she didn't sell.

You'd think she had enough stuff to play with, but she started messing with my things, as well: prancing around the room in nothing but my sword belt, playing childish games with my dragon candlesticks, going through all my shirts looking for holes, over and over . . . When she tried to mess with my good knives, I'd had it. Those edges are perfect, and needed to remain that way. "They're not toys," I told her; "and they're not yours. Leave them be."

So she picked up the glass dagger, and wound her bright, heavy hair up off her neck with one hand, pinning it in place with the blade. It looked good, and I told her so. She just tossed her head—"Glad you like it"—and went out.

From then on, I kept both knives on me, the weight balancing my hips.

It was a warm evening, and I was practicing. Jessamyn and I had woken early that morning and taken our pleasure together slowly and lazily for once, until the sun blazed through the cracks in the shutters, and we unstuck ourselves from the sweaty unit we had become. I lay in bed, drying myself with a corner of the sheet, watching Jessamyn sponge herself off with the water in the basin. She was like an ivory statue herself, pale body with its smooth and perfect curves, hair pale in the shadows, falling like a river carved by a careful hand.

She didn't ask me for help braiding her hair. Quickly and efficiently, she did it in one long, thick plait, and then she gave it a twist and secured it with the glass dagger. She dressed in a white linen smock, and a blue linen kirtle and bodice, then started draping herself with some of the trinkets she'd been collecting. I thought they looked garish, but I didn't say anything; she didn't like it when I had opinions. She said she knew her business best.

"I'm off," she said.

I said, "D'you have to go?"

"Oh, yes," she answered brightly. "He's taking me to luncheon at the King's Head."

I'd never heard of the place. I fell back asleep for a bit. Then I got up, and washed in the courtyard, dressed and went out to find something to eat. There were no messages of employment for me at the Maiden's Fancy. Rosalie hadn't heard of any stray jobs, either. So I went home to practice.

I was working on a new move that a blade in my last duel had nearly taken me down with. First I had to see my opponent clearly, and then I had to become him, executing the sequence so slowly that a child could have pierced through it, before speeding up, faster and faster.

The light was fading when Jess came waltzing in with a bright, fringed shawl. She tried to tickle me with the fringe. I shook her off, the way you do a fly: She knew better than to disturb me when I was working, I'd told her a dozen times.

"Rich-a-ard," she sang, "how do you like my new duds?"

"Later." Sweat was pouring down my chest. But I had to get the new move solid in my body so I knew it was there to count on next time, so fast my next opponent would never even see it coming.

"Oh, come on," she teased. She darted in to flick me with that shawl, like a kid taking a dare, and darted back out.

"Stop it, Jess." It's not wise to come at a swordsman unannounced.

"No, *you* stop it!" She started marching around the edges of my vision, in a distracting little semicircle. "You can practice later. Don't you want to have some fun?"

"I don't like 'fun.'"

"You don't, do you? Not anymore." She worked her bodice loose, bared a shoulder to me like some girl on the street. I saw it out of the corner of my eye, but I ignored her. "Like what you see?"

"Will you please—"

"I'm not just here to decorate the room, you know."

"I know." I tried to keep my sharpness and attack for my drill, but it came out in my voice: "I know, I know, now will you please shut up?"

"I will not shut up!" she shrieked, a sudden explosion, and she grabbed my free arm, a move I was not expecting. "You *look* at me! And you listen to me!"

Sweat was dripping into my eyes so I could hardly see. *"You don't care about me, you country son of a bitch! All you care about is your sword. You'd be dead if it weren't for me!"* I don't know how I even understood the words, they were so loud and high. *"You think you're too good to go out and earn your living like the rest of us, well, let me tell you, I do what I can to survive, do you even notice? You think you're some nobleman? You think you're too fine to do anything but practice until your next big duel?"* The noise was intolerable. *"When did you get so fancy, huh? When did you get too good for the rest of us?"* I didn't know how to make her stop. *"Look at you, waiting here at home for me to come back with whatever I can get for whatever I have to do and it's hard but you think I've lost my style I've got plenty of style, more than you'll ever have, you can't even get a job I haven't lost my nerve I have plenty of nerve left when it comes to whoresons like you Riverside doesn't want you I don't want you."*

She pulled the glass dagger from her hair. Silver tumbled all around her, so there must have been moonlight. She was coming at me with the knife still saying those things. I had to make her stop.

The moon was so bright it cast shadows all around.

Kathy Blount came by in the morning, with the sun barely up. She knocked on the door again and again, and when she opened it she stared at what she saw and stuck both fists in her mouth.

"She was screaming," I tried to tell her, and Kathy turned and ran.

After that, people steered clear of me for a while. It was a respectful distance, and I didn't mind. I never like it when people crowd me. Then a new swordsman came to town, flashy and boastful, annoying as hell. I challenged him on the street, killed him clean and fair with one blow, straight to the heart, and after that I was Riverside's own true blade again. Ginnie Vandall was annoyed because she'd just taken up with Hugo Seville, and it would be dangerous to dump him now, not to mention foolish. Hugo did weddings; Hugo did demonstration bouts; Hugo would fight a golden retriever if it made him popular with the nobles, or the merchants paid him enough.

I didn't go back to the Maiden's Fancy, even at summer's end. The stew at Rosalie's was better, and my credit seemingly inexhaustible.

So it was there that Marco and Ivan found me, back from their summer jaunt up north, and greeted me like a long-lost friend. Did I want to go back on the highway? they asked. Did I want to make some real money, this time? The summer had been tough on me, they'd heard, and hardly any of the nobles back in town yet, so jobs must be scarce, and the nights were getting cold. They'd missed me, up in Hartsholt, truly they had, though my style would be wasted up there, and now they were back in the city, how about it?

I told them *No*. It didn't matter what they offered, or how hard up I was.

I wasn't doing that again.

It leads to things I'd rather not think about.

And it wasn't any fun.

Scott Lynch

Fantasy novelist Scott Lynch is best known for his Gentleman Bastard series, about a thief and con man in a dangerous fantasy world, which consists of *The Lies of Locke Lamora*, which was a finalist for both the World Fantasy Award and the British Fantasy Society Award, *Red Seas Under Red Skies*, and *The Republic of Thieves*. His most recent book is another Gentleman Bastard story, *The Thorn of Emberlain*. He maintains a website at scottlynch.us. He lives with his wife, writer Elizabeth Bear, in Massachusetts.

Here he takes us along on an insanely dangerous quest with a down-on-his-luck thief who has nothing left to lose, and who finds that by finding everything, he gains nothing—except for a rousing story to tell on a cold winter's night.

THE SMOKE OF GOLD IS GLORY

Sail north from the Crescent Cities, three days and nights over the rolling black sea, and you will surely find the tip of the Ormscap, the fire-bleeding mountains that circle the roof of the world like a scar. There in the shallows, where the steam rises in a thousand curtains, you'll see a crumbling dock, and from that dock you can still walk into the scraps and tatters of a blown-apart town that was never laid straight from the start. It went up on those rocks layer after layer, like ten eyeless drunks scraping butter onto the same piece of bread.

The southernmost Ormscap is still called the Dragon's Anvil. The town below the mountain was once called Helfalkyn.

Not so long ago it was an enchantment and a refuge and a prison, home to the most desperate thieves in all the breathing world. Not so long ago, they all cried out in their sleep for the mountain's treasure. One part in three of every gleaming thing that has ever been drawn or dredged or delved from the earth, that's what the scholars claimed.

That's what the dragon carried there and brooded over, the last dragon that will ever speak to any of us.

Now the town's empty. The wind howls through broken windows in roofless walls. If you licked the stones of the mountain for a thousand days, you wouldn't taste enough precious metal to gild one letter in a monk's manuscript.

Helfalkyn is dead, and the dragon is dead, and the treasure might as well have never existed.

I ought to know. I'm the man who lost a bet, climbed the Anvil, and helped break the whole damn thing.

I tell this story once a year, on Galen's Eve, and no other. Some of you have heard it before. I take it kindly that you've come to hear it again. Like any storyteller, I'd lie about the color of my eyes to my own mother for half a cup of ale-dregs, but you'll affirm to all the new faces that to this one tale I add no flourishes. I deepen no shadows and gentle no sorrows. I tell it as it was, one night each year, and on that night I take no coin for it.

Heed me now. Gather in as you will. Jostle your neighbors. Spill your drinks. Laugh early at the bad jokes and stare at me like clubbed sheep for all the good ones, and I shall care not, for I am armored by long experience. But this bowl of mine, if we are to part as friends, must catch no copper or silver, I swear it. Tonight pay me in food, or drink, or simple attention.

With that, let me commence to tell:

FIRST, HOW I FELL IN WITH THE CHARMING LUNATICS WHO ENDED MY ADVENTURING CAREER

It was the Year of the Bent-Wing Raven, and everything went sour for me right around the back side of autumn.

One week I was in funds, the next I was conspicuously otherwise. I'm still not sure what happened. Bad luck, worse judgment, enemy action, sorcery? Hardly matters. When you're on the ground getting kicked in the face, one pair of boots looks very much like another.

I have long been candid about the nature of my previous employment. Those of you who find this frank exchange of purely historical details in any way disturbing are of course welcome to say a word or two to Galen on my behalf, and I shall thank you, as I doubt an old thief can really collect such a thing as too many prayers. In those days I would have laughed. Young thieves think luck and knee joints are meant to last forever.

I started the summer by lifting four ivory soul lanterns from the Temple of the Cloud Gardens in Port Raugen. Spent a few weeks carving decent wooden replicas and painting them with a white cream wash, first. I made the switch at night, walked out unnoticed, presented the genuine articles to my client, and set sail on the morning tide as a very rich man. I washed up in Hadrinsbirk a few weeks later with a pounding headache and a haunting memory of money. No matter. I made the acquaintance of an uncreatively guarded warehouse and appropriated a crate of the finest

Sulagar steel padlocks. I sold the locks and their keys to a corner-cutting merchants' guild, then sold wax impressions of the keys to their bitter rivals for twice that sum. So much for Hadrinsbirk. I cast off for the Crescent Cities.

There I guised myself as a gentleman of leisure, and wearing that mask, I investigated prospects and rumors, looking for easy marks. Alas, the easy marks must have migrated in a flock. I took the edge off my disappointment by indulging all the routine questionable habits, and that's when the bad time crept up behind me. The gaming tables turned. Easy credit went extinct. All the people who owed me favors locked their doors, and all the people I needed to avoid were thick in the streets. Before I knew it I was sleeping in a stable.

I stretched a point of courtesy then and slipped an appeal to the local practitioners of my trade. My entreaty was coolly received. There was a sudden plague of honesty in the land, and schemes simply weren't hatching, or so they claimed. Nobody needed to arrange a kidnapping, or a vault infiltration, or have a barrow desecrated.

This was a bind, and I confess that I partly deserved it. For all my hard-earned professional fame, I was still an outsider, and doubtless should have paid my respects to the thieves of the Crescent Cities a few weeks earlier. Now they were wise to me and watchful for the sorts of jobs I might pull on my own. The wind was sharpening, my belly was flat, and my belt was running out of notches. I needed money! Yet honest employment was out of the question too, as word of my presence spread. Who would make a caravan guard of Tarkaster Crale, bane of a dozen caravan runs? Who'd set Crale the Cracksman to stand guard over a money changer's strongboxes? Awkward! I couldn't beg for so much as an afternoon hauling wash buckets behind a tavern. A larcenist of my caliber and experience? Any sensible local thief would assume it had to be a cover for some grand scheme, which they would have to interrupt.

It's hard to be poor at the best of times, but in my old line of work, to be poor and famous—gods have mercy.

I had no prospects. No friends. I could have won an empty-pockets contest against anyone within a hundred miles. All I had left was youth and a sense of pride that damn near glowed like banked coals.

These were the circumstances that led me to seriously consider, for the first time in my life, the words of the Helfalkyn Wormsong.

I can see some of you nodding, those of you without much hair left. You heard it, too. Nobody repeats it these days, the fortunes of Helfalkyn having diminished so profoundly. But in my youth there wasn't a child in any land who didn't know the Wormsong by heart. It was a message from the dragon itself, the last and greatest of them, the Shipbreaker, the Sky Tyrant. Glimraug.

It went like this:

> *High-reachers, bright-dreamers, bright-enders,*
> *Match riddlesong, venom, and stone.*
> *Carry ending and eyes up the Anvil,*
> *Carry glorious gleanings back home.*

Isn't that a fine little thing?

Friends, that's how a dragon says, "Why not climb up my impenetrable treasure mountain and let me kill you?"

From the first day Glimraug claimed the Anvil, it took pains to welcome and entice us. Don't mistake that for a benevolent and universal hospitality, for of course Glimraug raided half the earth and spread dismay for centuries. No dragon ever deigned to smelt its own gold. But even as Glimraug fell on caravans and broke castles like eggs, it tolerated a small community of outcasts and lunatics in the shadow of its home. Once in a rare while it would even seize someone and haul them to the crest of the Anvil, to make a show of its growing treasure, then set them free to sing the Wormsong louder than ever.

Thousands of people accepted the dragon's invitation over the years. None of them lived. Some very canny customers in that crowd, too, great heroes, names that still ring out, but none of them were ever quite a match for riddlesong, venom, and stone. Still, for every one who dreamed the impossible dream and cacked it hard, two more showed up. The Dragon's Anvil was the last roll of the dice for those who'd played their lives out and bet poorly. It was equally attractive to the brilliant, the mad, and the desperate. I was at least two of those three, and by that simple majority the vote carried. I was on a ship that night, the *Red Swan*, and I scrubbed decks and greased ropes to pay for my passage to the end of the world.

That's what Helfalkyn looked like when I finally saw it—like the last human habitation thrown down by the last human hands at the far end of some mad priest's apocalypse. The sun was the color of bled-out entrails, edging the hulking mountain, and the bruised light showed me a gallimaufry of dark warrens, leaning houses, and crooked alleys down below. We sailed in through veils of warm breath from the mountain's underwater vents, and the air was perfumed with sulfur.

Many of you must be thinking the same thing I was as I trod the creaking timbers of the Helfalkyn docks—how did such a place ever come to thrive? The answer lies at the intersection of greed and perversity. Here came the adventurers, the suicides, the mad ones intent on climbing the mountain and somehow stealing the treasure of ten thousand lifetimes. But were they eager to go all at once? Of course not. Some needed to lay their plans, or drink their brains out, or otherwise work themselves into fits of enthusiasm. Some waited days, or weeks, or months. Some never went at all, and clung to Helfalkyn forever, aging sourly in the shadows of failed ambition. After the adventurers came the provisioners, of inebriation and games and rooms and warm companionship, and the town became a sputtering, improvised machine for sifting the last scraps of currency from those who would surely never need them again. The captains of the few ships that made the Helfalkyn run had a cordial arrangement with the town. They would haul anyone there for the price of a few days' labor, and charge a small fortune in real valuables for passage back to the world. Any newcomer trapped in Helfalkyn would thus be forced to try the mountain, or toil for years to the great advantage of the town's masters if they ever wanted to escape.

Mountebanks swarmed as I and a few other neophytes examined the town warily. The junk-mongers outnumbered us three to one. "Don't breathe the dragon air without taking a draught of Cleansing Miracle Water," shouted a bearded man, waving a stone pitcher of what was clearly urine and mud. "Look around! The dragon air gives you clisters, morphew, wretched megrims, and the flux like a black molasses! Have the advantage when you challenge the Anvil! Protect yourself at a fair price!"

I did look around, and it seemed that none of the other natives were downing miracle mudpiss to keep their lungs supple, so I judged none of us likely to perish of the megrims. I moved on, and was offered enchanted blades, enchanted boots, enchanted cheese, and enchanted handfuls of mountain rock, all for a fair price. How fortunate I felt, to discover such simple generosity and potent magic in the meanest of all places! Even if I'd had money, I would have reciprocated this cordial selflessness by refusing to take advantage of it. Two gracious humanitarians of Helfalkyn then attempted to pick my pockets; the first I merely spurned with a scolding. The second mysteriously incurred a broken wrist and lost his own purse at the same time, for in those days my fingers were considerably faster than the contents of my skull. I worried then about constables, or at least mob-fellowship against outsiders, but I quickly realized that the only law in Helfalkyn was to win or stay out of the way. No more creeping fingers tried my pockets after that.

Cheered by the acquisition of a few coins, I hunted for a place to spend them and tame my tyrant stomach. Ale dens of varying foulness offered themselves as I strolled, and street hawkers made pitches even less appetizing than the prospect of Cleansing Miracle Water. Sooner rather than later, for while Helfalkyn was encysted with diversions it was not terribly vast, its twisted streets naturally funneled me to the steps of the grandest structure in town, Underwing Hall. Here would be food, though the smell wafting out past the cold-eyed guards beside the doors promised nothing delicate.

Outside it was morning, but inside lay a perpetual smoky twilight. The entrance hall was decorated with bloody teeth and the slumped bodies of those who'd recently had them knocked out of their mouths. Porters, working with the bored air of long practice, were levering these unfortunates one by one out a side entrance. I saw more fisticuffs under way at several tables and balconies in the cavernous space. Given the relaxation of the door guards, I wondered what it took to rouse their interference. The servers, stout men and women all, wore ill-fashioned armor as they heaved platters about, and the kitchen windows were barred with iron. Rough hands thrust forth tankards and wine bottles like castle defenders dispensing projectiles through murder-holes. Though I'd enjoyed some elevated company in my career, this crowd was still an intimately familiar sort, comprised of equal parts stupid, cruel, cunning, blasphemous, and greedy faces. Every corner of the known world had skimmed the scum of its scum to populate Helfalkyn. I resolved to step warily and attract no attention until I learned the order of things.

"CRALE!" bellowed someone from a balcony overhead.

Ah, the feeling of receiving unsought the attention of a great room full of brawlers and carousers. Heads turned, conversations quieted, and even some of the servers halted to stare at me.

"Tarkaster Crale?" came a disbelieving shout.

"Bullshit. Tarkaster Crale's a tall handsome bastard," muttered a woman.

I was about to say something that would have, in all candor, improved nobody's situation, when I was seized from above and hauled into the air. The sheer power of my appropriator was startling, and I kicked helplessly as I was spun a disagreeable number of feet above the stones of the tavern floor. My assailant hung from a balcony rail by one arm and dandled me with the other. I prepared fresh unhelpful commentary and reached for the knives in my belt; and then I saw the man's face.

"Your highness!" I whispered.

"Don't give me the courtesies of cushion-sitters unless you want to get dropped, Crale." Still, there was warmth in his voice as he heaved me over the railing and set me on a stool as easily as anyone here might hang a tunic on a drying line. Here was a man with shoulders as broad as a boat's rowing-bench and arms harder than the oars. He was dark of skin and darker of hair, with gray setting some claim to his temples and beard, and all the lines in his face had been carved by either the sea-winds or the wild grin he wore when facing them. The other patrons of Underwing Hall rapidly lost interest in me, for I had been claimed for the table of none other than my old adventuring companion, Brandgar Never-Throned, King-on-the-Waves, Lord of the Ajja.

Like Helfalkyn, the King-on-the-Waves is little more than a story these days, though it's a good one and an Ajja skald who'll sing it for you is worth the asking price. All the Ajja clans had kings and queens, and keeps and lands and suchwise, but once a generation their mystics would read the signs and proclaim a King-on-the-Waves. This lucky bitch or bastard would be gifted a stout ship to crew with sworn companions, and set sail across the Ajja realms, calling upon cousin monarchs, receiving full courtesy and hospitality. Then they'd usually be asked to undertake some messy piece of questing that would end in unguessable amounts of death and glory. Thus charged was a King-on-the-Waves, to hold no lands, but to slay monsters, retrieve lost treasures, lift curses, and so forth, until they and all their companions had met some horrible, beautiful fate on behalf of the Ajja people. Brandgar was the last so-named, nor is there like to be another soon, for he and his companions were uncommonly good at the job and left few messes for others to clean up. I had fallen in with them on two occasions and done some reaving, all for the best of causes, I assure you, though I am sworn to utter no details. Even my sleeping sense of honor sometimes rolls over in bed and kicks. Onward!

"There's fortune in this. We had not thought to see an old friend here." Brandgar settled himself back on his own stool, over the half-eaten remains of some well-fatted animal I couldn't identify, sauced with sharp-smelling mustard and brown moonberry preserves. "What say you, Mikah?"

I gave a start, for sitting there in the darkness at the rear of the balcony was a shape I hadn't previously noticed. Yes, indeed, here was Mikah King-Shadow, rarely seen unless they chose the time and place. Mikah, my better in all the crafts of larceny, who could pass for man or woman in a hundred disguises, but in their own skin was simply Mikah, good friend and terrible enemy. They leaned into the light, and it seemed the years had not touched that lean angular face or the cool gray eyes that smiled though the lips below them never so much as twitched.

"Friend Crale has a hungry look, lord."

"They're in fashion hereabouts." Brandgar waved casually to the remains of his morning fast-breaking, and I fell to with a grateful nod. "Have you been here long, Crale?"

"I'm fresh-landed as a fisherman's catch," I said between bites of rich greasy something. I did not scruple to avoid licking my fingers, for I knew the table manners of a King-on-the-Waves were shaped for the tossing deck of a longship. "And I thank you for the sharing. This latest chapter in the book of my life has been writ mostly on the subject of empty bellies."

"And empty pockets?" said Mikah.

"I have offended some power unknown to me." I took a bone and greedily sucked the marrow of some animal also unknown to me. "An ill fate has swept me here to play a desperate hand."

"No," said Brandgar, and there was that damned grin I mentioned, a follow-me-over-the-cliff grin. "A kind fate has joined friend to friends. Give us your skills. We mean to climb the Dragon's Anvil and crown our lives with the glory of a treasure claimed. The Wormsong bids us to carry ending and eyes, eh? Ending we carry in our steel. Eyes we still need! You were ever a fine and cunning lookout."

"When do you intend to go?"

"Tonight."

I dropped my bone then and wiped my mouth with a scuffed jacket cuff. I'm not best pleased to shine a light on my hesitation, friends, but I vowed to give every truth of this tale as much illumination as it's due. I had gone to Helfalkyn in a desperate fever, yes, and by happy fate found two of the few people alive whom I might have chosen if given my pick of fellows. Still, with the weight of satisfying meat in my belly for the first time in recent memory, I found myself less than eager to set the hour of my doom so close.

"I had thought to spend a few days preparing myself," I began, "and learning whatever useful information might be—"

"You're no craven," rumbled Brandgar. "Yet any man might feel the sting of fear when he sits in comfort and thinks of peril. Come, I know you would never run from a duty bound in honest wager! Lay a simple bet with me. Should I win, join us tonight. Else we wait three days, and you may seek whatever 'useful information' you like before we climb."

Now here was a salve to all my several consciences, gentle listeners, by which I could keep faith with useful companions and still have time to ease myself into a frightful enterprise. I asked the means of the wager.

"See the attic-skorms that cling high upon the wall there?"

Gazing across the wide tavern, squinting past smoke and flickering brazier-light, I did indeed see a pair of the dark-scaled lizards motionless below the ceiling. Arm length and even-tempered, attic-skorms creep down from the mountains in all the northern countries, and are either eaten as food or tolerated as rat-catchers.

"The wager is this. Long have those two sat unmoving; sooner or later one of them will doubtless creep down in search of food. If the dark one on your side moves soonest, we go in three days. If the red-rippled one on my side moves, we go tonight. Is it sealed?"

"My oath," I said, and we sat at ease to watch this yawn-inducing spectacle unfold. This was not as odd as it might seem, for out upon the waves the Ajja will pass the time in friendly wagers on anything that catches the eye, from which way gulls will fly to which sailor on another ship will next use and empty a dung bucket over the side. I have eased fierce boredom with bets on some ludicrous trifles in my time.

Not five heartbeats after I spoke, the red-rippled skorm on the king's side pulled in its legs. It didn't so much climb down as fall directly off the wall like a grieving suicide in an old romantic tale.

I sputtered without dignity while Brandgar and Mikah laughed. Then there was a flash of silver light in the shadows where the king's choice had plunged; a thin mist rose into the air, a mist I recognized.

"No!" I shouted. "That was no honest bet! That was a skin-shifting sorceress of low moral character who is—"

"Standing right behind you," said Gudrun Sky-Daughter, appearing in silver light and mist. She ruffled my hair affectionately, for yes, I still had some in those days. Hers was seven braided spills of copper, now lined with the color of iron like her king's, and her round, flushed face was all mischief and mirth.

"That was unworthy," I scowled.

"That was fair as anything," said Brandgar. "For if your eyes had been working as a fine and cunning lookout's should, you'd have seen that there was only one beast upon the wall until a moment before my proposal. Come, Crale. We need you, and you won't find better company if you wait here a hundred years! This is fate."

I partly hated him for being right and was partly thrilled that he was. A warrior-king, a master thief, and a sorceress. Great gods, hope was a terrible and anxious thing! They were indeed allies who had as much chance on the Dragon's Anvil as any mortal born. I pondered my recent poverty and pondered the treasure.

"I have never in my life behaved with any particular wisdom," I said at last. "It would make little sense to start now."

"Ha!" Brandgar pounded the table, stood, and leaned out over the balcony. His voice boomed out, echoing from the rafters and startling the raucous commotion below into instant attention. "HEAR ME! Hight Brandgar, son of Orthild and Erika, King-on-the-Waves! Tonight we go! Tonight we climb the Dragon's Anvil! We, the Never-Throned, the King-Shadow, the Sky-Daughter, and the famous Tarkaster Crale! We go to claim a treasure, so take this pittance! Drink to us, and wait for the word! Tonight we break a legend!"

Brandgar opened a purse, and shook out a stream of silver into the crowds below, where drinkers cheered and convulsed and clutched at his largesse. Gods! If I'd had even that much money just a week before, I'd never have left the Crescent Cities. As the near riot for the coins subsided, a voice rose in ragged chant, and was joined by more and steadier voices, until nearly everyone in Underwing Hall was gleefully serenading us, a single verse over and over again:

> *Die rich, dragon's dinner!*
> *Play well the game that has no winner!*
> *Climb the mountain, greedy sinner!*
> *Die rich, dragon's dinner!*

The chant had the sound of a familiar ritual that had been much practiced. I liked it not a whit.

NEXT, HOW WE PROVED OUR RESOLVE AND BROKE A FEW HEARTS ALONG THE WAY

I dozed fitfully most of the day, in a hired chamber guarded by some of Gudrun's arcane mutterings. Terrified or not, I was still an experienced man of fortune and knew to try to catch a bit of rest when it was on offer.

At dusk the moons rose red, like burnished shields hanging on the wall of the brandywine sky. The mountain loomed, crowned with strange lights that never came from any celestial sphere, and it seemed I could hear the hiss and rumble of the stone as if it were a hungry thing. I shuddered and checked my gear for the tenth time. I had come light from the Crescent Cities, in simple field leathers, dark jacket, and utility belts. I carried a sling and a sparse supply of grooved stones. My longest daggers were whetted, and I wore them openly as I headed for the north-eastern side of town with my companions, pretending to swagger. Denizens of Helfalkyn watched from every street, every rooftop, every window, some jeering, some singing, but most standing quietly or hoisting cups to the air, as one might toast a prisoner on the way to the gallows.

Brandgar wore a fitted coat of plate under a majestically ragged gray cloak with parti-colored patchings from numerous cuts and burns over the years; he claimed it was as good as enchanted and that he had sweated most of his considerable luck into it. Gudrun had never offered a professional opinion on this, so far as I knew. She was as scruffy as ever, a study in comfortable disrepute. Strange charms and wooden containers rattled on leather cords at her breast, and she bore a pair of rune-inscribed drums on her back. Mikah were lightly dressed in silks and leather bracers, moving with their familiar fluid grace, concealing their real thoughts behind their even more familiar mask of calculating bemusement with the world. They carried a few coils of sea-spider silk and some climbing gear wrapped in muffling cloth. However detached they seemed, I knew they were fanatics about the selection and care of their tools, more painstaking than any other burglar I had ever worked with, and any professional jealousy I might have felt was rather drowned in comfort at their preparedness.

The only real oddity was the extra weapon Brandgar carried. His familiar spear, Cold-Thorn, had a bare and gleaming tip, and its shaft was worn with use. The other spear looked heavy and new, and its point was wrapped in layers of tightly bound leather like a practice weapon. When asked about this, Brandgar smiled, and said, "Extra spear, extra thief. Aren't I growing cautious in my old age?"

At the northeast edge of Helfalkyn lay our first ascent, an unassuming path of dusty dark stone that was marked by a parallel series of lines, half a foot deep, slashed across the walkway. Though time and weather had softened the edges of these lines, it was not hard to see them for what they were, the claw-furrows of a dragon. An unequivocal message to anyone who wanted to step over them. I suddenly wished I could forget our mutual agreement to go up the Anvil with clear heads and find something irresponsible to pour down my throat.

One by one we crossed the dragon's mark, your nervous narrator lastly and slowly. After that we walked up in silence save for the occasional rattle of gear or boot-scuff on stone. As the odors of the town and the harbor steam faded below us, the indigo edges of evening settled overhead and stars lit one by one like distant lanterns. It would be a clear night atop the mountain, and I wondered if we would be there to appreciate it. This first part of the climb was not hard, perhaps three-quarters of an hour with the switchback path offering nothing more than agreeable exercise. As the light sank the way roughened and narrowed, and when full dark came on it ceased to be a path and became a proper climb, up a sloping black rock-face of crags and broken columns. Rugged as it was, this was the only face of the Anvil that could be approached at all.

Brandgar shook Cold-Thorn and muttered something to Gudrun, who muttered something in return. A moment later the tip of Cold-Thorn flared with gentle but far-reaching light, and by that pale gleam we made our way steadily up.

"What happened to everyone else?" I asked on a whim during one of our brief pauses. When last I'd sojourned in the Never-Throned's company, he'd had eight of his original boon companions yet unslain, enough to crew his ship and drink up truly heroic quantities of something irresponsible whenever they paid call to a landed king or queen. "Asmira? Lorus? Valdis?"

"Asmira was pitched from the mast during a storm," said Brandgar. "Lorus challenged a vineyard wight to a game of draughts and kept it occupied 'til dawn. It killed him in its fury just before the first light of the sun slew it in turn. Valdis died in the battle against the Skull Priests at Whitefall."

"What about Rondu Silverbeard?"

"The Silverbeard died in bed," chuckled Gudrun.

"Under a bed, to be precise," added Mikah. "The defenders dropped it on us at the siege of Vendilsfarna."

"I hope our friends know joy in the Fields of Swords and Roses," I said, for that is where worthy Ajja are meant to go when they die, and if it's true I suppose it keeps all of our own heavens and hells a bit quieter. "Though I hope I give no offense if I wish we had a few more of them with us tonight."

"They died to bring us here," said Brandgar. "They died to teach us what we needed to know. They died to show us the way, and when our numbers dwindled and our duties grew lean, we three knew where we were called." Gudrun and Mikah nodded with that sage fatalism I had long lamented in my Ajja friends, and though my presence on that mountain reinforced my assertion that I had never in my life behaved with any particular wisdom, neither was I boorish enough to voice my concerns with their philosophy. Perhaps they had always mistaken this tact for fellow feeling. No, I admit I could fight with abandon when cornered, but when I could see a meeting with Death obviously scrawled in the ledger, I always preferred to break the appointment. How any of the Ajja ever survived long enough to span the seas and populate their holdings remains a mystery of creation.

We resumed our climb and soon heaved ourselves over the edge of a cleft promontory where a hemispherical stone ceiling, open to the night like a theater, overhung a darkness that led into the depths of the mountain. The wind had risen and the air was sharp against my skin. We gazed out for a moment at the lights of the town far below us, and the white-foamed blackness of the sea capped with mists, and the hair-thin line of sunset that still clung to the horizon. Then rose a scraping, shuffling noise behind us, and Brandgar turned with Cold-Thorn held high.

Red lights glowed in answer, throbbing like a pulse beat within the cavern. Whether they were lanterns or conjurations I could not discern, but in their rising illumination I saw an arched door wide enough to admit three wagons abreast. I wondered whether the dragon had left itself ample room in setting this passage, or if it could tolerate a tight squeeze. Unhelpful conjecture! In the space between us and the door stood two straight lines of pillars, and beside each pillar stood the shape of a man or woman.

Brandgar advanced, and the man shape nearest us held up a hand. "Bide," it whispered in a hoarse sickbed voice. "None need enter."

"Unless you propose to show us a more convenient door," said Brandgar, "this path is for us."

"Time remains to turn." There was enough light now to see that the hoarse speaker and all of its companions were unclothed, emaciated, and caked with filth. A paleness shone upon their breasts, where each on their left side bore a plate of something like dull nacre, sealed to the edges of the bloodless surrounding flesh by the pulsing segments of what seemed to be a milk-white centipede. The white segments passed into the body like stitches and emerged in a narrow, twitching tail at the back of the neck. From these extremities hung threads, gleaming silver, connecting each man or woman to a pillar. Atop those, in delicate brass recesses, pulsed fist-sized lumps of flesh. I'd been near enough death to know a human heart by sight, and felt a tight horror in my own chest. "The master grudges you nothing. You may still turn and go home."

"Our thanks to your master." Brandgar set his leather-wrapped spear down and spun Cold-Thorn, casting about a light like the sun's rays scattering from rippling water. "We are here on an errand of sacred avarice and will not be halted."

Some enchanted guardians never know when to shut up, but this one had a reasonable sense of occasion, so it nodded and proceeded directly to hostilities. Each of the heart-wraiths took up handfuls of dust, and in their clenched fists this dust turned to swords. Eight of them closed on four of us, and with a merry twirl of my daggers I joined most of my companions in making royal asses of ourselves.

It was plain to Mikah, Brandgar, and me, as veterans of too many sorcerer's traps and devices to enumerate here, that the weakness of these creatures had to be the glittering threads that bound them to their heart-pillars. Dodging their attacks, we wove a dance of easy competence and with our weapons of choice swung down nearly simultaneously for the threads of our targets. What it felt like, to me, was swinging for dande-lion fuzz and hitting granite. I found myself on the ground with my right hand spasming in cold agony, and was barely able to seize my wits and roll aside before a blade struck sparks where my head had just been.

"I had thought," muttered Brandgar (shaking Cold-Thorn angrily, for either his rude health or some quality of the spear had let him keep it when Mikah and I had been rendered one-handed), "the obvious striking point—"

"So did we all," groaned Mikah.

"Speak for your cloddish selves," shouted Gudrun, who had cast lines of emerald fire upon the stones, where they flashed and coiled like snakes in response to the movements of her hands, and were holding several of the heart-wraiths at bay.

I sidestepped a new assault, rebalanced my left-hand dagger, and judged the distance to the nearest pillar-top heart. If the threads had been a distraction, the weakness of the magic animating our foes surely had to lie there. I was not left-handed, but I threw well, and my blade was a gratifying blur that arrived dead on target, only to be smacked aside by one thrown with even greater deftness by Mikah, aimed at the same spot.

"Damnation, Crale, we're supposed to be better than this," said the King-Shadow as they whirled and weaved between onrushing heart-wraiths.

"If I live to tell this story in taverns, I shall amend this part to our advantage," I said, though you apprehend, my friends, that I have done otherwise and will sleep soundly in my conscience tonight. Mikah found a fresh dagger and made another cast, this time without my interference. The blade struck true at the visibly unprotected heart, and rebounded as though from an inch of steel. We all swore vicious oaths. Magic does from time to time so boil one's piss.

Mikah rolled one of the silk ropes off their shoulders, and with a series of cartwheels and flourishes deployed it as a weapon, lashing and entangling the nearest heart-wraiths, quickstepping between them like the passage of a mad tailor's needle. I had no such recourse, and my right hand was still useless. I scrambled across the stones, swept up a dropped blade in my left hand once more, and whirled toward the two wraiths assailing me. "Hold," I cried, "Hold! I find I'm not so eager for treasure as I was. Would your master yet give me leave to climb back down?"

"We are here to slay or dissuade, not to punish." The heart-wraith before me lowered its weapon. "Living with yourself is your own affair. You may depart."

"I applaud the precision and dedication of your service," I said, and as the heart-wraith began to turn from me, no doubt to join the fray against my companions, I buried my dagger in its skull with an overhand blow. The segments of the insectoid thing threaded into its abdomen shook, and something like creamy clotted bile poured from the mouth and ears of what had once been a man. It collapsed.

"That was a low trick," rasped the other heart-wraith, and came for me. I wrenched my dagger free, which wafted a sickly vinegar odor into my face, and waved my hands again.

"Hold," said I. "It's true that I'm a gamesome and unscrupulous rogue, but I feared you were playing me false. Are you really prepared to let me go in good faith?"

"Despite your unworthy—"

I never learned the specifics of my unworthiness, as I took the opportunity to lunge and sink my dagger into its left eye. It toppled beside its fellow and vomited more disgusting yellow soup. I am the soul of pragmatism.

"Enough!"

I saw that only one heart-wraith remained, and before my eyes the sword in its hand returned to dust. I had slain two, Gudrun had scorched two with her fire-serpents, and Mikah had at last bound their pair tightly enough to finish them with pierced skulls. Brandgar had beaten one of his foes to a simple pulp, breaking its limbs and impaling it through the bony plate where its heart had once been. As for those hearts, I saw at a glance that those atop seven of the eight pillars had shriveled. Dark stains were running down the columns beneath them.

"You have proven your resolve," rasped the final heart-wraith. "The master bids you onward."

The eerie red lights of the cavern dimmed, and with the crack and rattle of great mechanisms the arched doors fell open. Brandgar advanced on the surviving heart-wraith, spear held out before him, until it rested gently on the white plate set into the thing's chest.

"Onward we move," said Brandgar, "but how came you to the service of the dragon?"

"I sought the treasure and failed, threescore years past. You may yet join me, when you fail. If enough of your flesh remains, the master may choose to knit watch-worms into the cavern of your heart, so be advised . . . to consider leaving as little flesh as possible."

"After tonight your master Glimraug will have no need of us." Smoothly and without preamble, Brandgar drove his spear into the wraith's chest. "Nor any need of you."

"Thank . . . you . . ." the wraith whispered as it fell.

"Did we amuse you in our stumblings, sister Sky-Daughter?" said Mikah, massaging their right hand. My own seemed to be recovering as well.

"Spear-carriers and knife-brains love to overthink a problem," laughed the sorceress. "Feeds your illusionary sense of finesse. The truly stupid and the truly wise would have started with simply bashing at the damn things, but since you're somewhere in between, you tried to kill everything else in the room first. Good joke. This dragon knows how adventurers think." She looked up at the mountain and sighed. "Tonight could be everyone's night to stumble, ere we're through."

THIRD, HOW I PUT MY ASS ON THE LINE AND HOW WE SOUGHT THE SONG BENEATH THE SONG

Past the arched doors we found ourselves in a vaulted hall, lit once more by pale scarlet fires that drifted in the air like puffs of smoke. For a moment I thought we stood in an armory, then I saw the jagged holes and torn plates in every piece displayed, tier on tier and rank on rank, nearly to the ceiling. Broken blades and shattered spears, shields torn like parchment sheets, mail shirts pierced and burnt and fouled with unknown substances—here were the fates of all our predecessors memorialized, obviously. The dragon's boast.

"Perhaps a part-truth," responded Mikah, when I said as much. "Surely all dragons are braggarts after a fashion. But consider how this one seems determined to play fair with its challengers. The ascent up the mountain, with its gradual reduction of ease. The guardians at the door, willing to forgive and forget. Now this museum show for the fainthearted. At every step our host invites the insufficiently motivated to quit before they waste more of anyone's time."

Proud to be numbered among the sufficiently motivated, no doubt, I followed my companions through the dragon's collection, uneasily noting its quality. Here were polished Sulagar steel breastplates and black Harazi swords of the ten thousand folds. Here were gem-studded pauldrons of ageless elven silver, and gauntlets of sky iron that glowed faintly with sorcery, and all of these things had clearly been as useful as an underwater fart against the fates that had overtaken their wielders. At the far end of the hall lay another pair of great arched doors, and nested into one like a passage for pets was a door more suited to those of us not born as dragons. On this door lay a sigil that I knew too well, and I seized Brandgar by his cloak before he could touch it.

"That is the seal of Melodia Marus, the High Trapwright of Sendaria," said I, "and I've had several professional disagreements with her. Or, more precisely, the mechanisms she devises for the vaults and offices of her clients."

"I know her work by reputation," said Mikah. "It seems Glimraug is one of those clients."

"She's the reason I once spent three months unconscious in Korrister." I twitch at the memory, friends, but not all of one's ventures can end in good fortune, as we have seen. "And six weeks in a donjon in Port Raugen. And why I only have eight toes."

"Another fair warning," said Gudrun. "A frightful spectacle for all comers, then a more specific omen for those professionally inclined to thievery."

"We have two master burglars to test our way," said Brandgar, who seemed more cheerful with every danger and warning of greater danger.

"And if this woman's creations were perfect, surely she'd have more than two of Crale's toes by now."

The craft of trap-finding is much sweat and tedium, with only the occasional thrill of accident or narrow escape, and we spent the next hour absorbed in its practice. All the stairs and corridors in that part of the dragon's domain were richly threaded with death. Some halls were sized to us and some to the transit of larger things, and these networks of passages were neither wholly parallel nor entirely separate. This was no citadel made for any sensible court, but only a playing field for Glimraug's game, a stone simulacrum of what we would call a true fortress. Up we went floor by floor, past apertures in the walls that spat razor-keen darts, over false floors that gave way to mangling engines, through cleverly weighted doors that sprang open with crushing force or sealed themselves behind us, barring retreat from some new devilment.

In one particularly narrow hall both Mikah and I had a rare bout of all-consuming nincompoopery, and one of us tripped a plate that caused iron shutters to slam down before and behind us, sealing our quartet in a span of corridor little bigger than a rich merchant's water closet. An aperture on the right-hand wall began to spew a haze at us, the stinging sulfur reek of which was familiar to me from a job I'd once pulled in the mines of Belphoria.

"Dragon's breath," said Brandgar.

"More like the mountain's breath," I cried, and with a creditable leap I braced myself like a bridge across the narrow space and jammed my own posterior firmly into the aperture. The thin cloud of foulness that had seeped into the hall made my eyes water, but was not yet enough to cause us real harm. Though once a few minutes passed and I could no longer maintain such an acrobatic posture, my well-placed buttocks would no longer avail us. "It's what miners call the stink-damp, and it will dispatch us with unsporting speed if I can't hold the seal, so please conjure an exit."

"Fairly done, Crale!" Brandgar waved a hand before his face and coughed. "To save us, you've matched breach to breeches!"

"All men have cracks in their asses," said Gudrun, "but only the boldest puts his ass in a crack."

"Henceforth Crale the Cracksman will be celebrated as Crale the Corksman," said Mikah.

I said many unkind things then, and they continued making grotesque puns which I shall not torture any living soul with, for apparently to ward off a stream of poisonous vapor with one's own ass is to summon a powerful muse of low comedy. Eventually, moving with what I considered an unseemly attitude of leisure, Mikah tried and failed to find any mechanism they might manipulate. Then even the strength of Brandgar's shoulder failed against the iron shutters, and our salvation fell to Gudrun, who broke a rune-etched bone across her knee and summoned what she called a spirit of rust.

"I had hoped to reserve it for some grander necessity," said she. "Though I suppose this is a death eminently worth declining."

In a few moments the spirit accomplished its task, and the sturdy iron shutters on either side were reduced to scatterings of flaked brown dust on the floor. I unbraced with shudders of relief in every part of my frame, and we hurried on our way, kicking up whorls of rust in our wake to mingle with the lethal haze of the broken trap. We moved warily at first, then with more confidence, for it seemed that we had at last cleared that span of the mountain in which Melodia Marus had expressed her creativity. I do hope that woman died in a terrible accident, or at least lost some toes.

The red lights the dragon had graciously provided before were not to be found here, however, so we climbed through the darkness by the silver gleam of Gudrun's sorcery on our naked weapons. Eventually we could find no more doors or stairs, and so with painful contortions and much use of Mikah's ropes we ventured up a rock chimney. I prayed for the duration of the ascent that we had discovered nothing so mundane as the dragon's privy shaft.

Eventually we emerged into a cold-aired cavern with a floor of smooth black tiles. Scarlet light kindled upon a far wall, and formed letters in Kandric script (which I had learned to read as a boy, and which the Ajja had long adopted as their preference for matters of trade and accounting), spelling out the Helfalkyn Wormsong.

"As if we might have forgotten it," muttered Mikah. At that instant, a burst of orange fire erupted from the rock chimney we had ascended and burned like a terrible flickering flower twice my height, sealing off our retreat. White-hot lines spilled forth from the ragged crest of this flame, like melted iron from a crucible, and this burning substance swiftly took the aspect of four vaguely human shapes, lean and graceful as dancers. Dance they did, whirling slowly at first but with ever-increasing speed, and toward us they came, gradually. Inexorably.

"*Seek the song beneath the song,*" rang a voice that touched my heart, a voice that echoed softly around the chamber, a voice blended of every fine thing, neither man's nor woman's but something preternaturally beautiful. To hear it once was to regret all the years of life one had spent not hearing it. Even now, merely telling of it, I can feel warmth at the corners of my eyes, and I am not ashamed. The four fire-dancers glided and spun, singing with voices that started as mere entrancement and became more painfully beautiful with every verse.

> *"The fall of dice in gambling den*
> *The sporting bets of honest men*
> *Will bring them round again, again*
> *To their fairest friend, distraction . . ."*

It was not the words that were beautiful, for as I recite them here I see none of you crying or falling over. But the voices, the voices! Every hair on my neck stood as though a winter wind had caught me, and I felt the sorcery, sure as I could feel the stones beneath my feet. There was a compulsion weighing on us. The voices drew us on, all of us, cow-eyed, yearning to embrace the gorgeous burning shapes that called with such piercing loveliness. And that was the horror of it, friends, for I knew with some small part of my mind that if I touched one of those things, my skin would go like candle wax in a bonfire. Still, I couldn't help myself. None of us could. With every moment they sang, the pull of the fire-dancers grew, and our resolve withered.

> *"When beauties into mirrors gaze*
> *Nor look aside for all their days*
> *Until they lose all chance for praise*
> *They wake too late from distraction . . ."*

I groaned and forced myself backwards, step by step, though it felt like hooks had been set in my heart and it was ten hells to pull against them. I saw Mikah, reeling dizzily, seize Brandgar by the collar.

"Forgive me, lord!" Mikah cuffed their king hard, first across one cheek then the other. Terrible fury flared for an instant beneath Brandgar's countenance, then he seemed to remember himself. He clutched at his King-Shadow like a man being pulled away from a pier by a riptide.

"Gudrun," yelled Brandgar, "give us strength against this sorcery, or we are all about to consummate very painful love affairs!"

Our sorceress, too, had steeled her will. She swung the strange drums from her back, gasping as though she'd just run a great distance, and began to beat a weak, hesitant counter rhythm in the casual Ajja style:

> *"Heart be stone and eyes be clear*
> *Gudrun sees the puppeteer—*
> *Fire sings eights, Gudrun sevens*
> *This spell your power leavens . . ."*

I felt the rhythm of Gudrun's drumming like the hoofbeats of cavalry horses, rushing closer to bring aid, and for a moment it seemed the terrible lure of the fire-dancers was fading. Then they spun faster, and glowed fiercely white, and ribbons of smoke curled from their feet as they pirouetted across the tiles. Their voices rose, more lovely than ever, and I choked back a sob, balanced on the edge of madness. Why wasn't I embracing them? What sort of damned fool wouldn't want to hurl himself into that fire?

> *"The fly with hateful flit and bite*
> *The swordsman's feint that wins the fight*
> *The thief enshrouded in the night*
> *The world's true king is distraction . . ."*

Mikah knelt and punched the tiles, hard, screaming as their knuckles turned red. "I can't think," they cried, "I can't think—what's the song beneath the song?"

> *"The lasting truths poets compose*
> *The lowly tavern juggling shows*
> *Friends over card games come to blows*
> *You're chained like dogs to distraction . . ."*

"Fire!" bellowed Brandgar, who was stumbling with the eerie movements of a sleepwalker toward his destined fire-dancer, which was a scant few yards away. "Fire is beneath the song! No, stone! Stone is below the dancers! No, the mountain! The mountain is below us all! Gudrun!"

None of Brandgar's guesses loosened the coils of desire that crushed my chest and my loins and my mind. Gudrun shifted tempo again, and beat desperately at her drums in the stave rhythm of formal Ajja skaldry:

> *"Now to sixes singing,*
> *Ajja Gudrun knows well:*
> *Hellfire dancer's contest*
> *Can be met with no spell.*
> *Grimly laughs the king-worm,*
> *Mortal toys must burn soon;*
> *Fly now spear of Wave-King,*
> *Breaking stones before ruin!"*

With that, Gudrun fixed herself like a slinger on a battlefield and pitched her rune-stitched drums straight at Brandgar's head. Their impact, or the repeated shock of such treatment at the hands of his companions, brought him round to himself one final, crucial time.

"The wall," shouted Gudrun, falling to her knees. "The song of distraction is the distraction! The song beneath the song . . . is beneath the song on the wall!"

Heat stabbed the unprotected skin of my face like a thousand darting needles. Smoke curled now from the sleeves and lapels of my jacket; I breathed the scent of my own burning as my fire-dancer leaned in, looming above me at arm's reach, and I had never known anything more beautiful, and I had never ached for anything more powerfully, and I knew that I was dead.

In the corner of my vision, I glimpsed Brandgar steady on his feet, and with the most desperate rage I ever saw, he charged howling past his grasping fire-dancer and drove the point of Cold-Thorn into the center of the Helfalkyn Wormsong that glowed upon the chamber wall. Rock and dust exploded past him, and revealed there beneath the fall of shattered stone were lines of words glowing coldly blue. Quickly, clumsily, but with true feeling Brandgar sang:

> *"From the death here, all be turning*
> *Still the song, forsake the burning*
> *Chance at mountaintop our earning*
> *Though golden gain is distraction!"*

Instantly the blazing heat roiling the air before my face vanished; the deadly whites and oranges of the fire-dancers became the cool blue of the new song on the wall. An easement washed over me, as though I had plunged my whole body into a cold, clear river. I fell over, exhausted, groaning with pleasure and disbelief at being alive, and I was not alone. We all lay there gasping like idiots for some time, chests heaving like the near drowned, laughing and sobbing to ourselves as we came to terms with our memories of the fire-song's seduction. The memory did not fade, and has not faded, and to be free of it will be both a wonder and a sorrow until the day I die.

"Well sung, son of Erika and Orthild," said one of the gentled fire-dancers in a voice nothing like that which had nearly conquered us with delight. "Well played, daughter of the sky. The gift you leave us is an honor. Your diminishment is an honor."

The blue shapes faded into thin air, leaving only the orange pillar of fire which still poured from the rock chimney; it seemed our host was done with offering chances to escape. Then I saw that Brandgar was on his feet, staring motionless at a pair of objects, one held in each hand.

The two halves of the broken spear Cold-Thorn.

"Oh, my king," sighed Gudrun, wincing as she stood and retrieved her drums. "Forgive me."

Brandgar stared down at his sundered weapon without answering for some time, then sighed. "There is nothing to forgive, sorceress. My guesses were all bad, and your answer was true."

Slowly, reverently, he set the two parts of Cold-Thorn on the floor.

"Nine-and-twenty years, and it has never failed me. I lay it here as a brother on a battlefield. I give it to the stories to come."

Then he hefted his second spear over his shoulder, though he still refused to unbind the leather from its point, and his old grin appeared like an actor taking a curtain call.

"Bide no more; the night is not forever, and we must climb. With every step, I more desire conversation with the dragon. Come!"

FOURTH, HOW WE PASSED FROM THE BRITTLE BONES OF THE MOUNTAIN TO THE SNOW OF DEATH

Shaken but giddy, we wandered on into many-pillared galleries, backlit by troughs and fountains of incandescent lava that flowed like sluggish water. The heat of it was such that to approach made us mindful of the burning we had only narrowly escaped, and by unspoken agreement we stayed well clear of the stuff. It made soft sounds as it ran, belching and bubbling in the main, but also an unnerving glassy crackling where it touched the edges of its containers, and there darkened to silvery black.

"A strangeness, even for this place," said Gudrun, brushing her fingers across one of the stone pillars. "There's a resting power here. Not merely in the drawing up of the mountain's boiling blood, which is not wholly natural. There are forces bound and balanced in these pillars, as if they might be set loose by design."

"A new trap?" said Brandgar.

"If so, it's meant to catch half the Dragon's Anvil when it goes," said Gudrun. "Crale won't be shielding us from that with his bottom."

"Is it a present danger to us?" I asked.

"Most likely," said Gudrun.

"I welcome every new course at this feast," said Brandgar. "Come! We were meant to be climbing!"

Up, then, via spiral staircases wide enough for an Ajja longship to slide down, assuming its sails were properly furled. Into more silent galleries we passed, with molten rock to light our way, until we emerged at last beneath a high ceiling set with shiny black panes of glass. Elsewhere they might have been windows lighting a glorious temple or a rich villa, but here they were just a deadness in the stones. A cool breeze blew through this place, and Mikah sniffed the air.

"We're close now," they said. "Perhaps not yet at the summit, but that's the scent of the outside."

This chamber was fifty yards long and half as wide, with a small door on the far side. Curiously enough, there was no obvious passage I could see suited for a dragon. Before the door stood a polished obsidian statue just taller than Brandgar. The manlike figure bore the head of an owl, with its eyes closed, and in place of folded wings it had a fan of arms, five per side, jutting from its upper back. This is a common shape for a *barrow-vardr,* a tomb guardian the Ajja like to carve on those intermittent occasions when they manage to retrieve enough of a dead hero for a burial ceremony. I was not surprised when the lids of its eyes slowly rose, and it regarded us with orbs like fractured rubies.

"Here have I stood since the coming of the master," spoke the statue, "waiting to put you in your grave then stand as its ornament, King-on-the-Waves."

"The latter would be a courtesy but the former will never happen," said Brandgar, cheerfully setting his wrapped spear down. "Let us fight if we must though I will lose my temper if you have another song to sing us."

"Black, my skin will turn all harm," said the statue. "Silver skin forfeits the charm."

"Verse is nearly as bad," growled Brandgar. He sprinted at the statue and hurled himself at its midsection, in the manner of a wrestler. I sighed inwardly at this, but you have seen that Brandgar was one part forethought steeped in a thousand parts hasty action, and he was never happier than when he was testing the strength of a foe by offering it his skull for crushing. The ten arms of the barrow-vardr spread in an instant, and the two opponents grappled only briefly before Brandgar was hurled twenty feet backwards, narrowly missing Gudrun. He landed very loudly.

Mikah moved to the attack then with short curved blades, and I swallowed my misgivings and backed them with my own daggers. Sparks flew from every touch of Mikah's knives against the thing's skin, and the air was filled with a mad whirl of obsidian arms and dodging thieves. Mikah were faster than I, so I let them stay closer and keep the thing's attention. I lunged at it from behind, again and again, until one of the arms slapped me so hard I saw constellations of stars dancing across my vision. I stumbled away with more speed than grace, and a moment later Mikah broke off the fight as well, vaulting clear. Past them charged Brandgar, shouting something brave and unintelligible. A few seconds later he was flying across the chamber again.

Gudrun took over then, chanting and waving her hands. She threw vials and wooden tubes at the barrow-vardr, and green fire erupted on its arms and head. Then came a series of silver flashes, and a great ear-stinging boom, and the thing vanished in an eruption of smoke and force that cracked the stones beneath its feet and sent chips of rock singing through the air, cutting my face. Coughing, wincing, I peered into the smoke and was gravely disappointed, though perhaps not surprised, to see the thing still standing there quite unaltered. Gudrun swore. Then Brandgar found his feet again and ran headlong into the smoke. There was a ringing metallic thump. He exited the haze on his customary trajectory.

"I believe we might take this thing at its word that we can do nothing against it while its substance is black," said Mikah. "How do we turn its skin silver?"

"Perhaps we could splash it with quicksilver," said Gudrun. "If we only had some. Or coat it with hot running iron and polish it to a gleam, given a suitable furnace, five blacksmiths, and most of a day to work."

"I packed none of those things," muttered Mikah. Little intelligent discourse took place for the next few minutes, as the invulnerable statue chased us in turns around the chamber, occasionally enduring some fresh fire or explosion conjured by Gudrun without missing a step. She also tried to infuse it with the silvery light by which we had made our way up the darker parts of the mountain, but the substance of the barrow-vardr drank even this spell without effect. Soon we were all scorched and cut and thinking of simpler times, when all we'd had to worry about was burning to death in dancing fires.

"Crale! Lend me your sling!" shouted Mikah, who were badly beset and attempting not to plunge into a trough of lava as they skipped and scurried from ten clutching hands. I made a competent handoff of the weapon and a nestled stone, and was neither swatted nor burned for my trouble. Mikah found just enough space to wind up and let fly—not at the barrow-vardr, but at the ceiling. The stone hit one of the panes of black glass with a flat crack, but either it was too strong to break or Mikah's angle of attack was not to their advantage.

I admit that I didn't grasp Mikah's intent, but Gudrun redressed my deficiency. "I see what you're on about," she shouted. "Guard yourselves!"

She gave us no time to speculate on her meaning. She readied another one of her alarming magical gimmicks and hurled it at the ceiling, where it burst in fire and smoke. The blast shattered not only the glass pane Mikah had aimed for, but all those near it, so that it rained sharp fragments everywhere. I tucked in my head and legs and did a creditable impersonation of a turtle. When the tinkling and shattering came to an end, I glanced up and saw that the sundering of the blackened windows had let in diffuse shafts of cold light, swirling with smoke. Mikah had been right; we were indeed close to open sky, and in the hours we had spent making our way through the heart of the Anvil the moons had also risen, shedding the red reflection of sunset in favor of silvery-white luster. This light fell on the statue, and Brandgar wasted no time in testing its effect.

Now when he tackled the barrow-vardr it yielded like an opponent of ordinary flesh. The king's strength bore it to the stones, and though it flailed for leverage with its vast collection of hands, Brandgar struck its head thrice with his joined fists, blows that made me wince in over-generous sympathy with our foe. Imagine a noise like an anvil repeatedly dropped on a side of beef. When these had sufficiently dampened the thing's resistance, Brandgar heaved it onto his shoulders, then flung it into the nearest fountain of molten rock, where it flamed and thrashed and quickly sank from our sight.

"I shall have to look elsewhere for a suitable watch upon my crypt." Brandgar retrieved the wrapped spear he had once more refused to employ and wiped away smears of blood from several cuts on his neck and forehead. "Presuming I am fated to fill one."

The small door swung open for us as we approached, and we were all so battle-drunk and blasted that we made a great show of returning the courtesy with bows and salutes. The room beyond was equal in length to the chamber of the barrow-vardr, but it was all one great staircase, rising gently to a portal that was notable for its simplicity. This was no door, but merely a passage in stone, and through it we could see more moon-light and stars. The chamber was bitterly cold, and drifting in flurries across the stairs were clouds of scattered snow that came from and passed into thin air.

"Hold a moment," said Gudrun, kneeling to examine a plaque set into the floor. I peered over her shoulder and saw more Kandric script:

> *Here and last cross the serpent-touched snow*
> *In each flake the sting of many asps*
> *To touch skin once brings life's unmaking*

"To be stymied by snow in the heart of a fire-mountain," I said, shuddering at the thought of death from something as small as a grain of salt brushing naked skin. "That would be a poor end."

"We won't be trying it on for fit," said Gudrun. She gestured, and with a flash of silver light attempted the same trick I had seen in Underwing Hall, to move herself in the blink of an eye from one place to another. This time the spell went awry; with an answering flash of light she rebounded from some unseen barrier just before the stairs, and wound up on her back, coughing up pale wisps of steam.

"It seems we're meant to do this on foot or not at all," she groaned. "Here's a second ploy, then. If the snow is mortal to this flesh, I'll sing myself another."

She made a low rumbling sound in her throat and gulped air with ominous croaks, and with each gulp her skin darkened and her face elongated, stretching until it assumed the wedge shape of a viper's head. Her eyes grew, turning greenish gold while the pupils narrowed to dark vertical crescents. In a moment the transformation was complete; she flicked a narrow tongue past scaled lips and smiled.

"Serpent skin and serpent flesh to ward serpent bite," she hissed. "And if it fails, I shall look very silly, and we can laugh long in the Fields of Swords and Roses."

"In the Fields of Swords and Roses," intoned Mikah and Brandgar.

But there would be no laughing there, at least not on this account, for wearing the flesh of a lizard Gudrun hopped up the stairs, clawed green hands held out for balance, through twenty paces of instant death, until she stood beside the doorway to the night, unharmed. She gave an exaggerated curtsy.

"And can you do the same for us?" shouted Mikah.

"The changing-gift is in the heart of the wizard," she replied, "else I would have turned you all into toads sometime ago and carried you in my pack, loosing you only for good behavior."

Mikah sighed and pulled on their gloves. They studied the waft and weft of the snow for some time, nodding and flexing their hips.

"Mikah," I said, kenning their intentions, "this seems a bit much even for one of your slipperiness."

"We've each come here with all the skills of lives long lived," they said. "This is the test of those lives and skills, my friend."

Mikah went up the steps, fully clothed, but still their face and neck and wrists were unprotected. I understand it must be hard to credit, but that is only because you never saw Mikah move, and any attempt to describe it with words must be a poor telling, even mine. Swaying and weaving, whirling at a speed that made them seem half ghost, they simply dodged between the falling snowflakes as you or I might step between other people walking slowly along a road. In less time than it takes for me to speak of it they had ascended the deadly twenty paces and stood safe beside Gudrun. They stretched idly, in the manner of a cat pretending it has always been at rest, and that no mad leap or scramble has just taken place.

"Well done!" said Brandgar. "This is embarrassing, Crale. Those two have raised the stakes, and I am not sure how to make a show to match theirs, let alone surpass it."

"My concerns are more prosaic," I said. "I have no powers or skills I can think of to get myself out of this room."

"We would be poor friends to leave you here at the threshold," said Brandgar. "And I fear it would disappoint our host. I have a notion to bear us both across; can you trust me, as I have trusted you, absolutely and without objection?"

"You needn't use my affections as a lever, Brandgar," said I, though truthfully, in the face of the serpent-touched snow, he rather did. "Anyway, I am famous among my friends for having never in my life behaved with any particular wisdom."

"Be sure to make yourself small in my arms. Ho, Mikah!" Brandgar threw his wrapped spear up and over the snow, and Mikah caught it. Without taking any further measures to brace my resolve, Brandgar unclasped his cloak. Then he seized me, crushing me to his chest as if I were an errant child about to be borne away for punishment. Apprehending his intentions, I clung to him with my legs, tucked my head against his armored coat, and once again commended my spirit to whichever celestial power was on guard over the souls of fools that night. Brandgar spun his cloak over the pair of us like a tent, covering our arms and heads, blotting out my vision as well as his. Then, shouting some Ajja battle blather that was lost on me, he charged blindly up the steps. My world became a shuddering darkness, and I vow that I could hear the hiss and sizzle of the venomous snow as it met the cloak, as though it were angry at not being able to reach us. Then we bowled over Gudrun and Mikah, and wound up tangled in a heap, cloak and spear and laughing adventurers, safe and entirely bereft of dignity at the top of the steps. Save for a lingering smell in our clothes and gear, the power of the snow seemed to promptly evaporate outside the grasp of the sorcerous flurries.

We were all gloriously alive. The light of moon and stars drew us on.

FINALLY, WHAT AWAITED US AT THE
TOP OF THE DRAGON'S ANVIL

Atop the mountain lay a caldera, a flat-bottomed cauldron of rock wider than a longbow shot, and the stars were such brilliant figures of fire overhead that we could have seen well by them had it been necessary. But it was not, for here was the treasure of the dragon Glimraug, and the dragon was clearly much taken with the sight.

Arched pavilions of wood and stone ringed the caldera, each multiply tiered and grand as any temple ever set by human hands. A thousand glass lanterns of the subtlest beauty had been hung from the beams and gables of these structures, shedding warm gold and silver light that scintillated on piles of riches too vast to comprehend, even as we stood there gaping at them. Here were copper coins in drifts twenty feet high and silver spilling like the waters of an undammed river; gold nuggets, gold bars, gold discs, gold dust in ivory-inset barrels. Here were the stolen coins of ten centuries, plunder from Sendaria, the Crescent Cities, Far Olan, and the Sunken Lands. Here were the cold dead faces of monarchs unknown to us, the mottos stamped in languages we couldn't guess, a thousand currencies molded as circles, squares, octagons, and far less practical shapes. There were caskets beyond counting, rich varnished woodcrafts that were treasures in themselves, and each held overflowing piles of pearls, amethysts, citrines, emeralds, diamonds, and sapphires. To account it all in meanest summary would double the length of my telling. Here were gilded thrones and icon-tables, gleaming statues of all the gods from all the times and places the human race has set foot, crowns and chalices and toques and periapts and rings. Here were weapons crusted with gems or gleaming enchantments, here were bolts of silk and ceramic jars as tall as myself, full of gauds and baubles, drinking horns and precious mechanisms. All the mountaintop was awash in treasure, tides of it, hillocks of it the size of houses.

There was nothing pithy to say. Even getting it down would become the work of years, I calculated. Years, and hundreds or thousands of people, and engineers and machinery, and ships—if we could indeed force the dragon to part with this grand achievement, Helfalkyn would have to double in size just to service the logistics of plunder. I would need galleons to carry a tenth part of my rightful share, and then vaults, and an army to guard the vaults. These riches loosed upon the world would shake it for generations. My great-great-great-great-grandchildren would relieve themselves in solid gold chamber pots!

"Gudrun," said Brandgar, "is all here as we see it? Is this a glamour?"

The mere thought broke me from the hypnotic joy of my contemplation. Gudrun cast a set of carved bones on the ground. We all watched anxiously, but after consulting her signs only briefly she giggled like a giddy child. "No, lord. What's gold is gold, as far as we can see. And what's silver is silver, and what's onyx is onyx, and thuswise."

"This is the greatest trap of all," I said. "We shall all die of old age before we can carry it anywhere useful."

"We are missing only one thing," said Brandgar. "And that is our host, who will doubtless prefer to see us die of other causes before we take any of it. But I am content to let it come when it will; to walk amidst such splendor is a gift. Let us stay on our guard but avail ourselves of the courtesy."

And so we wandered Glimraug's garden of imponderable wealth, running our hands over statues and gemstones and shields, caught up in our private entrancements. So often had I won through to a rumored treasure in some dusty tower or rank sewer or mountain cave, only to discover empty, rusting boxes and profitless junk. It was hard to credit that the most ridiculous legend of wealth in all the world had turned out to be the most accurate.

Plumes of smoke and mist drifted from vents in the rock beyond the treasure pavilions, and my eyes were drawn to another such plume rising gently from a pile of silver. From there my attention was snared by a scattering of dark stones upon the surface of the metal coins. I approached, and saw that these were rubies, hundreds of them, ranging in color from that of fresh pumping blood to that of faded carnations. I have always been a particular admirer of red stones, and I shook a few into my hands, relishing the clink and glimmer of the facets.

The silver coins shifted, and from within them came a blue shape, a yard wide and as long as I was tall. So gently did it rise, so familiar did it seem that I stared at it for a heartbeat before I realized that it was a hand, a scaled hand, and the dark things glistening at the near ends of its digits were talons longer than my daggers. Delight transmuted to horror, and I was rooted with fear as the still-gentle hand closed on mine from beneath, trapping me with painless but inescapable pressure. The difference in scale? Imagine I had elected to shake hands with a cat, then refused to let go.

"Tarkaster Crale," rumbled a voice that was like a bolt of the finest velvet smoldering in a furnace. "The rubies are most appropriate for contemplation. Red for all the blood that lies beneath this treasure. The million mortals who died in vaults and towers and ships and armies so that we could take these proud things into our care."

The pile of silver shuddered, then parted and slid to the ground in every direction, displaced by the rising of the creature that had lain inside it, marked only by steaming breath curling up from nostrils as wide as my head. The arms rose, each a Brandgar-weight of scaled strength. I gaped at the lithe body the color of dark sapphire, its back ridges like the thorns of some malevolent flower, its impossibly delicate wings with membranes that glistened like a steel framework hung with nothing more than moonlight. Atop the sinuous neck was a head somehow vulpine and serpentine at once, with sharp flat ears that rang from their piercings, dozens of silver rings that would have encircled my neck. The dragon had a mane, a shock of blue-white strands that vibrated with the stiffness of crystal rather than the suppleness of hair or fur. The creature's eyes were black as the sky, split only by slashes of pulsing silver, and I could not meet them; even catching a glance made my vision flash as though I had stared at the sun. I could not move as the dragon's other hand reached out and closed around my waist, again with perfect care and unassailable strength. I was lifted like a doll.

"I . . . I can put the stones back," I burbled. "I'm sorry!"

"Oh, that is not true," said the dragon. Its breath smelled like burning copper. "And if it were, you would not be the sort of mortal to which we would speak. No, you are not sorry. You are terrified."

"Hail, Glimraug the Fair!" shouted Brandgar. "Hail, Sky Tyrant, Shipbreaker, and Night-Scathe!"

"Hail, King-on-the-Waves, Son of Erika and Orthild, Landless Champion, Remover of Others' Nuisances," said Glimraug, setting me down and nudging me to run along as if I were a pet. I gladly retreated to stand with my companions, judging it prudent to toss the rubies back onto the dragon-tossed pile of silver first. "Hail, companions to the king! You have endured every courtesy provided for our visitors, and glimpsed what no mortal has for many years. Have you been dispatched here to avenge some Ajja prince? Did we break a tower or two in passing? Did we devour someone's sheep?"

"We have come for our own sakes," said Brandgar. "And for yours, and for your treasure as a last resort. We have heard the Helfalkyn Wormsong."

I had no idea what Brandgar meant by any of that, but the dragon snorted and bared its teeth.

"That is not the usual order in which our visitors lay their priorities," it said. "But all who come here have heard the song. What is your meaning?"

"There are songs, and there are songs beneath songs, are there not?" Brandgar removed the leather wrappings of his unused spear. Ash-hafted, the weapon had the lethal simplicity of a boar spear, with a pyramidal striking tip forged of some dark steel with a faint mottle, like flowing water. "Others heard the song of gold, but we have heard the song of the gold-taker, the song of your plan, the song of your hope. We have brought ending and eyes."

"Have you?" whispered the dragon, and it was wondrous to see for an instant, just an instant, a break in its inhuman self-regard. It caught its breath, and the noise was like a bellows priming to set a furnace alight, which might have been closer to the truth than I preferred. "Are you in earnest, o king, o companions? Are we in sympathy? For if this is mere presumption, we will give you a death that will take five lifetimes to unravel in your flesh, and while you rot screaming in the darkness we will pile the corpses of Ajja children in a red mound higher than any tower. Your kinfolk will gray and dwindle knowing that their posterity has been ground into meat for the flies! This we swear by every day of every year of our age, and we have known ten thousand."

"Hear this. For long months we sought and strove," said Brandgar, "in Merikos, where the dragon Elusiel fell, where the wizards were said to keep one last jar of the burning blood that had seeped from her wounds."

"We lost many companions," added Gudrun. "The wizards lost everything, including the blood."

"For another year we dispensed with a fortune in Sulagar," said Mikah, "engaging the greatest of the old masters there in the crafting of black-folded steel."

"Twenty spears they made for me," resumed Brandgar. "Twenty I tested and found wanting. The twenty-first I quenched in the blood of Elusiel, and carried north to Helfalkyn, and have carried here to be used but once. Its makers called it *Adresh*, the All-Piercing, but I am the one who gave it purpose, and I have named it Glory-Kindler."

Glimraug threw back its head and roared. We all staggered, clutching our ears, even Brandgar. The sound rattled the very air in our lungs, and I did not merely imagine that the mountain shook beneath us, for I could see the lanterns bobbing and the treasure piles shaking. Lightning flashed at the rim of the caldera, bolt after bolt, splitting the darkness and painting everything in flashes of golden white, and the thunder that followed boomed like mangonel stones shattering walls.

"Perhaps it is you," said the dragon, when the terrific noises of this display had faded. "Perhaps it *is* you! But know that we are not so base as to tip the scales. Achieve us! Hold nothing back, for nothing shall be held in turn."

"This is an excellent doom," said Brandgar, "and we shall not take it lightly."

The dragon flared its wings, and for an instant their translucence hung like an aura in the night. Then, with a fresh roar of exultation, Glimraug hurled itself into the air, raising a wind that lashed us with dust and shook lanterns from their perches. I felt something close to seasickness, for in the manner of my profession I had blithely presumed we would make some effort to trick, circumvent, weaken, or even negotiate with our foe rather than honorably baring our asses and inviting a kick.

"Brandgar," I yelled, "what in all the hells are we supposed to be doing here?"

"Something beautiful. Your only task is to survive." He gave me a powerful squeeze on the shoulder, then pushed me away. "Run, Crale! Keep your wits loose in the scabbard. Think only of living!"

Then Glimraug crashed back down, and treasure fountained in a fifty-yard radius. Brandgar, Gudrun, and Mikah evaded the snapping jaws and the buffet of the wings, and now they commenced to fight with everything they had.

Gudrun chanted and scattered glass vials from her collection of strange accoutrements, breaking them against the stone, loosing the powers and spirits bound therein. She held nothing back for any more rainy days— seething white mists rose at Glimraug's feet, and in their miasmic tatters I saw the faces of hungry things eager to wreak harm. The dragon reared, raised high its arms, and uttered darkly hissing words in a language that made me want to loose my bowels. I ran for one of the treasure pavilions, hid behind a stout wooden pillar, and peered around the side to watch the battle unfold.

Brandgar struck for Glimraug's flank but the sapphire-scaled worm flicked its tail like a whip, knocking Brandgar and his vaunted new spear well away. Mikah fared better, dashing under the dragon's forelimbs and heaving themselves into a wing joint, and from there to the ridges of its back. The whorls of Gudrun's spirit-mist became a column, bone-white, wailing as it surged against Glimraug's face and body. It seemed as if the dragon were attempting to climb a leafless winter tree, and failing—but only for a moment.

With a sound like a river rushing swollen in spring's first melt, Glimraug opened wide its maw and sucked Gudrun's ghost-substance into its throat as a man might draw deeply from a pipe. Then it reared again, and blasted the stuff high into the air, trailing flickers of blue-and-white fire. The spirit-mist rose like smoke and quickly faded from sight against the stars, whatever power it had contained either stolen or destroyed. Then the dragon lunged with foreclaws for Gudrun, but with a flash of silver she was safe by twenty yards, and hurling her fire gimmicks without dismay. Orange fire erupted at Glimraug's feet, to little effect.

Now Gudrun sung further spell-songs, and hurled from a leather bag a thousand grasping strands of spun flax, which sought the dragon's limbs and wove themselves into bindings. Glimraug snapped them in a trice, as you or I might break a single rotten thread, and the golden fibers floated to the ground. Then the dragon's dignity broke, for Mikah had made their way up into its gleaming mane, and from there stabbed at one of its eyes. The blade met that terrible lens, I swear, but either luck wasn't with the thief or the weapon was too commonplace to give more than a scratch. Still, neither you nor I would appreciate a scratch against an eye, and the dragon writhed, trying to fling Mikah off. They kept their perch, but only just, and could do little else but hold fast.

Glimraug whirled and leapt away from Gudrun with the easy facility of a cat, once more scattering delicate objects far and wide with the shock of its landing. It struck at a pile of silver coins, jaws gaping, and took what must have been tons of the metal into its mouth as a greedy man might slurp his stew. Then it breathed deep, hissing breaths through its nostrils, and its neck bulged with every passage of air. A glow lit the gaps of the scales in the dragon's chest, faint red at first but swiftly brightening and shifting to blue, then white. Mikah cried out and leapt from the dragon's mane, trailing smoke. Their boots and gloves were on fire.

The dragon charged back toward Gudrun, mighty claws hammering the stones. The sorceress chanted, and a barrier of blue ice took shape before her, thick and overhanging like the crest of a wave. Glimraug drew in another long breath, then expelled it, and for an instant the blazing light of its internal fire was visible. Then the dragon breathed forth a stream of molten silver, all that it had consumed and melted, like the great burst of a geyser, wreathed in crackling white flame. The wave of burning death blasted Gudrun's ice shield to steam and enveloped her in an instant. Then came eruption after eruption of green-and-orange fire as the things she had carried met their fate. I recoiled from the terrible heat and the terrible sight, but to the last she had not even flinched.

I was forced to run to another pavilion as rivulets of crackling metal flowed toward me. Glimraug chuckled deep in its throat, orange-hot streams still dripping from between its fangs and cooling silver-black beneath its chin, forming a crust of added scales. Mikah howled furiously. They had quenched the flames, and however much pain they must have been bracing against, they did not reveal it by slowing down. Glimraug's claws came down twice, and Mikah was there to receive the blow neither time. Once more the thief leapt for the dragon's smoking back, but now they rebounded cannily and clung to the leading edge of the dragon's left wing. Before the dragon was able to flick them away, Mikah pulled out one of their blades and bore down on it with both arms, driving it into the gossamer substance of the dragon's wing membrane. This yielded where the eye had not. Mikah slid down as the stuff parted like silk, then fell to the ground when they ran out of membrane, leaving a flapping rent above them.

Glimraug instantly folded the hurt wing sharply to its side, as an unwary cat might pull back a paw that has touched hot fireplace stones. Then, heaving itself forward, it whirled tail and claw alike at the Ajja thief, whip-smack, whip-smack. Nearly too late I realized that the next stroke would demolish my place of safety. I fled and rolled as Glimraug's tail splintered the pavilion; a hard-flung wave of baubles and jewelry knocked me farther than I'd intended. I slid to a halt one handspan from the edge of a cooling silver stream, and hundreds of coins rolled and rattled past me.

I looked up just in time to see Mikah's fabled luck run its course. Stumbling over scattered treasure, at last showing signs of injury, they tried to be elsewhere for the next swipe of a claw but finally kept the unfortunate rendezvous. Glimraug seized them eagerly and hauled them up before its eyes, kicking and stabbing to the last.

"Like for like," rumbled the dragon, and with two digits of its free hand it encircled Mikah's left arm, then tore it straight out of the socket. Blood gushed and ran down the dragon's scales; Mikah screamed, but somehow raised their remaining blade for one last futile blow. The dragon cast Mikah into a distant treasure pavilion like a discarded toy. The impact was bone-shattering; the greatest thief I have ever known was slain and buried in an explosion of blood-streaked gold coins.

"One died in silver, one died in gold," said Glimraug, turning and stalking toward me.

"Tarkaster Crale won't live to be old," I whispered.

Up went the bloodstained claw. I heaved myself to my knees, wondering where I intended to dodge to, and the claw came down.

Well short of me, clutched in pain.

Brandgar had recovered himself, and buried the spear Glory-Kindler to the full length of its steel tip in the joint of Glimraug's right wing. The blood that spilled from the wound steamed, and the stones burst into flames where it fell on them. Brandgar withdrew the smoking spear and darted back as the dragon turned, but it did not attack. It shuddered, and stared at the gash in its hide.

"The venom of Elusiel, kin of our kin," said the dragon with something like wonder. "A thousand wounds have bent our scales, but never have we felt the like."

Brandgar spun Glory-Kindler over his head, pointed it at the dragon in salute, and then braced himself in a pikeman's stance. "Never have you *faced* the like," he shouted. "Let it be here and now!"

Ponderously the dragon turned to face him; some of its customary ease was gone, but it was still a towering foe, still possessed of fearsome power. With its wings folded tight and burning blood streaming from one flank, it spread its taloned arms and pounced. Brandgar met it screaming in triumph. Spear pierced dragon breast, and an instant later the down sweep of Glimraug's talons shattered the haft of Glory-Kindler and tore through Brandgar's kingly coat-of-plate. The man fell moaning, and the dragon toppled beside him, raising a last cloud of ashen dust. Disbelieving, I stumbled up and ran to them.

"O king," the dragon murmured, wheezing, and with every breath spilling more fiery ichor on the ground, "in all our ten thousand years, we have had but four friends, and we have only met them this night."

"Crale, you look awful." Brandgar smiled up at me, blood streaming down his face. I saw at once that his wound was mortal; under smashed ribs and torn flesh I could see the soft pulse of a beating heart, and a man once opened like that won't long keep hold of his spirit. "Don't mourn. Rejoice, and remember."

"You really didn't want the damned treasure," I said, kneeling beside him. "You crazy Ajja! 'Bring ending and eyes,' meaning, find a way to kill a dragon ... and bring a witness when you do it."

"You've been a great help, my friend." Brandgar coughed, and winced as it shook his chest. "I was never made to retire quietly from valor and wait for the years to catch me. None of us were."

"It comes," said Glimraug. Shaking, bleeding fire, the dragon hauled itself up, then lifted Brandgar gently, almost reverently in its cupped hands. "We can feel the venom tightening around our heart. The long-awaited wonder comes! True death-friend, let our pyre be shared, let us build it now! To take is not to keep."

"To take is not to keep," answered Brandgar. His voice was weakening. "Yes, I see. It's perfect. Will you do it while I can see?"

"With gladness, we loose our holds and wards on the fires bound within the mountain." Glimraug closed its eyes and muttered something, and the stone shifted below my feet in a manner more ominous than before. I gaped as one of the more distant treasure pavilions seemed to sink into the caldera floor, and a cloud of smoke and sparks rose from where it had gone down.

Then another pavilion sank, then another. With rumbling, cracking, sundering noises, the dragon's treasure was being spilled into reservoirs of lava. Flames roared from the cracks in the ground as wood, cloth, and other precious things tumbled to their destruction.

"What by all the gods are you doing?" I cried.

"This is the greatest of all the dragon-hoards that was ever built," said Brandgar. "A third of all the treasures our race has dug from the ground, Crale. The plunder of a million lives. But there's no true glory in the holding. All that must come in the taking . . . and the letting go."

"You're crazier than the Ajja!" I yelled at Glimraug, entirely forgetting myself. "You engineered this place to be destroyed?"

"Not so much as a shaving of scented wood shall leave with you, Tarkaster Crale." Glimraug carefully shifted Brandgar into one palm, then reached out and set a scimitar-sized talon on my shoulder. Spatters of dragon blood smoked on my leather jacket. "Though you leave with our blessing. Our arts can bear you to a place of safety."

"Wonderful, but what the hell is the *point*?"

Cold pain lashed across my face, and I gasped. Glimraug had flicked its talon upward, a casual gesture—and all of you can still see the result here on my cheek. The wound bled for days and the scar has never faded.

"The point is that it has never been done before," said Glimraug. Another treasure pavilion was swallowed by fire nearby. "And it shall never be done again. All things in this world are made to go into the fire, Tarkaster Crale. All things raise smoke. The smoke of incense is sweet. The smoke of wood is dull haze. But don't you see? The smoke of gold . . . is glory."

I wiped blood from my face, and might have said more, but Glimraug made a gesture, and I found that I could not move. The world began to grow dim around me, and the last I saw of the caldera was Brandgar weakly raising a hand in farewell, and the dragon holding him with a tenderness and regard that was not imagined.

"Take the story, Crale!" called Brandgar. "Take it to the world!"

After a moment of dizzy blackness, I found myself back at the foot of the Dragon's Anvil, on the gentle path that led up to it from Helfalkyn. The sky was alight with the orange fire of a false dawn; no sooner did I glance back up at the mountaintop than it erupted in an all-out confla-gration, orange flames blasting taller than the masts of ships, smoke roiling in a column that blotted out the moons as it rose.

Glimraug the Sky Tyrant was dead, and with it my friends Brandgar, Gudrun, and Mikah. And I, having lost my purse somewhere in the confusion, was now even poorer than I had been before I successfully reached the largest pile of assorted valuables in the history of the whole damn world.

I don't know how I made my way down the path without breaking my neck. My feet seemed to move of their own accord. I could perhaps believe that I was alive, or that I had witnessed the events of the night, but I could not quite manage to believe them both at the same time. A crowd came up from Helfalkyn then, armed and yammering, bearing lanterns and an unwise number of wine bottles, and from their exclama-tions I gathered that I looked as though I had been rolled in dung and baked in an oven.

They demanded to know what had happened atop the Anvil; most of Helfalkyn had roused itself when the thunder and lightning rolled, and by the time the flames were visible there wasn't anyone left in bed. My occasionally dodgy instinct for survival sputtered to life then; I realized that the denizens of a town entirely dedicated to coveting a dragon's treasure might not handle me kindly if I told them I had gone up with my friends and somehow gotten the treasure blasted out of existence. The solution was obvious—I told them I had seen everything, that I was the sole survivor, and that I would give the full and complete story only after I had received passage back to the Crescent Cities and safely disembarked from my ship.

Thus I made my first arrangement for compensation as a professional storyteller.

That, then, is how it all transpired. I heard that various scroungers from Helfalkyn sifted the shattered Anvil for years, but the dragon had its way—every last scrap of anything valuable had been dropped into the molten heart of the mountain, either burned or sunk from mortal reach forever. I retired from adventuring directly and took up the craft of sitting on my backside at the best place by the fire, telling glib confabulations to strangers for generally reasonable prices.

But one night a year, I don't tell a single lie. I tell a true story about kindred spirits who chose a doom I didn't understand at all when I walked away from it. And one night a year, I turn my bowl over, because the last thing I want to see for my troubles is a little pile of coins reminding me that I am an old, old man, and I sure as hell understand it now.

Rich Larson

Rich Larson was born in West Africa, has studied in Rhode Island and Edmonton, Alberta, and worked in a small Spanish town outside Seville. He now lives in Grande Prairie, Alberta, in Canada. He won the 2014 Dell Award and the 2012 Rannu Prize for Writers of Speculative Fiction. In 2011 his cyberpunk novel *Devolution* was a finalist for the Amazon Breakthrough Novel Award. His short work appears or is forthcoming in *Asimov's Science Fiction*, *The Magazine of Fantasy & Science Fiction*, *Clarkesworld*, *Interzone*, *Lightspeed*, *DSF*, *Strange Horizons*, *Apex Magazine*, *Beneath Ceaseless Skies*, *AE*, and many others, including the anthologies *Upgraded*, *Futuredaze*, and *War Stories*. Find him online at richwlarson.tumblr.com

In the tense and atmospheric story that follows, he takes us along to the gritty industrial city of Colgrid in company with two rogues seeking to unlock the secret of a fabulous treasure, and who find that the situation gets stranger and the knots they have to unravel more and more complicated with every step they take.

THE COLGRID CONUNDRUM

The channel was skinned with dark ice that squealed and crackled away under the ship's prow; apart from that they entered Colgrid in silence.

For Crane, it was uncharacteristic. He sat spider-like on an overturned crate, elbows resting on bony knees, wide mouth hidden under a thick-knit scarf. His watery blue eyes narrowed to slits as he watched Colgrid's sprawling factories slide closer. Gilchrist stood, sinewy arms folded, breath escaping as a tendril of steam. He was comfortable in silence, but his dark eyes, normally always scanning, always measuring, looked off to nowhere.

On the deck between them sat the strongbox. It was a dull gray cube resting on four small clawed feet, one of which had been cracked in the escape. The sides were filigreed with a carefully crafted pattern of whorls and ripples. The top was ringed with concentric grooves, and in the deepest of them, where Crane's scrubbing hadn't reached, there was still a crust of dried-black blood.

As the ship moved deeper into the city, the smells of oil and machinery spiked through the cold air. Half the factories still churned, belching smog that hung over the city like an inky cloak, blotting out the stars overhead.

"Acrid as ever," Crane finally said. He adjusted his scarf with one long, pale hand. "But from what I've heard of this lock breaker, I surmise our stay will be brief. We should leave with only partially devastated lungs."

"Lucky," Gilchrist said, toneless.

The dock approached, lit by phosphor lanterns that glowed bright green in the darkness. The ship's crew stirred to action, cutting speed, making shouted calculations with the dockhands before the pitons launched with a muzzle flash and sharp crack. Thick cables winched them out of the current, reeling them into the mooring, making the ship's frame shiver and groan.

"It was unavoidable, Gilchrist," Crane said, as gangplanks thumped down and the hubbub of debarking grew around them. "You know that as well as I do."

Gilchrist made no reply, but his hands clenched more tightly. Under one thumbnail, where his scrubbing hadn't reached, there was still a sliver of dried-black blood.

They slipped away from the dock like shades, with the strongbox slung in a makeshift harness between them. The ship's captain had been paid for his averted eyes, and persuaded even further by the feathery white Guild scar Crane had exposed while adjusting his sleeve—no need for him to know that the criminal organization had been more or less dissolved for months now.

Tall lampposts lined Colgrid's streets, topped with the same glowing phosphor as on the dock, lighting a way through thickening smog. A mask vendor was hawking shrilly at the next corner.

"We should," Gilchrist said. "Not many gypsies up here."

Colgrid's denizens were pale-skinned and dark-eyed—Crane blended well enough, but Gilchrist's dusky skin could stick in a passerby's memory. If all went well, they would have the strongbox opened and be sailing for far warmer climes before anyone could identify them.

Crane flicked the vendor two silver coins and received two masks from the stall in return, flimsier versions of the bug-eyed creation that concealed her entire face.

"I'm told they now wear these in the courts," Crane said, slipping the mask over his mouth and nose. "Fashion is an unpredictable beast, is it not, madam?"

"Them ones just for show, they don't have a good filter." The vendor's voice came high and tinny through her mask. "Mine have the best filters."

Gilchrist kept a hand on the strongbox while Crane adjusted his mask, then swapped places to don his own. They continued on, moving deeper into the city, following the directions Gilchrist had memorized in a small filthy bar on Brask's wharf. The hour was late and the streets mostly empty. Both tensed when a tall figure emerged from the gloom on impossibly long, skeletal legs, but it was only a lamplighter, using the clicking mechanical stilts that were still a rarity everywhere but Colgrid. Each metal shin was painted with a scarlet circle.

The same insignia appeared a dozen more times as Crane and Gilchrist wound their way through the twisting streets: sometimes stenciled onto signboards above shops, sometimes painted raggedly straight onto the brick. In the neater versions, they could see it was meant to be a fine-toothed gear.

"I admit I'm unfamiliar with this particular cipher," Crane puffed, nodding his chin toward the closest. "What do you make of it, Gilchrist? A mark of allegiance?"

Gilchrist touched his arm momentarily, where a Guild scar twin to Crane's own was hidden under his sleeve. The Guild had never had a strong hold on Colgrid, and now, not at all. "Vacuums fill quickly," he said.

Crane massaged his shoulder and tightened his grip on the sling. A transient snow was starting to fall, small dirty flakes that didn't touch the ground. They turned into a narrow alley, not marked by any red gear, and startled a small bundle of rags. The child was bony thin, soot-smeared. He, or maybe she, gave a choked sound of surprise and scuttled backward.

Gilchrist blinked. He stuck a hand into his pocket and retrieved a handful of crusts from their last meal on board the ship. "It's too cold tonight," he said, squatting. "You'll lose your toes. There's a heating pipe around back of that smithy two streets over."

The child snatched the bread away and forced all of it at once into a scabby mouth, then scrambled out of the alley, darting past Crane's knees. Gilchrist's dark eyes trailed after. He took a silver coin from his other pocket and wrapped it in the nest of rags the child had left behind.

Crane only watched, expressionless, until Gilchrist stood up and hefted his side of the strongbox. They walked on.

The lock breaker's shop was small, ensconced in shadows, the nearest lamppost smashed. Smoke coiled from a small stack on the roof and grease-yellow light leaked from slits in the barred windows. No light escaped the door, which was a thick slab of reinforced iron that looked better suited to a gaol or a fortress.

"A deceiver imagines everyone is out to deceive him," Crane said, yanking his mask down around his neck. "Perhaps a similar logic applies to lock breakers."

They set the strongbox down on the cobblestone with a dull thunk. Crane rubbed his aching shoulder again; Gilchrist studied the door. There was an ornate sort of knocker, shaped like a jaw, that seemed out of place on the otherwise unadorned surface. Crane blew into his reddening hands, then reached for it and took hold.

A disguised second jaw sprang from underneath and clamped his wrist in place. Crane flinched, but barely. His lips twisted into a smile as he looked down at his trapped extremity.

"How fortunate it has no teeth," he said. Gilchrist snorted. The quick-knife had slid from his sleeve into his fist and he was tensed, scanning for ambush. Crane gave an experimental wiggle and shook his head. The metal jaws were tight as a vise.

The scratch of moving feet came from behind the door, and a slit shuttered open. An eye ringed with kohl appeared in the gap. "Who the fuck are you?" came a woman's hoarse voice.

"A man with a great many uses for his left hand, most of which would be severely diminished by frostbite or broken bones," Crane said. "I am called Crane. My companion is Gilchrist. A mutual acquaintance in Brask informed us you might be able to solve a particularly vexing toy puzzle, for a price."

There was a muffled *click-chunk* from some internal mechanism, and the jaws opened. Crane retrieved his hand, rubbing ruefully at his blue-veined wrist. The cold metal had left a purplish welt.

"He said someone was going to try hitting the Thule Estate. You pulled it off?" The lock breaker's eye widened and her scratchy voice carried a hint of admiration.

"We are gentlemen and I resent the suggestion," Crane said blithely. "Will you aid us with the puzzle or not? It's rather conspicuous and we would prefer to have it off the streets, and out of sight, as soon as possible."

The lock breaker hesitated. "Show me."

Gilchrist slipped the strongbox from its harness and hefted it up to eye level. Its filigreed design gleamed in the yellow light. The lock break-er's eye narrowed. Then another *click-chunk,* a series of rattling scrapes as bolts retracted, and the door swung open at last with a slink of steam.

The lock breaker was wide-shouldered, narrow-hipped, dressed all in black. Her pale hair was slicked backward off an angular face. She had deep-set eyes, made more so by the kohl, that seemed older than the rest of her. There was a gray smudge on her forehead from an unwashed finger.

"Didn't think anyone would actually have the stones to rob that place," she said. "Heard they flay thieves."

"Do you greet all your customers so vigorously?" Crane asked, rubbing his wrist again as they stepped inside with the strongbox, smelling gunpowder and old metal.

"I'm closed," the lock breaker said. "Been closed three weeks now. And I'm careful." She turned back to the door and set to locking it again, spinning a brass wheel that drove the bolts into place. From the back, the simple iron door was a patchwork of moving mechanisms. Crane observed it keenly while Gilchrist scanned the shop's interior.

Oil lamps provided the yellow light, pulling strange shadows over the objects littering the workbench and hanging from the walls. There were glinting skeleton keys, hooks and thick needles, what looked like a hand-cranked drill. Dissected locks sat beside their intact neighbors in a scattering of pins and springs. A floor-to-ceiling rack contained hundreds on hundreds of keys, large and small, sleek and spiky, cheap copper and ornate silver and everything in between.

Traces of the lock breaker's personal effects were scant, but a small table carrying a cracked mug and half-eaten bowl of food was tucked into one corner, and a few shirts dangled from improvised hooks in the ceiling. A shabby rug was tacked unevenly to one wall and a cylindrical urn sat above the hissing heating pipe.

The lock breaker picked out a square of space on the bench; Crane and Gilchrist set the strongbox down. She examined it with an almost hungry expression on her face, leaning in close, peering from every angle.

"Haven't crossed paths with one of these little bastards for a long time," she said. "It's a dead-box. You know that, I hope. You try to force this open with a pry bar, it's spring-loaded to crush whatever's inside."

"We know that," Gilchrist said flatly, pulling off his mask.

"If it was within my abilities, we would not have come seeking yours," Crane said. "You've encountered its like before. I assume you can solve this one as well."

The lock breaker's eyes narrowed again. Her mouth thinned. "I can, yeah," she said. "For a price, I can."

"Of course," Crane said. "An expert of your caliber demands suitable compensation. With that in mind, we might be willing to negotiate up to—"

"A third," Gilchrist cut in.

Crane's face soured. "Yes. That."

The lock breaker was silent for a moment, considering. A muscle twitched in her cheek. "No," she said.

"No?" Crane echoed, a needle tenting the silk of his voice.

"Without me, that box isn't worth a pig's shit," she said. "Without me, you did that job for nothing, so I figure I get to name my own price, thanks."

Behind her, the quick-knife rippled down Gilchrist's sleeve again.

"But I don't want money," she continued. "I want something else. I want the pair of you to do something for me." She looked across the room, to the gray urn, and came slightly unfocused. Her thumb drifted up to her forehead, where the ash stained her skin. "How we mourn a lover, in the north," she said. "A little every day until the ash is gone. I want you to help me avenge him."

The lock breaker dragged a pair of splintering stools over to the heating pipe where Crane and Gilchrist were warming their hands, and told them, like an afterthought, that her name was Merin.

"A pleasure," Crane said.

Merin squatted down, nodding her chin toward the urn. "And his name was Petro. He was my husband. More or less. He's been dead eighteen days now."

"We extend our sincerest condolences," Crane said warily. His gaze flickered back toward the unattended strongbox. Gilchrist, by contrast, was rapt.

"I bet you do." Merin snorted. "I don't need you to care. Just need you to understand the situation, is all." She folded her arms on her knees. "Do you know who runs Colgrid?"

"The Dogue, officially," Crane said. "But I imagine the balance of power now shifts in favor of the merchants and industrialists. The same change has begun in Brask."

"Men of business." Merin's voice was thick with contempt. "Brutes, all of them. They worship money and see the world all in numbers." She clenched her teeth for a moment. "Here in Colgrid, we have the very worst of them. He calls himself Papa Riker. He's nearly as rich as the Dogue himself now. Ten times as ruthless."

"How did he attain his wealth?" Crane asked.

"The New World," Merin said. "Same as the rest of them. He was with the trading companies. Mostly narcotics."

Crane and Gilchrist exchanged a glance that did not go unnoticed.

"You know the trade?" Merin asked.

"A brief foray that proved ill-fated," Crane said. "For a variety of reasons."

"There was a fire," Gilchrist said.

Merin nodded, tonguing her teeth. "You know shiver?"

"Not my preferred vice," Crane said, but his eyes brightened. "But yes. We're quite familiar. Distilled powder from the xoda plant. Hones the nerves to a razor's edge." He tapped the side of his nose.

"Riker is the one who introduced it to the factories," Merin said. "They use it to keep the workers from falling asleep. He owns almost half the city, now. Competition is bought off or killed off. He's ruthless, how I said. Always looking for a new advantage." She looked at the urn again. "Twenty-six days ago, he wanted me to do some work for him. Petro set up the meeting."

"Sabotage?" Gilchrist guessed.

"Security," Merin said. "Not to keep anyone out. To keep the little imps in. Wanted me to rig up a design for adjustable manacles. Their wrists are too skinny, see. And some of them lose a hand altogether in the machinery." Her nostrils flared. "I told him to go fuck himself."

Crane looked over to Gilchrist. "This Riker employs children in his factories?"

"Sweeps them off the streets and puts them to work, yeah, mostly on the south side," Merin said. "Always looking for an advantage, how I said. As close to the devil as you can get. So I refused."

"And there was retribution," Crane surmised.

"Not the kind I was ready for." Merin glared at the urn. "My husband was a strong man in many ways. Weak, in some ways. When it came to drink, or to drugs, Petro was weak." She blinked hard. "The last few years, it was shiver. Never too bad. Never bad enough to make me put a stop to it. I even did it with him, every so often." Her voice turned fierce.

"A week after I refused the job, I found Petro in our bed, pale as snow. Dead. With shiver smeared around his nose. I tested some of the powder on a rat the next day, and it was how I thought. Someone gave him a tainted pinch. Laced it with cyanide."

Silence seeped into the cramped space. Crane glanced to Gilchrist again, but Gilchrist was staring at the urn almost as intently as Merin. "And in what manner did the rat die?" Crane asked.

The lock breaker's face darkened. "Badly," she said. "So that's my price. That's how Riker has to die. Badly."

"Vengeance is a natural proclivity," Crane said. "I indulge in it myself from time to time. But we are only three, and of the three, only you are familiar with this Riker and with the general environ. Gilchrist and I are strangers here."

"Better that way," Merin said. "Walls have ears these days. Don't know who to trust. That's why not another soul in Colgrid knows what I've got planned."

"To speak frankly, Madam Merin." Crane picked a piece of lint from his knee, peered at it, and cast it aside. "You would do better to open the strongbox and use your more than generous allotment of the contents to hire an assassin. We may even be able to put you into contact with one."

Merin's gaze was defiant. "If you got into that estate, and out in one piece, you can do this job easy. The price stands."

Crane opened his mouth to riposte.

"We'll do it," Gilchrist said. His black eyes were gleaming. "You have a plan?"

Merin exhaled a long breath. She looked more closely at Gilchrist, then nodded. "Yeah. Haven't thought about much else since Petro." She turned to Crane. "You're the talker, he's the doer. Is that it?"

"Such things are never so simple as they first appear," Crane said flatly. "But if no other payment can satisfy you, then Mr. Gilchrist speaks for us both. We will aid you in your revenge."

"Good." Merin rose and went to the urn, hesitating only a moment before she dipped her fingers inside. She turned back to them. The ash was smooth and cool against Gilchrist's hand, then Crane's, as they shook.

The queue of workers stretched from the factory gate all the way around the corner, ragged men and women stamping their feet and rubbing their arms against the cold. Some of them pulled their filter masks down long enough to puff at the clay pipe being passed from hand to grimy hand. Crane and Gilchrist kept theirs on as they tacked themselves to the end of the line.

"A rather ghastly piece of architecture, isn't it?" Crane remarked, tipping his head back to observe the factory. Its high brick walls were stained jet-black from soot and displayed no windows, the wrought-iron gates were topped with wicked-looking spikes, and the scaly roof was dominated by several enormous smokestacks already leaking their ink into the sky.

"Not many points of egress," Gilchrist said.

They stepped out of the queue and reinserted themselves farther along, aided by Crane opening the tin of snuff from his coat pocket and Gilchrist delivering a winding elbow to the gut of the one worker who protested. Up close, they could see the gate itself, guarded by a pair of scowling watchmen with truncheons. The red gear was painted on their chest plates.

Both guards snapped to attention as the clockwork clatter of a strutter echoed up the cobblestones. One of them made his way along the line, brandishing his truncheon, snarling for single file. The workers shuffled themselves; so did Crane and Gilchrist. All of them turned to watch the strutter clack up the street like a massive black insect, limbs churning in perfect synchronization, pulling a black carriage behind.

Whispers traveled up and down the queue as the carriage passed with curtains drawn. The top of it was racked and loaded with three squat barrels, all of them secured tightly by cables. The strutter shuddered to a halt at the gate and its driver dismounted, yanking off her grease-stained gloves before opening the carriage door.

The man who descended was massive, thick-shouldered with a broad chest and sizeable paunch only somewhat disguised by the precise tailoring of his black-and-scarlet waistcoat. His fine clothes were at odds with his bulk, and with the boxer's hands, gnarled and scarred, that escaped his sleeve cuffs. The wide ruff splayed around his neck might have looked affected on another man; on Riker, it gave him the look of a cannibal lizard from the New World. The impression was strengthened by his ornate filter mask, angled like the snout of a beast and inlaid with silver teeth locked in a razor-sharp grin.

Riker adjusted his cuffs while a pock-faced porter started unloading the barrels from the top of the carriage. When he wobbled under the last of them, Riker gave a snort of impatience and took it from his grasp, setting it on one bow-broad shoulder as if it weighed nothing at all.

"Merin failed to mention the man was a virtual colossus," Crane said, watching closely as Riker, accompanied by a swirl of attendants, strode toward the factory doors.

"Moves light," Gilchrist said, watching his gait.

A tremor of anticipation moved through the queue as the other two barrels passed by. One of the men whose thumb was stained from snuff broke into a gapped grin. "Big shipment," he said. "Heard it's purer than last one. Pure, pure."

Crane sucked air between his teeth. "That is a rather extravagant quantity of narcotic, Gilchrist," he murmured. "Three barrels, already processed. Worth a small fortune, I imagine."

Gilchrist calculated. "Double and a half the weight in silver."

"How the conflagration still haunts me," Crane said mournfully.

"Only pennies to what's in the strongbox," Gilchrist reminded him.

One attendant handed Riker a manifest on thick parchment; another stretched to mutter something into his ear. Riker turned toward the line of workers, all of whom fell dead silent. "Fifty only today," he said, in a voice thinned by the filter mask. "Preference to those already marked. Rest of you, fuck off."

Half the queue surged forward excitedly, nearly bowling Crane and Gilchrist over in their hurry to bare their wrists, scratching away grime to expose the blotted red ink stamped there. Others howled in disappointment; a few furtively tried to spit and rub the ink from a neighbor onto their own skin. Small scuffles broke out where the guards moved to establish the cutoff point.

An emaciated woman with wild gray hair broke through and darted at Riker. "My Skadi, my little Skadi, where is she?" she wailed, grabbing for him. "She has a cough, let me in, I'll work harder than anyone, I swear, I swear I will . . ."

Riker half turned and swatted her away with the back of his fist, sending her sprawling. Her skull bounced off the cobblestone with a wet smack. He looked down at her for a moment, watching impassively as she moaned and babbled. Then a guard hurried to drag her away, and Riker continued through the factory gate, returning his attention to the parchment.

Crane and Gilchrist stood still a second longer, then melted back through the clamoring workers, back the way they'd come. Gilchrist's hands were clenched to fists.

They were around the corner and out of sight, moving down a dirty alley, when Crane spoke.

"There is no ledger, Gilchrist."

Gilchrist looked up. "Meaning what, Crane?" His voice was brusque.

"You have a marvelous way with accounts and balances," Crane said. "But in matters of morality, there is no ledger. You cannot wash one man's blood off your hands using another's."

Gilchrist's broad back stiffened. He stopped walking. "You think that's what I'm doing."

Crane yanked the filter mask down from his mouth. "Assuaging your guilt, yes, by assuring yourself there are men far more evil than we are and by removing one from existence," he said. "It's delusional. Self-indulgent. It doesn't become you."

"It's how we get the strongbox open," Gilchrist said.

Crane scoffed. "You were ready to force her to do it," he said. "At knifepoint. It was her tragic tale that swayed you. That and the fact that our target employs children. Or do I misremember?"

Gilchrist gave a tight shrug. "I saw threats wouldn't work. Not on her. She has nothing to lose."

"So she would have us believe," Crane grated. "Yet she was unable to correctly describe the effects of cyanide poisoning. Why is that?"

Gilchrist started to walk again. "Not everyone knows poisons, Crane."

"We would do better to take the strongbox elsewhere." The blue veins of Crane's neck were taut and his voice was ice. "We are working in unfamiliar territory with an ally who, I believe, is not entirely forthcoming." He strode after his companion. "Dealing with the individual we just observed, I suspect any error at all might be disastrous. Riker does not strike me as a man one attempts to kill twice."

Gilchrist kept his eyes forward. "Lucky we only need to do it once."

Crane's long legs overtook him. "Your reticence is growing tiresome," he snapped. "I want to discuss what occurred during our escape from the Thule Estate."

"I remember what happened."

"You slit a man's throat before he could cry warning," Crane said. "Had you not, we would both be dangling from the gallows even now. You exchanged his life for ours, as I would have done in the same situation." He reached to seize onto Gilchrist's shoulder.

Gilchrist whirled and locked his arm, slamming him into the soot-stained brick of the alleyway. His lips pulled back off his teeth. "The watchman had children," he said. "I saw their shoes after. Outside the guardhouse. You did the reconnaissance. You never mentioned it."

Crane blinked down at the unfamiliar sight of Gilchrist's forearm under his windpipe. Rage twisted across his face for a moment, then receded. "It wasn't pertinent," he said, enunciating each word.

"To you," Gilchrist finished. "And he had ash on his forehead. Saw it while I was stashing the body. That means no mother for them. That means they end up in the street or sold off to some factory."

"There are worse fates," Crane said defiantly. "You survived similar beginnings." His expression was calm but his ears were scarlet red.

Gilchrist stepped back. Dropped his arm. "That's what I mean, Crane." He croaked a half laugh. "The last thing I want is to make more of me."

Crane rubbed his throat. He said nothing.

When they arrived back at the lock shop, Gilchrist forewent the knocker and rapped out the agreed-upon pattern against the door with his fist instead. This time Merin was quicker to let them inside. There was new ash on her forehead.

"You saw him? Saw his mask?" she asked, pulling a rubbery cup away from her ear and flopping its attached tube over her shoulder. The strongbox was sitting in the center of the workbench, surrounded by an array of skeleton keys and picks, one of which was sticking out from the locking groove. "Been listening," she explained, shutting the door behind them. "It's sticky in there. Something spilled on it."

"Wine," Gilchrist said. He took a seat on one of the stools; Crane stood, pale hands sunk in his pockets. "We saw the mask."

"He hardly takes it off," Merin said. "Had it specially made by an artisan from Lensa." She reached under the workbench and produced a thin tracing in carbon. "This wasn't easy to nab. Don't spill no wine on it."

Crane and Gilchrist looked down at the tracing, which showed the mask's design from the front, then in profile, then cross-sectioned.

"It's bigger than it needs to be," Merin said. "Room to make improvements." She overlaid the sheet with another, this one bearing her own pen strokes. Coiled springs and wedges folded against themselves, some sort of trigger mechanism. It was only when she brought the realized product from under the workbench, unwrapping wax paper from its metal shell, that they saw the sharpened spikes studding the inside.

Crane touched his wrist where the spring-loaded knocker had clamped down on it the night before. "How ingenious."

"These won't be visible after I line it," she said, running a finger down one of the spikes. "Hand me that bowl, would you?"

Gilchrist passed her the thick-bottomed clay bowl without speaking. She flipped it over, then set the metal shell down on top of it. The spiked jaws snapped with a deep crack. When she lifted the shell, the bowl fell to the bench in fragments and powder. Her expression was both eager and slightly ill.

"How do we get ahold of the mask?" Gilchrist asked.

Merin chewed the inside of her cheek. "Not from his quarters," she said. "Where he lives, it's a fucking labyrinth and it's locked down tighter than anyplace I've ever seen." She swept the remnants of the bowl off the bench's surface with one hand. "But there's a bathhouse he goes to. That's where you plant it. Then you leave without him ever even seeing you."

Crane looked down at the device. "Remote assassinations do not always go as planned," he said. "What if the mechanism were to fail?"

"It won't," Merin said firmly. "It's been tested plenty."

"Very well." Crane looked down at the schematic, avoiding Gilchrist's eye. "But leaving the sabotaged mask in its proper place, without arousing suspicion, fulfills our contract. If your device fails, it is no responsibility of ours. You will open the strongbox regardless."

"It'll work," Merin said, running her tongue along her gums. "But yes. I open the box regardless."

She inserted a crank into a slot in the metal shell and began to wind it tight again, click after rasping click.

The bathhouse was an incongruous slab of gleaming black stone amid the scab-colored brick and slant roofs that surrounded it. Geometric hieroglyphs carved over the doorway and the roof's beveled edges evoked the abandoned ziggurats of the New World, as if the building had been cleaved whole from the rain forests and dropped in the center of Colgrid.

It was a clumsy imitation at best—Crane and Gilchrist had seen the sleeping cities, with their towering temples and intricate catacombs deep under the earth, and knew no living architect could ever approximate them. But perhaps Riker had seen them too, and the bathhouse served him as a small reminder.

"Strutter's coming," Gilchrist said.

Crane drew himself up to his full height, adjusting the brim of a scooped hat with a sewn-in filter mask. The stolen clothes were slightly baggy on his frame, but of good quality, and Merin had assured him many gentlemen's clothes were ill fitting ever since shiver caught on in the courts.

The two of them had spent the better part of the day observing the bathhouse comings and goings, checking its exterior against the stained parchment where Merin had sketched a layout, all with a garrote-wire silence stretched between them.

It was a simple enough plan. According to a former attendant they'd bribed, Riker always went to the steam rooms first, near the back, then made a quick cold plunge before leaving—the whole visit took no more than fifteen minutes. That was time enough for Crane to crack the locked cupboard with Riker's effects in it, especially with Merin's superior tools. Gilchrist would be monitoring the steam room from the outside, ready to call warning should Riker leave early.

Now the distinctive black strutter was rounding the corner, and it was time to part ways: Gilchrist into the alley, Crane toward the bathhouse entrance.

As he swaggered toward the entry, Crane put a thumb to his reddened nostril and snorted sharp. The rush of powder through membrane made him shudder. It wasn't his drug of choice, but shiver was cheap and temptingly plentiful here. He'd bought a pinch in the factory queue and another behind the bathhouse while Gilchrist was otherwise occupied.

Colgrid's dirty streets turned clear and bright and slightly vibrating, the effect that gave the narcotic its name. He felt the high like a razor blade, like his every step and motion was slicing through a slower, thicker world. Riker seemed to move through syrup as he stepped from the strutter, trailed by a sole attendant carrying a fabric bag.

At the entrance, Crane paused his stride, bowed at the precise angle that hid his face entirely, and let the giant man pass first. He managed to seem even larger on shiver, as if the bunched muscles of his arms and shoulders were swelling and straining to escape his skeleton. He gave Crane a brief glance through the lenses of his filter mask.

Crane had an unbidden image of Riker's head imploding and spattering the insides of the lenses with greasy blood and gray matter. He had to lash down his chemical smile as he followed him into the antechamber, flicking a coin to the boy waiting by the door and receiving a cupboard key in return. He took one side of the coal-heated benches and Riker took the other. Riker was half-shielded by his attendant as he stripped down, but from the glimpse Crane caught, the whole of his bulk was netted with scars.

Gilchrist wedged himself into the corner of the furnace room and steam room, cramming low and yanking off his filter mask to put an eye against the knothole he'd drilled earlier. He breathed through his mouth; the back alley had a strong stink of tanning chemicals that he hoped would keep passersby to a minimum. If anyone did see him, the ragged coat he'd fished from the gutter would make him look like a beggar seeking warmth as the sunlight waned.

He blinked. He could see a few silhouettes lounging on the benches, steam swirling around their midsections, but none with Riker's size.

"What are you doing?"

Gilchrist whirled. There was less soot on the child's face this time; he could tell she was a girl. She rocked back and forth on the balls of her feet. Rubbed at her left shoulder.

"You gave me the coin, didn't you," she said vaguely. "Think it was you. Not the tall one." She peered between him and the hole in the wall, then made a wanking gesture in the air. "You a pervert, then?"

Gilchrist took another coin from his pocket. When she snatched for

it, he closed his fist and put a finger to his lips. Tapped his wrist where
a timepiece would sit, once, twice, three times. She nodded solemnly and
clapped a dirty hand over her mouth.

He hunkered down again, squinting through the knothole.

Crane peeled off his stolen clothes and walked to the warm baths, smooth
stone whispering against the soles of his feet. He nodded to the other
occupants, then lowered himself in at a stretch of gleaming black wall
polished reflective. The hot water tingled and stung at his cold skin. His
reflection was ghostly, distorted. Deep dark circles beneath the eyes and
a bruise blooming at his collarbone where Gilchrist had pinned him.

He traced it gently with one finger, then dug into it and made it sear.
Behind his reflection, Riker passed by like a thunderhead, the attendant
trailing behind with towel and scrubber. No bather looked up. Crane
waited a beat in the water, was tempted to wait longer. But he got out
and doubled back to the antechamber. Empty, aside from the boy wiping
down the benches.

"What slobbering ignoramus runs the furnace today?" Crane demanded,
punching out his syllables in the harsh Colgrid accent.

The boy flinched, nearly dropping the rag.

"I could better warm the baths with my piss," Crane said. "Tell them:
more coal. Tell them: a fucking plenitude of coal."

The boy scrambled away. Crane went to his own cupboard first, pulling
on his oversized trousers and knotting them with one hand. He took
Merin's picks from the inside of the hat, where the skull-crusher was
concealed, and moved to the cupboard he'd watched Riker's attendant
wrestle shut. The shiver had receded to a clear singing focus that would
keep his hands smooth.

Crane eyeballed the lock and selected the second-narrowest pick.

"Were you born in the desert?" the girl asked, for the third time. "You're
dark all over."

Gilchrist wiped a trickle of sweat before it could slide into his eye. He
focused through the steam. Riker had the room mostly to himself—the
other bathers had drifted away when he entered, their body language

twitching nervous. Through the other wall, he could hear voices arguing in the furnace room about the definition of a plenitude.

"You and the tall one, you staying in the widow's shop," the girl said, scratching her shoulder. "Followed you from there. Best be careful."

The words prickled the back of his neck, but Gilchrist kept watching the knothole. "Why's that?" he asked, keeping his voice low and even.

The girl's reply came in a solemn whisper. "Because she got a musket, and she shot her husband dead."

Gilchrist looked up. The girl made the shape of a muzzle with her fingers.

"Bam. His skull went all apart like an old fruit." She screwed up her face. "So, best be careful."

"Who told you that story?" Gilchrist asked.

"It's not a story," the girl said scornfully, scratching at her shoulder again, more vigorously. "I seen it. Papa Riker sent me to keep my eyes on her. I seen it happen." She gave a devilish smile. "Made an awful mess on the wall."

Gilchrist stared straight ahead for a moment, recalling the interior of the lock shop. "Crane's a bastard when he's right," he muttered, then put his fingers to his mouth and whistled three long, mournful notes.

Crane was a tumbler away, two at most, when the faint but unmistakable call of a New World carrion bird reached his ears. He froze. Cursed. The clear-out call meant something had gone wrong, meant Riker could be barreling in at any moment, but he was so close. He steadied his hands and leaned in, feeling for the next catch.

The wet slap of approaching feet sounded from the corridor. Close. Crane gritted his teeth. He tore the pick free, seized his shirt and shoes and hat last as he slipped out the door.

The inside of the lock shop was thick with shadows. Merin had only lit one lamp. When Gilchrist set the skull-crusher down on the workbench, just inside the pool of light, she stared at it blankly for a moment before she spoke.

"What happened?"

"We have a similar query," Crane said. "Regarding your husband's death. Your version of events is under dispute, and if we cannot trust your information, we cannot trust you to maintain your end of our bargain."

"Why did you kill him?" Gilchrist asked.

Merin gave a choked laugh. "The fuck are you talking about?"

"A musket ball at close range," Crane said. "Here in this very shop." He circled the cramped room in a few long strides, stopping at the threadbare rug hanging on the wall. "Such a death would leave traces." He reached for the corner of the rug.

"Don't." Merin's voice came in a snarl. She was standing, breathing hard, her hands balled into fists. Then all at once, her face crumpled. She dropped back down onto the stool, laying both hands flat on the bench. One of her fingers jumped. "I never meant to fire it," she said, looking at her hands first, then up at Crane and Gilchrist. Her black-rimmed eyes were hollow. "Only to keep him back." She blinked. "He was given laced shiver. That was the truth. But it wasn't laced with poison. It was ichor."

Gilchrist didn't flicker at the word, but Crane's eyes narrowed. "The rage drug," he clarified. "Secreted by a particularly venomous New World toad. Extremely rare."

"That's how I know it was Riker who did it," Merin said. "Only he'd have access to that stuff."

"Describe it." Crane's voice was intent, almost eager. "Describe the effects."

Merin's nostrils flared. "Fuck you."

"You've attempted to deceive us once already," Crane said. "Why would we accept your word now without—"

"His veins were like ropes." Merin paused. Took a shuddering breath. "When he came down the stairs, he was sweating and all his veins were thick like ropes. His cock was hard. And he was talking. Not in any language, just talking. Gibberish."

"How did he behave?" Crane asked, folding his arms.

"Tranced, at first," Merin said thickly. "I tried to get him to sit down. Then, angry. Like an animal. Like an animal in my husband's body." She waved a hand over her eyes. "There was nothing back there. He was gone in the head. I tried to calm him down." She swallowed. "Tried to calm him down, couldn't. He got his hands around my throat. I barely slipped him. Musket was on the table. He chased me." Her gaze raked around the room, seeing ghosts in motion, then came to rest on the hanging rug. "Told him to back up. He didn't. He grabbed my wrist and I pulled the trigger."

Crane nodded with something like reverence. "Ichor is incredibly potent," he said. "Even in the smallest doses it causes violent hallucinations. Inflames the carnal urges. Occasionally induces a form of glossolalia, as well." He drummed his long fingers against his elbow. "Little wonder it was considered a myth in the early years of exploration."

"Riker helped cover up Petro's killing," Gilchrist said. "Told everyone he'd gone south to dodge a debt. That right?"

"Yes," Merin said bitterly. "He'll ask me for another job someday, and he knows I'll do it if I don't want to end up imprisoned for Petro's murder. You see why I hate him. See why I have to kill him. Don't you?"

Gilchrist looked at her for a moment, then nodded. "You have to kill him because you aren't sure," he said. "You aren't sure if he gave Petro the ichor. Or if Petro took it himself and misjudged the potency."

Merin snarled. "He wouldn't."

"The barflies of the inner city say otherwise," Crane interjected. "By all accounts, your husband was not sound in mind or in spirit during the months leading up to his disappearance. He experimented with the more exotic narcotics. He spoke often of death."

"I know that," Merin snapped. "I know he wasn't well. But he would never."

"Riker might have spread the rumor of your husband's debt in order to deflect attention from his own role," Crane said. "The Dogue would not react kindly to Riker selling ichor to Colgrid's citizenry."

"If you kill Riker without knowing the truth, you'll wonder," Gilchrist said. "Forever."

Merin's eyelids dropped shut. "What are you suggesting, then?" she asked, voice cracked.

"An amendment to our bargain," Crane said. "You need a confession, not a mere execution. Confessions can be extracted with the proper leverage."

"If you think Riker would ever confess to giving Petro the ichor, you're a simpleton."

"Leverage," Crane repeated. "As of this morning, Riker is storing three barrels of shiver in the south-side factory. That represents a sizeable investment."

Merin opened her eyes. "What, steal it?"

"More take it hostage," Gilchrist said. "We know someone who can get us inside. Tonight." He cocked his head toward the sound of a small fist rapping low on the door. "That'd be her."

When the night was sufficiently dark, they trooped out of the shop into the cold streets. The girl scampered ahead of them. Her name was Skadi, and the shoulder she always scratched had a messy red gear tattooed into the skin. She'd shown it to them with a mixture of pride and resentment.

Then, without ever looking at Merin directly, she'd explained how Riker had ordered her to watch the lock shop on the day of Petro's death, and how after relaying the news to him she'd never returned to the factory how she was supposed to.

But she still knew how to get back in without anyone seeing her. She knew where the guards patrolled and half of their names. She knew the third smokestack was no longer in use. She'd hovered over Gilchrist's shoulder, chewing dates from Merin's larder, as he sketched out the factory's dimensions.

Their shadows stretched long and slender as they passed under the first phosphor lamppost. Gilchrist carried coiled rope and the improvised grapple Merin had put together. Crane's long fingers toyed with the phial he'd mixed over the heating pipe. Merin was strapped with her lock-breaking tools.

All of them wore filter masks, and Merin had dug out one for Skadi, too, after the girl emptied her pockets of all the keys she'd filched while they were sketching out the factory's dimensions and arguing about entry and egress.

They stopped a street behind the south-side factory. Crane took out the glass phial and tapped one frayed fingernail against it. Tendrils of luminous yellow swirled inside. Skadi watched with undisguised fascination as he capped it with a tiny pipette.

"I want to use it, too," she said, yanking her mask down.

"Lamprey extract requires successive doses to be effective," Crane said, tipping his head back, peeling back an eyelid. "I'm afraid you would see only a blur." He squeezed a drop into one eye, then the other. When he finished blinking his pupils were swollen wide with a silvery gleam to them. Gilchrist took the phial from him and did the same.

"What do you see?" Skadi asked.

"The light human eyes miss," Gilchrist said. "You ready, Merin?"

Merin pulled down her mask. Her face was drawn, but her voice came steady. "Haven't done a break-in for about a decade," she said. "Always feel a bit sick until the entry. Let's get on with it."

One of the night watchmen was sauntering along the back of the factory, singing hoarsely and occasionally tapping his truncheon against the brick for percussion. They watched from the shadows until he rounded the corner, then Skadi led the way to the wall, almost skipping.

"See the cracks?" she whispered. "You should be able to see 'em. I can barely, but I know where they all are anyways."

Crane and Gilchrist looked up the brick wall to see where the mortar had eroded, leaving the cracks Skadi used for her climb. Large enough for a child's hand- and toeholds, nothing more, but they'd anticipated as much. Gilchrist unspooled the rope and handed the grapple off to Crane. He judged the distance to the carved gutter that rimmed the roof, made two practice swings, and cast it.

The grapple sailed up through the dark, rope ribboning out behind it like a startled snake. Its hooks clattered against the angled surface, sliding, scraping, finally catching. Soot caked on the roof softened the noise, but they still waited, breath bated, for watchmen voices. A moment passed. Another.

Crane tugged the rope taut and offered it to Merin. She dusted her hands with chalk from her pouch and stretched her arms, then started to climb. She was barely over the top when Skadi followed, quick as a cat. Gilchrist reached for the rope next, but paused.

"Why'd you agree to hit the factory?" he asked.

Crane snorted. "Your sketch of the exterior was remarkably detailed, considering it was done from memory," he said. "You would have ended up here whether I agreed or not. In order to liberate a cadre of orphans."

Gilchrist fixed him with a long look. "You came to skim some of the shiver," he said.

"I suppose we are each in our own way predictable." Crane paused. "Will this balance your ledger, then? Will you be satisfied?"

"More than the drug ever satisfies you."

"Two entirely different matters," Crane said, but quietly, as Gilchrist churned up the rope with his feet barely grazing the wall for support. Crane followed, coiling the rope up behind him as he went.

From the top, they could see Colgrid's crooked roofs and belching chimneys spilling into the distance, dotted with the green phosphor blaze of streetlamps. They only lingered long enough for Crane to unhook the grapple before making their way along the factory's spine, to the disused smokestack Skadi had pinpointed on Gilchrist's crude map.

"Rungs on the inside for when we used to go up to clean it," the girl said. "Nice and easy for you."

Crane cast again, but this time the grapple bounced, clanging off the rim of the smokestack and back to the roof. Merin had to hop backward to avoid its impaling her foot. She hissed a curse; Crane only gave an irritable shrug. He retrieved the grapple, measured, and this time found the edge of the smokestack.

The descent was cramped and slow, the rungs all slippery with soot, the cloying smell of chemical leaking through their masks' filters. Crane and Gilchrist led the way, their augmented vision painting the pipe with silvery brushstrokes, letting them see the accumulated sediment scabbing the walls and pass up whispered warnings of the rungs that were rusted weak or missing entirely.

Before the bottom, where the shaft connected to the boiler, they found a small metal door in the dark as Skadi had promised. It came open with a sharp creak and Gilchrist squeezed through, twisting his wide shoulders. Crane next, easily as an eel, then Merin contorted herself to follow. Skadi levered herself through last.

It was a short drop to the base of the boiler, and after the tight confines of the smokestack the vaulted factory interior felt the size of a cathedral. Rows of spiky black machinery stretched from back to front, looming out of the dark like mechanical monsters, their bared cogs grinning teeth. Skadi's shoulders hunched at the sight; she rubbed furiously at the left one.

"Storeroom's back there," she murmured, pointing with her whole hand. "Locked up good." She looked around the factory again and shook herself. "I hate this place lots."

She led the way down the row, and as they walked, soles scuffing on soot, pale faces poked out from the machinery. Some of them whispered; one called Skadi's name in a wavering question. Crane put a bony finger to the place where his mask covered his lips. There was straw spread out underneath the machinery, moth-eaten blankets, too. A few of the children huddled alone; most tangled together for body heat or for comfort.

"Hush, hush, hush," Skadi said. "How asleep is the nanny?"

"Two and some," one of the children whispered. "Amalia took the some."

They found the nanny slumped up ahead in a carved wooden chair, three empty bottles lined beside him, grizzled chin resting on his chest. Crane paused long enough to pour laudanum into his half-open mouth, to make sure he stayed that way. More of the children were waking, now, and there was a sound of scraping metal as they shifted.

Merin pointed down at a foot that wasn't tucked under blankets. The child's ankle was cuffed in a heavy iron attached to a long cable that ran the length of the factory floor. "Bastards," she said softly. "Looks like an easy pick, though."

They moved on to the storeroom, which was bricked into the back corner of the factory and secured by a heavy wooden door.

"Go faster with a bit of light," Merin said, running her fingers over its thick lock. "I don't have lamprey shit in my eyes."

Gilchrist turned. "Skadi. Get a candle."

The girl vanished and returned a moment later with a burned-down nub of wax. She crouched, watching intently as Merin laid out her tools on the floor in a neat line. The lock breaker held out a few simple picks. Gilchrist and Crane took one each, then went back down the row. Gilchrist worked one side and Crane the other, rousing the children who were still asleep, muffling the occasional startled yelp, pointing to the ankle iron, jiggering it open.

They'd made it nearly all the way down when voices came from the factory entrance.

"See if the old drunk's got something for us, too," a watchman coughed. "Go on, just check. Fucking dull out here."

Crane and Gilchrist exchanged a look. Crane motioned the children to cover their ankles and be still, then swept toward one side of the entry, pulling on his gloves. Gilchrist took up position at the other, moving like a shadow. The quick-knife was in his hand, the blade telescoping and clicking into place. His jaw clenched.

The iron door swung open, and the watchman's lantern pierced the gloom. In the same instant, Crane sucked in his breath, pulled a burnt-orange pellet from his pouch, and crushed it between his palms.

The watchman took a few steps inside, then hesitated. He fumbled with the strap of his filter mask. Motes of powder from Crane's stained gloves were clouding into the air, a foul peppery smell accompanying. One of the children started to sneeze. Crane's eyes were leaking tears and mucus was spotting his mask. He still hadn't breathed in.

The watchman took another faltering step, then spun. "Ask him your-self, you sheepfucker," he said, hauling the factory door shut behind him, his voice turning faint. "You didn't tell me there was a spill today. Smells like the devil in there."

They waited another heartbeat, another. They waited for the sound of boots to disappear. As soon as the watchmen were gone back to the gate, Crane darted over to the barrel of drinking water and plunged his face inside. He emerged with a curse that made the children's ears prick up as Gilchrist picked the last few cuffs.

"Rather more potent than my previous recipe," Crane muttered, strip-ping off the stained gloves.

"Good." Gilchrist used the ladle to splash water into his bloodshot eyes. Then they moved back down the row, the freed children trailing after them, murmuring to each other, some of them knuckling their eyes still from the pellet. When they got to the storeroom, Merin was lifting her mask to wipe sweat off her forehead.

"Close thing, that watchman coming in," she said. "Good work. Whatever you did."

She shoved the wooden door and it swung open smoothly on its hinges. Inside, among the crates and stacked metal, the three barrels of shiver stood clustered together.

"They look heavy," Merin muttered.

"Then let's not waste time," Crane said, eyes gleaming. He tipped the first barrel and Gilchrist caught it from the other side, lowering it to the floor to be rolled. The three of them worked quickly, moving the barrels into position by the smokestack. Skadi and a few older girls managed to herd the children into a group, quieting the talkers with hissed admonishments or smacks up the head.

When all three barrels of shiver were in place, Crane gingerly fished more of the orange pellets from his pouch and passed them out among the older children. "These are intended to be thrown, not crushed in hand, and certainly not ingested," he said. "Not for eating. Understood?"

A few nods.

"I have a query, children," he continued. "What happens when one pokes a ball of cave spiders?"

The children looked at each other for a moment. "Go everywhere," one of the boys finally mumbled. Others made scurrying motions with their fingers.

"Yes," Crane said. "So, when we open the factory door, all of you must be little cave spiders. Scattering in all directions." He lifted one of the pellets between two fingers. "And should a watchman move to grab you, these are your stingers."

The children nodded, every single one of them, and Skadi's grin gleamed in the dark.

Morning over Colgrid. The rising sun drenched the sky red outside Merin's window. The lock breaker was boiling a pot of tar-black coffee; Crane and Gilchrist were sitting by the heating pipe, the blankets they'd slept on briefly now piled at their feet. During the chaos created by the fleeing children, they'd gone back up the smokestack and down from the roof. The last they'd seen of Skadi was her leading her little band into the streets, whooping and shrieking.

"Bet he's flogging the watchmen," Merin said. "Bet he thinks they helped us."

"All the better," Crane said, tapping a pen against his cheekbone as he considered the letter lying in midcomposition across his lap. "Ambiguity is our ally. How does this strike you both?" He stroked out the final sentence and raised the parchment to the light. "My dearest Mr. Riker, you are cordially invited to join me at the Corner of the Four Angels at midnight, unaccompanied and unarmed, so that we might negotiate an exchange of goods and services. If I sight anyone in your employ within a block of our meeting point, or sense any threat to my person, your barrels will burn. Signed, your loving thief."

Merin snorted. "Won't think it's me, that's for certain."

"Seal it," Gilchrist said. "With a pinch of the shiver."

Crane grudgingly opened one of the tiny bags he'd filled from the last barrel. He tapped a bit of powder onto the flat of Merin's kitchen knife, then held it over the heating pipe until it bubbled and melted to a distinctive tarry brown Riker would recognize. It smeared like hot wax over the fold of the letter.

"He won't come alone," Merin said, taking the letter as it cooled and stiffened. "Or unarmed."

"You won't, either," Gilchrist said.

Merin hesitated for a moment. Then she set the letter aside and reached under the workbench, hauling the strongbox out into the light and lifting the rough-spun shroud overtop of it. The locking grooves were pinned with calipers and a tiny section of metal had been peeled back, exposing part of the mechanism where two skeleton keys speared inside.

"Had it cracked yesterday already," she admitted. "Once you know the trick to them, they're not so bad." She pointed at the keys. "That one clockways, the other opposite. You can do the honors, if you like."

The men exchanged a glance. Then Crane took the left, Gilchrist the right, and they twisted without hesitation. Rather than simply falling open, the strongbox seemed to bloom. The intricate filigree of the cube's four sides came unlocked and peeled outward onto the floor like the petals of a mechanical flower, revealing a simple mesh cage, and inside that cage . . .

"My lexicon fails me," Crane said. "Gilchrist?"

Gilchrist only shook his head.

"Fucking beauty, isn't it," Merin said. "I peeked earlier." Her mouth twisted. "I can see why you went to the trouble."

The crown was a heavy ring of unblemished gold that turned fiery in the lamplight, veined with new silver and set with gemstones the color of a sparkling clear sea.

"The Thule clan's last link to the ancient kings," Crane murmured. "Far older than the elected Dogues. Older than Colgrid or even Brask." He yanked a work glove over his hand and removed the crown gently, so gently, as if it might shatter under his fingers. Gilchrist's eyes were fixed to it as it revolved gleaming in the light.

"Miraculous," Crane said. "To be in such condition. After so many years." His gaze hardened as he looked up. "You realize we have no compulsion to stay now that you've solved our toy for us. We could leave you and Riker to the fates."

"I realize, yeah." Merin managed half a smile. "But I figured you would want to see it through. Just to see how it all ends." She looked from the crown to the splayed-open strongbox. "And if things go to shit tonight, I wanted to make sure I'd held up my end of the bargain."

News of the factory break-in diffused through Colgrid over the course of the day; Gilchrist and Crane heard snatches of it both times they left the concealment of the shop to buy twine, resin, gunpowder. They never removed their filter masks, and they took circuitous routes back to Merin's to ensure they weren't followed. By the time night fell, a stiff wind was building in the streets, enough to shift part of the smog. It flapped at their clothes as they made their way to the Corner of the Four Angels.

Gilchrist circled the block to ensure none of Riker's men were lying in wait, then the three of them stepped into the sculptures' shadow. They were angels in the style of Brask, harsh and inhuman with geometric faces, archaic script carved into their spindly limbs and spread wings. In the gusting wind, they seemed ready to take flight. Merin climbed up to spread the resin in the crook of a stone elbow. Crane paced out the distance.

It wasn't long before the tap-tap-tap of a strutter echoed up the cobblestone. They took their positions: Crane stood loose and insolent, Gilchrist and Merin spread their feet and clasped their hands behind their backs, a military stance to keep Riker guessing. Gilchrist was massaging his hands in slow patterns, keeping his fingers warm and ready, but Merin's were clenched white.

A silhouette hulked through the gloom, then Riker strode into view, a phosphor lantern clutched in his massive hand like a ball of witch's fire, illuminating the sharklike teeth of his filter mask. The strutter's driver followed him like a shadow, dressed in a long black jacket with the shape of a musket bulging underneath.

"Mr. Riker," Crane greeted. "You've failed to follow instructions. Do you not recall the consequences?"

Riker halted five steps away from them, a gap that his long arms could close in an instant, and planted his feet. The tips of his boots were sharp and pointed toward them like knives. He surveyed them in silence through the lenses of his mask, then passed the lantern backward to his driver.

"Nobody burns three barrels of the pure shit," he said. "Not even a lunatic."

"You seem quite convinced of their value," Crane said. "And yet they were so poorly secured. Removing them was child's play, frankly."

"You think it was clever." Even through the mask, Riker's thin voice was taut with anger. "Using the children."

"Clearly you think the same."

"Everyone in Colgrid knows better than to steal from me," Riker said. "That means you're not from here. Means you don't know winter. If those children stay on the street, they'll all be frozen fucking corpses in a couple months."

"You keep them chained," Gilchrist said, speaking for the first time.

"At night. Better that than have another one climb into a boiler." Riker tapped a gnarled finger against his ornate mask. "Half the little shits are addled in the head right out the womb, from their mothers breathing the smog. They won't last outside."

"They left," Gilchrist said. "First chance they had."

"You didn't do them a fucking favor," Riker snapped. "I feed them. I keep them off the shiver. Out of the whorehouses. The ones with any sense will come back to the factory. The others will freeze."

Crane cleared his throat. "We digress," he said. "Fortunately for you, Mr. Riker, the shiver we stole was not our primary target. Our reconnaissance was flawed, you see." He paused. "We were told there might be ichor."

Riker didn't react.

"We are opportunists, of course, so we took what we found," Crane continued. "But as you ascertained, we are not from Colgrid. Our buyers lie farther south, and receive shiver through more established channels. They want ichor for the fighting pits in Vira and Lensa. That was what we intended to steal. Now we are open to an exchange."

"You'd trade my own shit back to me." Through the mask, Riker's laugh was a dead thing. "You do have some fucking balls on you."

Crane managed a careless shrug. "Assuming you *do* have ichor. And that you've tested it."

Riker regarded them for a long minute through his lenses. "How'd you get the barrels out?"

"With considerable difficulty," Crane said. "The method is irrelevant."

Another long pause, then Riker spoke. "I have ichor. As a curiosity. There's not a market for it up here."

Merin twitched; reined it in. Riker didn't seem to notice.

"Then I propose a deal: your shiver for your ichor. And if our buyers approve of your product, we might be able to establish a standing arrangement lucrative for all parties." Crane's voice hardened. "But we've encountered many would-be vendors returning from the New World, and their product is invariably a crude stimulant mixture that lacks the ... *specific* ferocity of true ichor."

Riker cocked his head to the side for a moment. "It's real," he said. "Gave it to a few mad beggars. One killed the other and fucked his corpse raw for an hour or so. I put him down as it wore off. More merciful than his having to remember it."

Merin was so still she might have been a statue herself. Crane drew a breath through his mask. "How marvelous," he said. "Though you would have been better served testing it on a more stable individual."

"Those are hard to come by in Colgrid." Riker waved a dismissive hand. "Half this fucking city is mad. But there was one other trial, yeah. When I first got my hands on the stuff. I cut some wastrel's shiver with it and sent him home to his woman."

The words drifted on the cold air. The angels seemed to bend forward, blank faces awaiting revelation.

"Did he know it was tainted?" Crane asked softly. "One must always be wary of the placebo response."

"He didn't," Riker said. "And when it came on, she shot him in the head. Clever cunt must have been waiting for an excuse to do that."

Merin ripped her filter mask down; the sudden motion triggered a flurry as the strutter driver drew her weapon, dropping the phosphor lantern. It smashed, painting a tableau in a burst of pale green: Crane had stepped back, Gilchrist's blade was out, the driver was aiming at Merin's chest ...

Riker peered at her. His flat laugh was contemptuous. "The clever cunt. The locksmith."

Merin had one hand still behind her back. The other trembled at her side as she spoke. "You know my fucking name."

"I forgot it," Riker said. "But I remember you needed a lesson."

Merin's face was twisted, half anger, half anguish. "You wanted me dead."

Riker looked at Crane and Gilchrist again, then back to Merin. "No," he said coldly. "The beggars got a full dose. Your Petro got barely a trace. He would have fucked you good and hard. Roughed you a bit. Came to his senses and wondered where he'd gotten a spine all of a sudden."

Behind her back, Merin pulled the twine that wrapped around her fist and stretched like spiderweb to the sculptures looming over them.

"All you had to do was take your lesson," Riker said. "Maybe you would've even liked it."

The crack of the concealed musket was deafening. Riker sank; Gilchrist lunged over him. A second crack, splitting the night air and sending shards of stone flying from an angel's ruined face. Gilchrist drove his quick-knife through the driver's arm and the smoking musket spun away in the dark. Then Riker was on his feet again, despite a ragged hole punched through his thigh, and his silence was more terrifying than anything else as he hurtled at Merin.

Crane leapt from the side but Riker swatted him away; Merin was backpedaling as Riker's fist glanced her jaw, snapping her head back. She crumpled to the cobblestone. Gilchrist was tangled with the driver, who was keening and bleeding as she scrabbled for the dropped gun. Riker swung at Merin again, enough force behind it to shatter her face, and Merin slid a metal shell from under her coat and thrust it up like a shield.

Riker's hand caught in the mechanism. He made to pull back, and—

"Don't fucking move," Merin said, thick through a syrup of blood. "Or you'll lose it. Feel the spikes?"

Riker didn't move. Merin got slowly to her feet, still holding her end of the skull-crusher. Crane picked himself up. Gilchrist joined them, delivering a last kick to the strutter driver. He had the musket in hand, first wiping blood off the grip with the edge of his shirt, then loading the second ball.

"You can have the fucking shiver," Riker said, not taking his eyes off his trapped hand. "And I'll get you the ichor, too. For your southern buyers."

"Oh, we have our sights set on far more exotic locales than Vira and Lensa," Crane said, mildly apologetic. "We are bound for the New World once more, you see. Funded by a certain object worth more than all the ichor you could supply." He massaged his chest where Riker's blow had landed. "As for the shiver, it's currently piled in the bottom of your factory's third smokestack."

Gilchrist placed the loaded musket in Merin's free hand. He hesitated. "Do what you want," he said. "But remember there's always a worse man."

"Our ship awaits us," Crane said. "We bid you farewell, Madam Merin. Mr. Riker. The hospitality of your fair city was very ..." He trailed off, wrapping his coat more tightly around himself.

"You ever need another dead box opened," Merin said vaguely. She held the musket trained on Riker's forehead. Her hand was perfectly steady.

Gilchrist pried the other musket from its hiding place and disassembled it with three smooth motions. Then he and Crane departed, plunging back into the winding streets, retrieving their things from a particular alley before heading toward the docks. Both of them listening for the sound of a final gunshot.

The strongbox sat between them on the rail, shifting precariously as the ship began to move. The crown's gemstones had been hidden in various boots, pockets, and pouches, while the crown itself resided inside Crane's wide-brimmed hat. Now the box was empty and stuck halfway open, a bat unsure of whether to unfurl its wings.

"Think she did him?" Gilchrist asked.

Crane cocked his head to the side, contemplating. "I heard no third report," he said. "Though it's possible she marched him to a more secluded location first."

Gilchrist was silent for a moment. "Skadi's tattoo, that was from the factory. But she had older marks on her, too. Scars. From her mother, she said." He grimaced. "Maybe Riker was right about the children. And I only freed them to freeze to death. Maybe in the end I'm worse than he was."

"We are all composed of light and darkness, Gilchrist," Crane said. "Which in turn renders us all the same muddled gray as we stumble toward our respective graves. Better to not meditate long on such matters." He retrieved the bag of shiver he'd scooped from the top of Riker's barrel and tapped a fat white trail onto the back of his hand. "The design of this box is remarkable. I imagine we could resell it."

Gilchrist shook his head. "Not worth finding a fence. We're rich enough as is."

"Indeed." Crane snorted, rubbed his nose. "It's time we started making arrangements for our passage across the ocean. The New World awaits our return. The infamous Crane and Gilchrist, seeking further fortunes, battling the fates ..."

Gilchrist said nothing. Then he reached forward and pushed the strongbox off the edge of the rail. The winds caught its delicate mechanisms, wrenching it fully open, and it settled on the dark slushy water like a metal flower. Crane fell into uneasy silence, stroking his bruised collarbone, as they watched it sink.

Elizabeth Bear

Here's a daring raid on a cursed, monster-haunted island by as odd and mismatched a trio of treasure hunters as ever rowed themselves hopefully ashore—only to find that they have no idea at all what they're getting themselves into. If they had, they might have rowed *back* again just as quickly . . .

Elizabeth Bear was born in Connecticut, and now lives in South Hadley, Massachusetts. She won the John W. Campbell Award for Best New Writer in 2005, and in 2008 took home a Hugo Award for her short story "Tideline," which also won her the Theodore Sturgeon Memorial Award (shared with David Moles). In 2009, she won another Hugo Award for her novelette "Shoggoths in Bloom." Her short work has appeared in *Asimov's Science Fiction*, *Subterranean*, *SCI FICTION*, *Interzone*, *The Third Alternative*, *Strange Horizons*, *On Spec*, and elsewhere, and has been collected in *The Chains That You Refuse* and *Shoggoths in Bloom*. She is the author of the five-volume New Amsterdam fantasy series, the three-volume Jenny Casey SF series, the five-volume Promethean Age series, the three-volume Jacob's Ladder series, the three-volume Edda of Burdens series, and the three-volume Eternal Sky series, as well as three novels in collaboration with Sarah Monette. Her other books include the novels *Carnival* and *Undertow*. Her most recent book is an acclaimed novel, *Karen Memory*.

THE KING'S EVIL

"I am a servant of King Pale Empire," Doctor Lady Lzi muttered to herself, salt water stinging her lips. "My life at his command."

Brave words. They did not quiet the churning inside her, but her discomfort did not matter. Only the brave words mattered, and her will to see them through.

Lzi told herself it was enough, that this will would see her through to the treasure she sought, and further yet. She held a long, oiled-silk package high and dry as she turned back in the warm surf to watch the metal man heave himself, streaming, from the aquamarine waters of the lagoon. He slogged up the slope beneath breakers rendered gentle by the curving arms of land beyond. The metal man—his kind were a sort of Wizard's servant common in the far West, called a Gage—had a mirrored carapace that glittered between his tattered homespun rags like the surface of the water: blindingly.

Behind him, a veiled man in a long red woolen jacket held a scimitar, a pistol, and a powder horn aloft as he sloshed awkwardly through the sea, waves tugging at the skirts of his coat. He was a Dead Man, a member of an elite—and disbanded—military sect from the distant and exotic West. Right now, ill clad for the heat and the ocean, he looked ridiculous.

Afloat on the deeper water, the *Auspicious Voyage* unfurled her bright patchwork wings and heeled her green hull into a slow turn. The plucky little vessel slid toward the gap where the lagoon's arms did not quite complete their embrace of the harbor. She took with her three hands, a ship's cat, and the landing party's immediate chance of escape from this reputedly cursed island. Even royal orders would not entice the captain to keep her in this harbor while awaiting the return of Lzi and her party.

They could signal with a fire in the morning if they were successful.

And if not, well. At least it was a pretty place to die and a useful cause for dying in.

Birds wheeled and flickered overhead. A heavy throb briefly filled the air, an almost-mechanical baritone drone. A black fin sliced the water like a razor, then was gone. Lzi sighed to herself, and wondered if she had made a terrible mistake. True, her feet were on the sand and she hadn't been afflicted with Isolation Island's purported royal death curse yet, but there was water yet foaming around her thighs. Maybe the eaten-alive-by-maggots part wouldn't kick in until she was properly beached.

Or maybe the blessing of her royal mission was enough to protect her. And maybe even the mercenaries, too. She had only hope—and the store of sorcery promised by her honorific.

Determination chilled in her belly. She turned her back on the sea and the splashing mercenaries and marched through the water to the dark gray beach, so different from the pink coral sand of most of the Banner Isles. Each roll of the sea sucked sand from under her, as if the waves themselves warned her away. She forced herself not to hesitate as she stepped from the surf: waiting wouldn't alter anything.

When the solid, wet sand compacted under her bare toes, though, she still held her breath. And . . . didn't die. Didn't sense the gathering magic of a triggered hex, either, which was a good sign. She paused just above the tide line and turned back. While she waited for the mercenaries, she unwrapped her long knife and wrapped the silk around her waist as a sash, then stuck the knife in its scabbard through the sash, where she could reach it easily.

By the time she was done, the Dead Man had also gained the beach. The Gage was still heaving himself forward step by sucking step, his great weight a tremendous handicap.

Lzi threw back her head and laughed. "Well, here I am! Foot upon the sand, and no sign of warbles yet, you cowards!"

Whether the retreating sailors heard her or not, she could not tell. The only one she could spot on deck was Second Mate, and he seemed busy with the sail.

"This was a terrible idea," the Dead Man said, as he found his stability in the sandy bottom. Water pumped from the top of his boots with every stride. He didn't dignify their marooners with a backwards glance. Lzi supposed from the stiffness of his shoulders that the stiffness of his neck was quite intentional.

"At least you'll dry out fast in the heat," the Gage said, conversationally.

"Crusted in such salt as will rub one raw in every crevice."

"You should strip down," said Lzi. "I don't know how you stand it." She wrung out her own bright gauze skirt between her hands.

The Dead Man ignored her and thrust his sword through the sash binding his coat closed.

"I'll be crusted in salt, too, very shortly," the Gage said. Lzi wondered if it would flake and freckle off his metal hide. He didn't seem to have corroded yet. He pointed with a glittering hand to the dark blue water the *Auspicious Voyage* was already slicing through. "How does a coral atoll form in such deep water?"

The Dead Man swept a hand around. "Ah, my friend. You see, this island is unlike the others. It is volcanic. The black sand reveals its nature. That's not a coral ring. It's the caldera."

"You aren't as ill educated as you look," Lzi said. She kept her face neutral, hoping the mercenaries would know she meant to include herself in their bantering. "That's the reason the King from this island chose the name King Fire Mountain Dynasty."

"Is it extinct?" the Gage asked.

Lzi shook out her orange-patterned wrapped skirt so it would dry in the breeze. "It hasn't erupted since about 1600, I think."

The Gage paused—she supposed he was doing a date conversion to his weird Western system of dating by Years After the Frost—and came up with what Lzi hoped was a comforting thousand-year cushion. "That could just mean that it's biding its time."

"I've heard volcanos are so wont." The Dead Man tugged his veil more evenly across his face. According to the books, such soldiers revealed their faces only when they were about to kill. "Do you not care to discover if your magical, impervious hide is magically impervious to molten stone, my brother?"

"Oh," said the Gage. "I think I'll pass on being smelted."

"Anyway," Lzi interrupted, pretending to be impervious to the smirk showing at the corners of the Dead Man's eyes, "there's plenty of fresh water on the island for you to rinse yourself in. There's a stream right there."

A braid of clear water trickled over steel-colored sand. When she stepped toward it, her bare feet left prints like pearls had been pressed into the wet, packed beach beside their parent oyster shells.

The Gage called her attention to the answering marks on the far side of the freshwater rill at the same moment that she noticed them herself—and just an instant after the Dead Man invoked his Prophet and her Goddess. A furrow, as if a boat had been dragged up the beach to be hidden in the greenery, with the divots of striving feet beside it.

Fresh.

"Isn't it a strange thing," the Dead Man said conversationally, "that we should not be the only visitors to such an out-of-the-way, shunned, supposed cursed and abandoned island on the very same day?"

Lzi stopped, staring at the furrow. "Strange indeed."

"I don't suppose there's any significance to this particular date on the calendar?"

After a day's acquaintance, Lzi had already learned that the more casually curious the Dead Man sounded, the more likely he was to have his hand on his wheel lock. She checked. Yes, there it was, resting on the ornately elaborate pistol butt.

She slapped at a mosquito that was insufficiently discouraged by the sea breeze and the brightness of the sun burning white in the rich blue sky.

"Well," she said resignedly. "Now that you mention it. But before we talk about that, I'm going to wash the salt off."

The outrigger was inside the jungle's canopy, screened and shaded by ferns and vines. Lzi and the Gage stood over it, touching nothing, counting the seats, estimating the provisions cached under canvas for when the paddlers returned. Four seats, and they seemed to have all been filled. Leaving not much room for spoils . . .

Lzi slapped another mosquito and bent down to peer. She found that what was under the canvas was not food, but blown-glass fishing floats. Perhaps they too were here to steal the dead King Fire Mountain Dynasty's treasure, and they intended to float the treasure back? Or sink it and mark its location? But then anyone could come along and claim it.

"So it's possible," Lzi said, "and perhaps even likely, that His Majesty King Pale Empire was overheard making preparations to rescind the old King's curse on his island, and perhaps they decided to try to beat us to the treasure. If this interloper should succeed, of course, it would be disastrous for the poor, as King Pale Empire means to use these resources to provide for the needy."

"That is a thing that still confounds my understanding. How is it that such treasure has come to be left in a tomb?"

"It's not a tomb," Lzi said, for what felt like the five hundredth time. "It's a palace."

"A tomb," said the Dead Man patiently, "is perforce where a corpse is maintained . . ."

"Look at the bright side," the Gage interrupted, coming back. "We just got significantly less marooned."

"You design to steal their canoe and abandon them to the haunted island?" The Dead Man slapped at a mosquito as well, less patiently.

"Well," the Gage said, "I'd still have to walk back. That won't carry me. But I was thinking that they could take a message to the *Auspicious Voyage* for us, if they turn out to be polite. And maybe they'd let you straddle the outrigger."

"Much to the amusement of the sharks," the Dead Man said, slapping. "Doctor Lady Lzi. You're a natural philosopher. Can't you do anything about these mosquitoes?"

"Welcome to the tropics," the Gage said lightly. "Tell him about the parasites, Doctor Lady Lzi."

Lzi paused within the canopy and found long-leaved zodia plants. They had a pungent, fecund scent, and a handful of leaves stuffed into a pocket or waistband did a fairly good job of keeping the mosquitoes at bay.

"The fact is," she said a few moments later while holding a tangle of vines aside for the Dead Man, "having all this gold tied up in mausoleums is murder on the economy." Her knife was still sheathed in her sash. Whoever had come before them had done a good job cutting a path. While it was regrowing already, it would be useful for a few days more.

"So the current King wants to rob his ancestor's tomb to put a little cash back into the system?" It was hard to tell when the Gage was being sarcastic. Unless he was always being sarcastic. He was a wicked and tireless hand with the machete, however.

"Not so much rob the tomb as . . . put the treasure back into circulation.

To use as relief for the poor. And, King Fire Mountain Dynasty was not King Pale Empire's Ancestor," said Lzi. "Our Kings are not hereditary. Only their Voices are, and that's because of magic. A retired King can only speak through his female relatives."

"It would be less hassle if your Kings all came from the same lineage," the Gage suggested. "Then at least the money would still be in the family, and the new King could use it, instead of its all going to sustain a relic. And the current Kings would keep siring Voices for their Ancestors."

"Sure," said Lzi. "There are absolutely no problems with hereditary dynasties. And everybody wants to spend all eternity being bossed around personally by their Ancestors. Smooth sailing all the way."

"Well," said the Gage. "When you put it like that . . ."

The Dead Man looked at Lzi shrewdly over his veil. "Will you be an interlocutor for the current King, when he is gone?"

"Not gone, exactly, either," Lzi said. "The Kings drink certain sacred potions, which are derived by natural philosophers such as myself. Abstain from most foods, and many physical pleasures. If they have the discipline to stay the course, the flesh hardens and becomes incorruptible. The *processes* of life stop, but . . . the life remains. They may continue for a long time in such a state, far beyond a mortal life span. But eventually the flesh hardens to the point where they cannot move or speak on their own. And then they need interlocutors. Voices."

"Interlocutors like you."

"King Pale Empire has successfully attained the blessed state," she said, aware her voice was stiff. "But he does not yet require a Voice. Once he does, a new King will rule, and he will retire to the position of honored antecedent. In the meantime, I am merely his servant, and a scientist. I am not of his blood, though in his kindness he adopted me into the royal family, and only women of the royal line may serve as Voices to the Ancestors."

"How can you be sure the Kings are actually saying anything through their Voices that the Voices did not think up themselves? It seems like one of the few ways a woman could get a little power around here."

Lzi had wondered that herself, on occasion. She chose to answer obliquely. "There are stories of Voices who did not do the will of their Kings."

"Let me guess," the Gage said. "They all end in tragedy and fire."

"Stacks of corpses. As must always the ambitions of women."

"So. This old dead King is not dead, but has no living female descendants willing to serve as his interlocutors," the Dead Man said. "He's a King with no Voice. What we are embarked upon, well, sounds like robbery to me, begging your pardon."

Lzi shrugged. "Politics as usual. The voiceless are always powerless."

The Gage said, "And is that the future you desire for yourself?"

Lzi opened her mouth to temporize, and wasn't sure what it was about the Gage's eyeless gaze that paralyzed her voice inside her. Maybe it was simply the necessity of regarding her own face, stretched and strangely disordered, in the flawless mirror of his face. She shut her mouth, swallowed, and tried again, but what came out was the truth. "I have no people beyond the King."

"What became of the family of your birth?" the Dead Man asked, so formally she could not take offense. It was prying in the extreme ... but the Dead Man was a foreigner, and probably didn't know any better.

"My parents and brother were killed," Lzi said, which was both the truth and devoid of useful information.

"I'm sorry," the Dead Man said. He paused to allow that heavy throbbing sound to rise and fade again, then added, as a small kindness, "I lost my family too."

"Do you miss them?" Lzi asked, surprising herself with her own rudeness in turn. She had, at best, jumbled memories of her kinfolk: warmth, a boy who teased her and took her sweets but also comforted her when she fell and hurt herself. Two large figures with large calloused hands. Sweet rice gruel served in a wooden bowl.

"The first family, I was too young to remember," the Dead Man said without breaking stride. Nimbly, he leaped a branch. "The second family—yes, I miss them very much."

Lzi looked away, wondering how to get out of this one. The Dead Man's voice had been so matter-of-fact ...

The Gage sank up to the knees in the compost underfoot. Lzi thought it was a good thing brass didn't seem to feel tiredness the way bone and muscle did, or he'd have worn himself out just walking on anything except a paved road.

The Dead Man, kindly, took the opportunity to change the subject. "It's amazing you ever get anywhere." The Dead Man crouched on a long low branch, his soft boots still leaving squelching footprints. The wetness of the soles did not seem to impede his footing.

"I may not get there quickly," the Gage replied, his voice as level as if he sat on cushions in a parlor. "But I have yet to fail to wind up where I intended, and when I pass through a place, few fail to remember where I have been."

Lzi hid a shiver by shrugging her pack off her shoulder. She drank young coconut water. As she capped the canteen, she shrugged to herself. What else had she to spend her life on? More musty, if fascinating, research? More monographs that no one but other naturalists would ever even care about, much less read? More theory on the function of the body and deriving the essential principles from certain plants? More service to an ideal because she had no ambition of her own to work toward?

Perversely, ironic fatalism made her feel a little less empty inside. If she had nothing of her own to live for, it was surely better to find a purpose in life in serving others, rather than increasing suffering and chaos. If you were alone, wasn't it the choice of the Superior Woman to serve those who were not?

The Dead Man shrugged. He stood up on his bough, pivoted on the balls of his feet, and ran lightly along the rubbery gray bark while the branch dipped and swayed under him until he reached a point where another limb crossed the first at midthigh. He stepped up onto the other without seeming to break stride and ran along it in turn, toward some presumed trunk invisible through the foliage ahead. The sound of his footsteps faded into the jungle noise before he vanished from view.

He had the sort of physique that grew veins instead of muscles, and it made his strength seem feral and weightless. In so many ways, the opposite of the Gage.

And yet Lzi could not shake the feeling that in every essential way the two were identical. Except that one wore his armor on the outside, and the other beneath his skin.

She did not desert the Gage. She couldn't have kept up with the Dead Man's branch-running, and it seemed a poor idea to allow their little party to become strung out. She wasn't sure if the Gage noticed, because he labored along without comment.

She was relieved, though, when the Dead Man dropped through the canopy above and ran down a broad bough, his tight-wrapped veil fluttering at the edges. He skidded sideways on his insteps until he was just a foot or two above eye level, far enough away that Lzi didn't need to crane her head back to see him.

"I found the tomb," he announced.

"Palace," she corrected, automatically.

He shrugged. "It resembles a tomb to my eye."

Lzi insisted they pause to eat before pushing any further into unknown dangers—which was easy, in the rich lands of the Banner Islands. They had not even packed supplies: Lzi and the Dead Man simply scanned the earth under the enormous canopy of a breadfruit tree to find ripe, scaly globes, pulled them open, and dined on the mild, custard-like innards. She expected complaints—raw, fresh breadfruit was generally regarded as a bland staple at best—but the foreigner spread a linen cloth that was clean but no longer white across his lap and ate without comment, raising his veil with one hand while scooping morsels from the fruit with the other. Maybe there was no way to eat a ripe breadfruit daintily, but that did not stop him from trying. Lzi wondered what exquisite manners looked like where he came from. Something like this, she imagined.

The Gage didn't seem to care about food.

The Dead Man finished and wiped his fingers daintily on the cloth. He was rolling the cloth so that the soiled portion would not smirch the clean when that searching drone rose once again.

The Dead Man glanced around, cupping a hand behind his veil to better localize the sound. "What *is* that?"

Doctor Lady Lzi had a hypothesis, but she didn't like it very much, and anyway she wasn't confident enough yet to advance it for discussion. One did not become a Lady Doctor by making assertions in public of which one was not confident, and which one could not back up with facts. "Insects?" she asked.

"Well, no maggot curse yet," the Gage said as lightly as a seven-foot-tall brazen bass could be expected to say anything.

The Dead Man shook his jacket clean of nonexistent crumbs. "Mayhap we've not yet gone far enough in."

Lzi followed him through the forest. He stayed on the ground this time, and paused at one point to show her four sets of footprints in a marshy place. They were fresh, filling with water but still sharp-edged. One set was smaller than the others.

The Gage looked at the swampy bit and took the long way around. By the time he rejoined them, Lzi and the Dead Man were already paused behind a screen of greenery, staring across a yard of crushed seashells toward a temple, or a palace, or—she had to admit—a mausoleum. The whole was constructed of pillars—pillars upon pillars upon pillars—stacked in tiers with black basalt in the middle, white coral at the center, and red coral at the top with intermediate shades between so the effect, rather than stripes or bands, was as of the fade from black night to crimson sunrise, only in reverse.

Lzi had expected the palace to be overrun with verdancy, the pillars stumpy and jagged. But it was at least somewhat intact and, if not mani-cured, she could see where the long knives had recently been at work.

"Maybe King Fire Mountain Dynasty is still aware," she said. "Someone is tending this place."

"Not the people from the canoe?" the Gage asked.

She shrugged. "They probably had machetes."

Something burst into the clearing from the jungle to their left without warning, with such speed and force that Lzi stifled a cry of surprise. It was high up, oil-iridescent, as big and darkly barbed as a bluefin tuna and as sleekly shaped for speed. A blur of glistening wings surrounded it, and Lzi had a confused momentary perception of faceted sapphires glittering as big as her two fists before she realized they were eyes.

She hated being right.

"Well," said the Gage complacently, "that'll be the thing, then, that's been making your buzzing sounds."

"Well, it's better than a maggot curse, right?" the Gage offered, when they had withdrawn a hundred yards or so and were considering their options. Crossing that crushed-shell barren seemed much, much less appealing than it had previously.

"Giant wasps?" The Dead Man shook his head emphatically. "I think not."

"Hornets," said Lzi.

The Dead Man looked at her. The Gage might have also: it was hard to tell in a creature that did not need eyes to see and did not seem to turn his head except when he remembered to.

"They're called corpse-wasps," Lzi said, feeling pedantic even as she embarked upon the explanation. "But taxonomically speaking, they are hornets. They form nests. Colonies."

The Dead Man leaned forward. "So we must expect a great many of these creatures?"

She nodded.

The Gage said, "But they're probably not interested in humans unless you threaten their nest, right? They eat fruit or something?"

"The adults eat fruit," she agreed. "But ..."

The weight of their attention stopped her, then compelled her to continue.

"... they do sting animals, including people, and carry them back to the nest for the larvae to feed on. That's why they're called corpse-wasps. Although, technically, they're not feeding on corpses, at least not to start, because the prey animals are just ... well, paralyzed."

"Oh, there's your maggots," the Gage said to the Dead Man.

The Dead Man rocked back explosively. "You *knew* about these things?"

"I know they exist," Lzi said defensively. "I didn't know there were any *here*. Anyway, if you separate the infertile workers from the hives, they become really docile."

She had a sense they were both staring at her though with the Gage it was hard to tell.

"They make great pets."

"Pets," the Dead Man said. "People use them like ... watchdogs?"

"Oh, no. They're far too tame for that."

"Ysmat's bright pen," the Dead Man said, and closed his eyes above his veil.

They discussed waiting until nightfall, but Lzi pointed out that many insect species were more active at dusk and after dark, and the hornets could probably sense warmth anyway, so moving by daylight would actually afford them more protection.

"Theoretically," the Gage said.

"Theory is what we have," Lzi answered. "I think it's unlikely, however, that they will be able to carry *you* off, Brass Man."

He chimed like a massive clock: his mechanical laughter. "That does not, however, solve the problem of how to get you two past them."

"Mud," Lzi said, the excitement of an idea upon her. "And more zodia. The pillars of the palace look too close together for the wasps to fly or crawl through, so I think if we reach it, we should be mostly safe inside. But to get us there—"

"Mud," the Dead Man said.

Lzi nodded. "And lots of it."

The first half of their approach across the barren to the palace went, Lzi thought, surprisingly well. The green, heady scent of the zodia surrounded them densely, almost palpable on the air, making her light-headed. Their skin was invisible under a layer of pounded plant pulp and mud.

The only problem was that the mud/leaf compound, which had stayed pliable in the moist shade under the leaves, began to dry and whiten almost immediately as they came out into the punishing sun. She thought they would be all right if they hurried, but the mud cracked and flaked off, and they had not thought to plaster the Gage. It might not be possible for the corpse-wasps to sting him or carry him off, but it seemed as if the sunlight dazzling from his brazen hide nevertheless attracted the giant insects.

They had been walking, crouched down under camouflage improvised from handfuls of palm fronds she'd cut with her long knife, the saw-toothed-stem edges wrapped in torn cloth to protect their hands. The heavy thrumming heralded a shadow passing over: first one, then another, and another, until the crushed shells underfoot were darkened with blurry blotches. The corpse-wasps swirled down toward the Gage, who uttered what Lzi assumed was an ungentlemanly word in his own tongue and drew his ragged homespun robes and hood close about his featureless form.

Lzi ducked. "I should have thought of that."

"So should I," the Gage answered. A wasp as long as he was tall veered down, rumbling like a charging elephant, and clanged against his upstretched arm. Lzi stared for a moment. She thought of drawing her knife, then thought how laughable a blade merely as long as her forearm would be against something like that.

Then, as a second shadow swelled around her, she found her feet and glanced over at the Dead Man, who beckoned with an outstretched hand, too polite to grab her elbow and drag her with him. His eyes were white-rimmed, and as she started toward him, bent almost double, he turned and fled beside her.

She was getting the impression that he held no real love for bugs.

Another clang and a heavy, squashing thud followed them. Lzi stumbled while trying to look back and this time the Dead Man did touch her shoulder. "He'll be fine."

She had to trust him. Side by side, they ran toward the completely theoretical safety of the palace.

They were doing all right until they tripped over the corpse. It was just inside the pillars, where the shadow of the roof made it nearly impossible to see through the glare of the sun without. In retrospect, Lzi realized that she'd smelled it before she found it, but between the stench of the tomb, that of the festering mud, and the reek of the zodia her memory hadn't automatically supplied the information that this particular terrible odor belonged to some sort of large and very dead thing.

The body had probably been that of a man, but it was bloated with stings now, the skin stretched and crackling with the products of decomposition. Lzi was startled to see that no maggots writhed through its flesh: surely the smell should have attracted every blowfly on the island by now.

Lzi hadn't fallen, but she'd sprawled against a pillar in the second rank and her palm fronds had gone everywhere. She turned back, the breath knocked out of her, looking for the Dead Man. She wheezed in horror, her spasming lungs unable to shriek a warning, as the corpse lurched and twitched and began to push itself upright behind him.

Fortunately, Lzi's wits, even scattered, were sufficient. With her right hand, she fumbled for her blade and shook it free of the sheath, which fell at her feet. She'd worry about that if she lived. Her bruised and scraped left hand, she raised, waving it frantically to get the Dead Man's attention and pointing past his shoulder.

He had good reflexes, and must have decided she was worthy of at least some trust. He ducked even as he turned, and the corpse's clumsy, club-handed swipe whistled over his head and thudded against the pillar with a noisome splatter.

"He isn't dead!" the Dead Man yelped.

"Oh, he's dead all right," Lzi answered. "And mercifully, too." She could see what the Dead Man could not. The corpse's spine had been eaten away, and beneath the shredding skin pulsated the translucent segments of a great larva.

She hoped he was dead, anyway. Hoped with all the force of her rising gorge even though thick blood welling slowly from some of the fresh tears in the necrotic flesh seemed to give the lie to her desire.

Even as Lzi recoiled, the innate curiosity that had led her to natural philosophy made her focus her attention on the grub. It had a glossy black head like polished obsidian, and Lzi could see the pincery mouth parts embedded in the base of the dead man's skull. The visible part of each was long as her finger, and the gentleness of the taper suggested that they continued for some distance more within the base of the brain. Segmented legs were visible here and there, grasping deep within the festering body.

The larva contracted along its length, a sick, rippling pulse. The corpse convulsed, whirling toward Lzi now in its staggering, seizing dance. The foul arms windmilled and she glimpsed, with ever-increasing horror, that the eyes within the slipping skin were clear, not clouded and dead.

Storm dragons cleanse it with thunder, she thought, and lunged out of the way. She swung with the knife, but the floor under a layer of plant detritus was mosaic, and what had once been smooth was now heaved by roots. Chunks of stone littered it from the collapsing roof. They snagged her feet and slammed her toes so sharp pain shot up her legs. She wasn't sure how she kept her feet, then she wasn't sure how she had lost them. She twisted, falling, and landed on her ass, looking up at the deliquescing face of the horror that pursued her.

The thing staggered like a drunk, dragging one leg and stomping wildly with the other, swaying and wavering. She stuck her long knife out like a ward. Over the blade, she saw the Dead Man raise his right hand. Something glinted bright against the blue of his veil, followed by a stone-cracking retort and the cleansing reek of black powder. The parasite jerked with the impact and collapsed unceremoniously across Lzi's lower legs, twitching faintly.

Lzi screamed through clenched teeth, in disgust as much as pain, and yanked her ankles clear. She huddled, panting, while the Dead Man swiftly reloaded his gun. A shadow fell over her and she looked up, pulse accelerating.

It was the Gage, his robe and brass carapace streaked with fluids of two or three colors. Ichor, she judged, and probably venom. He was wiping his big metal gauntlet-hands on the robe, leaving unidentifiable streaks. Then he bent and picked up her soft leather scabbard from where it had fallen among the litter.

"Well," he said, offering a cleaner gauntlet to Lzi, "that seems to have got their attention. Get up. There's a flight headed this way and they might be able to squeeze through the pillars."

"Or," said the Dead Man, without holstering his pistol, "there might be more of those." He gestured at the thing on the ground, which still quivered faintly. "There were four sets of footprints."

Lzi pulled herself up with the Gage's help, bruises stiffening. She stowed her knife. Then she bent down and with both hands hefted a sizeable chunk of rubble, one that made her grunt to lift. She thought of the brown, clear eyes in the parasitized thing's melting face.

She lifted the rock to chest height, and threw it toward the ground. It struck the host's skull with a terrible sound and the quivering stopped.

"Now we can go."

The droning buzz of the corpse-wasps grew heavier, more layered, until Lzi felt the vibrations in the hollowness that had been her chest. She imagined she could watch the tremors shimmer across the Gage's surface. If she looked back, she could see that the light was dimming not simply because they picked their way deeper into the palace complex, but also because the bodies of enormous wasps layered one over another blocked the white glare of the sun. The insects had a smell, in such quantities: musty, like dry leaves. But not so clean.

None of the travelers asked how they would be able to leave the palace now that they had won entrance to it, but Lzi was thinking about it. Maybe they could wait until it rained. A soaking thunderstorm was never far, in the Banner Islands, where the dragons roamed the Sea of Storms. Flying insects took shelter in rough weather, lest they be blown out to sea.

She hoped that applied to insects eight feet long.

There was light ahead and they made for it. The Dead Man's teeth

chattered behind his veil, but his gun hand was steady. He held a scimitar drawn in his off-hand, and that seemed steady too. The Gage moved
with surprising delicacy between the columns, though his carelessness
could probably have knocked the whole moldering palace down.

They came to an open space, unroofed, where the drone of the swarm
was pronounced but distant, rising and falling like the mechanical noise
of cicadas. Litter-filled ornate fountains and statuary bore witness that
this had been a formal courtyard. A gigantic tree rumpled the surrounding
paving stones and clutched benches it must once have shaded in gnarled
roots, as if at any moment it might heave itself free of the earth and come
forward, swinging them as weapons. Beyond, a tall building was surrounded
by the litter of its own crumbling verandas. Like the pillars, it was shaded
from black through white to red. It had once had glass windows, a
profound luxury for the era and the place when it was built, and a few
unbroken panes still gleamed.

"Can we cross that?" the Gage asked, stopping within the shelter of
the penultimate rank of pillars.

"We must," the Dead Man answered, with a glance at Lzi. She was
the employer, she remembered. She could call this off right now.

But her life was service. And besides, they could not go back.

"We must," Lzi agreed. And was looking about her for a plan, or at
least a cluster of zodia plants, when the painted door up the steps behind
the wreckage of the veranda opened, and a woman dressed in a white
skirt and twining sandals, her long hair braided back as thick as Lzi's
wrist, stood framed against interior darkness.

Lzi touched the hilt of her long knife. "Well, don't just stand there,"
the woman said. "It's safe to cross the open space right now as long as
you move quickly. I spent a long time studying the corpse-wasps. I know
a great deal about parasites."

The darkness inside the doorway, once they had scrambled over the rubble
of the wrecked courtyard and climbed gingerly up the steps—which
settled under the Gage's weight but did not crack—was less absolute than
Lzi had anticipated. It was only the contrast with the glare of the direct
sun that had made it seem pitch-black behind the woman. In reality, the
interior of the palace was comfortably dim and cool.

And the interior of the palace was in much better repair than the courtyard or the pillared colonnade.

Ropes of necklaces and heavy bangles shifted and shone as she closed the door behind them, the gold rich against her brown skin. She was tanned—Lzi could see the paler brown behind the waistband of her skirt—but there were no tan lines behind the jewelry. There were wooden amulets sewn into the wrap cloth, though, and those looked long established, with frayed threads and bits of mud in the fine lines of the designs.

"The Emperor is waiting for you. I am the Lady Ptashne, his Voice." She spoke with awkward dignity, worn like those unaccustomed jewels, and gestured them to follow her.

The woman's feet and ankles were dirty under the sandals, as if she had walked through soupy mud then shod herself without being able to first clean her feet. Lzi saw the Dead Man gazing at them speculatively over his veil, and she knew he was comparing their size to the footprints beside the canoe. She was about to ask how a Voice came to be so presently arrived in a deserted kingdom, but words interrupted her.

Someone spoke . . . her name.

She glanced around. There was no one present except the Gage, the Dead Man, and this Ptashne. They were in an entrance hall of crumbling grandeur, hung with silk brocade so brittle it was shredding under its own weight and stacked with furniture coated in layers of dust. The walls were pale coral in shades of pink and white. They had once been hung with tapestries, but the tapestries had broken their threads and fallen from their rings. No one could be hiding behind them.

And the voice that said her name again was like a rustle of wasp wings in her mind. :*Doctor Lady Lzi. Have you too come to disturb my rest, Granddaughter?*:

She blinked with shock, and though the floors here were smooth, she stumbled so the Gage had to steady her elbow. She saw the Lady Ptashne glance over her shoulder speculatively and frown. Lzi kept her face carefully blank. Experimentally, she thought, *King Fire Mountain Dynasty?*

:*You serve the new King.*:

How is it that you are speaking to me, your majesty? I am not your descendant.

:*Are you sure?*: She could sense his amusement. :*Descent through a mother's line is often forgotten. And what person can say for certain who is his father? You have enough of my blood in you for the palace to awaken to your steps.*:

Lzi considered that for a moment. She allowed herself to drift to the end of the group trailing Lady Ptashne, where Lzi could just follow the shoulders in front of her and not concern herself too much with what her features showed.

Who was the man with the wasp inside him?

:Lady Ptashne's companion. One of them. There are two others. I think one was her husband.:

Do you control the wasps? Did you do ... that ... to him?

:The wasps are my guardians, but I do not control them. Long ago, I did bind their ancestors to this place. He and the others trespassed and the wasps defended me.: He sounded matter-of-fact.

If he was Lady Ptashne's companion, how did he come to trespass?

:She was yet Ptashne,: the old King said. *:But not yet Lady when it happened. She brought the men with her as a sacrifice, and she has some little talismans that give her certain powers. Will you be my Voice, Granddaughter?:*

So the Lady Ptashne was, as the canoe had suggested, a recent addition to the royal household. How had she come to pass unscathed through the corpse-wasps, Lzi wondered, apparently alone of her party of four? And why did she seem so calm, despite the deaths?

I spent a long time studying the corpse-wasps. I know a great deal about parasites.

Lzi said—or thought, hard and clearly—*You have a Voice.*

:So I do,: the dead King answered. *:One Voice. After a fashion. Is it not better to have a choice, than to have no choices?:*

But ... you have a Voice. Already.

:And you have one, too. Do you speak out with it in your own words? Or do you silence it except when commanded to its use by another?:

It was the same question he had asked before, which she had dodged, but more provocatively phrased this time. Was the dead King needling her? Trying to get her to rise to the bait?

What if I don't have anything to say?

The undead King did not answer. She wondered if she needed to intend to speak to him for him to hear her, or if he were politely ignoring her own interior monologue.

I serve King Pale Empire, she said. *But he does not own my voice.*

:That is good to hear, Granddaughter. Ah, you are nearly to the presence chamber. Do not allow Lady Ptashne to know that you can speak to me, Doctor Lady Lzi. Not yet. It would be ... unwise.:

Well, *that* painted Lzi with a wash of unease.

Ahead, Lady Ptashne had stopped before an ironbound door. It seemed recently maintained, and there were fresh scratches around the keyhole, which was sized to admit an enormous old-fashioned key. Ptashne lifted just such a key from inside her skirt pocket. A ribbon connected it to the material of her garment: it had been sewn into place with hasty stitches and thread that did not match.

She turned the key, struggled with the weight of the door before prevailing, and led them into another space, shadowy and echoing from its depths.

Nuggets of glass turned under Lzi's feet. She was distracted keeping her balance and watching the Gage pick his way carefully until she realized that if the glass did not crush into powder under his feet, then it was not glass at all, but gemstones. Rubies and sapphires in every color of the rainbow littered the floor: a priceless trip hazard.

Lzi thought with frustration of kingdoms where such riches would not be left uselessly to molder as symbols of the bygone might of dead Emperors, but used to support trade, to buy medicines, to feed the poor. How much had her island home suffered through the centuries because of waste such as this? This ... all this treasure ... How much linen could it buy from the mainland for sails? How much hemp for ropes? The Sea of Storms protected the Banner Islands from any raiders more significant than the occasional pirate. But the Banner Islands, though rich in foodstuffs and spices and hardwood, were otherwise natural-resource poor. Trade was their lifeline. This would pay for trade.

As they reached the center point of the hall, lights flared in sconces along both sides. They looked like torch flames but burned strikingly violet and blue, and there were no torches beneath them. Their light stained the Gage's bronze hide a most unearthly color and sent thick, watery, reflected bands of radiance rippling across everything in the hall.

More wealth gleamed on every side, and before them, another fifty steps or so along the enormous hall, was a throne whose golden seat hung suspended between two mammoth ivory tusks that crossed at the top in barbaric splendor.

The throne stood empty.

The Dead Man's step checked. Lady Ptashne, though, seemed to have anticipated it. Without turning her head, she said, "His Majesty is in the Presence Chamber."

She turned them to the right and brought them to a small door, much more human in scale than the one she had struggled with, recessed between two pillars in the side wall. This one was unlocked, apparently, for she simply manipulated the handle and opened it.

It revealed a small, comfortably furnished room that was lit with the same eerie blue flames, but did not need them. At the far end, two multipaned windows big as doors framed a Song-style ox-yoke armchair of carved wood and cracking leather, fragile with age but still strong enough to support the slight weight of the corpse who slouched in it. He was little more than a collection of brown sticks wrapped in moldering silken brocades, decorated with ropes of jewels. Over the robes, the corpse wore a dust-coated cloak. There were places where the heavy, feathery dust had been disturbed— brushed or blown off—and beneath them Lzi glimpsed the iridescent, translucent wings of insects, sewn together in tiers like the feathers of a bird.

The corpse was mummified, the skin glossy brown as lacquered leather. White bits of bone showed through where the fingers had crumpled or been gnawed by rats.

Following Ptashne, Lzi and the others approached. The Gage's footsteps made a heavy careful sound on the flagstones. The dead King smelled of moths and attics, dry fluttery things.

:*I never could stand that throne room,*: said King Fire Mountain Dynasty, and Lzi swallowed and tried not to think too much about the fact that she was in a close little room with his thousand-year-old body. :*Drafty old pile. This is a much better place to wait for eternity.*:

Lzi bowed low before the chair. After a confused glance, the Gage and the Dead Man did as well.

"King Fire Mountain Dynasty bids you welcome, and rise."

Lzi hadn't heard him say any such thing. But perhaps he just hadn't spoken to her.

Lzi turned to the Lady Voice, and said, "Your friend is dead."

Ptashne frowned at her in mild distaste. "My husband?" She shrugged.

How had Ptashne known which of her companions they had encountered? The Gage made his chiming chuckle, and Lzi thought of King Fire Mountain Dynasty's warning about talismans.

Ptashne twisted a hand in the folds of her white skirt. "His Majesty commands your assistance. He wishes to be carried from this place, and to the beach."

Lzi held her breath for a moment, gathering her courage. "What are the floats for?"

"Floats?"

"The fishing buoys. In your canoe."

"Oh," Ptashne said. "For floating King Fire Mountain Dynasty back to the big island, of course."

"Back to the big island?"

"Of course," she repeated. "You don't think he wants me to stay here forever, do you? With his treasure and my status as his granddaughter . . ." Ptashne smiled. "We will have a good life. Of course, if you help me, I will share some of my wealth with you. Now, please have your soldier and your"—she waved a hand vaguely at the Gage—"lift him, and carry him down to the lagoon."

:*That is not what I require of you, Granddaughter.*:

And in a flash of comprehension, as if he had shown her a map, Lzi understood what the dead King did require of her. It came on a tremendous warmth, a sense of belonging. Of being part of something.

She rebelled against his request.

I have only found you!

:*And would you, too, use me for power and wealth?*:

She felt deep shame. *Wealth is why I came here. But not for me. For the current King.*

:*And will he not reward you?*:

He has . . . she stopped. Thought. *Given me service. Given me a place.*

:*Well,*: the old King answered. :*If that is all you want, Granddaughter.*:

I want you, she answered. *I have only just found you. Do not make me give you up so soon.*

:*I am tired. And you see what I've had to contend with in certain branches of the family.*:

He didn't move, of course. He couldn't. He hadn't moved in a thousand years. But she still had a sense of a dismissive flick of his fingers in the direction of the Lady Ptashne.

"Pick him up!" Ptashne demanded, increasingly shrill.

"Is that what you require us to do?" the Dead Man asked. "It is you who holds our contracts, Doctor Lady."

You are my only family. She stopped herself from saying it—thinking it—out loud. Whatever she was or was not, she would not guilt-trip a man who had been alone for six hundred years because she was lonely.

"Well, no, actually," Lzi said. She closed her eyes. She *liked* this long-undead ancestor whom she had so swiftly become acquainted with. She felt a great, tearing sense of loss as she took a deep breath and said, "I want you to destroy him."

If she expected an outraged outburst, she didn't get it. The Dead Man just said, curiously, "So there is in truth no curse?"

"Of course there's a curse," she scoffed. "Do you think any of this stuff would still be in there if there wasn't a *curse?* But he wanted to be left alone, not protected. And now, he has been alone a very long time, and what he wants is to be *gone.*"

"How can you know that?" Ptashne said. "*You* can't talk to him. I am his Voice!"

"She's got the contracts," the Gage said tiredly. "Or rather, her King does. Please stand aside, Lady Ptashne."

The Brass Man took a step forward. The lady in the white skirt did not step aside. She wheeled and fell to her knees, clutching the mummified legs of the ancient King. They flaked and crumbled at her touch.

"Let me serve you, ancestor!" Ptashne cried.

Lzi felt her mouth shape words, her throat stretch to allow a voice of foreign timbre to pass. :The only service I require is destruction, child,: she said aloud. :What service you offer is for yourself, and not for the kingdom.:

Ptashne's sobs dried as if her throat had closed on them. She rose gracefully, the cultivated daintiness of a lady. Lzi wondered where she had come from, and what had brought her here. It itched in her conscience and her curiosity that she would probably never know.

Ptashne turned to face the Gage. He towered over her, and she seemed frail and small. Her hands twisted in the waistband of her skirt, clutching at the amulets sewn there.

Her mouth pressed together until no red was left, and Lzi thought if there hadn't been flesh and teeth in the margin, bone would have rasped on bone. It was the expression of an unwanted child who is reminded that there are children for whom parents make sacrifices.

Lzi felt it in her bones, and knew the interior shape of it intimately.

There *are* children for whom parents make sacrifices. It's a thing some take a long while to understand in their hearts even if they see it with their eyes.

Experience is a more potent teacher than observation. And Lzi had never had a sacrifice made for her sake either. A terrible pity took her.

Ptashne looked Lzi in the eyes, forward as a lover, and spoke to her as if to King Fire Mountain Dynasty. "Let me serve you, Grandfather. You are my family. I need you. You are my ancestor, Grandfather. I honor you. I have honored you, and all my ancestors, all my life. With my sorcery and with my search. You owe me this small thing."

Lzi's lips moved around that voice that came not from her lungs, but somewhere else. :I am tired, Granddaughter. Take half my jewels. Make a life with that.:

Why do you speak through me? Lzi asked. *Why not her?*

:*She has protections in place for that, as well. I can speak to her, but not through her, and these words need to be spoken aloud.*:

"I do not want your jewels, Grandfather." Ptashne straightened up, her muddy feet in their laced sandals set stubbornly on carpet that was more moth-hole than knot and warp. "I want to be your Voice." The hard line of her mouth softened. She looked up at the Gage, who had stopped just out of his own ability to reach her, like a man trying not to frighten a cornered kitten.

She said to the giant metal man, "I've come all this way for him and it's not fair, women are only allowed to hold power through men, why won't he *help* me?"

It was a child's voice. It cut Lzi like a knife. The ridges of wound, gummed cloth on the hilt of her machete were rough against her palm.

And then Ptashne steeled herself, and said, "Then I shall help myself."

She twisted her hands in her skirts. She shouted, a shrill and wavering scream. One of the amulets at her waistband swelled with a green glow like light through young leaves. It streamed between her fingers in rays like the sun parting clouds. The Gage took a step forward, ornate tiles powdering under his foot. The Dead Man reached for his gun.

They were both too late.

The sidelight windows flanking the dead King's chair of estate shattered in a hail of glass and buzzing. Two infected, flailing men stumbled into the room, followed by a half dozen corpse-wasps. The men both waved

machetes haphazardly. The wasps brandished daggerlike stingers damp at
the tip with droplets of paralytic poison.

Lzi, with her hand on her sheathed knife, froze. She made one startled
sound—a yelp of surprise rather than a moan of terror—and then her
body locked in place as surely as if the wasps had already had their way
with her. She watched her reflection grow in a gargantuan, glossy green-
black thorax. The part of the brain that screams *run, run* in those dreams
where your body seems immured in glass was informing her calmly that
this was the last instant of her life.

The Dead Man stepped in front of her and shot the corpse-wasp
between the eyes.

Dust sifted from between the stones overhead. The shot wasp tumbled
to the floor and buzzed, legs juddering, the spasms of its wings trembling
the stones under Lzi's feet. The sound . . . the sound of the gun was enormous. It filled Lzi's ears and head and left room for nothing else. No
other sound, no thought—and not even the paralyzing fear.

She fumbled her machete into her hand. She hacked at the nearest
threatening thing—the convulsing wasp's stinger. She severed it in two
sharp whacks and looked up to see the Dead Man still standing before
her, parrying wild swings by one of the parasitized men. The Gage was
fending off two wasps, their stingers leaving venom-smeared dents in his
carapace. Ptashne, her hair escaping its thick braid, had fallen back to
stand before the chair of estate of the corpse she would have be her King.
She had her own long knife drawn from its sling at the small of her back,
but was holding it low and tentatively, as if she did not know how she
would fight with it.

And between Lzi and Ptashne were five angry hornets and two pathet-
ically disgusting not-quite-corpses. So that wasn't really a solution.

A wasp came in from the left, furiously intent on the Dead Man as
he drove Ptashne's parasitized companion back, step by step. Its wings
and the back of its thorax struck the ceiling as it curved, bringing its
stinger to bear.

Lzi stepped forward and brought the machete down hard and sharp,
as if she were trying to cut a poison-sap vine with one blow. It struck
the underside of the heavy chitinous abdomen and stuck there with a
sound like an axe buried in wood. Splinters of the insect's carapace and
splatters of pulpy interior flew, and the machete stuck fast.

With an angry buzz and a clatter of its mandibles, the sapphire-eyed insect tried to turn on her. Its feet scratched at her face and hair. She ducked to shield her eyes and held frantically to the long knife's handle, locking her elbow and pushing the pulsing, seeking stinger away. The Dead Man was too busy with his maggot man and another of the wasps to come to her aid.

Lzi screamed with all her might and twisted the blade sharply.

The wasp's carapace shattered with a crack, and the stinger twisted and went slack. The thing made a horrible buzz and tried to bite. She hammered at the jeweled eye with the pommel of the long knife, as it was too close to use the blade. Now she screamed, or at least yelled vigorously.

There was a revolting crunch, and the enormous wasp—which was terribly light, she realized, for its size, as if it were mostly hollow inside— scrabbled at her once more and fell away. She looked up into the featureless face of the Gage, smeared with ichor and more nameless things.

"The wasps are protecting the larvae," Lzi said, as sure of the truth behind the inspiration as if she had learned it at her father's knee. "Ptashne doesn't control the adults. Just the larvae in the corpses."

"Destroy the King." The Gage's head did not turn as his left hand flashed out to snatch at the wing of another wasp as it darted toward the Dead Man. He used its own momentum to slam it into the ceiling, his metal body pivoting inhumanly, like a turret, at the waist. He continued in a level tone—or maybe it was just that all its nuances were flattened by her deafness. "If Ptashne has nothing to fight for, she'll stop."

Dragon's breath, I hope so. Lzi thought she might be desperate enough to keep fighting anyway, having nothing else to live for. "Get me through."

The Gage did not respond in words. Instead it turned again, seamlessly, and lurched forward, flailing with its enormous arms. It didn't attempt to prevent the enemies from striking it, and it didn't seem to care if it struck them. It just created a flurry of motion that surrounded Lzi and fended the enemies away. It walked sideways, crabwise, toward the dead King and his Voice.

He turned, still keeping her in the shelter of his parries, and Lzi was next to the place where King Fire Mountain Dynasty slumped in his finery. She could smell him: not rot, but salt and natron and harsh acetone.

Ptashne seemed to realize what they were about and whirled on them. "No," she shouted. She would have rushed at Lzi, but the Gage caught her effortlessly around the waist and held her tight. She hammered at him with the pommel of her long knife, and the room might have rung like a bell if Lzi's ears had not still felt stuffed with wool. Holding on to Ptashne limited the Gage's effectiveness in fending the wasps away from Lzi, but the Dead Man was between her and the enemy, a whirl of blades and faded crimson coat-skirts.

It was hard, so hard, to turn her back on the fight, on the slashing stingers and whirling blades, the clang of machete on scimitar, the screaming and flailing of the would-be Voice. But she did, ran two steps through the chaos, hefting her long knife, and stopped by the chair of the King.

:*That will not do the job, Granddaughter. For this, you need fire.*:

"Fire," she said aloud. She didn't look, but somehow there was a powder horn in her hand, and a flint and steel.

The Dead Man's powder horn.

Fire. Black powder would burn nearly anything.

She poured it over the dead King, his rotting robes, his ropes of gold and jewels, his crooked slipping crown. His face drawn tight to the skull, the nose a caved-in hole. His eye sockets empty with the withered lids sagging into them.

She poured the contents of the horn over him, into his lap, into the tired wisps of his staring hair. She dropped the horn. She clutched the flint and iron and raised them over the corpse of the King.

Behind her, all the sounds of battle ceased. The buzzing continued, but when Lzi risked a glance, she saw that the one remaining parasite host had staggered back and was leaning against the wall by the door, and the two adult wasps that were still alive and mobile crouched in front of him, one on the ceiling and one on the floor, protecting the young of the hive but not, themselves, immediately attacking.

"Please," Ptashne said. She had stopped struggling as well, and now just hung in the Gage's grasp, bedraggled and bruised, her long knife on the floor where it had fallen from her hand.

"All this for a family," Ptashne said, tiredly.

:My family is gone,: King Fire Mountain Dynasty said, through Lzi. :And you gave yours to the wasps in exchange for a weapon, Grandchild.:

The Dead Man looked at him, head sideways. At the mummy, Lzi noticed, and not at the Voice. Used to marvels, this mercenary. "You have family in this room."

I would have given you my life.

:*Keep it for yourself,*: he counseled. :*End this.*:

Lzi struck a spark. She had been too cautious and kept her hand too far away. It fell and fizzled. Ptashne screamed.

Lzi struck again. This time it flared, and the powder caught. She backed hastily away from a shower of sparks and the strange dry smoke of burning mummy. King Fire Mountain Dynasty burned like a torch once he caught, and said nothing further in Lzi's head. Not even the whisper of a *thank-you*.

Well, it was what she should have expected of a King.

"You ruined me," Ptashne said dully. "You have ruined everything."

Lzi glanced at the wasps, which seemed to have no intention of charging these dangerous creatures again. They buzzed menace and held the door. Lzi and her mercenaries were going to have to climb out a window.

"He gave you jewels," she said to Ptashne. "Take whatever you can carry. May you find joy in it."

Lzi sat alone on the beach beside a tree, waiting for the sun to rise and the *Auspicious Voyage* to return. She fretted the edge of her machete with her thumbnail. It was, understandably, dull.

She looked up as two silhouettes approached. "Did you get him?"

The Gage shook his head, which gleamed softly in the moonlight. He sat down on her left, the Dead Man on her right. "We looked. The wasps must have taken their last offspring somewhere safe from the likes of us."

"Poor man," Lzi said.

After a while, the silence of lapping waves was broken by the Dead Man's voice. "So," he said. "We shall collect our pay soon, and be traveling on. And then, where do *you* go from here, Doctor Lady?"

"It's not hard to live here," she said. She gestured to the jungle behind them, the sea before beyond. "Many people are content with the breadfruit, the harvest of the lagoons, the coconuts and mangoes and the pounded hearts of palm. Many people are content to sail, and swim, and find somebody to fight and make babies with."

"But it was never enough for you."

Lzi heard the length of her own pause, and the snort that followed. "Maybe the restlessness runs in the blood like the sea. My parents sailed off in search of an uncharted island and never returned, did you know that? Into the dragon-infested Sea of Storms. They took my brother with them. I was judged too young. They had ambition and it killed them. I had ambition . . . and also I was afraid."

"So you studied the arts of science?"

"I learned to read," she said. "I learned to heal. I learned to kill by poison and by blade, because you cannot learn to create without learning to destroy, and the reverse of course holds true as well. I made a place for myself in the service of King Pale Empire. My life at his command."

The Dead Man nodded, perhaps sympathetically. He leaned against the tree she sat beside. "But."

"But it wasn't enough. I felt like I was scraping mud from the bottom of the well, that it was filling with salt water from beneath."

"You can only give so much from a well until you fill it again. With rain or with buckets, or with time and the water that rises from within. When you are doing something entirely for somebody else—out of altruism, or out of a need to feel some purpose—"

"What else is there?"

"What are you good for?" He might have smiled. In any case, the shadowy stretch of the veil across his face altered. "You could try wanting something. For yourself. For its own sake. Or getting mad enough about something unfair to decide to do something about it."

She considered it. So strangely attractive. Find something worth fighting for, then fight for it.

"But what?"

He blinked sleepily. "Doctor Lady Lzi, if you come to that under-standing, you will have exceeded the accomplishments of fully half of humanity. And now please excuse me. It will be day before long, and I am going to look for some dry wood for the signal fire."

She sat on the beach beside the Gage and watched the sun go down. The wind off the water grew chill; the sand underneath her stayed warm.

The Gage spoke before she did. "Do you want to wind up like maggot man back there? That's what service to the unappreciative gets you. Ask a Gage how he knows."

She decided not to. "What if you don't have anything but service?" she asked starkly.

There was a silence. The stars burned through it, empty and serene as Lzi wished she could be.

"I had a family for a time as well," said the Gage, over the hush of the waves.

"You?" Lzi's expression of confusion was making her forehead itch. "But you are . . ."

"Gages are born before we're made," said the Gage. "The Wizard needs something to take apart, to animate the shell when she puts it back together again."

"By the Emperor's wings," Lzi said softly.

"I volunteered."

She stared at him, rude though it was. The light of the moons made blue ripples on his hide.

"Well," the Gage said, reasonably, "would you want something like me around if it hadn't decided it wanted to be made and serve you?"

"Were you dying?" Lzi covered her mouth with her hands. She was catching rudeness from these foreigners.

"Not yet. But I needed to live long enough to exact a kind of justice. For *my* family."

Lzi hadn't heard the Dead Man come up behind her. His voice made her jump. "I did live for service. Very like you. And then the service was taken from me." He thumped a pile of sticks down on the sand. "In this life, one cannot rely on anything."

"What kept you going past that point?"

"For me," the Dead Man said, "it was also revenge."

The Gage had called it *justice*. Lzi asked, "Revenge for your Caliph?"

The naïve might have mistaken his bark of pain for a laugh. "For my daughters," he said. "And my wife."

Lzi couldn't think what to say, and said nothing, for so long that the Dead Man collected himself and went on.

"That desire kept me alive long enough for others to assert themselves."

The Gage tilted his polished head. It gleamed with a soft luster in the tropic dark. "Revenge led me to become a Gage," he admitted. "Since then, I have not met anything that could put a stop to me. So here I am."

"Is that the only effective purpose? The only way to make a space for yourself in the world that is not . . . serving someone else's whim?" Lzi asked. "Vengeance?"

"It is the worst one," the Gage replied. "But it's something to go forward on."

"I don't have anyone to punish." Not even the parents who had abandoned her, she realized. For how do you punish those who are dead and gone? But she realized also that she could never make herself good enough, small enough, useful enough to lure them home. Because they were dead, and they were gone.

"All this for family?" Lzi said, and felt that expression push her mouth thin. "She was right, you know. This is the only power of her own that she would ever have had."

"Yes," said the Gage quietly. "I know."

He was silent for a moment or two.

"Then a harder question. What would you be, beyond a servant?" the Dead Man asked her. "What else would you seek?"

Lzi shrugged. "I am not giving up my service. I am useful where I am."

"What does your soul crave, though, besides being useful?" There was enough light now to see him shift slightly from foot to foot. Morning was coming.

"I suppose the first thing I seek is what I am seeking."

He touched his nose through the veil, which she thought signified a smile. "Write me a letter when you find it."

"You're not staying?"

He shrugged.

The Gage rolled his enormous shoulders, as if settling his tattered homespun more comfortably. Lzi would have to see if the Emperor's gratitude for the sapphires in her pack would extend to a new raw-silk robe for the brazen man.

He didn't turn his polished metal egg, but Lzi had a sense that he was looking at the Dead Man . . . fondly?

"Not here," the Gage supplied for his partner. "He's seeking . . . something else." He waited a moment, watching a pale line creep across the bottom of the sky. "You could come with us. We're short a naturalist."

He's seeking a home, she thought. *Does the destination matter, or is the value in the journey and whom you make it with?* "Let me think about it," she said, and watched the *Auspicious Voyage*'s silhouette approach across the broken mirror of the lagoon.

Lavie Tidhar

I had to think hard about whether it was proper to include one of Lavie Tidhar's tales of "guns & sorcery," featuring the bizarre and often ultra-violent adventures of Gorel of Goliris, a "gunslinger and addict" in a world full of evil sorcery and monstrous creatures. Did a story without swords belong in a Sword & Sorcery anthology? But swords or no swords, the Gorel stories are true to the spirit of Sword & Sorcery, and their antecedents are clear—there's the strong influence of Stephen King's Gunslinger stories, obviously, but equally strong are the traces of C. L. Moore, Michael Moorcock, Jack Vance, and Robert E. Howard. The Gorel stories especially remind me of Howard's early Conan the Barbarian stories. What they are is almost the pure essence of Sword & Sorcery—violent, action-packed, paced like a runaway freight train, politically incorrect and socially unredeemable, in your face. They're also a lot of fun, and yet another example, along with the work of many of the other writers here, of the interesting and sometimes surprising directions this particular subgenre is evolving in as we progress deeper into the twenty-first century.

So let yourself be swept along with Gorel on his latest dark and twisted quest, but buckle your seatbelts—it's going to be a bumpy ride.

(Further adventures of Gorel can be found in the chapbook novella *Gorel and the Pot Bellied God* and in the collection *Black Gods Kiss*.)

Lavie Tidhar grew up on a kibbutz in Israel, has traveled widely in Africa and Asia, and has lived in London, the South Pacific island of Vanuatu, and Laos; after a spell in Tel Aviv, he's currently living back in England again. He is the winner of the 2003 Clarke-Bradbury Prize (awarded by the European Space Agency), was the editor of *Michael Marshall Smith: The Annotated Bibliography*, and the anthologies *A Dick & Jane Primer for Adults*, the three-volume The Apex Book of World SF series, and two anthologies edited with Rebecca Levene, *Jews vs. Aliens* and *Jews vs. Zombies*. He is the author of the linked story collection *HebrewPunk*, and, with Nir Yaniv, the novel *The Tel Aviv Dossier*, and the novella chapbooks *An Occupation of Angels*, *Cloud Permutations*, *Jesus and the Eightfold Path*, and *Martian Sands*. A prolific short-story writer, his stories have appeared in *Interzone*, *Asimov's Science Fiction*, *Clarkesworld*, *Apex Magazine*, *Strange Horizons*, *Postscripts*, *Fantasy Magazine*, *Nemonymous*, *Infinity Plus*, *Aeon*, *The Book of Dark Wisdom*, *Fortean Bureau*, *Old Venus*, and elsewhere, and have been translated into seven languages. His novels include *The Bookman* and its two sequels, *Camera Obscura* and *The Great Game*, *Osama: A Novel* (which won the World Fantasy Award as the year's Best Novel in 2012), *The Violent Century*, and *A Man Lies Dreaming*. His most recent book is a big, multifaceted SF novel, *Central Station*.

WATERFALLING

A Guns and Sorcery Novelette

1.

Gorel of Goliris rode slowly, half-delirious in the saddle of his graal. The creature lumbered beneath him, moving sluggishly. It was a multilegged beast, native to the sands of Meskatel, which lay far to the south. Its tough carapace would turn a pleasing green in sunlight, as it depended on the solar rays for sustenance: but right now its skin was a dark and unhealthy-looking mottled grey, as the storm clouds had been amassing steadily over the deadlands and the creature was starved of nutrition just like its master, in his own way, was. Its tail was raised like the stem of a flower, the better to catch moisture in the air, the sting at its end naked like a spur.

They were much alike, master and beast. Hardy, obstinate, durable, and deadly. Gorel's head hung limp on his chest. His gums hurt and his eyes felt fused shut, and everything ached. His hands shook uncontrollably.

Withdrawal.

He needed it.

He needed the Black Kiss.

What drove him into the deadlands was a mixture of heartache, desire, and need. Somewhere far behind him lay the Black Tor, and its enigmatic master, the dark lord whom Gorel knew only as Kettle. The Avian mage was a small, slight being, his fragile bones like those of a bird. The two had been together when great Falang-Et fell, and the river Thiamat flooded, its god dead ...

Kettle had used Gorel, and Gorel could not forgive his onetime lover for that betrayal.

His journey since had taken him far and wide: to the great cemetery of Kur-a-len, where the dead still walk, and to the Zul-Ware'i mountains, where the remnants of an ancient war still littered the glaciers with deadly unexploded ordnance. What drove him, always, was his quest. The search for lost Goliris, that greatest of empires, the biggest and most powerful the World had ever known. His home, from which he had been taken as a child, to which he must return, and claim his throne . . .

Yet in all the World, in all of his searching, throughout the long years, he had never found a trace of his homeland, as though—he sometimes thought, in dark moments—it had been erased entirely from the memory of all living beings.

But the World was large—infinite, some even claimed. And Gorel would not rest until he found it once again.

Goliris . . .

Heartache, then, and need. Yet, what of desire?

It had happened long before, in the jungle lands where the Urino-Dag, the ghouls of the bush, haunt the unwary traveller in the thicket. Where the smell of rotten leaves and decay fills the still air, where a village once stood, where Gorel had come in his search . . . only to encounter the twin goddesses, Shar and Shalin, who bit him, laughing, with the Black Kiss . . . and even as he murdered them both, and all their followers, their curse was in him, and he was forever hooked.

Gods' Dust.

But there were no gods in the deadlands. There were barely any human habitations to attract them, no subsequent illicit transaction of pleasure for faith. And Gorel was driven on blindly, across a land cracked with drought, under a black sky, driven as much *away* as *towards*, growing weak, growing delirious . . .

And in his *delirium tremens*, he remembered.

He remembered Goliris.

2.

The great towers of dread Goliris rose like an infection out of the fertile ground. They were not so much built as *cultivated*, planted there in aeons past by the magus-emperor Gon, the fungimancer. Where he had bought these spores, at what cost, or in what far-flung corner of the great empire of Goliris, was lost to the mists of time, but the towers grew, tall graceful stems with bulbous caps, gills protruding, and a small army of wizard-gardeners tending to their constant maintenance.

Goliris, mother-city, sat atop the shores of a great ocean. Its black ships, unequalled in all the World, departed from its shores to all corners and returned laden with goods and pillage. The hot, humid air was cooled by the sea breeze, and in its wide avenues and canals there strode, flew, and swam the ambassadors of a thousand races, come to pay tribute.

Gorel remembered standing at the top of the palace, holding his father's hand. The room was cool and dark, and through the gills one could see the ocean spread out to the horizon, where a blood-red sun was slowly setting. Its dying light illuminated the great fleet, black sails raising over-head the seven-pointed-star flag of Goliris.

"Where are they going, Father?" the young Gorel had asked.

"To conquer new lands," his father said. "To further spread the fame and power of Goliris. Gorel . . . one day, all this will be yours. For untold generations our bloodline held pure and strong, commanding empire. To rule is your destiny, as it was mine. Will you be ready?"

The young Gorel held his father's hand and stared out to sea. The thought of his future, the terrible responsibility, both excited and fright-ened him. But he could not disappoint his father, could not reveal his inner turmoil.

"Yes," he said. "Yes, Father, I will be ready."

"Good boy!" his father said. Then he scooped him in his arms, and for one brief, wondrous moment Gorel felt warm, and safe, and loved.

. . . but already their downfall was underway. And that terrible night came not long after, though he could no longer remember the exact sequence of events, what followed what . . . he was only a boy, and they had schemed in secret, in the shadows, the mages of Goliris, servants burning with a hatred of mastery. He remembered that awful night, the screams, the cruel, laughing faces. The stench of wizardry.

Then he was taken. Taken from his home, from his World, from all that he knew and loved. Transported, in the blink of an eye, away from there, the screams still echoing in his ears, and that awful smell, until he woke and found himself in a foreign land, by the side of a hill, and he was crying, for he was only a boy . . .

Now he lolled in the saddle, and his hands caressed the six-guns hanging on his sides. He had fashioned them himself, and each bore the seven-pointed stars of Goliris.

The land he found himself in as a boy was called the Lower Kidron, and the couple who had found and adopted him were gunsmiths. In that wild, untamed land the boy Gorel learned the ancient way of the gun, and it was from there that he set out on his journey, to claim back his ancient throne—though the journey had been taking longer than anticipated, and though he had killed many on the way, he was no closer to his goal . . .

Overhead, the clouds amassed. Somewhere, no doubt, the Avian called Kettle was planning the next stage in his inexplicable conquest of this part of the World. There had always been dark mages, and they were always bent on conquest, yet there was something different about Kettle, a hidden purpose, as though he alone could see some grand and troubling design no one else could discern . . .

But this was no longer Gorel's concern. In truth, he had a job. And, despite all the current set-backs, he was intent on following it through.

The job was simple, as such jobs usually were. Find a man—and then kill him. And Gorel was good at the first, and very, *very* good at the second . . .

3.

The client had tracked Gorel down at an Abandonment on the edge of the deadlands. He was, unusually, an Apocrita.

The Apocrita were benign parasites, starting off small, attaching to a human host's lower abdomen and gradually growing with their hosts until reaching puberty, when they began discarding and changing their humans with some frequency. Other than that unfortunate habit, the Apocrita were considered a highly civilized species, with a fine taste in wine and music and an almost fanatical devotion to the writing of poetry. What one was doing this far away from their natural habitat, a small monarchical feudatory state on the edge of the Yanivian Desert, Gorel had no idea, but nor did he care.

"I say," the Apocrita said. "Are you the gunslinger fellow?"

Gorel was sitting down with a small cup of draeken, that rare wine, from the far western principality of Kir-Bell, which is made by slowly bleeding the indentured tree-sprites of that place and fermenting their blood. He stared at the Apocrita and made a noncommittal grunting sound and struck a match to light his cigar.

"Depends who's asking," he said, at last.

The Apocrita sat down opposite without being invited. He clicked his fingers for service and gruffly ordered, "Whatever that gentleman is drinking." The server, a grave-wraith from Kur-a-len, gave an ugly leer but fetched the drink without comment. The Apocrita had nodal growths spread over the human host's body and its own large, black sack-like mass was fused to the man's back and spread round his hips to the front.

"There's a man," the Apocrita said.

"There usually is," Gorel allowed.

"He stole something from me," the Apocrita said. "The goods would most likely be spoiled by now, but that's immaterial. What is important is that a message is sent. Do you understand?"

"What's in it for me?" Gorel said.

The Apocrita shrugged. From his bespoke tailored jacket he took out a small black money-bag tied with a string. He pushed it across the table, casually and almost contemptuously, at Gorel.

Gorel picked it up, untied it, and stared at the powder inside.

Gods' Dust.

The Black Kiss.

He took a pinch, snorted.

It hit him like an open slap to the face and he rocked back in his seat. Across from him, the Apocrita dust merchant looked at him with that same mild contempt.

"You will take the job?"

And Gorel said, "Yes."

4.

The man he was tracking was hard to find. Gorel's payment had long ago gone up his nose, and now, away from any gods, withdrawal hit him hard.

But he was nothing if not a professional. He followed the trail, for even in the deadlands there were pockets of habitation, Abandonments and ruins, strange little hamlets where the destitute and the near dead sought shelter in isolation. The man he was seeking had used many names, but he only had four fingers . . .

He'd lost him several times, but he sensed that he was finally close. Gorel always carried a job through. And so now, delirious, half-starved, and in a thoroughly bad mood, he and his graal at last approached the ruins of an old stone building, which might have once been a temple, though who had built it, and for what inexplicable reason, here in the middle of the deadlands, Gorel didn't know.

Not that he cared.

As he approached he slipped softly from the graal's hide. The beast sank gratefully to the ground, folding its legs under itself and withdrawing its head inside the dark carapace. It would remain motionless now until the sun came out again and it could once again absorb enough energy to bring it into waking.

Gorel drew both his pistols. He trod softly on the ground. He crept towards the building. Dark ivy grew in the cracks between the old stones, and inside he could hear murmured voices . . .

The door was nothing but a rotting wooden slab. Gorel kicked it open and went inside, where it was dark and dank.

A figure lying on a mattress scrambled up, said, "What do you—?" and stopped.

"Devlin Fo-Fingga," Gorel said, grinning. His hand was around the man's throat. The man's skin felt slimy. His breath came and went through Gorel's palm. "I *thought* it was you."

"Who—what?" Devlin's small eyes peered up at Gorel's face, panicked. Then—recognition, followed by shock.

"*Gorel?* Is that *you?*"

"Still alive," Gorel said, dryly.

"No, no no no no no," Devlin said, speaking quickly, his hands weaving a dance of denial in the air. "That wasn't my fault, no no no, I wasn't even there when the—"

There had been figures in the mist. Ancient carved totems with malevolent eyes. Buried Eyes, they called those stones. Seeing eyes. Gorel's company had wandered through the mist, but every time it closed, men were missing . . . and the totems had a habit of appearing, out of nowhere, looming out of the mist and staring at you, calling to you . . .

Few had survived the Mosina Campaign.

"You cut a deal with them," Gorel said, flatly. "They let you live—for a price ..." He smiled grimly and shoved the gun in Devlin's face. "How many did you sacrifice to the old ones of Mosina?" he said.

Beneath him, Devlin Fo-Fingga shook and shivered. Spittle came out of his mouth. "No no no no no," he said, in plea or apology, it was hard to tell. "I never ... I didn't ..."

"So imagine my surprise when a certain Apocrita merchant cornered me in a bar and mentioned he was looking for a four-fingered thief. Funny that, I thought. That description tends to stick in one's mind. So I thought to myself, I might take this job. It is good to have friends, isn't it, Devlin? Old friends, from the old days. I wondered, could it be my old friend, Devlin Fo-Fingga, alive after all these years?"

"Gorel, it wasn't—!"

"The only thing I don't quite get," Gorel said, "is what exactly it was that you stole off that tight-ass merchant. He was surprisingly vague on the details. I only ask, because, if it's still worth something ... I might not kill you *quite* so slowly."

His hands shook suddenly as the craving overtook him, and though he tried to cover it, Devlin's small, sharp eyes noticed it—and suddenly the man was grinning.

"He never said, did he?" Devlin's rotten teeth sucked what little light there was in the room. "Then come, I will show you, I will ... For old times' sake, Gorel."

Gorel's finger tightened on the trigger, and yet he couldn't shoot. The craving was upon him then, and at last, reluctantly, he released Devlin. The man rose swiftly, like a rat.

"Come," he said. "Come!"

A second, sturdier door separated the antechamber from the main body of the ruined temple. From his belt, Devlin selected a rusted metal key and unlocked the door. When he pushed it open, the darkness beyond was greater still.

Gorel hesitated on the threshold—

But he could feel it.

It lay thick and hard on the air. It suffocated the breath, tantalising and rich, the very scent of it almost enough.

Almost.

But it was never enough.

Ablution. Faith. Call it what you will.

The curse bestowed upon him by the goddesses Shalin and Shar.

Devlin hurried into the darkness. And now lights were coming alive, one by one, small candles being lit along the walls.

In the dim light Gorel could see they were not alone.

It was a large room, and the women and men lying on the floor seemed near death. Only the gentle rising and falling of chests gave indication that they still breathed, still retained a tenuous link to life. He could taste god-sorcery in the air, feel keenly the thin membrane between the two worlds stretching, here . . .

He had crossed it before and could never truly get back.

"What have you done?" he said—but even as he spoke he already knew the answer.

"Come, come come come!" Devlin said. His grin was manic, his eyes dancing wildly in his face. "It is waiting, It is ready, It is near!"

He took Gorel by the hand. The gunslinger followed him, helpless to resist. They walked, deeper into the room, stepping over the sleepers, Devlin putting a finger to his mouth in an exaggerated warning to be quiet. Here and there, groans from the sleepers. One propped herself up and stared at them. "Is it time, Devlin? Is it time, yet?"

"Not for you, Gammy Steel!" Devlin cackled. "Gammy Gammy, ugly Gammy, your time is not yet come!"

"I have money"—the woman said, then—"I . . . I can get some. I can get more."

"Then do so."

Ignoring her, he led Gorel on. The woman's eyes followed them, then, with a sigh, she lay back down. Gorel could hear her stifled sobs.

They came to the end of the hall. Devlin let go of Gorel's hand and knelt down, lighting a semicircle of candles facing the wall. One by one they came alive, and trapped within them was a god.

5.

It was chained to the wall with bands of steel. It had the breasts of a woman, the sex of a man. It was naked. The god's eyes were two dark orbs, and its lips were thick and bruised and glistened wetly. There was no hair upon the body, and the god's cock was a small, shrivelled thing. Sweat glistened upon the god, as fine as grains of dust.

Dust.

Gorel knelt before the god. Devlin's hand was on his head, then, stroking. Gorel stared at the captive god, and the god stared back through eyes like bottomless holes ...

"Better than dust," Devlin whispered. "You want to know what I *stole*, Gorel? I took only that which was promised to me! Do you like it, Gorel? I see the mark on you, I can taste your need, *old friend*, your desire! Do you *want* it?"

"Yes!" Gorel said. "Yes!"

"Then the Black Kiss itself is yours for the taking, Gorel of Goliris."

He was no longer fully aware of Devlin. The world contracted to the half-circle of candlelight. Gorel could *smell* the god, that rancid, sweet, overpowering scent of dust, and he knew he wanted it, *needed* it, the way he never needed anything else. On hands and knees, slowly, he crept towards the god. If the flames of the candles hurt him, if it burnt his flesh, he didn't know, nor care. The chained god thrashed against his chains but he was held fast. Dimly, Gorel was aware of the others coming alive, felt their desire joining his. He crawled to the naked god and offered him his lips.

The first hit was always the best.

Flashes of light, flashes of consciousness. Gorel was fading in and out of the World. Rarely had it been this good, this ... *direct*. Even the pain of losing his home, of being vanquished from proud Goliris—the betrayal, the hurt, the fear—they were all gone, and there was only bliss.

Flashing images, disconnected from each other. Strange sensations. The sweet and sour taste of the god's mouth ... a taste of blood, and sorcery.

He was only briefly aware of hands—Devlin's?—going through his clothes, relieving him of non-essentials, coin and guns. A chuckle, close in his ear, hot rotting breath. A murmur: "Only the first taste is free ..."

None of these things mattered. His lips fastened on the god's.

Nothing mattered anymore. Nothing but the Black Kiss, the terrible Kiss of the gods.

6.

How long he lay so he didn't, later, know. Time did not matter. Nothing did. The dark hall was Heaven, the only kind of Heaven man could hope for in this World. The dirty mattress that he lay on was his home, grander even than vanished Goliris. He had no need for money, for guns, for knowledge or desire. All was as it should be, here in the Hall of the Naked God.

The naked god . . . the chained god . . . from what dark place did it arise, what primordial bog did it crawl out of, with Fo-Fingga as his prophet and disciple? It was a question unimportant to Gorel—all questions were. He needed nothing, *was* nothing.

Only dimly, therefore, was he aware at last of someone moving through the bodies of the lost, of shouts, and a laugh, and steps again, and a hand reaching down and shaking him roughly awake.

A voice from far-away said, "You stupid fool."

Gorel grinned, or tried to. The hand slapped him, once, twice.

Gorel tried to hit back but couldn't lift his hand.

The voice said, "Devlin, if he's dead, you're next in line."

"He is alive, alive!" a whiny voice replied. "A dead man's no use to me, no use to anyone but the gods beyond the veil."

"Gods," the other voice said. "Save me from gods and their addicts."

"You won't—you won't hurt him, will you?" the wheedling voice, Fo-Fingga's voice, said.

"Gorel?"

"My *god*," Devlin said. "Screw Gorel and those who ride with him."

"Watch your language, little man. Now get him up and sober. I need him."

"He's good for nothing but another dose of dust."

"Then get me dust. And hurry. My patience's running thin."

Hands tugging at Gorel, lifting him. He tried to fight them, but the Black Kiss was upon him again, and he soon enough subsided.

"He'll have to sleep it off. As for the dust—"

"I'll pay the going rate."

"Why didn't you say so to begin with?"

"Just get him ready, or you'll lose another finger."

Darkness, light. He was being carried. The stench of sorcery subsided, gradually. Cold water hit him, made him cry out. He was being scrubbed, none too gently, then hit with cold water again.

Then something soft. A towel.

A voice said, "Dry yourself. Think you can manage that?"

He wasn't sure.

The voice sounded familiar. He dried himself as best he could. Hands dragging him, something soft beneath. A bed, no roaches there this time.

He slept.

When he woke up the room was bright with light. Gorel blinked back tears.

"Good to see you back in the land of the living," a voice said.

The voice from his dreams. A familiar voice ...

He sat up and stared at the small man sitting by his bedside. The man gave him a sardonic smile. His left eye was missing and covered by a plain leather patch. His hair was grey, and bald along the line of an old scar ...

He was smoking a thin, home-made cigar.

Gorel said, *"Mauser?"*

"Were you expecting Fo-Fingga?"

"I was expecting no one." He examined the smaller man. His fingers bunched into fists. "You took me from *there*?"

"I need you functioning." A curious glance. "When did you ..."

Gorel shook his head. "An itinerant god. Far south from here ... it's a long story."

Mauser shook his head. "It's good to see you again, Gorel."

"You, too." Gorel touched his head. It felt sore. His hands, he noticed, were covered in bites. Bed-bugs.

He scratched, half-heartedly. "I thought you were dead."

His friend merely smiled at that. He said, "I heard you were around."

"How?"

"Fo-Fingga tried to sell me your guns."

"That little—"

Mauser gestured with his head. "They're there. Are you fit enough to use them?"

The guns were on the table by the bed, the seven-pointed stars of Goliris shining on their handles. Gorel said, "I just . . ."

"Yes?"

"I need just a little bit."

There was silence between them. Mauser's smile evaporated. He took a drag on his cigar, held the smoke in before releasing it. His face was wreathed in blue smoke.

He said, "Perhaps you're no good to me after all."

"Screw you," Gorel said. He stood up, reached for his guns. Mauser didn't move. Gorel took the guns, began checking first one then the other. Mauser smoked, and watched. After he was satisfied with the guns, Gorel dressed himself, shaved, and stretched. He didn't think he could stomach any food . . . but he'd try. When he turned around to Mauser, the smaller man had finished his cigar and in its place was holding a small packet of folded paper. He threw it to Gorel.

Gorel caught it, opened it carefully, and took a pinch of dust. He put it up his nose, snorted it, and smiled.

"What's the job?" he said.

7.

"There's really nothing to it," Mauser said. They were standing outside the ruined temple. Devlin Fo-Fingga was on his hands and knees in the mud, with Gorel's gun pressed painfully against his forehead.

"Please, Gorel . . . It's all just a terrible mistake!"

Gorel pressed the muzzle of the gun harder against the man's greenish skin. "I'm listening," he said, to Mauser.

"A grab and run, a heist. *You* know what it's like."

"Aha. And what's the target?"

"Gorel, *please*, let me go! What happened in Mosina wasn't my fault!"

"Shut up," Gorel said. "Mauser?"

"An ikon, that's all. Look, are you going to finish him off, or what?"

"Haven't decided."

"He could be useful," Mauser said, meditatively.

"A thief's no good, with just four fingers."

"He can still hold a gun, Gorel. You only need one finger to pull a trigger."

"So, a rough job."

"Did you expect anything else?"

Gorel chewed on his cigar.

"A *religious* ikon?" he said.

"You know any other kind?"

"And *where* exactly is this ikon?"

"In a temple, Gorel," Mauser said. "Isn't that where they usually are?"

"I see, I see," Gorel said. He chewed on his cigar, then casually back-handed Devlin on the side of the head with the butt of the gun. The man fell down on the ground holding his face. He stared up in hatred at the muzzle of the gun.

"Oh, get up," Gorel said. "I'm not going to kill you . . . today."

The man slowly got up. He wiped the blood with his fingers, then sucked on them. Gorel looked away in disgust and Devlin grinned.

"You're not?" he said.

"Hey, it's your lucky day," Mauser said.

"You need me, huh?"

Gorel shrugged. "Where exactly *is* this temple?" he said.

"Ever heard of Waterfalling?"

"No, no," Devlin said. He shook his head from side to side and began to back away from them. "No no no no no. I'm not going to no—"

This time it was Mauser's gun pointed at his face. Gorel looked at him, spat out the cigar, and smiled.

"Do you want the job?" he said. "Or not?"

His gun, pointed unwaveringly at Devlin's face, was all the answer anyone needed.

They rode away from that abandoned place that day. They had left the dying god behind, and its worshippers clustered around it, feeding. Who knew, Gorel thought. Perhaps the god would thrive on its worshippers' need. Perhaps it would grow, not diminish, and in years to come that lonely spot would be the birthplace of a new religion.

Stranger things have happened.

Though Devlin complained bitterly and at length about the loss of his property and its derivative income.

They had served together on the ill-fated Mosina Campaign, in the Romango lands far from there. Gorel had been young, had only recently left the Lower Kidron. He'd sought employ with a group of mercenaries, each more savage and unruly than the other. They were a group of young bloods with a taste for murder: there was Gorel, and the half-Merlangai, Jericho Moon, and there was Devlin Fo-Fingga ...

But as tough as they thought they were, nothing could prepare them for the swamps of Mosina.

... where tendrils of fog permeated the air.

... where the landscape constantly shifted about them.

... where people simply ... *disappeared*.

You could not fight what wasn't there. And, separated from the main body of troops, their company sank deeper and deeper into the domain of the old ones.

... what they were, these *things* which haunted the nightmarish swamps, he never learned. All he could remember was a circle of totemic poles rising suddenly out of the fog, hideous carved faces staring down on them, the eyes alive, and glinting ... the mouths were cruel slashes, gouged into the wood.

When they got hold of you ...

There was no getting away, and the screams of their victims pierced the fog and the eternal twilight of that place, lasting for hours, all through their slow and terrible sacrifice.

It was this that he remembered, most of all. The endless screams, across the bogs.

Only one got away.

Devlin got away.

He'd not lost so much as a finger.

Only later did they realise what terrible bargain the thief had struck with the old ones. How he'd paid for his freedom with his comrades' lives.

A rat and a thief and a traitor, and Gorel wanted to kill him, but Mauser was right: they might need him for the job.

They rode away from that desolate place and across the deadlands, heading towards the fertile places beyond.

Gorel was no fool. He knew when he was being sold a dummy. But he owed Mauser, just as Mauser owed him, and the man *had* come looking for him specifically . . . the truth was he was curious. He had heard of this place they were travelling to.

Waterfalling.

8.

They heard it long before they saw it.

The great waterfall which gave the city its name fell down from the high plateau of Tarsh, which borders the deadlands on one side and reaches as far as the Zul-Ware'i mountains. In those mountains, where the twin and ancient races of the Zul and the Ware'i had died in their war of complete annihilation, the glaciers provided the water which fed the Nirian. It was a long, wide, and stately river, which flowed across that vast distance without undue hurry until reaching the sheer drop of rock that led its water, without warning, to plunge for a great distance down until it hit the Sacred Pool. It was not so much a pool, of course, as a wide if miniature lake. From there, the water flowed more gently, away from the Sacred Pool and into a carefully crafted series of canals and water-ways and an ingenious system of locks, around which there formed the numerous islands, embankments, and aits which formed the sprawling city itself.

A rough-hewn path was cut into the side of the mountain, twisting and turning at a steep angle as it rose all the way up to the Tarsh plateau, allowing any resident of the city, when their time was due, to traverse it to the top of the waterfall. That path was long, and tortuous, and steep; and yet it was used. It was called the Path of Ascension.

The sky was calm. The air smelled fresh and clear. A kingfisher flew against the sky. The colour of the water, as one approached, was a startling blue, and against it, the well-ordered flora of the city was in a range of vivid greens. Flowers bloomed everywhere in a cacophony of red and blue and yellow, and their scent filled the air like perfume. The houses were neat and built of wood and stood on stilts, and children ran laughing along the many bridges.

It was, in nearly every way, a peaceful and idyllic scene, and it was only mildly spoiled, Gorel felt, by the still, serene, and perfectly preserved corpses in the water.

But that came a little later.

They approached the city just after dawn. A day's ride away they had come to Mauser's dead drop. There, Gorel found clothes, a stack of weapons that impressed even him, and a small, gaily painted wagon with the legend *Mimes* on it.

Along with the wagon was a donkey.

Gorel stared at the donkey, then he stared at Mauser.

"All this just happened to be here?"

"It pays to be prepared."

"But who's doing the paying?"

Mauser shrugged. "Does it matter, to you? A client's a client."

"I don't like the smell of this job, much," Gorel said. Mauser grinned and tossed him a twisted packet of paper. Gorel unfolded it and stared at the powder . . .

"Besides," Mauser said. "It's an old city, the foundations go back . . . who knows what arcane knowledge they have hidden there? Perhaps they would know of your homeland."

It was bait; Gorel knew it; Mauser knew it; Fo-Fingga, for sure, knew it.

Yet that didn't make it untrue.

Gorel took a pinch, only a pinch of dust; just enough to quiet the craving. "All right," he said. "But what about the wagon? No one is going to believe we're anything other than what we are. Or fail to notice the weapons."

"I've got that covered, too," Mauser said. Gorel stared at him in suspicion as the other man reached into a hidden bag the colour of bark and brought out three amulets. He handed one to Devlin and one to Gorel and kept one for himself.

Gorel stared at the amulet. It was made of a warm metal and was light to the touch, and intricately carved with circles and lines that seemed to spell something to him, if only he could read their meaning . . .

He knew what it was, of course. It reeked of sorcery.

"They're one-use," Mauser said, almost apologetically. "But they'll be enough to get us through. Just don't put it on until we get close to the city."

"And this was provided . . . ?"

Mauser shrugged. "It's not too late to back out," he said. "If you don't want the job."

"And what would you do without me?"

"No one's irreplaceable, Gorel."

They stared at each other, but there was no real question about the outcome.

The next morning, early, three humble mimes made their way in their gaudily painted cart across the plain to the city of Waterfalling. They were pulled by the small and patient donkey. They were not much to look at, three weather-beaten entertainers brought down by life on the road. One of them was missing a finger. They rode in silence and they could hear the city long before they reached it, the never-ceasing sound of an incredible volume of water falling from a great height until it hit the down-below.

There were always rainbows over Waterfalling. The constant spray of water in the air broke the light into joyous colour, while at night one witnessed the silvery form that comes when moonlight interacts with that same fog.

To get to the city one had to cross the largest canal, which served as an effective moat around the city, barring invaders, and it was there that Gorel first saw the corpses. They floated just underneath the surface, their eyes open and serene, their noses pressed against the surface of the water as though ready, at any moment, to rise through and resume their lives. But their skins were leeched white, near translucent, and their depth never varied though sometimes they were pushed by the current as more corpses came down from . . .

"The Sacred Pool," Devlin whispered, and shuddered.

"Shut up, fool!"

Gorel's hand was on the butt of his gun. He hoped the enchantment would do its work and conceal them.

There were guards on the only gate, which blocked entry to the only bridge into the city. The guards were Ebong mercenaries, large beetle-like creatures with great helmet-like heads as opaque as polished black stone, and they held rifles.

"Stop."

The mimes stopped obediently.

"Purpose of visit?"

"We are but humble entertainers, seeking to ply our humble trade—"

"Do a mime."

"Excuse me?"

"I said, do a mime!"

The next five minutes were some of the worst of Gorel's life. Which was saying something. He, Mauser, and Devlin pranced and pretended to be trapped in invisible glass jars and to climb invisible ladders and to go down invisible stairs, and all in silence. They were terrible. Every moment Gorel expected the ruse to be discovered, and to enter a deadly shoot-out with the Ebong. They were not a race he liked to tangle with, at least, not without gaming the odds.

When they were finished, however, there was a short hiss of noxious air which, for the Ebong, must have passed for enthusiastic clapping.

"You can go. Warn you, though, not much call for mimes round here."

"And the rents are steep," added his colleague.

"Ask me, you'd be better off striking for the lowlands," said a third. "Besides, you want to watch out you don't hear the Call."

His colleagues turned their black helmet heads on him at that and the mercenary slunk away, or as much as an Ebong could ever be said to slink. The three mimes thanked the guards humbly, and rode through the open gate and across the bridge and into the city . . .

And Gorel could hear it, now. And he realised he had been hearing it for some time, all through their approach to the city, though it was clearer now.

A sort of faint crystal peal . . .

A little sound of summoning, just at the edge of hearing.

9.

Once they were inside, the talismans began to lose their power. The three would-be robbers found a ramshackle inn that stood on an ait in the confluence of two of the smaller canals. There they checked their weapons while Mauser outlined the plan.

How and when Gorel had met Mauser was a long and not entirely interesting story. It was during that unfortunate episode with the Demon-

Priests of Kraag. Needless to say, both of them had barely escaped with
their lives, and Mauser still had a neat little scar to show for it. Where
he came from, Gorel was never entirely sure. He was a rare white-face,
of a race of barbarians who lived high in the snow-peaked mountains of
the Beyaz. Gorel trusted him—as much as he could be said to trust
anyone. Devlin he didn't trust at all, but then the man's untrustworthiness
was a sort of assurance in itself.

The city was ... strange.

It was clean and prosperous and ordered, a little haven of peace in a
violent world.

He had had a chance to examine the corpses in the canals as they
wended their slow way to the inn.

There were the bodies of many races in the water. Human and
Avian and Merlangai, Ebong and numerous others. Who could tell
where they had come from, or how long they had been lying there,
submerged, perfectly preserved in the cold water that flowed from
the Sacred Pool?

Even as he watched, he'd see a new body arrive from up-stream, fed
into the system of canals, until it found a place and there remained,
suspended. And always, at the edge of hearing, there was that faint peal
of a bell, a sort of muted laughter, an invitation ...

And as he watched, he saw a woman stop in the middle of her shopping, and drop her bags, and stand, transfixed. Her child stood beside
her, a little girl. A beatific smile filled the woman's face, then she began
to walk away, leaving behind both her shopping and her child. The little
girl began to run after her mother, but the woman paid her no mind,
and a shopkeeper and a flower seller with a kindly face held the girl from
following, and tried, awkwardly, to comfort her.

The mother went away.

The plan was simple.

There was only one god in Waterfalling.

The God of the Waterfall had many small temples scattered throughout
the city, and one main one. The Grand Temple occupied the entirety of
an island high up-stream. The path to the Drop passed close to it as it
led farther up until it reached the plateau.

It was not heavily guarded, for who would dare disturb the temple of the god in its own domain?

"The ikon is inside the temple," Mauser said. "It is a small, blue, amorphous shape faintly resembling a human figure. It is made of Ice VII. Some say it holds the soul of the god within it. Others that it is merely an artistic representation. We are going to go on the first assumption. The job's to get in and get the ikon. The ultimate target's—"

"Assassination," Devlin said, and leered.

Gorel stared at the two of them. Devlin's ugly grin and Mauser's grim determination.

"Assassination?"

"Come on, Gorel. It's not like it would be the first god you've killed. In fact, you're almost uniquely qualified."

"Is that why I'm here?"

"Would you rather be somewhere else? Are we keeping you from some urgent appointment?"

Gorel lit a cigar and stared at the two of them. He began to wonder just *who* the mysterious Apocrita merchant who'd first hired him was, and just *how*, exactly, Mauser had then found Gorel . . .

But Mauser was right. A job was a job and, besides, Gorel had his own purpose in being there. So he just nodded, affably enough, and said, "I'm going to look around. You two try to stay out of trouble."

"I think the trouble part's going to come later," Mauser said, and Devlin sucked on his wet, green teeth noisily and leered at Gorel. He left them there, checking and cleaning the weapons.

10.

Of course he'd known about the God of the Waterfall.

11.

Gorel was no fool. And the fame of Waterfalling had spread far and wide . . .

Now he followed the Path of Ascension. Initially the road was paved, as he followed city thoroughfares and traversed small bridges. People stared after him but said nothing. He saw the temple then, a large, imposing complex of beautiful white stone. He skirted the temple and soon reached the first incline and there the city stopped and the Path proper began.

It was cut into the very rock, and it rose steeply, at a sharp incline. Small pebbles rolled underfoot. The climb was slow and hard but there were places to stop and rest along the way, small alcoves cut into the rock. Gorel did not hurry. He enjoyed the climb, the cooler air up there, and when he turned he could look down on Waterfalling and far beyond, across the plains and to the deadlands where, far away, loomed the Black Tor.

He thought of Kettle, then. There wasn't a day gone past when he didn't think about Kettle.

As he climbed he saw almost no people. One he passed, and he realised with some surprise it was the woman he had seen earlier. She was resting in one of the alcoves, with that same happy, vacant look on her face. She didn't seem to see him, and he walked on, discomfited.

The call ... no.

The Call.

He could hear it more clearly now. And as the Path wound its way up, and up, and up, he could hear the thunder of the waterfall, and feel the spray of its roar on his face, and his eyes were dazzled by an explosion of rainbows; *Come, come!* said the Call but it was faint, still; it was not meant for him but for another. Gorel of Goliris traversed the Path of Ascension until he reached, at last, the Plateau of Tarsh, where the Nirian river flows until it reaches the escarpment.

He saw it all, now. He stood in that place called the Drop. The river moved almost sluggishly as it neared the edge. A series of rocks slowed down the flow of water, and it tumbled over the edge almost reluctantly. When it did, it became a great thundering waterfall. Way down below, he could see the mist rising out of the impact of the water into the Sacred Pool.

He stood there for a long time.

When the woman at last reached the Drop she seemed as beatific as before. Though her journey must have been physically exhausting for her, nevertheless there was no change in her demeanour. For a long moment she merely stood there, smiling that vacant, enigmatic smile. She seemed indifferent to or unaware of Gorel's presence. Then she took one step, and another, until Gorel felt compelled to shout a warning: for she was headed straight for the sheer drop beyond which was the fall. But the woman ignored him as though he weren't there, and when he went to stop her she shrugged him away, not angrily but the way one would shrug off a mild irritant.

Come . . . Come!

For one moment the Call was so clear that it overwhelmed Gorel's senses. Too late, he saw the woman step to the edge of the rocks. Then she took one step more—and, just like that, she was gone.

He crawled to the edge and peered over. He saw her fall. She fell without grace through the air until the waterfall claimed her, the water engulfing her unto itself, then she was gone from sight.

Gorel of Goliris remained at the Drop for a long while more, and his thoughts were troubled. He was not idle, though. When he was done, he wended his way down the Path and returned to the inn, where his two companions waited. It was night, by then. The stars shone down cold and indifferent, and the air was filled with the stench of the Black Kiss. He realised he had not needed a hit since they got to the city. It was all about them, as natural and as plentiful as water.

And he realised they were all, here, as much in slavery to the Kiss as he was.

When the city began, when the first jumper jumped, that no one knew. The city grew, and the god with it. The city prospered, and the god with it. They fed on each other.

And now someone wanted the god dead.

When he had returned, Mauser and Devlin were ready. There was no need for speech. All three men were armed.

They stepped out lightly; and only a fleeting egret saw them pass into the night.

12.

Later, when he was running, with Devlin lying on the canal bank with half his brains blown out and Mauser on his hands and knees trying to crawl away from the Speakers-to-Water as they closed in on him, there was no one to see him then, too. The good people of Waterfalling knew when to close their doors and when to draw the blinds on their windows, and the whole city lay silent and slumbering in the moonlight.

The job was botched from the very beginning. The very air of the city had whispered that this was all folly.

Nevertheless, they went in.

Over the bridge, into the temple complex.

Where the waft of incense and the chanting of priests could be heard . . .

Where ducks and geese congregated in the canals where the dead men lay.

Deep into the temple, searching for the inner sanctum . . .

A novice surprised them, innocently watering lilies, and Mauser shot her, the blast echoing loudly over the islet . . .

Devlin shot two further novices as they emerged, blinking off sleep, to see what was happening . . .

The blue ikon was there just as Mauser said it would be.

A small and amorphous representation of a vaguely human shape that could have been a waterfall.

The three men made for the idol . . .

The Speakers-to-Water emerged then. The priests of the God of the Waterfall. Dressed in flowing white robes, with water flowers in their hair. Their eyes were vacant and they moved in perfect unison. In their hands they held swords of ice.

Their lips moved as one. They said: "You shall not steal."

"Screw that," Devlin said, and he began firing. Blades of ice moved in perfect harmony, deflecting shots. Devlin screamed in rage and snatched the shotgun from his back and fired, once, twice, until he hit one of the Speakers in the guts. The Speaker collapsed to the ground, but his lips still moved, and with his fellow Speakers he said, "You shall not *steal*!"

Gorel and Mauser spread out, and it was then that he saw the corpses. They emerged out of the water, out of the dank canal. One at first, and then another, and another. Humans, Ebong, two Merlangai, an Avian shivering water off her feathers. The perfectly preserved bodies in the water. Now their eyes opened and a single force animated them, and they reached into the canal and pulled out blade-sharp staffs of ice. They advanced on the three men.

"You bring *swords*?" Devlin screamed. "What good are damn swords against *guns*?"

Gorel fired. He fired cleanly, methodically, without emotion. It was a scientific sort of extermination, a matter of numbers, not blood. The creatures in the water must have been living once, but they lived no longer, and the corpses were only that. He shot not to kill but to *destroy*, inflicting damage on skulls and knee-caps and finger bones, shooting to disable, if possible to annihilate. He was good at what he did. He had to be, to have survived this long. Perhaps he wasn't the *best*—the World was filled with the stories of legendary gun masters such as Sixgun Smel of the Upper Kidron, or Yi-Sheng the Unbeatable, who killed the sea serpent, Og, or the wizard, Der Fliegenmelker, who collected the heads of his enemies and whose mound of skulls was said to be taller than a mountain by the time of his disappearance—but these were just that, legends, stories told around the camp-fire in hushed voices. They were of some distant past, and Gorel was of the present. As far as he was concerned, he *was* the best, and would remain so until someone finally managed to shoot him down, if they ever did. He wouldn't have given them odds.

The men kept pulling more guns out of the bags they'd brought with them. But more and more of the bodies came, and their swords of ice flashed cold in the moonlight, and Devlin cried out when one just missed slicing off his arm, and Gorel was pushed back, back as they came, and Mauser fired with a calm intensity on his face, like a card-player calculating the odds of his hand.

There was so very little blood. The things that climbed out of the water had been in there too long, Gorel thought. What ran in their veins, if it ran at all, was a sort of amethyst liquid, and as it left their bodies it congealed and tried to slither back into the canal.

"We can't hold them forever!" Mauser shouted. All the while the Speakers-to-Water were chanting, their lips moving in unison, the canal dwellers between them and the three shooters.

"Cover me!" Gorel shouted, then he was running, bodies blasted on either side of him as Devlin and Mauser fired. Gorel slid in the purple ichor and his forward momentum pushed him along, until he bounced off an Ebong and was through. He came right up to the Speakers in one fluid motion and with his two guns drawn. For a moment he looked into their eyes. What he saw in them it was hard to say.

He pulled both triggers.

With the fall of the Speakers the onslaught abruptly ceased. The preserved corpses did not fall but remained standing, motionless and eerie in the moonlight. The three men looked at one another, their ears still ringing with the sound of gun-shots.

Then they moved as one: racing for the prize, their enemies forgotten.

Gorel got to it first. He snatched the blue idol a moment before Mauser.

When he turned, Devlin had his guns pointed at the two of them and was he grinning his ugly grin. "It's about time we settled this," Devlin said.

Mauser fired but Devlin was quicker and Mauser was thrown back, hurt. The other shot missed Gorel. He had moved behind Mauser and the shot meant for him missed. Devlin's smile dissipated and Gorel's smile bloomed and he fired.

Devlin's body fell back and he lay on the bank of the canal, his skull blown to pieces and his brain leaking slowly into the water.

Gorel was briefly pleased at a job finally brought to conclusion.

"Gorel ..." Mauser said. He was still alive. The shot had opened an ugly wound in his stomach and he was trying to hold his intestines in. "Help me ..."

Gorel held up the ikon. He said, "How do you destroy it?"

"I don't ... know. He said ..."

"Who bought you off, Mauser? Who hired you?"

"Does it ... matter ..."

"It does to me."

"It was him! It was that mage from the Black Tor! The one who brought down Falang-Et and killed Tharat ... He said you ..."

Cold fury rose in Gorel. "Kettle?" he said. "Kettle sent you?"

"Gorel, please ..."

The Speakers-to-Water Gorel had shot rose up from the ground then. They looked at Gorel with broken eyes. And all the corpses that had risen from the water turned, as one, and focused their attention on the two men, the one living and the one dying.

Then the Speakers spoke.

They said: "*Gorel of Goliris.*"

Mauser said: "Help me!"

The preserved corpses advanced one step, then another.

"We *know* you, Gorel of Goliris. Come, now. *Come!*"

"Help me! Gorel, Please!"

Gorel ran.

He ran without destination in mind, yet the destination had always been there, waiting for him. He was not followed. Few saw him pass. And yet his feet led him inexorably upwards, and the voice in his head grew stronger and stronger until it was like a raging storm, and it said, *Come to me . . . come!*

It knew his name. In his hand, the blue idol was still. Gorel's feet would not obey him. He felt a calmness descend on him then, and his face assumed a beatific aspect. He came to the Path of Ascendance and began to climb it.

It has been many centuries since I had last encountered a man of Goliris . . . the voice said.

"You know of Goliris?"

His lips moved, but whether sound emerged or not was immaterial. It was night. He was alone on the Path. Behind him, Devlin lay dead, Mauser dying. Another botched job in a long line of such. None of it mattered to Gorel.

Many have heard of, yet none had seen, Goliris . . . said the voice in his head. *You seek it, still?*

"Always."

Yet now you must come to rest, Gorel. Let go of desire, of need. I will be all that you require.

"No!" his lips protested. His legs obeyed the orders of the god. "Tell me. Tell me how to find my home."

Sooner or later, all things must come to an end, Gorel of Goliris. All empires pass.

"Including yours?"

But the god was not amused by the retort.

Gorel climbed, and climbed, and climbed. The physical effort of the rise meant nothing to him, for now he truly was under the Black Kiss, and every fibre of his being was bliss, and he was happy; as happy as a man could ever be.

Yet still he resisted. Yet still he fought the insidious Black Kiss of the god. And still: his feet led him on, step by inexorable step.

Until he found himself once more standing at the Drop.

The waterfall thundered nearby. Rainbows of moonlight sparkled in the rising cloud of spray.

Come to me, Gorel of Goliris, said the god. *Come!*

There was no resisting the Call.

And yet he dallied. And it was good, he thought, that he had prepared himself for this eventuality. And he busied himself with the things that he had left there, at the Drop, earlier, for just such an eventuality. And the voice of the god grew mistrustful in his head and it said, *What are you doing?*

But Gorel did not answer. And the Call of the god grew stronger and more insistent, until there was no resisting it further.

For one fleeting moment, Gorel thought of all the countless lives that had come here before him, had worn the rock smooth with the passage of their feet. Then he, too, took those last few, finite steps, to the edge; and fell to his doom.

13.

What did you do? said the god.

14.

The first impact was the worst. He hit the roaring mass of water on his way down and all his protective clothing couldn't stop him from feeling the impact. Then the ropes tied to his harness *pulled*, and he shot upwards then back down and impacted again: but then the bouncing slowed, until he could at last control his descent.

What did you do*!* roared the god.

The water fell and fell and tried to push him down, down, down into the Sacred Pool, and the rocks beat at him, but Gorel welcomed the pain and used it to his advantage. The Kiss no longer held him. The god's Call was never meant to last beyond the final Drop, and now it had no more power to hold Gorel in thrall. Slowly, slowly, he released more rope, hoping it would hold, and he lowered himself down the cliff.

"Tell me," Gorel demanded. "Tell me what you know of Goliris."

Then join me. Become a part of me! And you will know all that I know.

"No."

Please, the god said. *Please.*

How long he journeyed this way he didn't know. The bottom was a blur far down below. The cliff rose impossibly high overhead. At last he found it. He hit empty air and flailed, then he was through the screen of water and inside a hollow cave, hidden behind the water. He took off the harness and fell to the dry stone floor.

He lay there for some time, breathing heavily.

You have come to kill me! the voice accused. It sounded frightened, now.

"Tell me what I want to know."

It was a natural cave in the rock, Gorel saw. Once, millennia ago, it had been explored, and the skeletons of humans and Ebong still remained in recesses in the wall.

Then, it had become a temple, of a sort. An altar sat against the far wall, and on it was a crude stone figure. Something living hid in the dark behind it, a creature like a ferret or a water rat. Baleful eyes glared at Gorel from the shadows but he paid them no mind. He held the blue ikon in his hand.

"Tell me," he said.

I could only show you.

His mind flickered then. It went through countless rapid lives: he saw an Ebong mercenary arrive at the cliffs and look down, curiously, for the first time; an Avian flying overhead, who plunged down towards the water with a glad cry; an expedition of vanished Zul, searching for a weapon, who had come upon the place and fell victim to the Call; water-dwelling Merlangai who swam down the Nirian, a hunting party, until, too late, they too became a part of the god . . .

He saw the crude village underneath grow and prosper, become a town, then at last a city. The dead resided in the water, their eyes forever open. He saw people drawn from all over to this city, where the Kiss lay like an enchantment over the streets and houses. It was a small price to pay, for happiness, he thought. From time to time some would hear the Call, and climb the Path until they were one with their god. It was a small price to pay.

Do you see? Join me! said the god.

"Show me Goliris."

Then he saw it. A small figure trudging in from the deadlands, a sorcerer of Goliris, and Gorel knew him, then: it was one of his father's servants, a minor war-mage with the fleet—just another face in the corridors of the palace, a man who might have once smiled politely at the boy, this future king.

He came, and he dwelled in the city for some time, then he heard the Call and heeded it.

And Gorel saw deep into his heart, for the man was with the god now, and he saw the hatred and the loathing deep within the man's mind, and he saw that the hatred and loathing were directed inwards, at the traitor's own self. He saw then the sorcerers of Goliris gathered in a dark room, saw them plot the downfall of the royal family. He saw himself, the boy, taken while his father was murdered, saw his mother cry, but soundlessly, and he saw the empty throne, and cobwebs, and bleached skulls.

"How will I find it again?" he said, demanded, of this ghost.

And only the faint echo came back—*You never will . . .*

A great fury took hold of Gorel of Goliris then, and for a time he knew not where he was. Gradually he came back to awareness, and the god's voice, weak, panicked, demanded, over and over, *What did you do? What did you do?*

Gorel sat there in the cave, cross-legged, and looked out at the waterfall. But the water, strangely, seemed to grow less fierce. Its flow was easing. The screen of water slowly parted, and the god's voice cried, *What did you do? You are killing me!*

But Gorel had done nothing.

Beside him, the small, blue ikon was slowly melting.

The waterfall was dying.

As less and less water fell, Gorel could now look out from the cave, into clear air. At last it was all over and he went to the edge and looked down, and saw the pool, no longer sacred, and the corpses below lying still in the water. He looked up, then, and saw no water, falling.

Behind him, behind the altar, the mindless creature that might have been a ferret or a water rat growled, but Gorel paid it no mind. He sat, cross-legged, on the floor and lit a cigar, and he waited.

15.

The small, delicate shape fluttered in the air before coming to rest inside the cave. It leaned against one wall and crossed its arms and cocked its head and looked at Gorel of Goliris.

"Kettle," Gorel said.

"Gorel."

"It was you? You set it up, from the beginning. It was so convenient, how that trader found me, how Mauser just happened to be in the right place at the right time."

"I would have asked you, but you would have turned me down."

"You lied to me. From the very start, you always *lie*."

A look of pain crossed the Avian's face. "Gorel, I . . ."

"You'd tell me you *love* me?"

"You know how I feel."

"And yet you'd use me."

"Isn't that what love is?"

The Lord of the Black Tor looked at Gorel of Goliris and Gorel of Goliris looked away, so that Kettle would not see his tears.

"What was it all for?"

"I needed a distraction. Something to focus the God of the Waterfall's attention on. Something crude and obvious, and effective."

"You used me as *bait*."

"Yes."

"And all the meanwhile you—"

"My engineers had done their work. We dammed the Nirian. My army dug a new channel for the river."

"And starved the waterfall."

"Yes."

"Clever."

Kettle shrugged.

"*Why?*" Gorel said.

"Why?"

"Yes."

Kettle looked at Gorel of Goliris and his eyes were filled with pain.

"There's a war coming," he said. "And an enemy against which even I am helpless. I have been trying to consolidate territories, to prepare ... Gorel, I *need* you. I need you by my side. Help me. Come back with me."

"Never."

"Will I ever be able to apologise enough? I love you."

Gorel did not reply.

After a time, the small and delicate figure of the mage flew away. After a time longer, Gorel put on the harness, pulled on the ropes, and began the long, slow climb down the side of the cliff, and back towards the ground.

16.

The Dark Mage's army came into the city of Waterfalling at sunrise. They came quietly and with purpose and they were not opposed. The city's residents looked at them with numb surprise, as though waking from a long and pleasant dream that was now, inexplicably, over. Gorel of Goliris was stopped only once, on his way out of the city. But the people who held him must have received orders from high up, for they let him go, and he rode away from there, to continue his search for vanished Goliris.

High above the city, at the place that was once called the Drop, the Lord of the Black Tor looked down on his conquest, but his attention was elsewhere:

Far away, figures moved, numerous beyond count. They marched like shadows but they were not shadows. They marched in rows. They marched upon the World.

He saw them conquer cities, he saw them burn down temples, bring down gods, for gods and sorcery meant nothing to these soulless things. What they were, he didn't know. They moved like automata. They were a wizardry of a sort he'd never known. Something ancient, and deadly, and newly awakened.

They came from the desert. They brought with them the smell of burnt cardamoms.

And as they moved, they spoke.

It was a roar, a cry of triumph, and despair.

A single word.

Goliris.

Cecelia Holland

Cecelia Holland is one of the world's most highly acclaimed and respected historical novelists, ranked by many alongside other giants in that field such as Mary Renault and Larry McMurtry. Over the span of her thirty-year career, she's written more than thirty historical novels, including *The Firedrake, Rakóssy, Two Ravens, Ghost on the Steppe, The Death of Attila, Hammer for Princes, The King's Road, Pillar of the Sky, The Lords of Vaumartin, Pacific Street, The Sea Beggars, The Earl, The Kings in Winter, The Belt of Gold,* and more than a dozen others. She also wrote the well-known science-fiction novel *Floating Worlds,* which was nominated for a Locus Award in 1975, and of late has been working on a series of fantasy novels, including *The Soul Thief, The Witches' Kitchen, The Serpent Dreamer, Varanger, The King's Witch, The High City, Kings of the North,* and *The Secret Eleanor.* Her most recent novel is *Dragon Heart.*

Here a shipwrecked voyager finds himself in a situation dangerous enough that he might have been better off taking his chances with the raging sea—but a situation in which he must remain if he has any chance to satisfy the thirst for vengeance burning in his heart.

THE SWORD TYRASTE

From the first blow, the iron sang under the hammer. Tvalin sang along with it, pounding out the blade, long and straight and keen. He knew already this would be a noble sword, and it tore his heart to think who would own it.

He thrust the iron back into the forge, and said to his nephew, "Heat it up."

Tulinn worked the bellows. Tvalin wiped his hands on his apron. His shoulders ached. He went to the back of the cave and got a stoop of ale. Galdor at least kept them well fed. Tvalin was soaked with sweat from the work, which felt good, and he loved the smell of the iron heating and the sound of the bellows.

He called the sword Tyraste, darling of the god of battles, but he never said the name aloud, to keep it strong. He said it in his mind often. He drank another long draught of the ale, and going back to the forge, he drew the white-hot blade from the coals. Lifting the hammer in his hand, he beat against the iron, and even through the tongs, the blade's high voice rang true.

High overhead, a door creaked. Tulinn said, "He comes," and backed away into the shadows. Tulinn was afraid of Galdor. Tvalin laid the sword across the anvil, between him and the stairs, and down the steps came the king, massive in his bearskins, his feet scraping on the stone, and his eyes like a snake's. On his forefinger was a red jewel, and he carried a weight of gold around his neck.

The two dwarfs bowed down. Tvalin was cursing himself for allowing them to fall into Galdor's hands. He said, "We are doing the work, King Galdor. We are keeping our end of the bargain." Straightening, he gestured toward the sword on the anvil.

Galdor caught sight of it, and his face flushed red; his eyes gleamed.

He said, "Ah, yes." He put out his hand toward it, but the ungripped sword was still hot, and he drew back. Tvalin let out his breath between his teeth. Galdor faced him, narrow-eyed again.

"Finish it. And I will keep you no longer. Is that the bargain?" He looked from one dwarf to the other. Tvalin nodded. Galdor went back up the stair, heavy stepping.

Tvalin went back to the sword, cooling on the anvil, and laid it into the coals again. His chest felt too tight. He knew Galdor was treacherous and the king's last words rang with lies. He turned the sword again in the coals, and drew it out, and worked the fore edge.

With each stroke he thought, Tyraste, be evil. Tyraste, do evil. Tyraste, kill Galdor.

They quenched the blade and honed it, fit on wooden grips and a pommel of a piece of ocean-blood. Galdor would change those anyway to something gaudier. Tvalin lifted the sword in his hand, the balance perfect, the blade eager, and his maker's heart leapt at what he had done. Then the king came down again.

Tvalin laid the sword across the anvil and stepped back. Tulinn hovered next to him, wanting to be gone from here. Galdor threw back his cloak; he took the sword into his hand, and cocking it from side to side, he murmured under his breath.

"A prince of blades," he said. "Tvalin, you are better even than your name."

Tvalin swelled, pleased, and glanced at Tulinn to make sure he had noted that. Galdor said, "Now let's test the edge."

Too late, Tvalin saw what was happening. Galdor swung the sword around and in a single stroke sliced off Tvalin's head and that of his nephew.

"See," Galdor said, up there above them. "Now I don't have to keep you. I'll board this room up, so nobody bothers you." With the sword in his hand, he went back up the stairs.

With his full strength Vagn hauled his oar again through the water. Night was falling, they should have made landfall long ago, and now they were deep into the narrows, here, between two coasts they didn't know, with a storm bearing down on them. Around him his brothers and his friends were rowing as hard as he was, shouting the rhythm. A current fought them, the knarr jerking and bucking. Back over the stern he could see the rain blowing toward them, a shadow over the water. Above them a craggy headland loomed. The first rain struck him in the face. The light was bleeding out of the sky.

At the steerboard, his oldest brother suddenly called out and pointed. Vagn cast a quick glance over his shoulder and saw a light bobbing, in the dark below the headland, a signal, a buoy. His brother was already steering them that way. Vagn flung his body against the oar. The wind helped them, heaved them forward. The rain pounded his cheeks and his wet hair got in his eyes. He bent to his oar and the blade struck something, and just behind his bench he felt the hull shudder. The light had lured them into the rocks.

His brother yelled, "Hold on! Hold on!" Vagn cast his oar overboard and jumped after it.

He went feetfirst into the water, his hands out to fend off the rocks, and sank deep in over his head. When he came up a wave hurled him over, and with him the oar and a piece of a strake. In the murky darkness he could make out nothing but the waves' slap and churn. Then something huge loomed up before him, and his feet touched bottom and he scrambled up onto the side of a rock. The storm wind battered him. He was shivering and he clutched his shirt around him.

Even through the wind and the sea, a scream reached his ears, and shouting. The torch on the shore cast a glow out onto the surging water. He leaned around the side of the rock and saw, against the uncertain light, bare hands raised against swords. He heard his oldest brother calling out, "No, no," over and over. Then nothing. Men thrashed around in the shallows. A sharp voice rose, once, giving orders, directions—they were looking for pieces of the cargo. A keg bobbed in the slack water behind his rock. They would come to get that. He slid down into the rocking waves, in over his head, and waited there. Legs thrashed by him, close enough almost to touch, lifted the keg away, and moved on.

He raised his head above the surface and listened. He could hear voices, in there on the beach, but now they were moving off. He dragged himself up out of the water onto the rock, found a crevice out of the rain, and pulled his shirt around him as well as he could, and waited to die.

He did not die; the woolen shirt, which his mother had made, kept

him warm, and this being midsummer, the sun was soon up again. The
fierce waves of the night before had passed with the storm. He waded in
through little ruffles to the beach. As he came in the seagulls rose in a
cloud from his brothers and his friends. The robbers had taken even their
clothes away.

He went from one to the other of the dead men, saying each name,
noticing the wounds, and pulled them all together on the beach, as they
had been on the knarr together. He sat for a while beside his oldest
brother, who should have gotten them in to shore sooner, and should not
have believed the light. His brother's body was hacked and battered, he
had fought hardest of any of them.

Vagn piled up rocks over the bodies, making a boat shape, and putting
in what bits and pieces of the knarr had drifted in to the shore. There
was nothing left of the cargo, the furs, the salted fish, the casks of honey
and wax. As he went around, he stamped on crabs and ate them, ate
seaweed, dug up clams, and drank water that seeped out of the cliff.

He did not, for a long while, look up at the top of the cliff.

When he was done, he sat down on the sand, and thought about his
brothers and his friends and what had been done to them. Only he was
left alive, which put a hard charge on him. Now he stood up, and looked
up, at the top of the headland, and the tower there, looming behind its
wall. He rinsed the salt out of his shirt, slept a little in the sun while it
dried, and in the afternoon, he walked around the back of the headland
and made his way up.

King Galdor, lord of the Vedrborg, walked out to his high seat and laid
the sword on the table before him. Standing there, he looked out over
the hall at his men, all on their feet, all their faces turned toward him,
and he was still a moment, to feel his power, before he sat, and they could
all sit. The slaves brought in the bread and the ale and they fell to feasting.

Galdor thought of his enemies. He wished like Odin he had no use
for meat, and did not have to waste time in eating. A great dish came
onto the table before him, a mess of fish, likely from the ship they had
taken the night before. Peasants' food. He laid his hands instead on the
sword in its sheath, with its pommel and grips of chased gold.

The midsummer was on them, when Hjeldric the Dane had sworn to challenge him, to run the strait against his will, and Galdor meant to turn that to advantage. The Vedrborg grew too small for him. He wanted more than mere piracy. He pressed the sword under his hands. A man with his power should have a kingdom and not a rock and a handful of men. He longed to take the sword into his hand, to loose the strength he felt in it, on some cause great enough for him.

In the hall a stirring caught his eye. Someone had come in from outside. He talked to someone, who talked to someone else, the little passage of the words going up the hall along the outside of the table. At his place just below Galdor, his man Gifr heard it, nodded, and stood.

"There is a stranger here who asks to see you."

"A stranger. A messenger?"

"No—just a wayfarer."

Galdor lifted his eyes. In the middle of the hall, a half-grown gawky beardless boy stood, broad-shouldered, with curly black hair, startling blue eyes, in a filthy shirt.

Galdor said, "Come up in front of me. Who are you?"

The boy walked up to stand below the high seat, and spoke out, "My name is Vagn Akason. I have come over the sea because I have heard such of your power, King, that I would join you."

Galdor leaned back in the high seat. He knew at once that this was both true and untrue. In this he sensed some witchwork: the boy was both a danger and an opportunity. He laid his hands on the sword again.

"Vagn: what kind of name is that?" An outlander. Galdor thought again of Hjeldric. He could always use another fighter if this one was apt.

"Well, perhaps you would prove your mettle?" He looked around the table. "Thorulf Grimsson, stand."

At once, they all began to move. Thorulf got to his feet, a bear of a man, all hair and muscle. The others pulled the tables back to make room in the middle of the hall. The boy Vagn stood there looking around him, and when Thorulf lumbered toward him, drawing his sword, the boy wheeled toward Galdor.

"I have no sword."

Among the men now grouped along the wall there gusted some laughter. Galdor said, "What then do you offer me?" He smiled, thinking, for all his big talk, the boy was trying to back out of this. "But there are other ways—bring out staffs, let them fight that way." He nodded to the black-haired boy. "You still have your chance, see?"

He leaned on the arm of his high seat. He thought this could be amusing. Thorulf was a slacker and a stirpot. The boy was brawny and should have one good fight in him anyway. Galdor beckoned to the slave, who came quickly over to fill his cup again.

Vagn stood in the middle of the room, now a much wider space, and gripped the staff in both hands, his knuckles up. He had fought often with sticks with his brothers.

He knew the men who had killed his brothers were all around him.

The lumpy, shaggy man tramping across the floor toward him held the staff crosswise. They batted at each other a few times, shuffling around, and Thorulf didn't change his grip. The men watching began to hoot and call out, spurring them on. Thorulf was already sweating. Vagn took a step to one side and struck, going high, over the upside-down grip, and Thorulf blocked it, and with his counterstroke knocked Vagn flat.

The breath went out of him, but even dazed he knew to keep moving. He rolled. The following blow cracked on the rush-strewn floor beside him. He staggered to his feet. He had dropped his staff. He had made a mistake. He had to be keener. Thorulf was strong and knew how to do this. The big man plunged toward him, jabbing his stick at Vagn's belly, at his face, and Vagn dodged, ducked, jumped, flailing his arms out. The staff whipped past his ear and over his head. In the laughing, jeering crowd someone whistled. Thorulf was red-faced, panting, and his little eyes popped. Big as he was, he was already tired. He lunged around, swinging broad at Vagn's head, and Vagn dove past him into the middle of the room, rolled, and coming to his feet grabbed his own staff up off the floor.

The crowd roared. Thorulf plodded after him, out of breath, and Vagn danced around him, luring him into another rush. When the big man charged Vagn stepped sideways and thrust his staff in between Thorulf's knees and felled him like an ox.

A thundering yell went up from those watching. Thorulf sprawled across the rush-strewn floor, and Vagn bounded after him and battered at him until he crouched down, his knees to his chest, and covered his head with his arms.

Vagn swung the staff up. He knew Thorulf had been there the night before on the beach. He wanted to drive the staff straight through him. The men howling and stamping around him were ready for a death. But then he heard Galdor say, up there, "See if you can kill him."

At that, he lowered the staff. His blood cooled. They were all around him, he couldn't kill them all, now, anyway. He put out his hand to Thorulf to help him up. The other men yelled, disappointed, derisive, and Thorulf swatted away his hand and got to his feet and went off.

The other men were already moving the tables back into place, and the slaves were bringing in more food. Vagn stood watching all this. The others ignored him. He saw how they sorted themselves out, top to bottom, with Galdor up on the highest place. When everybody else had sat down again, he went to the lowest end of the table and sat on the end of the bench. The bread came to him and he ate. The ale came to him and he drank. Nobody paid him much attention.

He thought about what he had to do here. All these men were guilty of his brothers' blood, but it was Galdor who was the head. He looked up at the high seat, where the king sat fondling the sword. Wait, Vagn thought to himself.

He slept the short night on some straw in a corner of the hall. In the morning, he expected someone to come to him with work, as would have happened at home, but nobody was doing much of anything. Men came and went in the hall, rolling up their blankets, talking together, and sitting down at the tables to play chess, and drinking. Galdor did not appear. A slave brought in some bread.

Vagn went off around the place, seeing what was there. As he had marked the day before, on his way here, the tower rose on the high point of the headland. A stout stone wall fenced off a wide half circle of space around the foot of it, running from cliff edge to cliff edge. One high gate, braced and hinged with iron, pierced the wall, closed and barred.

He went around the inside of the wall and found a little stable and some storerooms built along it. In the yard some of the men were pitching axes; they paid no heed to him. Firewood stood in stacks along the foot of the tower and tools lay around the yard. In the far corner, where the wall bent to meet the cliff, he came on the kitchen.

In his experience the three things he needed most, bread, clean clothes, and a warm look, all came from women, and women were usually found in kitchens. This one was a narrow room under a turf roof, with two ovens set in the stone wall and a row of split tree trunks for tables. People came and went through it steadily, and he found a corner at the top of a passageway, at the back of it all, where he lurked around until a wan, sullen girl noticed him.

He wheedled her into giving him some bread; he was glad to see that girls were the same everywhere. Like cats, they loved to be stroked. He stroked her more, and she smiled, and then was pretty. He said so. She flustered and fluttered and went off to her work, kneading dough, her hands dusty white and her cheeks bright red, but a few minutes later she brought him mead in a little flagon.

As he took this, thinking he could kiss her, a rattling sound came up from the passageway behind him. The girl gave a violent start, her hands flying up. He looked around, into the dark throat of a corridor, stacked high with wood for the ovens.

"Where does that go?"

She turned her wide eyes on him. "Nowhere. Stay away from there." She leaned closer. "It's haunted," she whispered, and he kissed her.

Later, he squeezed in past the oven wood into the corridor. As he went he could hear the scurrying of rats and he thought that was the noise he had heard.

The corridor wound down steeply into the dark, but in a niche in the wall, under a dusty veil of cobwebs, he found a rush and a firebox. Someone had come down here often but not recently. He blew the dust off the rush and lit it and took it down into the dark.

Around a corner, he came to a door, blocked with a balk of wood. He moved the wood, and the door swung open. Holding the rush out before him he went down a long flight of steps, and the cold air that came to him smelled of an ancient fire, and of bricks, and of iron. This was a dead forge, hidden under the tower. He reached the last step and turned, looking around him.

Almost at his feet, something moaned.

He went cold. He could not move, every hair staring. The sound came again. Down on the thick dust of the floor lay a shaggy head.

Vagn knelt beside it. The head's eyes were closed. Its long thick hair was filthy with dirt and old blood and its raddled beard trailed away beyond the reach of the rush light. He knew it was a dwarf by its beard and its bristling eyebrows, its plug of a nose. Its lips moved but only a moan came out. Vagn remembered the flagon of mead, and took it from his belt and moistened the dwarf's lips.

The lips moved, greedy, and smacked. They spoke again, but he could not make out what they said, and he fed them more mead.

"Tyraste," the dwarf whispered. "Tyraste, remember."

"What." Vagn put his head down closer. "What are you saying? Who are you?"

"Tyraste, remember," the dwarf said, louder.

The rush light was going out. Vagn looked around to make sure he knew where the stair was. He bent to the dwarf's head again. "Tell me what you mean!"

But all the dwarf said was, "Tyraste, remember."

The light flickered out. Vagn turned and went up the steps, groping along in the darkness. At the top of the stair he shut the door and jammed the chunk of wood against it, and went on up to the light.

Beyond the kitchen a flight of steps went up the wall to a parapet over-hanging the sea. Vagn climbed up there, to the highest place, and stood looking out over the strait, where the wrinkled water spread out far into the distance. From here, Galdor had seen the knarr coming, had seen from here that the little cargo ship was struggling, and gone down to lure it in.

A foot scraped behind him, startling him, and he whirled around. Thorulf Grimsson was coming up the stair. Vagn went stiff all over. Two steps from the top, Thorulf stopped and looked up at him, squinting into the sun.

"You're going to need a sword. I'll help you get one."

Vagn said, "Very well. You go first."

The big man turned and went down the steps ahead of him. At the bottom, Thorulf waited for him to catch up, and said, under his breath, "That was Galdor, yesterday, who did that." He put his hand out, and said his name.

Vagn shook his hand. They were walking by the kitchen, by the passageway there. He said, "Who is Tyraste?"

"Is that a name? Some girl?" In the high stone wall beyond the kitchen was a wooden double-sided door. Thorulf pulled the two panels wide open. The sun shone in on a narrow room, the wheels and shafts of a wagon, a pile of round shields, and a barrel of sand. Out of the barrel there stuck up a forest of hilts and crosspieces. Thorulf gripped the barrel and rolled it forward; Vagn saw again how strong he was.

"Try this." The big man pulled a sword out of the barrel and handed it to Vagn.

The hilt was neatly leather-wrapped, with a round pommel, but the blade felt heavy to him. He looked for something to try the sword against and Thorulf pointed him out the door. In the yard just beyond was a stump of wood, notched and splintered, the ground around it caked with sawdust. Vagn hacked at it; the battered chunk of tree was too low and the angle was bad.

Thorulf said, "Here. Use this edge, see, that's the front edge. Try this one."

The next blade was spotted with rust and had a big notch out of the blade near the crossbar, but it felt better in his hand. He struck at the stump again, crouching to get the angle, and Thorulf said, "Good. Stiffen your wrist. Like that." He thumped Vagn hard on the back. "That's it."

Vagn stepped away from the stump, his breath short; he was thinking of his brother. Two other men came over toward them. "What, Thorulf," said one, "teaching him to beat you worse?" And smirked.

Thorulf said, "That's Ketil. Ketil Tooth. And that is Johan, who is not even Norse."

Ketil grinned at Vagn, displaying a jagged eyetooth pointing straight out from the gum. He said, "Don't get too cocky beating up on an old souse like him, boy." The fair-headed Johan, not much older than Vagn, gave him a nod. He stood watching everybody, his eyes sharp, but said nothing.

"You'll need a shield, too." Thorulf went back into the storeroom.

Ketil said, "You won't find much good steel in that barrel, boy." He bumped into Vagn, as if by accident.

"Oh, this suits me," Vagn said. He held his ground, and Ketil had to step back. Big Johan was staring at the sword in Vagn's hand; he pointed at the blade, where below the hilt now Vagn saw some old runes in the iron.

"Gut," Johan said. He nodded vigorously at Vagn. "Gut."

"What is the work here?" Vagn asked.

Johan looked over at Ketil to answer; obviously he had little Norse. Ketil said, "It's easy enough. We keep the narrows. All that come by must give us some of what they carry." Ketil stuck his chin out, pointing east. "The big market lies beyond, where the river flows in. Through here is the quickest way there."

Vagn knew this; he and his brothers had been on their way to this market. He had the sword in his hand. He could kill someone now. Thorulf brought him a leather sheath. Around him three of the men who had killed his brothers.

Then they stiffened, and all three were looking across the yard toward the hall. Vagn followed their eyes.

King Galdor had come out of the hall. He stood upon the threshold, his head thrown back. He wore a black bearskin cloak, a breastplate studded with metal. His sword swung at his hip. He stared at them a moment, saying nothing, and walked off across the yard. As he walked, his hand fell lightly to his sword. Thorulf muttered under his breath and made a sign with his fingers.

Ketil said, "Shut up, fool."

"He's after me," Thorulf said. "He's after me all the time."

"That's a fine sword," Vagn said. "Galdor's sword."

"No other has such a sword," Ketil said. "With that in his hand he does not lose."

In Vagn's mind the weapon in his hand shrank to a twig. A few other men walked out of the hall, yawned, stretched. Ketil and Johan started toward them, calling out. Vagn slid his new sword down into the scabbard. He could not kill them all. Galdor he should hate, not these. The girl from the kitchen was wandering by, a basket on her hip, her eyes not quite finding his. He followed Thorulf off to join the other men.

At undernmeal, he sat between Ketil and Thorulf, halfway up the table. While they were all eating, Galdor called out, "We should have some poetry. Thorulf! Give us a skalding!"

All around the hall the men laughed, and turned to stare at Thorulf, who had turned white as lambskin. He got to his feet. The jug was there and he took a big slurp of the ale. The laughing swelled, expecting some amusement. Galdor was lounging in his place, smiling.

"Give us a poem, Thorulf. Speak!"

Thorulf's chest heaved. He said, "On the swan's road—" and gulped. Around the room, the jeering rose; Vagn sat still, seeing this was an old practice. Thorulf's eyes bulged. "The raven lord came—battle-sweat— unh—"

The yells of the other men rose to a roar, and from all sides they threw bread and bones and cheese at Thorulf, who flung his arms up to ward off the volleys, and sank down on the bench. He covered his head with his arms. The table in front of Vagn was littered with bits of food.

Up there, Galdor said, "Well, that was disappointing."

The room hushed. Everybody waited, breathless, on the king, who looked around them all, and finally said, "Vagn Akason. Perhaps you can do better?"

Vagn stood up; he swiped the crumbs off his sleeves. He said, "Odin's match is the Vedrborg's king—"

A disappointed cheer rose. Beside Vagn, Ketil gave a cackle of a laugh. "Figured it out, did you?" On the high seat Galdor raised his head and beamed.

Vagn said, "Save he has both his eyes, his spears are bread, and his ravens are crows—"

The general mutter of approval broke off. Ketil snorted. Galdor's smile froze. Vagn was cobbling up another line, trying to work in a comparison of Valhalla and the Vedrborg. On either side, Ketil and Thorulf yanked Vagn down onto the bench. Around them the table rumbled up a hard-smothered laughter. Galdor tilted forward from the high seat, staring down at Vagn across the room, and his hands went to the sword lying on the table before him. The laughter stopped.

"Mighty king!" On the far side of the room, another man leapt to his feet. "Ring-breaker, feeder of the eagles—"

Every head in the room swung toward this one, and he went on so, for many lofty words. Vagn sat still; he thought maybe he had shown himself too soon. But he was glad. Already Galdor was making a big point of sending this new poet a golden cup of mead. Next to Vagn, Thorulf clapped him on the shoulder and leaned toward his ear. "Keep watch," he whispered. "Galdor won't forget." He straightened. Up there, Galdor had turned to glare at Vagn again. Ketil handed him the alehorn.

"You need this, fool?"

Vagn drank deep.

Later, he saw Galdor, still on his high seat, leaning on the arm to talk with a balding man, squat as a toad. After that one had gone away, Galdor sent a slave to fetch Vagn up. When Vagn stood before him, Galdor frowned at him.

"You are no skald. You annoyed me. So I want you to go up on the parapet and keep night-watch. It's cold up there, in the wind, and it's likely to rain. You can think about where your stupid tongue has gotten you." He sat back. The sword lay on the table between them.

Vagn said, "Yes, King Galdor," and went off.

There was some weather coming in, as the night fell; he could feel it in the air. He stood on the parapet, looking into the dark, listening to the wind boom and sigh over the walls around him. The rain began, light as a veil. He thought awhile of his brothers, dead down there, and he alive up here, and could not push this into any balance. He knew no one would come down the narrows on a night like this and he went down the stairs again, and away into the back of the kitchen, where the passage started down.

The kitchen slaves were asleep around the banked ovens. He took off his shoes, to make no noise, and kept watch on the yard. In the warmth he dozed a little. He dreamt of the dwarf, just down at the other end of the passage; he heard himself begging the dwarf to help him. He started awake, and heard someone scurry by outside, toward the stair.

He went up to the front of the kitchen, and saw the toad-man climbing up the stair; as he went he drew his dagger. Vagn climbed up two steps at a time behind him, his bare feet soundless. At the top, the toad was peering around.

"Looking for me?"

The toad wheeled, his dagger lashing out, but Vagn was already driving into him, shoulder first, hurling him back across the narrow walkway. The dagger nicked his cheek. The toad hit the waist-high parapet wall and tumbled over into the air. Vagn stood there a moment, and heard a thud. Then he went back down the stairs.

From the kitchen, the girl called him, and he went in there, and lay down with her in the warmth of the hearth.

———

Galdor came out of the hall door. The rain had stopped, and the sunlight blazed bright and clean over the world. To his surprise, across the yard, hacking at a barrel with a sword, was the black-haired boy Vagn Akason.

The king cast a look all around the yard, looking for his man Gifr, and didn't see him. He called Vagn to him.

"I see you made a night of it," he said, when the boy stood before him.

"Not much happened," Vagn said. There was a fresh cut on his cheek.

Galdor said, "You didn't see anything?"

"No. A blowfly bothered me, once, but I swatted it away."

Their eyes met. Galdor laid his hand on the hilt of his sword. "Where did you say you came from?"

"West of here. From the big island."

"Then how did you get here?"

"I walked."

"On the water?"

The boy opened his mouth with another lie, then, from the tower, the horn blew. Galdor said a round oath. "Get to the ships," he said. "Hjeldric is come at last."

Vagn loved being back on the water, where everything was simple: the stroke, his strength, and the sea. On the bench ahead of him Thorulf swung his oar; Ketil stood at the helm, steering them through the broken water. All around Vagn, the men were chanting the count.

He had rowed all his life, but always clunky little boats like the knarr. Never before a vessel like this one, this sea serpent of a ship, light and supple, skimming over the water. The rhythm carried him like great wings. He added his voice to the count, a glad part of this.

Through the corner of his eye he could see that they were racing to cut off another longship, streaking up the strait from the west. Ketil yelled out and the count quickened. Vagn pushed himself to match it, gasping at the effort; all around him the other men strained at the oars. The ship trashed across a rough current. The oncoming ship was fighting the same surface chop and lost half a length, and then Vagn's ship glided out onto a patch of easy water. The other longship stood up its oars and veered off.

A hoarse cheer rose from the benches around Vagn. Ketil laid them over. The jug came by and Vagn gulped down most of the water in it. His sword lay under his bench. Maybe now they would fight, ship to

ship. He longed to try the sword in a real fight. Over there, across the
open water, the other longship faced them, too far to see any of those
men. He dragged in a deep breath. Thorulf reached around and slapped
his shoulder, and someone else gave a random yell. Vagn felt his blood
beating through his body; he shook his muscles loose. He looked quickly
around at the other men, his crew. His brothers now. He thrust that
problem off. He looked out over the water toward the other ship, his
hand itching to pick up his sword.

Then a horn blew, behind them.

He twisted to look over his shoulder. Back there, Galdor had his other
two ships bow to stern across the narrows. Three more enemy ships lay
up the strait, waiting. Lean and low, they were beautiful, and it swelled
him to think he would fight in such a one. The horn sounded again and
Vagn felt his scalp prickle. This was the beginning of it. But none of the
other men even looked up. Back at the helm, Ketil suddenly gave over
the steerboard to somebody else and went forward.

Thorulf was sitting back. Another jug came. Vagn said, "What's
going on?"

"They're talking." The man across the way from him turned toward
him. "Nothing is going to happen for a while."

On the bench behind him, somebody said, "They outnumber us. Galdor
doesn't fight against the odds." Thorulf muttered something under his
breath.

Vagn looked around them. They were at the narrowest part of the strait.
He remembered the rocks that cluttered the water along the shore. It
seemed to him Galdor's three ships could hold off the four enemy ships
easily enough. Probably there was some piece of warcraft he was not
grasping here. Now Galdor was shouting from his ship toward one of
the others, and someone there was shouting back. They were arranging
to meet on the land. There would still be a fight. Vagn reached down to
touch the hilt of his sword.

Galdor had sent most of his men back up to the Vedrborg. The rest he
kept below, in a broad meadow just inland of the beach where Hjledric's
ships drew up, and he went among them and counted out seven of them.
Thorulf was among these seven and so was Vagn. When Ketil was not

counted in, he and the others went away. Galdor paced up and down past
the men who stayed.

He said, "I am staking the Vedrborg on this. I will reward good work
here." His eyes were hot and bright. He drew his sword; Vagn imagined
it hissed like a snake, coming out of the sheath. "Thorulf, take the weather
edge. I will take the middle."

Thorulf stepped back and leaned on his sword. Around him the other
men were gripping each other's hands, drinking deep of the alehorns.
Across the grass Hjeldric's eight men gathered. Vagn looked over his new
sword again. He had worked on the rusty parts with sheep's fat and a rag
and gotten some of it clean. The notch he could not fix. But the blade
felt good in his hand. He took a deep breath. The sun was warm on his
cheek. He told himself he might never see another sunrise; this seemed
a far-distant, unimportant matter.

Thorulf stood there, swinging his arms back and forth. He said, "Is
this the first time you've fought like this?"

Vagn said, "Yes." His voice had a squeak.

Thorulf said, "I think it is my last."

Ketil suddenly appeared again. To Vagn, he said, "Galdor will win this.
Keep your sword up." He thumped Thorulf on the back. "You'd better get
down there. Feed a few ravens for me." Thorulf walked heavily away across
the grass, and Vagn followed.

Vagn could not stop bouncing. He was gripping the sword too tight.
Beside him, Thorulf slouched, scratching his beard. He said, "Tonight
in Valhalla, Vagn Akason," and spat through his fingers. Galdor came
pacing along in front of them, calling their names and jabbing his sword
in the air.

He lifted his shield, and the horn blew.

They walked together in a row toward Hjeldric's men, who came toward
them in a row, each to each. In front of Vagn was a lanky body behind
a big round shield, red hair sticking out all around a leather helmet. Vagn
could not quite get his breath. Beside him, Thorulf gave a screech and
dashed forward.

The redheaded man lunged at Vagn, striking shoulder high, and Vagn
tore his attention away from Thorulf. He swung up the shield and the

blow struck so hard it numbed his arm. He slashed out with his sword, low, not seeing much, and felt it bang hard on the redheaded man's shield, and the other man sprang away. Vagn followed him, shield first, wanting him to strike first. Inside the leather helmet, above the thatch of red beard, the man's blue eyes locked with his. He jabbed with his sword, and when Vagn pulled his shield up, turned the stroke low, and hard.

The tip of the sword sliced toward Vagn's knee. He drove his own sword down, and the blades rang together. Vagn saw at once the other man had the longer reach. He crashed forward, shield first, into the tall, gangly body, closing the gap between them. For an instant, they were chest to chest together, the redhead's breath blasting in Vagn's face. He felt the other man's strength coil to throw him off, and as the other man shoved he slid sideways out of the way, laying out his sword. The redheaded man stumbled, fell across the blade and staggered to his knees.

Vagn bellowed, hot with triumph. Then another of Hjeldric's men was charging him, shorter, wider, swinging an axe.

He caught this on the shield, turning the edge a little, so the wide curved blade did not strike full on. With his sword he hacked down at the axeman's head. The axeman ducked back and away, and for an instant Vagn could look around.

The redhead was getting to his feet. Blood smeared his side but he was raising his sword again. Out there on the trampled grass, Thorulf lay in a heap.

The axeman barked some name, and he and the redheaded man fanned out and came at Vagn together. The redheaded man was breathing hard, the blood bright on his breastplate and shield arm. The other man, squatty, with his axe, bobbed back and forth then gave a howl and charged.

Vagn stood fast; he turned the first blow off with his shield and with his sword poked and cut, watching how the other man met that. He knew that the redheaded man was coming in behind him, and he backed up in a rush, getting out from between them. The redheaded man dropped to one knee again. The other one lifted his axe, moving sideways, circling around to Vagn's far side.

The redheaded man heaved himself up onto his feet and stumbled forward. Vagn cocked up his shield; his body felt huge and the shield the size of a pea. From the side the axe sliced at his head and he ducked and lunged and his sword glanced off the axeman's shield. He dodged away from them both again, and the axeman stepped back. The redheaded man lost his balance and fell to his hands and knees.

Vagn cast another look around. They had moved far along the meadow, somehow, almost to the wood; Thorulf's body was a long way back there. Nearer, Galdor and Hjeldric were circling each other. Galdor's sword swung out, and Hjledric dodged, then attacked, going against Galdor's shield hand.

Then from the wood there burst a tide of men.

Vagn stood, startled. They were Galdor's men, and they reached the redheaded man first and hacked him down, and then the axeman went down. Hjeldric wheeled toward them, and Galdor plunged the sword through his back. Vagn did not move. He saw Galdor fling his arms up, triumphant. He saw, down on the beach, two of Hjeldric's ships push away.

Ketil walked up to Vagn. He said, "I told you he would not leave it to chance." His eyes did not quite meet Vagn's. Vagn threw his shield down, and went off to see what had happened to Thorulf.

At undernmeal Vagn sat staring at his hands. Around him the voices purred and muttered but he heard nothing. The food came around and he ate nothing. He drank from the alehorn, which did him no good.

His mind was churning. Thorulf was dead, but Thorulf had died well, of hard wounds taken in front. Vagn thought over and over of the redheaded man, who had fought so hard, even wounded, merely to be cut down from behind like a coward. The gall burned in his belly. Ketil, beside him, spoke to him only once.

"We won, didn't we?"

Vagn grunted at him. After that Ketil said nothing, only glanced at him now and then, and passed him the horn.

In the high seat Galdor shouted out a name, and some warrior stood up, and Galdor pulled one of the gold rings from his arm and a slave brought it down and everybody cheered. Vagn stared at the table.

Then Galdor was calling out his name.

Vagn lifted his head, and all around saw faces watching him. A slave came trotting toward him, holding out a gold ring, and a long yell rose, his name in sixty voices.

He stood up, everybody's eyes turned on him, and hurled the ring across the room.

"No! There was nothing golden on that field, no honor—" He was shaking, the blood booming in his ears. "Better men than you died on that field, Galdor No-King, Galdor Cheat! I would be a better king here than you are."

The hall crashed into silence. Nobody moved.

Galdor said, "This is your end, Vagn Akason." He rose in his place and took the sword up off the table and drew it from the scabbard. Around Vagn the others were suddenly moving, pulling the benches and tables back, and he was alone, standing there. He drew his sword. Galdor was coming toward him down the hall.

He moved away, then Galdor was coming at him, sideways, the keen blade slicing toward him. He bounded backward. He got his sword crosswise of Galdor's and the shock rang up his arm. Galdor was pushing him along, darting here, there, poking at him, laughing. Vagn skittered backward, trying to get some room, and came up against the table.

Hands gripped him from behind. Somebody was holding him for Galdor, and the king moved in fast. Vagn dropped his sword. He reached back and got the wrists holding him, twisted and crouched down, and with all his weight he hauled the man behind him over his shoulder and into Galdor's thrust.

The sword came out through the falling man's chest. While Galdor was pulling it free Vagn grabbed up his own sword again and vaulted onto the table. The other men shied back, toward the walls. Galdor swung hard at his knees, and when he dodged that, the king leapt onto the table after him. Slashing and cutting up and down, he drove Vagn backward, through the bread and the cheese, tipping over the alehorns. Vagn kept his sword up, fending off the king's blows, groping along behind him with his feet.

Galdor stabbed at him, and Vagn saw something; he lunged toward the weakness, but it was a trap. The king wheeled his blow backward at him and struck the sword out of his hand.

A bellow went up. The king's eyes glowed. Vagn leapt down from the table, and raced out the door into the yard. Galdor was hot after him. Just beyond the threshold was a stack of firewood, and Vagn threw a chunk of it at Galdor and saw an axe among the wood. With a bound he caught it up. Galdor was right behind him and he wheeled around and swung the axe waist high, missing Galdor by a finger's breadth.

Galdor howled. His teeth showed. He hacked right, and Vagn dodged, then left and Vagn dodged. The axe was top-heavy and hard to manage. Galdor let him swing and came in behind the swing, and Vagn felt the blade crease his ribs through his shirt. He swung the axe around and hurled it straight at Galdor.

Galdor went down; the axe grazed his shoulder. Vagn raced across the yard, toward the storeroom with the barrel of swords. The doors were shut and barred. Galdor was pounding after him, yelling, derisive.

"Wait, little boy, I'm not done with you!"

Vagn swerved toward the kitchen, where there would be knives. Galdor was on his heels. On the ground out in the middle of the yard he saw a broom, and veered toward it. He could hear yelling, from a great distance; all he saw was the broom, and he snatched it up and wheeled just as Galdor closed with him.

The sword swung at his head; he thrust up the broom and the blade bit the wood and snapped it. Still clutching the short end, Vagn slid back, out of reach of the sword. Galdor stood a moment, the sword raised, the tip circling in the air as if it sniffed for him.

The others, packed up against the walls, were calling and whistling. Vagn watched only the tip of the sword. Sliding his feet along, the stub end of the broomstick poking out before him, he inched his way toward the wall. Galdor shifted as he shifted, the sword blocking him this way, herding him that, moving him backward, backward. Vagn gave a quick look over his shoulder. Just behind him was the stair up to the parapet. The blade ripped at him and he sprang backward, up onto the steps.

Galdor was below him now, but Vagn had no fit weapon. He lashed out with the short piece of the broom and the king coiled back, out of reach, and whipped the sword at his ankles. Vagn leapt up another step, and Galdor came after. The sword jabbed at him. Galdor lunged up the steps and Vagn scurried away across the parapet and came up hard against the rail.

"Nowhere to run now," Galdor said, breathless. He lifted the sword, and Vagn's gaze rose with it. "Aha! You admire my sword? You should. It's beyond price. It longs for blood." He waggled the sword in Vagn's face. "Its first blood was the dwarf who made it, who never made another like it. And now—" He cocked back the sword above Vagn's head. "It will have yours."

The dwarf. The dwarf. Braced against the wall, Vagn cried out, "Tyraste, remember!"

Galdor swung the blade down at his head, and the sword turned in Galdor's hand, struck the wall, and flew across the parapet.

Vagn yelled. Galdor lunged after the sword, both hands stretched out. Vagn was closer. His hand fastened on the sword hilt and without pausing he swung his arm with all his strength around and took Galdor across the body.

Somewhere far off a huge yell went up. Vagn stood. Galdor sagged to his knees, his hands on his ripped belly, his head back. Vagn said, "This for my brothers. And Thorulf. And the dwarf in the cellar." He drove the sword through Galdor's chest.

The yelling went on. Down in the yard the other people were shouting and waving their arms. Vagn stood, panting.

The sword in his hand felt light, quick; its power burned in it. He understood why Galdor had always been touching it. Vagn wanted right away to strike with it again. The dwarf had made it full of charms. He remembered how it had turned on Galdor.

He went on down the stair to the yard, crowded with people. They were all watching him, and when he came toward them they moved back out of his way. He went in through the kitchen. There he found a rush light, and followed the passageway into the dark.

In the forge, at the foot of the stair, he sank down on his heels, and held the rushlight up to see. In the dust was the dwarf's head, but now it was smiling.

Vagn laid the sword down beside it.

"I have brought this back to you."

The dwarf whispered, "Yours. Yours, now."

Eagerly he took it back in his hand. The dwarf's lips bent in a deeper smile. "But beware. It is still evil."

This was how Vagn Akason became king of the Vedrborg. But the life there was not to his liking, and soon he went off to join the Jomsvikings.

George R.R. Martin

Hugo, Nebula, and World Fantasy Award-winner George R.R. Martin, *New York Times* bestselling author of the landmark A Song of Ice and Fire fantasy series, has been called "the American Tolkien."

Born in Bayonne, New Jersey, George R.R. Martin made his first sale in 1971, and soon established himself as one of the most popular SF writers of the seventies. He quickly became a mainstay of the Ben Bova *Analog* with stories such as "With Morning Comes Mistfall," "And Seven Times Never Kill Man," "The Second Kind of Loneliness," "The Storms of Windhaven" (in collaboration with Lisa Tuttle, and later expanded by them into the novel *Windhaven*), "Override," and others, although he also sold to *Amazing, Fantastic, Galaxy, Orbit*, and other markets. One of his *Analog* stories, the striking novella "A Song for Lya," won him his first Hugo Award, in 1974.

By the end of the seventies, he had reached the height of his influence as a science-fiction writer, and was producing his best work in that category with stories such as the famous "Sandkings," his best-known story, which won both the Nebula and the Hugo in 1980 (he'd later win another Nebula in 1985 for his story "Portraits of His Children"), "The Way of Cross and Dragon," which won a Hugo Award in the same year (making Martin the first author ever to receive two Hugo Awards for fiction in the same year), "Bitterblooms," "The Stone City," "Starlady," and others. These stories would be collected in *Sandkings*, one of the strongest collections of the period. By now, he had mostly moved away from *Analog* although he would have a long sequence of stories about the droll interstellar adventures of Haviland Tuf (later collected in *Tuf Voyaging*) running throughout the eighties in the Stanley Schmidt *Analog*, as well as a few strong individual pieces such as the novella "Nightflyers"—most of his major work of the late seventies and early eighties, though, would appear in *Omni*. The late seventies and eighties also saw the publication of his memorable novel *Dying of the Light*, his only solo SF novel, while his stories were collected in *A Song for Lya*, *Sandkings*, *Songs of Stars and Shadows*, *Songs the Dead Men Sing*, *Nightflyers*, and *Portraits of His Children*. By the beginning of the eighties, he'd moved away from SF and into the horror genre, publishing the big horror novel *Fevre Dream*, and winning the Bram Stoker Award for his horror story "The Pear-Shaped Man" and the World Fantasy Award for his werewolf novella "The Skin Trade." By the end of that decade, though, the crash of the horror market and the commercial failure of his ambitious horror novel *The Armageddon Rag* had driven him out of the print world and to a successful career in television instead, where for more than a decade he worked as story editor or producer on such shows as the new *Twilight Zone* and *Beauty and the Beast*.

After years away, Martin made a triumphant return to the print world in 1996 with the publication of the immensely successful fantasy novel *A Game of Thrones*, the start of his Song of Ice and Fire sequence. A freestanding novella taken from that work, "Blood of the Dragon," won Martin another Hugo Award in 1997. Further books in the Song of Ice and Fire series, *A Clash of Kings*, *A Storm of Swords*, *A Feast for Crows*, and *A Dance with Dragons*, have made it one of the most acclaimed and bestselling series in all of modern fantasy. Recently, the books were made into an HBO TV series, *A Game of Thrones*, which has become one of the most popular and acclaimed shows on television, and made Martin a recognizable figure well outside of the usual genre boundaries, even inspiring a satirical version of him on *Saturday Night Live*. Martin's recent books include a massive retrospective collection spanning the entire spectrum of his career, *Dreamsongs*; a novella collection, *Starlady and Fast-Friend*; a novel written in collaboration with Gardner Dozois and Daniel Abraham, *Hunter's Run*; and, as editor, several anthologies edited in collaboration with Gardner Dozois, including *Warriors*, *Song of the Dying Earth*, *Songs of Love and Death*, *Down These Strange Streets*, *Dangerous Women*, and *Rogues*; as well as several new volumes in his long-running Wild Cards anthology series. In 2012, Martin was given the Life Achievement Award by the World Fantasy Convention. His most recent books are *High Stakes*, the twenty-third volume in the Wild Cards series, and *The World of Ice and Fire*, an illustrated history of the Seven Kingdoms.

Here he takes us to Westeros, home to his Ice and Fire series, and back in time for a look at things that happened long before *A Game of Thrones* begins, for the story of an unfortunate sibling rivalry that has tragic and disastrous effects on the entire world.

THE SONS OF THE DRAGON

King Aegon I Targaryen, as history records, took both of his sisters to wife. Both Visenya and Rhaenys were dragonriders, blessed with the silver-gold hair, purple eyes, and beauty of true Targaryens. Elsewise, the two queens were as unlike one another as any two women could be ... save in one other respect. Each of them gave the king a son.

Aenys came first. Born in 7 AC to Aegon's younger wife, Queen Rhaenys, the boy was small at birth, and sickly. He cried all the time, and it was said that his limbs were spindly and his eyes small and watery, so that the king's maesters feared for his survival. He would spit out the nipples of his wet nurse, and give suck only at his mother's breasts, and rumors claimed that he screamed for a fortnight when he was weaned. So unlike King Aegon was he that a few even dared suggest that His Grace was not the boy's true sire, that Aenys was some bastard born of one of Queen Rhaenys's many handsome favorites, the son of a singer or a mummer or a mime. And the prince was slow to grow as well. Not until he was given the young dragon Quicksilver, a hatchling born that year on Dragonstone, did Aenys Targaryen begin to thrive.

Prince Aenys was three when his mother, Queen Rhaenys, and her dragon Meraxes were slain in Dorne. Her death left the boy prince inconsolable. He stopped eating, and even began to crawl as he had when he was one, as if he had forgotten how to walk. His father despaired of him, and rumors flew about the court that King Aegon might take another wife, as Rhaenys was dead and Visenya childless and perhaps barren. The king kept his own counsel on these matters, so no man could say what thoughts he might have entertained, but many great lords and noble knights appeared at court with their maiden daughters, each more comely than the last.

All such speculation ended in 11 AC, when Queen Visenya suddenly announced that she was carrying the king's child. A son, she proclaimed confidently, and so he proved to be. The prince came squalling into the world in 12 AC. No newborn was ever more robust than Maegor Targaryen, maesters and midwives agreed; his weight at birth was almost twice that of his elder brother.

The half brothers were never close. Prince Aenys was the heir apparent, and King Aegon kept him close by his side. As the king moved about the realm from castle to castle, so did the prince. Prince Maegor remained with his mother, sitting by her side when she held court. Queen Visenya and King Aegon were oft apart in those years. When he was not on his royal progress, Aegon would return to King's Landing and the Aegonfort, whilst Visenya and her son remained on Dragonstone. For this reason, lords and commons alike began to refer to Maegor as the Prince of Dragonstone.

Queen Visenya put a sword into her son's hand when he was three. Supposedly the first thing he did with the blade was butcher one of the castle cats, men said . . . though more like this tale was a calumny devised by his enemies many years later. That the prince took to swordplay at once cannot be denied, however. For his first master-at-arms, his mother chose Ser Gawen Corbray, as deadly a knight as could be found in all the Seven Kingdoms.

Prince Aenys was so oft in his sire's company that his own instruction in the chivalric arts came largely from the knights of Aegon's Kingsguard, and sometimes the king himself. The boy was diligent, his instructors all agreed, and did not want for courage, but he lacked his sire's size and strength, and never showed himself as any more than adequate as a fighter, even when the king pressed Blackfyre into his hands, as he did from time to time. Aenys would not disgrace himself in battle, his tutors told one another, but no songs would ever be sung about his prowess.

Such gifts as this prince possessed lay elsewhere. Aenys was a fine singer himself, as it happened, with a strong, sweet voice. He was courteous and charming, clever without being bookish. He made friends easily, and young girls seemed to dote on him, be they highborn or low. Aenys loved to ride as well. His father gave him coursers, palfreys, and destriers, but his favorite mount was his dragon, Quicksilver.

Prince Maegor rode as well, but showed no great love for horses, dogs, or any animal. When he was eight, a palfrey kicked him in the stables. Maegor stabbed the horse to death . . . and slashed half the face off the stableboy who came running at the beast's screams. The Prince of Dragonstone had many companions through the years, but no true friends. He was a quarrelsome boy, quick to take offense, slow to forgive, fearsome in his wroth. His skill with weapons was unmatched, however. A squire at eight, he was unhorsing boys four and five years his elder in the lists by the time he was twelve and battering seasoned men-at-arms into submission in the castle yard. On his thirteenth name day in 25 AC, his mother Queen Visenya bestowed her own Valyrian steel blade, Dark Sister, upon him ... half a year before his marriage.

The tradition amongst the Targaryens had always been to marry kin to kin. Wedding brother to sister was thought to be ideal. Failing that, a girl might wed an uncle, a cousin, or a nephew; a boy a cousin, aunt, or niece. This practice went back to Old Valyria, where it was common amongst many of the ancient families, particularly those who bred and rode dragons. The blood of the dragon must remain pure, the wisdom went. Some of the sorcerer princes also took more than one wife when it pleased them, though this was less common than incestuous marriage. In Valyria before the Doom, wise men wrote, a thousand gods were honored, but none were feared, so few dared to speak against these customs.

This was not true in Westeros, where the power of the Faith went unquestioned. The old gods were still worshipped in the North, but in the rest of the realm there was a single god with seven faces, and his voice upon this earth was the High Septon of Oldtown. And the doctrines of the Faith, handed down through centuries from Andalos itself, condemned the Valyrian marriage customs as practiced by the Targaryens. Incest was denounced as vile sin, whether between father and daughter, mother and son, or brother and sister, and the fruits of such unions were considered abominations in the sight of gods and men. With hindsight, it can be seen that conflict between the Faith and House Targaryen was inevitable. Indeed, many amongst the Most Devout expected the High Septon to speak out against Aegon and his sisters during the Conquest, and were most displeased when the Father of the Faithful instead counseled Lord Hightower against opposing the Dragon, and even blessed and anointed him at his second coronation.

Familiarity is the father of acceptance, it is said. The High Septon who had crowned Aegon the Conqueror remained the Shepherd of the Faithful until his death in 11 AC, by which time the realm had grown accustomed to the notion of a king with two queens, who were both wives and sisters. King Aegon always took care to honor the Faith, confirming its traditional rights and privileges, exempting its wealth and property from taxation, and affirming that septons, septas, and other servants of the Seven accused of wrongdoing could only be tried by the Faith's own courts.

The accord between the Faith and the Iron Throne continued all through the reign of Aegon I. From 11 AC to 37 AC, six High Septons wore the crystal crown; His Grace remained on good terms with each of them, calling at the Starry Sept each time he came to Oldtown. Yet the question of incestuous marriage remained, simmering below the courtesies like poison. Whilst the High Septons of King Aegon's reign never spoke out against the king's marriage to his sisters, neither did they declare it to be lawful. The humbler members of the Faith—village septons, holy sisters, begging brothers, Poor Fellows—still believed it sinful for brother to lie with sister, or for a man to take two wives.

Aegon the Conqueror had fathered no daughters, however, so these matters did not come to a head at once. The sons of the Dragon had no sisters to marry, so each of them was forced to seek elsewhere for a bride.

Prince Aenys was the first to marry. In 22 AC, he wed the Lady Alyssa, the maiden daughter of the Lord of the Tides, Aethan Velaryon, King Aegon's lord admiral and master of ships. She was fifteen, the same age as the prince, and shared his silvery hair and purple eyes as well, for the Velaryons were an ancient family descended from Valyrian stock. King Aegon's own mother had been a Velaryon, so the marriage was reckoned one of cousin to cousin.

It soon proved both happy and fruitful. The following year, Alyssa gave birth to a daughter. Aenys named her Rhaena, and the realm rejoiced ... save, perhaps, for Queen Visenya. Prince Aenys was the heir to the Iron Throne, all agreed, but now an issue arose as to whether Prince Maegor remained second in the line of succession, or should be considered to have fallen to third, behind the newborn princess. Queen Visenya proposed to settle the matter by betrothing Rhaena to Maegor, who had just turned twelve. Aenys and Alyssa spoke out against the match, however ... and when word reached Oldtown's Starry Sept, the High Septon sent a raven, warning the king that such a marriage would not be looked upon with favor by the Faith. He proposed a different bride for Maegor: Ceryse Hightower, maiden daughter to the Lord of Oldtown (and the High Septon's own niece). Aegon, mindful of the advantages of closer ties with Oldtown and its ruling House, saw wisdom in the choice and agreed to the match.

Thus it came to pass that in 25 AC, Maegor Targaryen, Prince of Dragonstone, wed Lady Ceryse Hightower in the Starry Sept of Oldtown, with the High Septon himself performing the nuptials. Maegor was thirteen, the bride ten years his senior . . . but the lords who bore witness to the bedding all agreed that the prince made a lusty husband, and Maegor himself boasted that he had consummated the marriage a dozen times that night. "I made a son for House Targaryen last night," he proclaimed as he broke fast.

The son came the next year . . . but the boy, named Aegon after his grandsire, was born to Lady Alyssa and fathered by Prince Aenys. Lady Ceryse did not quicken in the years that followed, though other children came one after the other to Alyssa. In 29 AC, she gave Aenys a second son, Viserys. In 34 AC, she gave birth to Jaehaerys, her fourth child and third son. In 36 AC came another daughter, Alysanne. Each son pushed Prince Maegor further down in the succession; some said he stood behind his brother's daughters too. All whilst Maegor and Ceryse remained childless.

On tourney ground and battlefield, however, Prince Maegor's accomplishments far exceeded those of his brother. In the great tourney at Riverrun in 28 AC, Prince Maegor unhorsed three knights of the Kingsguard in successive tilts before falling to the eventual champion. In the melee, no man could stand before him. Afterward he was knighted on the field by his father, who dubbed him with no less a blade than Blackfyre. At ten-and-six, Maegor became the youngest knight in the Seven Kingdoms.

Others feats followed. In 29 AC and again in 30 AC, Maegor accompanied Osmund Strong and Aethan Velaryon to the Stepstones to root out the Lysene pirate king Sargoso Saan, and fought in several bloody affrays, showing himself to be both fearless and deadly. In 31 AC, he hunted down and slew a notorious robber knight in the riverlands, the so-called Giant of the Trident.

Maegor was not yet a dragonrider, however. Though half a dozen hatchlings had been born amidst the fires of Dragonstone in the later years of Aegon's reign, and were offered to the prince, Maegor refused them all. His brother's wife teased him about it one day in court, wondering aloud whether "my good-brother is afraid of dragons." Maegor darkened in rage at the jape then replied coolly that there was only one dragon worthy of him.

The last seven years of the reign of Aegon the Conqueror were peaceful ones. After the frustrations of his Dornish War the king accepted the continued independence of Dorne, and flew to Sunspear on Balerion on the tenth anniversary of the peace accords to celebrate a "feast of friendship" with Deria Martell, the reigning Princess of Dorne. Prince Aenys accompanied him on Quicksilver; Maegor remained on Dragonstone. Aegon had made the Seven Kingdoms one with fire and blood, but after celebrating his sixtieth name day in 33 AC, he turned instead to brick and mortar. Half of every year was still given over to a royal progress, but now it was Prince Aenys and his wife Alyssa who journeyed from castle to castle, whilst the aging king remained at home, dividing his days between Dragonstone and King's Landing.

The fishing village where Aegon had first landed had grown into a sprawling, stinking city of a hundred thousand souls by that time; only Oldtown and Lannisport were larger. Yet in many ways King's Landing was still little more than an army camp that had swollen to grotesque size: dirty, reeking, unplanned, impermanent. And the Aegonfort, which had spread halfway down Aegon's High Hill by that time, was as ugly a castle as any in the Seven Kingdoms, a great confusion of wood and earth and brick that had long outgrown the old log palisades that were its only walls.

It was certainly no fit abode for a great king. In 35 AC, Aegon moved with all his court back to Dragonstone, and gave orders that the Aegonfort be torn down, so that a new castle might be raised in its place. This time, he decreed, he would build in stone. To oversee the design and construction of the new castle, he named the King's Hand, Lord Alyn Stokeworth (Ser Osmund Strong had died the previous year), and Queen Visenya. (A jape went about the court that King Aegon had given Visenya charge of building the Red Keep so he would not have to endure her presence on Dragonstone.)

Aegon the Conqueror died of a stroke on Dragonstone in the thirty-seventh year after the Conquest. His grandsons Aegon and Viserys were with him at his death, in the Chamber of the Painted Table; the king was showing them the details of his conquests. Prince Maegor, in residence at Dragonstone at the time, spoke the eulogy as his father's body was laid upon a funeral pyre in the castle yard. The king was clad in battle armor, his mailed hands folded over the hilt of Blackfyre. Since the days of old Valyria, it had ever been the custom of House Targaryen to burn their dead, rather than consigning their remains to the ground. Vhagar supplied the flames to light the fire. Blackfyre was burned with the king, but retrieved by Aenys afterward, its blade darker but elsewise unharmed. No common fire can damage Valyrian steel.

The Dragon was survived by his sister Visenya, his sons Aenys and Maegor, and five grandchildren. Prince Aenys was thirty years of age at his father's death, Prince Maegor five-and-twenty.

Aenys had been at Highgarden on his progress when his father died, but Quicksilver returned him to Dragonstone for the funeral. Afterward he donned his father's iron-and-ruby crown, and Grand Maester Gawen proclaimed him Aenys of House Targaryen, the First of His Name, King of the Andals and the First Men, Lord of the Seven Kingdoms, and Protector of the Realm. The lords and knights and septons who had come to Dragonstone to bid their king farewell knelt and bowed their heads. When Prince Maegor's turn came, Aenys drew him back to his feet, kissed his cheek, and said, "Brother, you need never kneel to me again. We shall rule this realm together, you and I." Then the king presented his father's sword, Blackfyre, to his brother, saying, "You are more fit to bear this blade than me. Wield it in my service, and I shall be content."

Afterward the new king sailed to King's Landing, where he found the Iron Throne standing amidst mounds of rubble and mud. The old Aegonfort had been torn down, and pits and tunnels pockmarked the hill where the cellars and foundations of the Red Keep were being dug, but the new castle had not yet begun to rise. Nonetheless, thousands came to cheer King Aenys as he claimed his father's seat for his own. Thereafter His Grace set out for Oldtown to receive the blessing of the High Septon, traveling by way of Riverrun, Lannisport, and Highgarden on a grand royal progress. His wife and children made the journey with him, and all along the route the smallfolk appeared by the hundreds and thousands to hail their new king and queen. At the Starry Sept, the High Septon anointed him as he had his father, and presented him with a crown of yellow gold, with the faces of the Seven inlaid in jade and pearl.

Yet even as Aenys was receiving the High Septon's blessing, some were casting doubt on his fitness to sit the Iron Throne. Westeros required a warrior, not a dreamer, they whispered to one another, and Prince Maegor was the stronger of the Dragon's two sons. And foremost amongst the whisperers was Maegor's mother, the Dowager Queen Visenya Targaryen. "The truth is plain enough," she is reported to have said. "Even Aenys sees it. Why else would he have given Blackfyre to my son? He knows that only Maegor has the strength to rule."

The young king's mettle would be tested sooner than anyone could have imagined. The Wars of Conquest had left scars throughout the realm. Sons now come of age dreamed of avenging long-dead fathers. Knights remembered the days when a man with a sword and a horse and a suit of armor could slash his way to riches and glory. Lords recalled a time when they did not need a king's leave to tax their smallfolk or kill their enemies. "The chains the Dragon forged can yet be broken," the discontented told one another. "We can win our freedoms back, but now is the time to strike, for this new king is weak."

The first stirrings of revolt were in the riverlands, amidst the colossal ruins of Harrenhal. Aegon had granted the castle to Ser Quenton Qoherys, his old master-at-arms. When Lord Qoherys died in a fall from his horse in 9 AC, his title passed to his grandson Gargon, a fat and foolish man with an unseemly appetite for young girls who became known as Gargon the Guest. Lord Gargon soon became infamous for turning up at every wedding celebrated within his domains so that he might enjoy the lord's right of first night. A more unwelcome wedding guest can scarce be imagined. He also made free with the wives and daughters of his own servants.

King Aenys was still on his progress, guesting with Lord Tully of Riverrun, when the father of a maid Lord Qoherys had ruined opened a postern gate at Harrenhal to an outlaw who styled himself Harren the Red, and claimed to be a grandson of Harren the Black. The outlaws pulled his lordship from his bed and dragged him to the castle godswood, where Harren sliced off his genitals and fed them to a dog. A few leal men-at-arms were killed; the rest agreed to join Harren, who declared himself Lord of Harrenhal and King of the Rivers (not being ironborn, he did not claim the islands).

When word reached Riverrun, Lord Tully urged the king to mount Quicksilver and descend on Harrenhal as his father had. But His Grace, perhaps mindful of his mother's death in Dorne, instead commanded Tully to gather his banners, and lingered at Riverrun as they gathered. Only when a thousand men were assembled did Aenys march ... but when his men reached Harrenhal, they found it empty but for corpses. Harren the Red had put Lord Gargon's leal servants to the sword and taken his band into the woods.

By the time Aenys returned to King's Landing the news had grown even worse. In the Vale, Lord Ronnel Arryn's younger brother Jonos had deposed and imprisoned his loyal sibling, and declared himself King of Mountain and Vale. In the Iron Islands, another priest-king had walked out of the sea, announcing himself to be Lodos the Twice-Drowned, the son of the Drowned God, returned at last from visiting his father. And high in the Red Mountains of Dorne, a pretender called the Vulture King appeared, and called on all true Dornishmen to avenge the evils visited on Dorne by the Targaryens. Though Princess Deria denounced him, swearing that she and all leal Dornishmen wanted only peace, thousands flocked to his banners, swarming down from the hills and up out of the sands, through goat tracks in the mountains into the Reach.

"This Vulture King is half-mad, and his followers are a rabble, undisciplined and unwashed," Lord Harmon Dondarrion wrote to the king. "We can smell them coming fifty leagues away." Not long after, that selfsame rabble stormed and seized his castle of Blackhaven. The Vulture King personally sliced off Dondarrion's nose before putting Blackhaven to the torch and marching away.

King Aenys knew these rebels had to be put down, but seemed unable to decide where to begin. Grand Maester Gawen wrote that the king seemed unable to comprehend why this was happening. The smallfolk loved him, did they not? Jonos Arryn, this new Lodos, the Vulture King . . . had he wronged them? If they had grievances, why not bring them to him? "I would have heard them out," he said. He spoke of sending messengers to the rebels, to learn the reasons for their actions. Fearing that King's Landing might not be safe with Harren the Red alive and near, he sent his wife and children to Dragonstone. He commanded his Hand, Lord Alyn Stokeworth, to take a fleet and army to the Vale to put down Jonos Arryn and restore his brother Ronnel to the lordship. But when the ships were about to sail, he countermanded the order, fearing that Stokeworth's departure would leave King's Landing undefended. Instead he sent the Hand with but a few hundred men to hunt down Harren the Red, and decided he would summon a great council to discuss how best to put down the other rebels.

Whilst the king prevaricated, his lords took to the field. Some acted on their own authority, others in concert with the Dowager Queen. In the Vale, Lord Allard Royce of Runestone assembled twoscore loyal lords and marched against the Eyrie, easily defeating the supporters of the self-styled King of Mountain and Vale. But when they demanded the release of their rightful lord, Jonos Arryn sent his brother to them through the Moon Door. Such was the sad end of Ronnel Arryn, who had flown thrice about the Giant's Lance on dragonback. The Eyrie was impregnable to any conventional assault, so "King" Jonos and his die-hard followers spat down defiance at the loyalists, and settled in for a siege ... until Prince Maegor appeared in the sky above, astride Balerion. The Conqueror's son had claimed a dragon at last, and none other than the Black Dread, the greatest of them all.

Rather than face his fires, the Eyrie's garrison seized the pretender and delivered him to Lord Royce, opening the Moon Door once again and serving Jonos the kinslayer as he had served his brother. Surrender saved the pretender's followers from burning, but not from death. After taking possession of the Eyrie, Prince Maegor executed them to a man. Even the highest born amongst them were denied the honor of dying by sword; traitors deserved only a rope, Maegor decreed, so the captured knights were hanged naked from the walls of the Eyrie, kicking as they strangled slowly. Hubert Arryn, a cousin to the dead brothers, was installed as Lord of the Vale. As he had already sired six sons by his lady wife, a Royce of Runestone, the Arryn succession was seen to be secure.

In the Iron Islands, Goren Greyjoy, Lord Reaper of Pyke, brought "King" Lodos (Second of That Name) to a similar swift end, marshaling a hundred longships to descend on Old Wyk and Great Wyk, where the pretender's followers were most numerous, and putting thousands of them to the sword. Afterward he had the head of the priest-king pickled in brine and sent to King's Landing. King Aenys was so pleased by the gift that he offered Greyjoy any boon he might desire. This proved unwise. Lord Goren, wishing to prove himself a true son of the Drowned God, asked the king for the right to expel all the septons and septas who had come to the Iron Islands after the Conquest to convert the ironborn to the worship of the Seven. King Aenys had no choice but to agree.

The largest and most threatening rebellion remained that of the Vulture King along the Dornish marches. Though Princess Deria continued to issue denunciations from Sunspear, there were many who suspected that she was playing a double game, for she did not take the field against the rebels and was rumored to be sending them men, money, and supplies. Whether that was true or not, hundreds of Dornish knights and several thousand seasoned spearmen had joined the Vulture King's rabble, and the rabble itself had swelled enormously, to more than thirty thousand men. So large had his host become that the Vulture King made an ill-considered decision and divided his strength. Whilst he marched west against Nightsong and Horn Hill with half the Dornish power, the other half went east to besiege Stonehelm, seat of House Swann, under the command of Lord Walter Wyl, the son of the Widow-lover.

Both hosts met with disaster. Orys Baratheon, known now as Orys One-Hand, rode forth from Storm's End one last time, to smash the Dornish beneath the walls of Stonehelm. When Walter Wyl was delivered into his hands, wounded but alive, Lord Orys said, "Your father took my hand. I claim yours as repayment." So saying, he hacked off Lord Walter's sword hand. Then he took his other hand, and both his feet as well, calling them his "usury." Strange to say, Lord Baratheon died on the march back to Storm's End, of the wounds he himself had taken during the battle, but his son Davos always said he died content, smiling at the rotting hands and feet that dangled in his tent like a string of onions.

The Vulture King himself fared little better. Unable to capture Nightsong, he abandoned the siege and marched west, only to have Lady Caron sally forth behind him, to join up with a strong force of marchmen led by Harmon Dondarrion, the mutilated Lord of Blackhaven. Meanwhile Lord Samwell Tarly of Horn Hill suddenly appeared athwart the Dornish line of march with several thousand knights and archers. "Savage Sam," that lord was called, and so he proved in the bloody battle that ensued, cutting down dozens of Dornishmen with his great Valyrian steel blade, Heartsbane. The Vulture King had twice as many men as his three foes combined, but most were untrained and undisciplined, and when faced with armored knights at front and rear, their ranks shattered. Throwing down their spears and shields, the Dornish broke and ran, making for the distant mountains, but the marcher lords rode after them and cut them down, in what became known after as "the Vulture Hunt."

As for the rebel king himself, the man who called himself the Vulture King was taken alive, and tied naked between two posts by Savage Sam Tarly. The singers like to say that he was torn to pieces by the very vultures from whom he took his style, but in truth he perished of thirst and exposure, and the birds did not descend on him until well after he was dead. (In later centuries, several other men would take the title "Vulture King," but whether they were of the same blood as the first, no man can say.)

The first of the rebels proved to be the last as well, but Harren the Red was at last brought to bay in a village west of the Gods Eye. The outlaw king did not die meekly. In his last fight, he slew the King's Hand, Lord Alyn Stokeworth, before being cut down by Stokeworth's squire, Bernarr Brune. A grateful King Aenys conferred knighthood on Brune, and rewarded Davos Baratheon, Samwell Tarly, No-Nose Dondarrion, Ellyn Caron, Allard Royce, and Goren Greyjoy with gold, offices, and honors. The greatest plaudits he bestowed on his own brother. On his return to King's Landing, Prince Maegor was hailed as a hero. King Aenys embraced him before a cheering throng, and named him Hand of the King. And when two young dragons hatched amidst the firepits of Dragonstone at the end of that year, it was taken for a sign.

But the amity between the Dragon's sons did not long endure.

It may be that conflict was inevitable, for the two brothers had very different natures. Kindhearted and soft-spoken, it was said of King Aenys that he loved his wife, his children, and his people, and wished only to be loved in turn. Sword and lance had long ago lost whatever appeal they ever had for him. Instead His Grace dabbled in alchemy, astronomy, and astrology, delighted in music and dance, wore the finest silks, samites, and velvets, and enjoyed the company of maesters, septons, and wits.

His brother Maegor, taller, broader, and fearsomely strong, had no patience for any of that, but lived for war, tourneys, and battle. He was rightly regarded as one of the finest knights in Westeros, though his savagery in the field and his harshness toward defeated foes was oft remarked upon as well. King Aenys sought always to please; when faced with difficulties, he would answer with soft words, whereas Maegor's reply was ever steel and fire. Grand Maester Gawen wrote that Aenys trusted everyone, Maegor no one. The king was easily influenced, Gawen observed, swaying this way and that like a reed into the wind, like as not to heed whichever councillor last had his ear. Prince Maegor, on the other hand, was rigid as an iron rod, unyielding, unbending.

Despite such differences, the sons of the Dragon continued to rule together amicably for the best part of two years. But in 39 AC, Queen

Alyssa gave King Aenys yet another heir, a girl she named Vaella, who sadly died in the cradle not long after. Perhaps it was this continued proof of the queen's fertility that drove Prince Maegor to do what he did. Whatever the reason, the prince shocked the realm and the king both when he suddenly announced that Lady Ceryse was barren, and he had therefore taken a second wife in Alys Harroway, daughter of the new Lord of Harrenhal. The wedding was performed on Dragonstone, under the aegis of the Dowager Queen Visenya. As the castle septon refused to officiate, Maegor and his new bride were wed in a Valyrian rite, "wed by blood and fire."

The marriage took place without the leave, knowledge, or presence of King Aenys. When it became known, the two half brothers quarreled bitterly. Nor was His Grace alone in his wroth. Lord Hightower, father of Lady Ceryse, made protest to the king, demanding that Lady Alys be put aside. And in the Starry Sept at Oldtown, the High Septon went even further, denouncing Maegor's marriage as sin and fornication, and calling the prince's new bride "this whore of Harroway." No true son or daughter of the Seven would ever bow to such, he thundered. Prince Maegor remained defiant. His father had taken both of his sisters to wife, he pointed out; the strictures of the Faith might rule lesser men, but not the blood of the Dragon. No words of King Aenys could heal the wound his brother's words thus opened, and many pious lords throughout the Seven Kingdoms condemned the marriage, and began to speak openly of "Maegor's Whore."

Vexed and angry, King Aenys gave his brother a choice: put Alys Harroway aside and return to Lady Ceryse, or suffer five years of exile. Prince Maegor chose exile. In 40 AC he departed for Pentos, taking Lady Alys, Balerion his dragon, and the sword Blackfyre (it is said that Aenys requested that his brother return Blackfyre, to which request Prince Maegor replied, "Your Grace is welcome to try and take her from me"). Lady Ceryse was left abandoned in King's Landing.

To replace his brother as Hand, King Aenys turned to Septon Murmison, a pious cleric said to be able to heal the sick by the laying on of hands. (The king had him lay hands on Lady Ceryse's belly every night, in the hopes that his brother might repent his folly if his lawful wife could be made fertile, but the lady soon grew weary of the nightly ritual and departed King's Landing for Oldtown, where she rejoined her father in the Hightower.) No doubt His Grace hoped the choice would appease the Faith. If so, he was wrong. Septon Murmison could no more heal the realm than he could make Ceryse Hightower fecund. The High Septon continued to thunder, and all through the realm the lords in their halls spoke of the king's weakness. "How can he rule the Seven Kingdoms when he cannot even rule his brother?" it was said.

Yet the king remained strangely oblivious to the discontent in the realm. Peace had returned, his troublesome brother was safely out of sight across the narrow sea, and a great new castle had begun to rise atop Aegon's High Hill: built all in pale red stone, the king's new seat would be larger and more lavish than Dragonstone, more beautiful than Harrenhal, with massive walls and barbicans and towers capable of withstanding any enemy. The Red Keep, the people of King's Landing named it. Its building had become the king's obsession. "My descendants shall rule from here for a thousand years," His Grace declared. And thinking of those descendants, in 41 AC Aenys Targaryen made a disastrous blunder, and gave the hand of his daughter Rhaena in marriage to her brother Aegon, heir to the Iron Throne.

The princess was eighteen, the prince fifteen. A royal wedding is a joyous event, the occasion for celebration, but this was the sort of incestuous union that the High Septon had warned against, and the Starry Sept condemned it as an obscenity and warned that children born of it would be "abominations in the sight of gods and men." On the day of the wedding, the streets outside the Sept of Remembrance—built by a previous High Septon atop the Hill of Rhaenys, and named in honor of the fallen queen—were lined with Warrior's Sons in gleaming silver armor, scowling at the wedding guests as they passed by, afoot, ahorse, or in litters. The wiser lords, perhaps expecting that, had stayed away.

Those who did come to bear witness saw more than a wedding. At the feast afterward, King Aenys compounded his misjudgment by granting the title Prince of Dragonstone to his heir Aegon. A hush fell over the hall at those words, for all present knew that title had hitherto belonged to Prince Maegor. At the high table, Queen Visenya rose and stalked from the hall without the king's leave. That night she mounted Vhagar and returned to Dragonstone, and it is written that when her dragon passed before the moon, that orb turned as red as blood.

Aenys Targaryen did not seem to comprehend the extent to which he had roused the realm against him. Thinking to win back the favor of the smallfolk, he sent Aegon and Rhaena on a royal progress, only to find that they were jeered wherever they went. Septon Murmison, his Hand, was expelled from the Faith in punishment for performing the nuptials, whereupon the king wrote to the High Septon, asking that His High Holiness restore "my good Murmison," and explaining the long history of brother/sister marriages in old Valyria. The High Septon's reply was so blistering that His Grace went pale when he read it. Far from relenting, the Shepherd of the Faithful addressed Aenys as "King Abomination," declared him a pretender and a tyrant, with no right to rule the Seven Kingdoms.

The Faithful were listening. Less than a fortnight later, as Septon Murmison was crossing the city in his litter, a group of Poor Fellows came swarming from an alley and hacked him to pieces with their axes. The Warrior's Sons began to fortify the Hill of Rhaenys, turning the Sept of Remembrance into their citadel. With the Red Keep still years away from completion, the king decided that his manse atop Visenya's Hill was too vulnerable and made plans to remove himself to Dragonstone with Queen Alyssa and their younger children. It was a wise precaution. Three days before they were to sail, two Poor Fellows scaled the manse's walls and broke into the king's bedchamber. Only the timely intervention of Ser Raymont Baratheon of the Kingsguard saved Aenys from death.

His Grace was trading Visenya's Hill for Visenya herself. On Dragonstone the Queen Dowager famously greeted him with, "You are a fool and a weakling, nephew. Do you think any man would ever have dared speak so to your father? You have a dragon. Use him. Fly to Oldtown and make this Starry Sept another Harrenhal. Or give me leave, and let me roast this pious fool for you. Vhagar grows old, but her fires still burn hot." Aenys would not hear of it. Instead he sent the Queen Dowager to her chambers in Sea Dragon Tower, and ordered her to remain there.

By the end of 41 AC, much of the realm was deep in the throes of a full-fledged rebellion against House Targaryen. The four false kings who had arisen on the death of Aegon the Conqueror now seemed like so many posturing fools against the threat posed by this new rising, for these rebels believed themselves soldiers of the Seven, fighting a holy war against godless tyranny.

Dozens of pious lords throughout the Seven Kingdoms took up the cry, pulling down the king's banners and declaring for the Starry Sept.

The Warrior's Sons seized the gates of King's Landing, giving them control over who might enter and leave the city, and drove the workmen from the unfinished Red Keep. Thousands of Poor Fellows took to the roads, forcing travelers to declare whether they stood with "the gods or the abomination," and remonstrating outside castle gates until their lords came forth to denounce the Targaryen king. Prince Aegon and his wife were forced to abandon their progress, and take shelter in Crakehall castle. An envoy from the Iron Bank of Braavos, sent to Oldtown to treat with Lord Hightower, wrote to the bank to say that the High Septon was "the true king of Westeros, in all but name."

The coming of the new year found King Aenys still on Dragonstone, sick with fear and indecision. His Grace was but thirty-five years of age, but it was said that he looked like a man of sixty, and Grand Maester Gawen reported that he oft took to his bed with loose bowels and stomach cramps. When none of the Grand Maester's cures proved efficacious, the Dowager Queen took charge of the king's care, and Aenys seemed to improve for a time . . . only to suffer a sudden collapse when word reached him that thousands of Poor Fellows had surrounded Crakehall, where his son and daughter were reluctant "guests." Three days later, the king was dead.

Like his father, Aenys Targaryen, the First of His Name, was given over to the flames in the yard at Dragonstone. His funeral was attended by his sons Viserys and Jaehaerys, twelve and seven years of age respectively, and his daughter Alysanne, five. Queen Alyssa sang a dirge for him. The Dowager Queen Visenya was not present. Within an hour of the king's death, she had mounted Vhagar and flown east, across the narrow sea.

When she returned, Prince Maegor was with her, on Balerion.

Maegor descended on Dragonstone only long enough to claim the crown; not the ornate golden crown Aenys had favored, with its images of the Seven, but the iron crown of their father set with its blood-red rubies. His mother placed it on his head, and the lords and knights gathered there knelt as he proclaimed himself Maegor of House Targaryen, First of His Name, King of the Andals, the Rhoynar, and the First Men, and Protector of the Realm.

Only Grand Maester Gawen dared object. By all the laws of inheritance, laws that the Conqueror himself had affirmed after the Conquest, the Iron Throne should pass to King Aenys's son Aegon, the aged maester said. "The Iron Throne will go to the man who has the strength to seize it," Maegor replied. Whereupon he decreed the immediate execution of the Grand Maester, taking off Gawen's old grey head himself with a single swing of Blackfyre. Queen Alyssa and her children were not on hand to witness King Maegor's coronation. She had taken them from Dragonstone within hours of her husband's funeral, crossing to her lord father's castle on nearby Driftmark. When told, Maegor gave a shrug . . . then retired to the Chamber of the Painted Table with a maester, to dictate letters to lords great and small throughout the realm.

A hundred ravens flew within the day. The next day, Maegor flew as well. Mounting Balerion, he crossed Blackwater Bay to King's Landing, accompanied by the Dowager Queen Visenya upon Vhagar. The return of the dragons set off riots in the city, as hundreds tried to flee, only to find the gates closed and barred. The Warrior's Sons held the city walls, the chaos that would be the Red Keep, and the Hill of Rhaenys, where they had made the Sept of Remembrance their own fortress. The Targaryens raised their standards atop Visenya's Hill and called for leal men to gather to them. Thousands did. Visenya Targaryen proclaimed that her son Maegor had come to be their king. "A true king, blood of Aegon the Conqueror, who was my brother, my husband, and my love. If any man questions my son's right to the Iron Throne, let him prove his claim with his body."

The Warrior's Sons were not slow to accept her challenge. Down from the Hill of Rhaenys they rode, seven hundred knights in silvered steel led by their grand captain, Ser Damon Morrigen, called Damon the Devout. "Let us not bandy words," Maegor told him. "Swords will decide this matter." Ser Damon agreed; the gods would grant victory to him whose cause was just, he said. "Let each side have seven champions, as it was done in Andalos of old. Can you find six men to stand beside you?" For Aenys had taken the Kingsguard to Dragonstone, and Maegor stood alone.

The king turned to the crowd. "Who will come and stand beside his king?" he called. Many turned away in fear or pretended that they did not hear, for the prowess of the Warrior's Sons was known to all. But at last one man offered himself: no knight, but a simple man-at-arms who called himself Dick Bean. "I been a king's man since I was a boy," he said. "I mean to die a king's man."

Only then did the first knight step forward. "This bean shames us all," he shouted. "Are there no true knights here? No leal men?" The speaker was Bernarr Brune, the squire who had slain Harren the Red and been knighted by King Aenys himself. His scorn drove others to offer their swords. The names of the four Maegor chose are writ large in the history of Westeros: Ser Bramm of Blackhull, a hedge knight; Ser Rayford Rosby; Ser Guy Lothston, called Guy the Glutton; and Ser Lucifer Massey, Lord of Stonedance.

The names of the seven Warrior's Sons have likewise come down to us. They were: Ser Damon Morrigen, called Damon the Devout, Grand Captain of the Warrior's Sons; Ser Lyle Bracken; Ser Harys Horpe, called Death's Head Harry; Ser Aegon Ambrose; Ser Dickon Flowers, the Bastard of Beesbury; Ser Willam the Wanderer; and Ser Garibald of the Seven Stars, the septon knight. It is written that Damon the Devout led a prayer, beseeching the Warrior to grant strength to their arms.

Afterward the Queen Dowager gave the command to begin. And the issue was joined.

Dick Bean died first, cut down by Lyle Bracken mere instants after the combat began. Thereafter accounts differ markedly. One chronicler says that when the hugely fat Ser Guy the Glutton was cut open, the remains of forty half-digested pies spilled out. Another claims Ser Garibald of the Seven Stars sang a paean as he fought. Several tell us that Lord Massey hacked off the arm of Harys Horpe. In one account, Death's Head Harry tossed his battle-axe into his other hand and buried it between Lord Massey's eyes. Other chroniclers suggest Ser Harys simply died. Some say the fight went on for hours, others that most of the combatants were down and dying in mere moments. All agree that great deeds were done and mighty blows exchanged, until the end found Maegor Targaryen standing alone against Damon the Devout and Willam the Wanderer. Both of the Warrior's Sons were badly wounded, and His Grace had Blackfyre in his hand, but even so, it was a near thing, the singers and maesters are agreed. Even as he fell, Ser Willam dealt the king a terrible blow to the head that cracked his helm and left him insensate. Many thought Maegor dead as well, until his mother removed his broken helm. "The king breathes," she proclaimed. "The king lives." The victory was his.

Seven of the mightiest of the Warrior's Sons were dead, including their commander, but more than seven hundred remained, armed and armored and gathered about the crown of the hill. Queen Visenya commanded her son to be taken to the maesters. As the litter bearers bore him down the hill, the Swords of the Faith dropped to their knees in submission. The Dowager Queen ordered them to return to their fortified sept atop the Hill of Rhaenys.

For twenty-seven days Maegor Targaryen lingered at the point of death, whilst maesters treated him with potions and poultices and septons prayed above his bed. In the Sept of Remembrance, the Warrior's Sons prayed as well, and argued about their course. Some felt the order had no choice but to accept Maegor as king, since the gods had blessed him with victory; others insisted that they were bound by oath to obey the High Septon, and fight on.

The Kingsguard arrived from Dragonstone in the nonce. At the command of the Dowager Queen, they took command of the thousands of Targaryen loyalists in the city and surrounded the Hill of Rhaenys. On Driftmark, the widowed Queen Alyssa proclaimed her own son Aegon the true king. In the Citadel of Oldtown, the archmaesters met in Conclave to debate the succession and choose a new grand maester. Thousands of Poor Fellows streamed toward King's Landing. Those from the west followed the hedge knight Ser Horys Hill, those from the south a gigantic axeman called Wat the Hewer. When the ragged bands encamped about castle Crakehall left to join their fellows on the march, Prince Aegon and Princess Rhaena were finally able to depart. Abandoning their royal progress, they made their way to Casterly Rock, where Lord Lyman Lannister offered them his protection. It was his wife, the Lady Jocasta, who first discerned that Princess Rhaena was with child.

On the twenty-eighth day after the Trial of Seven, a ship arrived from Pentos upon the evening tide, carrying two women and six hundred sellswords. Alys of House Harroway, Maegor Targaryen's second wife, had returned to Westeros . . . but not alone. With her sailed another woman, a pale raven-haired beauty known only as Tyanna of the Tower. Some said the woman was Maegor's concubine. Others named her Lady Alys's paramour. The natural daughter of a Pentoshi magister, Tyanna was a tavern dancer who had risen to be a courtesan. She was rumored to be a poisoner and sorceress as well. Many queer tales were told about her . . . yet as soon as she arrived, Queen Visenya dismissed her son's maesters and septons and gave Maegor over to Tyanna's care.

The next morning, the king awoke, rising with the sun. When Maegor appeared on the walls of the Red Keep, standing between Alys Harroway and Tyanna of Pentos, the crowds cheered wildly, and the city erupted in celebration. But the revels died away when Maegor mounted Balerion and descended upon the Hill of Rhaenys, where seven hundred of the Warrior's Sons were at their morning prayers in the fortified sept. As dragonfire set the building aflame, archers and spearmen waited outside for those who came bursting through the doors. It was said the screams of the burning men could be heard throughout the city, and a pall of smoke lingered over King's Landing for days. Thus did the cream of the Warrior's Sons meet their fiery end. Though other chapters remained in Oldtown, Lannisport, Gulltown, and Stoney Sept, the order would never again approach its former strength.

King Maegor's war against the Faith Militant had just begun, however. It would continue for the remainder of his reign. The king's first act upon resuming the Iron Throne was to command the Poor Fellows swarming toward the city to lay down their weapons, under penalty of proscription and death. When his decree had no effect, His Grace commanded "all leal lords" to take the field and disperse the Faith's ragged hordes by force. In response, the High Septon in Oldtown called upon "true and pious children of the gods" to take up arms in defense of the Faith, and put an end to the reign of "dragons and monsters and abominations."

Battle was joined first in the Reach, at the town of Stonebridge. There nine thousand Poor Fellows under Wat the Hewer found themselves caught between six lordly hosts as they attempted to cross the Mander. With half his men north of the river and half on the south, Wat's army was cut to pieces. His untrained and undisciplined followers, clad in boiled leather, roughspun, and scraps of rusted steel, and armed largely with woodsmen's axes, sharpened sticks, and farm implements, proved utterly unable to stand against the charge of armored knights on heavy horses. So grievous was the slaughter that the Mander ran red for twenty leagues, and thereafter the town and castle where the battle had been fought became known as Bitterbridge. Wat himself was taken alive, though not before slaying half a dozen knights, amongst them Loadows of Grassy Vale, commander of the king's host. The giant was delivered to King's Landing in chains.

By then Ser Horys Hill had reached the Great Fork of the Blackwater with an even larger host; close on thirteen thousand Poor Fellows, their ranks stiffened by the addition of two hundred mounted Warrior's Sons from Stoney Sept, and the household knights and feudal levies of a dozen rebel lords from the westerlands and riverlands. Lord Rupert Falwell, famed as the Fighting Fool, led the ranks of the pious who had answered the High Septon's call; with him rode Ser Lyonel Lorch, Ser Alyn Terrick, Lord Tristifer Wayn, Lord Jon Lychester, and many other puissant knights. The army of the Faithful numbered twenty thousand men.

King Maegor's army was of like size, however, and His Grace had almost twice as much armored horse, as well as a large contingent of longbowmen, and the king himself riding Balerion. Even so, the battle proved a savage struggle. The Fighting Fool slew two knights of the Kingsguard before he himself was cut down by the Lord of Maidenpool. Big Jon Hogg, fighting for the king, was blinded by a sword slash early in the battle, yet rallied his men and led a charge that broke through the lines of the Faithful and put the Poor Fellows to flight. A rainstorm dampened Balerion's fires but could not quench them entirely, and amidst smoke and screams King Maegor descended again and again to serve his foes with flame. By nightfall victory was his, as the remaining Poor Fellows threw down their axes and streamed away in all directions.

Triumphant, Maegor returned to King's Landing to seat himself once more upon the Iron Throne. When Wat the Hewer was delivered to him, chained yet still defiant, Maegor took off his limbs with the giant's own axe, but commanded his maesters to keep the man alive "so he might attend my wedding." Then His Grace announced his intent to take Tyanna of Pentos as his third wife. Though it was whispered that his mother the Queen Dowager had no love for the Pentoshi sorceress, only Grand Maester Myres dared speak against her openly. "Your one true wife awaits you in the Hightower," Myres said. The king heard him out in silence, then descended from the throne, drew Blackfyre, and slew him where he stood.

Maegor Targaryen and Tyanna of the Tower were wed atop the Hill of Rhaenys, amidst the ashes and bones of the Warrior's Sons who had died there. It was said that Maegor had to put a dozen septons to death before he found one willing to perform the ceremony. Wat the Hewer, limbless, was kept alive to witness the marriage. King Aenys's widow, Queen Alyssa, was present as well, with her younger sons Viserys and Jaehaerys and her daughter Alysanne. A visit from the Dowager Queen and Vhagar had persuaded her to leave her sanctuary on Driftmark and return to court, where Alyssa and her brothers and cousins of House Velaryon did homage to Maegor as the true king. The widowed queen was even compelled to join the other ladies of the court in disrobing His Grace and escorting him to the nuptial chamber to consummate his marriage, a bedding ceremony presided over by the king's second wife, Alys Harroway. That task done, Alyssa and the other ladies took their leave of the royal bedchamber, but Alys remained, joining the king and his newest wife in a night of carnal lust.

Across the realm in Oldtown, the High Septon was loud in his denunciations of "the abomination and his whores," whilst the king's first wife, Ceryse of House Hightower, continued to insist that she was Maegor's only lawful queen. And in the westerlands, Aegon Targaryen, Prince of Dragonstone, remained adamant as well. As the eldest son of King Aenys, the Iron Throne was his by right. Prince Aegon was but seventeen, however, and the son of a weak father besides; few lords cared to risk King Maegor's wroth by supporting his claim. His own mother Queen Alyssa had abandoned his cause, men whispered to each other. Even Lyman Lannister, the prince's host, would not pledge his sword to the young pretender though he did stand firm when Maegor demanded that Aegon and his sister be expelled from Casterly Rock.

And thus it was there at Casterly Rock that Princess Rhaena gave birth to Aegon's daughters, twins they named Aerea and Rhaella. From the Starry Sept came another blistering proclamation. These children too were abominations, the High Septon proclaimed, the fruits of lust and incest, and accursed of the gods.

The dawn of the year 43 AC found King Maegor in King's Landing, where he had taken personal charge of the construction of the Red Keep. Much of the finished work was now undone or changed, new builders and workmen were brought in, and secret passages and tunnels crept through the depths of Aegon's High Hill. As the red stone towers rose, the king commanded the building of a castle within the castle, a fortified redoubt surrounded by a dry moat that would soon be known to all as Maegor's Holdfast.

In that same year, Maegor made Lord Lucas Harroway, father of his wife Queen Alys, his new Hand ... but it was not the Hand who had the king's ear. His Grace might rule the Seven Kingdoms, men whispered, but he himself was ruled by the three queens: his mother Queen Visenya, his paramour Queen Alys, and the Pentoshi witch Queen Tyanna. "The mistress of whispers," Tyanna was called, and "the king's raven," for her black hair. She spoke with rats and spiders, it was said, and all the vermin of King's Landing came to her by night to tell tales of any fool rash enough to speak against the king.

Meanwhile, thousands of Poor Fellows still haunted the roads and wild places of the Reach, the Trident, and the Vale; though they would never again assemble in large numbers to face the king in open battle, the Stars fought on in smaller ways, falling upon travelers and swarming over towns, villages, and poorly defended castles, slaying the king's loyalists wherever they found them. Ser Horys Hill had escaped the battle at Great Fork, but defeat and flight had tarnished him, and his followers were few. The new leaders of the Poor Fellows were men like Ragged Silas, Septon Moon, and Dennis the Lame, hardly distinguishable from outlaws. One of their most savage captains was a woman called Poxy Jeyne Poore, whose savage followers made the woods between King's Landing and Storm's End all but impassable to honest travelers.

Meanwhile, the Warrior's Sons had chosen a new grand captain in the person of Ser Joffrey Doggett, the Red Dog of the Hills, who was determined to restore the order to its former glory. When Ser Joffrey set out from Lannisport to seek the blessing of the High Septon, a hundred men rode with him. By the time he arrived in Oldtown, so many knights and squires and freeriders had joined him that his numbers had swollen to two thousand. Elsewhere in the realm, other restless lords and men of faith were gathering men as well, and plotting ways to bring the dragons down.

None of this had gone unnoticed. Ravens flew to every corner of the realm, summoning lords and landed knights of doubtful loyalty to King's Landing, to bend the knee, swear homage, and deliver a son or daughter as a hostage for their obedience. The Stars and Swords were outlawed; membership in either order would henceforth be punishable by death. The High Septon was commanded to deliver himself to the Red Keep, to stand trial for high treason.

His High Holiness responded from the Starry Sept, commanding the king to present himself in Oldtown, to beg the forgiveness of the gods for his sins and cruelties. Many of the Faithful echoed his defiance.

Some pious lords did travel to King's Landing to do homage and present hostages, but more did not, trusting to their numbers and the strength of their castles to keep them safe.

King Maegor let the poisons fester for almost half a year, so engrossed was he in the building of his Red Keep. It was his mother who struck first. The Dowager Queen mounted Vhagar and brought fire and blood to the Reach as once she had to Dorne. In a single night, the seats of House Blanetree, House Terrick, House Deddings, House Lychester, and House Wayn were set aflame. Then Maegor himself took wing, flying Balerion to the westerlands, where he burned the castles of the Broomes, the Falwells, the Lorches, the Myatts, and the other "pious lords" who had defied his royal summons. Lastly he descended upon the seat of House Doggett, reducing the hall and stables to ash. The fires claimed the lives of Ser Joffrey's father, mother, and young sister, along with their sworn swords, serving men, and chattel. As pillars of smoke rose all through the westerlands and the Reach, Vhagar and Balerion turned south. Another Lord Hightower, counseled by another High Septon, had opened the gates of Oldtown during the Conquest, but now it seemed as if the greatest and most populous city in Westeros must surely burn.

Thousands fled the city that night, streaming from the gates or taking ship for distant ports. Thousands more took to the streets in drunken revelry. "This is a night for song and sin and drink," men told one another, "for come the morrow, the virtuous and the vile alike shall burn together." Others gathered in septs and temples and ancient woods to pray they might be spared. In the Starry Sept, the High Septon railed and thundered, calling down the wroth of the gods upon the Targaryens. The archmaesters of the Citadel met in Conclave. The men of the City Watch filled sacks with sand and pails with water to fight the fires they knew were coming. Along the city walls, crossbows, scorpions, spitfires, and spear-throwers were hoisted onto the battlements in hopes of bringing down the dragons when they appeared. Led by Ser Morgan Hightower, a younger brother of the Lord of Oldtown, two hundred Warrior's Sons spilled forth from their chapterhouse to defend His High Holiness, surrounding the Starry Sept with a ring of steel. Atop the Hightower, the great beacon fire turned a baleful green as Lord Martyn Hightower called his banners. Oldtown waited for the dawn, and the coming of the dragons.

And the dragons came. Vhagar first, as the sun was rising, then Balerion, just before midday. But they found the gates of the city open, the battle-ments unmanned, and the banners of House Targaryen, House Tyrell, and House Hightower flying side by side atop the city walls. The Dowager Queen Visenya was the first to learn the news. Sometime during the blackest hour of that long and dreadful night, the High Septon had died.

A man of three-and-fifty, as tireless as he was fearless, and to all appearances in robust good health, this High Septon had been renowned for his strength. More than once he had preached for a day and a night without taking sleep or nourishment. His sudden death shocked the city and dismayed his followers. Its causes are debated to this day. Some say that His High Holiness took his own life, in what was either the act of a craven afraid to face the wroth of King Maegor or a noble sacrifice to spare the goodfolk of Oldtown from dragonfire. Others claim the Seven struck him down for the sin of pride, for heresy, treason, and arrogance.

Many and more remain certain he was murdered . . . but by whom? Ser Morgan Hightower did the deed at the command of his lord brother, some say (and Ser Morgan was seen entering and leaving the High Septon's privy chambers that night). Others point to the Lady Patrice Hightower, Lord Martyn's maiden aunt and a reputed witch (who did indeed seek an audience with His High Holiness at dusk, though he was alive when she departed). The archmaesters of the Citadel are also suspected, though whether they made use of the dark arts, an assassin, or a poisoned scroll is still a matter of some debate (messages went back and forth between the Citadel and the Starry Sept all night). And there are still others who hold them all blameless and lay the High Septon's death at the door of another rumored sorceress, the Dowager Queen Visenya Targaryen.

The truth will likely never be known . . . but the swift reaction of Lord Martyn when word reached him at the Hightower is beyond dispute. At once he dispatched his own knights to disarm and arrest the Warrior's Sons, amongst them his own brother. The city gates were opened, and Targaryen banners raised along the walls. Even before Vhagar's wings were sighted, Lord Hightower's men were rousting the Most Devout from their beds and marching them to the Starry Sept at spearpoint to choose a new high septon.

It required but a single ballot. Almost as one, the wise men and women of the Faith turned to a certain Septon Pater. Ninety years old, blind, stooped, and feeble, but famously amiable, the new High Septon almost collapsed beneath the weight of the crystal crown when it was placed upon his head ... but when Maegor Targaryen appeared before him in the Starry Sept, he was only too pleased to bless him as king and anoint his head with holy oils, even if he did forget the words of the blessing.

Queen Visenya soon returned to Dragonstone with Vhagar, but King Maegor remained in Oldtown for almost half the year, holding court and presiding over trials. To the captive Swords of the Warrior's Sons, a choice was given. Those who renounced their allegiance to the order would be permitted to travel to the Wall and live out their days as brothers of the Night's Watch. Those who refused could die as martyrs to their Faith. Three-quarters of the captives chose to take the black. The remainder died. Seven of their number, famous knights and the sons of lords, were given the honor of having King Maegor himself remove their heads with Blackfyre. The rest of the condemned were beheaded by their own former brothers-in-arms. Of all their number, only one man received a full royal pardon: Ser Morgan Hightower. The new High Septon formally dissolved both the Warrior's Sons and the Poor Fellows, commanding their remaining members to lay down their arms in the name of the gods. The Seven had no more need of warriors, proclaimed His High Holiness; henceforth the Iron Throne would protect and defend the Faith. King Maegor granted the surviving members of the Faith Militant till year's end to surrender their weapons and give up their rebellious ways. After that, those who remained defiant would find a bounty on their heads: a gold dragon for the head of any unrepentant Warrior's Son, a silver stag for the "lice-ridden" scalp of a Poor Fellow.

The new High Septon did not demur, nor did the Most Devout.

During his time at Oldtown, the king was also reconciled with his first wife, Queen Ceryse, the sister of his host, Lord Hightower. Her Grace agreed to accept the king's other wives, to treat them with respect and honor and speak no further ill against them, whilst Maegor swore to restore Ceryse to all the rights, incomes, and privileges due her as his wedded wife and queen. A great feast was held at the Hightower to celebrate their reconciliation; the revels even included a bedding and a "second consummation," so all men would know this to be a true and loving union.

How long King Maegor might have lingered at Oldtown cannot be known, for in the latter part of 43 AC word of another challenge to his throne reached his ears. His nephew Aegon, Prince of Dragonstone, had emerged from the west at last to stake his claim to the Iron Throne. Mounted on his own dragon Quicksilver, the eldest son of the late King Aenys had denounced his uncle as a tyrant and usurper, and was marching across the riverlands at the head of an army fifteen thousand strong. His followers were largely westermen and river lords; the Lords Tarbeck, Piper, Roote, Vance, Charlton, Frey, Paege, Parren, and Westerling were amongst them, joined by Lord Corbray of the Vale, the Bastard of Barrowton, and the fourth son of the Lord of Griffin's Roost.

Though their ranks included seasoned commanders and puissant knights, no great lords had rallied to Prince Aegon's cause ... but Queen Tyanna, mistress of whisperers, wrote to warn Maegor that Storm's End, the Eyrie, Winterfell, and Casterly Rock had all been in secret communication with the widowed queen, Alyssa. Before declaring for the Prince of Dragonstone, they wished to be convinced he might prevail. Aegon required a victory.

Maegor denied him that. From Harrenhal came forth Lord Harroway, from Riverrun Lord Tully. Ser Davos Darklyn of the Kingsguard marshaled five thousand swords in King's Landing and struck out west to meet the rebels. Up from the Reach came Lord Rowan, Lord Merryweather, Lord Caswell, and their levies. Prince Aegon's slow-moving host found armies closing from all sides; each smaller than their own force, but so many that the young prince (still but seventeen) did not know where to turn. Lord Corbray advised him to engage each foe separately before they could join their powers, but Aegon was loath to divide his strength. Instead he chose to march on toward King's Landing.

Just south of the Gods Eye, he found Davos Darklyn's Kingslanders athwart his path, sitting on high ground behind a wall of spears, even as scouts reported Lords Merryweather and Caswell advancing from the south, and Lords Tully and Harroway from the north. Prince Aegon ordered a charge, hoping to break through the Kingslanders before the other loyalists fell upon his flanks, and mounted Quicksilver to lead the attack himself. But scarce had he taken wing when he heard shouts and saw his men below pointing, to where Balerion the Black Dread had appeared in the southern sky.

King Maegor had come.

For the first time since the Doom of Valyria dragon contended with dragon in the sky, even as battle was joined below.

Quicksilver, a quarter the size of Balerion, was no match for the older, fiercer dragon, and her pale white fireballs were engulfed and washed away in great gouts of black flame. Then the Black Dread fell upon her from above, his jaws closing round her neck as he ripped one wing from her body. Screaming and smoking, the young dragon plunged to earth, and Prince Aegon with her.

The battle below was nigh as brief, if bloodier. Once Aegon fell, the rebels saw their cause was doomed and ran, discarding arms and armor as they fled. But the loyalist armies were all around them, and there was no escape. By day's end, two thousand of Aegon's men had died, against a hundred of the king's. Amongst the dead were Lord Alyn Tarbeck, Denys Snow, the Bastard of Barrowton, Lord Jon Piper, Lord Ronnel Vance, Ser Willam Whistler ... and Aegon Targaryen, Prince of Dragonstone. The only notable loss amongst the loyalists was Ser Davos Darklyn of the Kingsguard, slain by Lord Corbray with Lady Forlorn. Half a year of trials and executions followed. Queen Visenya persuaded her son to spare some of the rebellious lords, but even those who kept their lives lost lands and titles and were forced to give up hostages.

The forty-fourth year After the Conquest was a peaceful one, compared to what had gone before ... but the maesters who chronicled those times wrote that the smell of blood and fire still hung heavy in the air. Maegor I Targaryen sat the Iron Throne as his Red Keep rose around him, but his court was grim and cheerless, despite the presence of three queens ... or perhaps because of it. Each night he summoned one of his wives to his bed, yet still he remained childless, with no heir but for the sons and grandsons of his brother Aenys. "Maegor the Cruel," he was called, and "kinslayer" as well, though it was death to say either in his hearing.

In Oldtown, the ancient High Septon died, and another was raised up in his place. Though he spoke no word against the king or his queens, the enmity between King Maegor and the Faith endured. Hundreds of Poor Fellows had been hunted down and slain, their scalps delivered to the king's men for the bounty, but thousands more still roamed the woods and hedges and the wild places of the Seven Kingdoms, cursing the Targaryens with their every breath. One band even crowned their own High Septon, in the person of a bearded brute named Septon Moon.

And a few Warrior's Sons still endured, led by Ser Joffrey Doggett, the Red Dog of the Hills. Outlawed and condemned, the order no longer had the strength to meet the king's men in open battle, so the Red Dog sent them out in the guise of hedge knights, to hunt and slay Targaryen loyalists and "traitors to the Faith." Their first victim was Ser Morgan Hightower, late of their order, cut down and butchered on the road to Honeyholt. Old Lord Merryweather was the next to die, followed by Lord Rowan's son and heir, Davos Darklyn's aged father, even Blind John Hogg. Though the bounty for the head of a Warrior's Son was a golden dragon, the smallfolk and peasants of the realm hid and protected them, remembering what they had been.

On Dragonstone, the Dowager Queen Visenya had grown thin and haggard, the flesh melting from her bones. Her nephew's widow, the former Queen Alyssa, remained on the island as well, with her son Jaehaerys and her daughter Alysanne. Maegor had made them his mother's wards, prisoners in all but name, but Prince Viserys, the eldest surviving son of Aenys and Alyssa, was summoned to court by Maegor. A promising lad of fifteen years, skilled with sword and lance, Viserys was made squire to the king . . . with a Kingsguard knight for a shadow, to keep him away from plots and treasons.

For a brief while in 44 AC, it seemed as if the king might soon have that son he desired so desperately. Queen Alys announced she was with child, and the court rejoiced. Grand Maester Desmond confined Her Grace to her bed as she grew great with child, and took charge of her care, assisted by two septas, a midwife, and the queen's sisters Jeyne and Hanna. Maegor insisted that his other wives serve his pregnant queen as well.

During the third moon of her confinement, however, Lady Alys began to bleed heavily from the womb and lost the child. When King Maegor came to see the stillbirth, he was horrified to find the boy a monster, with twisted limbs, a huge head, and no eyes. "This cannot be my son," he roared in anguish. Then his grief turned to fury, and he ordered the immediate execution of the midwife and septas who had charge of the queen's care, and Grand Maester Desmond as well, sparing only Alys's sisters.

It is said that Maegor was seated on the Iron Throne with the head of the grand maester in his hands when Queen Tyanna came to tell him he had been deceived. The child was not his seed. Seeing Queen Ceryse return to court, old and bitter and childless, Alys Harroway had begun to fear that the same fate awaited her unless she gave the king a son, so she had turned to her lord father, the Hand of the King. On the nights when the king was sharing a bed with Queen Ceryse or Queen Tyanna, Lucas Harroway sent men to his daughter's bed to get her with child. Maegor refused to believe. He told Tyanna she was a jealous witch, and barren, throwing the grand maester's head at her. "Spiders do not lie," the mistress of the whisperers replied. She handed the king a list of names.

Written there were the names of twenty men alleged to have given their seed to Queen Alys. Old men and young, handsome men and homely ones, knights and squires, lords and servants, even grooms and smiths and singers; the King's Hand had cast a wide net, it seemed. The men had only one thing in common: all were men of proven potency known to have fathered healthy children.

Under torture, all but two confessed. One, a father of twelve, still had the gold paid him by Lord Harroway for his services. The questioning was carried out swiftly and secretly, so Lord Harroway and Queen Alys had no inkling of the king's suspicions until the Kingsguard burst in on them. Dragged from her bed, Queen Alys saw her sisters killed before her eyes as they tried to protect her. Her father, inspecting the Tower of the Hand, was flung from its roof to smash upon the stones below. Harroway's sons, brothers, and nephews were taken as well. Thrown onto the spikes that lined the dry moat around Maegor's Holdfast, some took hours to die; the simple-minded Horas Harroway was said to linger for days. The twenty names on Queen Tyanna's list soon joined them, and then another dozen men, named by the first twenty.

The worst death was reserved for Queen Alys herself, who was given over to her sister wife Tyanna for torment. Of her death we will not speak, for some things are best buried and forgotten. Suffice it to say that her dying took the best part of a fortnight, and that Maegor himself was present for all of it, a witness to her agony. After her death, the queen's body was cut into seven parts, and her pieces mounted on spikes above the seven gates of the city, where they remained until they rotted.

King Maegor himself departed King's Landing, assembling a strong force of knights and men-at-arms and marching on Harrenhal, to complete the destruction of House Harroway. The great castle on the Gods Eye was lightly held, and its castellan, a nephew of Lord Lucas and cousin to the late queen, opened his gates at the king's approach. Surrender did not save him; His Grace put the entire garrison to the sword, along with every man, woman, and child he found to have any drop of Harroway blood. Then he marched to Lord Harroway's Town on the Trident and did the same there.

In the aftermath of the bloodletting, men began to say that Harrenhal was cursed, for every lordly house to hold it had come to a bad and bloody end. Nonetheless, many ambitious king's men coveted Black Harren's mighty seat, with its broad and fertile lands ... so many that King Maegor grew weary of their entreaties and decreed that Harrenhal should go to the strongest of them. Thus did twenty-three knights of the king's household fight with sword and mace and lance amidst the blood-soaked streets of Lord Harroway's Town. Ser Walton Towers emerged victorious, and Maegor named him Lord of Harrenhal ... but the melee had been a savage affray, and Ser Walton did not live long to enjoy his lordship, dying of his wounds within the fortnight. Harrenhal passed to his eldest son, though its domains were much diminished, as the king granted Lord Harroway's Town to Lord Alton Butterwell, and the rest of the Harroway holdings to Lord Dormand Darry.

When at last Maegor returned to King's Landing to seat himself again upon the Iron Throne, he was greeted with the news that his mother Queen Visenya had died. Moreover, in the confusion that followed the death of the Queen Dowager, Queen Alyssa and her children found their way to a ship and made their escape from Dragonstone ... to where, no man could say. They had even gone so far as to steal Dark Sister from Visenya's chambers as they fled.

His Grace ordered his mother's body burned, her bones and ashes interred beside those of her brother and sister. Then he told his knights to seize his squire, Prince Viserys. "Chain him in a black cell and question him sharply," Maegor commanded. "Ask him where his mother has gone."

"He may not know," said Ser Owen Bush, a knight of Maegor's Kingsguard. "Then let him die," the king answered famously. "Perhaps the bitch will turn up for his funeral."

Prince Viserys did not know where his mother had gone, not even when Tyanna of Pentos plied him with her dark arts. After nine days of questioning, he died. His body was left out in the ward of the Red Keep for a fortnight, at the king's command. "Let his mother come and claim him," Maegor said. But Queen Alyssa never appeared, and at last His

Grace consigned his nephew to the fire. The prince was sixteen years old when he was killed, and had been much loved by smallfolk and lords alike. The realm wept for him.

In 45 AC, construction finally came to an end on the Red Keep.

King Maegor celebrated its completion by feasting the builders and workmen who had labored on the castle, sending them wagonloads of strong wine and sweetmeats, and whores from the city's finest brothels. The revels lasted for three days. Afterward, the king's knights moved in and put all the workmen to the sword, to prevent them from ever revealing the Red Keep's secrets. Their bones were interred beneath the castle that they had built.

Not long after the completion of the castle, Queen Ceryse was stricken with a sudden illness, and passed away. A rumor went around the court that Her Grace had given offense to the king with a shrewish remark, so he had commanded Ser Owen to remove her tongue. As the tale went, the queen had struggled, Ser Owen's knife had slipped, and the queen's throat had been slit. Though never proven, this story was widely believed at the time; today, however, most maesters believe it to be a slander concocted by the king's enemies to further blacken his repute. Whatever the truth, the death of his first wife left Maegor with but a single queen, the black-haired, black-hearted Pentoshi woman Tyanna, mistress of the spiders, who was hated and feared by all.

Hardly had the last stone been set on the Red Keep than Maegor commanded that the ruins of the Sept of Remembrance be cleared from the top of Rhaenys's Hill, and with them the bones and ashes of the Warrior's Sons who had perished there. In their place, he decreed, a great stone "stable for dragons" would be erected, a lair worthy of Balerion, Vhagar, and their get. Thus commenced the building of the Dragonpit. Perhaps unsurprisingly, it proved difficult to find builders, stonemasons, and laborers to work on the project. So many men ran off that the king was finally forced to use prisoners from the city's dungeons as his workforce, under the supervision of builders brought in from Myr and Volantis.

Late in the year 45 AC, King Maegor took the field once again to continue his war against the outlawed remnants of the Faith Militant, leaving Queen Tyanna to rule King's Landing together with the new Hand, Lord Edwell Celtigar. In the great wood south of the Blackwater, the king's forces hunted down scores of Poor Fellows who had taken refuge there, sending many to the Wall and hanging those who refused to take the black. Their leader, the woman known as Poxy Jeyne Poore, continued to elude the king until at last she was betrayed by three of her own followers, who received pardons and knighthoods as their reward.

Three septons traveling with His Grace declared Poxy Jeyne a witch, and Maegor ordered her to be burned alive in a field beside the Wendwater. When the day appointed for her execution came, three hundred of her followers, Poor Fellows and peasants all, burst from the woods to rescue her. The king had anticipated this, however, and his men were ready for the attack. The rescuers were surrounded and slaughtered. Amongst the last to die was their leader, who proved to be Ser Horys Hill, the bastard hedge knight who had escaped the carnage at the Great Fork three years earlier. This time he proved less fortunate.

Elsewhere in the realm, however, the tide of the times had begun to turn against the king. Smallfolk and lords alike had come to despise him for his many cruelties, and many began to give help and comfort to his enemies. Septon Moon, the "High Septon" raised up by the Poor Fellows against the man in Oldtown they called "the High Lickspittle," roamed the riverlands and Reach at will, drawing huge crowds whenever he emerged from the woods to preach against the king. The hill country north of the Golden Tooth was ruled in all but name by the Red Dog, Ser Joffrey Doggett, and neither Casterly Rock nor Riverrun seemed inclined to move against him. Dennis the Lame and Ragged Silas remained at large, and wherever they roamed, smallfolk helped keep them safe. Knights and men-at-arms sent out to bring them to justice oft vanished.

In 46 AC, King Maegor returned to the Red Keep with two thousand skulls, the fruits of a year of campaigning. They were the heads of Poor Fellows and Warrior's Sons, he announced, as he dumped them out beneath the Iron Throne ... but it was widely believed that many of the grisly trophies belonged to simple crofters, field hands, and swineherds guilty of no crime but faith.

The coming of the new year found Maegor still without a son, not even a bastard who might be legitimized. Nor did it seem likely that Queen Tyanna would give him the heir that he desired. Whilst she continued to serve His Grace as mistress of whisperers, the king no longer sought her bed.

It was past time for him to take a new wife, Maegor's counsellors agreed ... but they parted ways on who that wife should be. Grand Maester Benifer suggested a match with the proud and lovely Lady of Starfall, Clarisse Dayne, in the hopes of detaching her lands and House from Dorne. Alton Butterwell, master of coin, offered his widowed sister, a stout woman with seven children. Though admittedly no beauty, he argued, her fertility had been proved beyond a doubt. The King's Hand, Lord Celtigar, had two young maiden daughters, thirteen and twelve years of age respectively. He urged the king to take his pick of them, or marry both if he preferred. Lord Velaryon of Driftmark advised Maegor to send for his niece Princess Rhaena, his brother's daughter and the widow of his brother's son, and take her to wife. By wedding Rhaena, the king would unite their claims and strengthen the royal bloodline.

King Maegor listened to each man in turn. Though in the end he scorned most of the women they put forward, some of their reasons and arguments took root in him. He would have a woman of proven fertility, he decided, though not Butterwell's fat and homely sister. He would take more than one wife, as Lord Celtigar urged. Two wives would double his chances of getting a son; three wives would triple it. And one of those wives should surely be his niece; there was wisdom in Lord Velaryon's counsel. Queen Alyssa and her two youngest children remained in hiding (it was thought that they had fled across the narrow sea, to Tyrosh or perhaps Volantis), but they still represented a threat to Maegor's crown and any son he might father. Taking Aenys's daughter to wife would weaken any claims put forward by her younger siblings.

After the death of her husband in the Battle Beneath the Gods Eye, Rhaena Targaryen had acted quickly to protect her daughters. If Prince Aegon had truly been the king, then by law his eldest daughter Aerea stood his heir, and might therefore claim to be the rightful Queen of the Seven Kingdoms ... but Aerea and her sister Rhaella were barely a year old, and Rhaena knew that to trumpet such claims would be tantamount to condemning them to death. Instead, she dyed their hair, changed their names, and sent them from her, entrusting them to certain powerful allies, who would see them fostered in good homes by worthy men who would have no inkling of their true identity. Even their mother must not know where the girls were going, the princess insisted; what she did not know she could not reveal, even under torture.

No such escape was possible for Rhaena Targaryen herself. Though she could change her name, dye her hair, and garb herself in a tavern wench's roughspun or the robes of a septa, there was no disguising her dragon. Dreamfyre was a slender, pale blue she-dragon with silvery markings who had already produced two clutches of eggs, and Rhaena had been riding her since the age of twelve. Dragons are not easily hidden. Instead the princess saddled her, and took them both as far from Maegor as she could, to Fair Isle, where Lord Farman granted her the hospitality of Faircastle, with its tall white towers rising high above the Sunset Sea. And there she rested, reading, praying, wondering how long she would be given before her uncle sent for her. Rhaena never doubted that he would, she said afterward; it was question of when, not if.

The summons came sooner than she would have liked though not as soon as she might have feared. There was no question of defiance. That would only bring the king down on Fair Isle with Balerion. Rhaena had grown fond of Lord Farman, and more than fond of his second son, Androw. She would not repay their kindness with fire and blood. She mounted Dreamfyre and flew to the Red Keep, where she learned that she must marry her uncle, her husband's killer.

And there as well Rhaena met her fellow brides, for this was to be a triple wedding. All three of the new queens-to-be were widows. Lady Jeyne of House Westerling had been married to Lord Alyn Tarbeck, who had marched beside Prince Aegon, and died with him in the Battle Beneath the Gods Eye. A few months later, she had given her late lord a posthumous son. Tall and slender, with lustrous brown hair, Lady Jeyne was being courted by a younger son of the Lord of Casterly Rock when Maegor sent for her, but this meant little and less to the king.

More troubling was the case of Lady Elinor of House Costayne, the fiery red-haired wife of Ser Theo Bolling, a landed knight who had fought for the king in his last campaign against the Poor Fellows. Though only nineteen, Lady Elinor had already given Bolling three sons when the king's eye fell upon her. The youngest boy was still at her breast when their father, Ser Theo, was arrested by two knights of the Kingsguard and charged with conspiring with Queen Alyssa to murder the king and place the boy Jaehaerys on the Iron Throne. Though Bolling protested his innocence, he was found guilty and beheaded the same day. King Maegor gave his widow seven days to mourn, in honor of the gods, then summoned her to tell her they would marry.

At the town of Stoney Sept, Septon Moon appeared to denounce King Maegor's wedding plans, and hundreds of townfolk cheered wildly, but few others dared to raise their voices against His Grace. The High Septon took ship at Oldtown, sailing to King's Landing to perform the marriage rites. On a warm spring day in the forty-seventh year After the Conquest, Maegor Targaryen took three wives in the ward of the Red Keep. Though each of his new queens was garbed and cloaked in the colors of her father's House, the people of King's Landing called them "the Black Brides," for all were widows.

The presence of Lady Jeyne's son and Lady Elinor's three boys at the wedding ensured that they would play their parts in the ceremony, but there were many who expected some show of defiance from Princess Rhaena. Such hopes were quelled when Queen Tyanna appeared, escorting two young girls with silver hair and purple eyes, clad in the red and black of House Targaryen. "You were foolish to think you could hide them from me," Tyanna told the princess. Rhaena bowed her head, and spoke her vows, weeping.

Many queer and contradictory stories are told of the night that followed, and with the passage of so many years it is difficult to separate truth from legends. Did the three Black Brides share a single bed, as some claim? It seems unlikely. Did His Grace visit all three women during the night, and consummate all three unions? Perhaps. Did Princess Rhaena attempt to kill the king with a dagger concealed beneath her pillows, as she later claimed? Did Elinor Costayne scratch the king's back to bloody ribbons as they coupled? Did Jeyne Westerling drink the fertility potion that Queen Tyanna supposedly brought her, or throw it in the older woman's face? Was such a potion ever mixed or offered? The first account of it does not appear until well into the reign of King Jaehaerys, twenty years after both women were dead.

This we know. In the immediate aftermath of the wedding, King Maegor declared Princess Rhaena's daughter Aerea his lawful heir, "until such time as the gods grant me a son," whilst sending her twin sister Rhaella to Oldtown to be raised as a septa. His nephew Jaehaerys, felt by many to be the rightful heir, was expressly disinherited in the same decree. Queen Jeyne's son was confirmed as Lord of Tarbeck Hall, and sent to Casterly Rock to be raised as a ward of House Lannister, and Queen Elinor's elder boys were similarly disposed of, one to the Eyrie, one to Highgarden. The queen's youngest babe was turned over to a wet nurse, as the king found the queen's nursing irksome.

Half a year after the wedding, Lord Celtigar, the King's Hand, announced that Queen Jeyne was with child. Hardly had her belly begun to swell when the king himself revealed that Queen Elinor was also pregnant. Maegor showered both women with gifts and honors, and granted new lands and offices to their fathers, brothers, and uncles, but his joy proved to be short-lived. Three moons before she was due, Queen Jeyne was brought to bed by a sudden onset of labor pains, and was delivered of a stillborn child as monstrous as the one Alys Harroway had birthed, a legless and armless creature possessed of both male and female genitals. Nor did the mother long survive the child.

Maegor was cursed, men said. He had slain his nephew, made war against the Faith and the High Septon, defied the gods, committed murder and incest, adultery and rape. His privy parts were poisoned, his seed full of worms, the gods would never grant him a living son. Or so the whispers ran. Maegor himself settled on a different explanation, and sent Ser Owen Bush and Ser Maladon Moore to seize Queen Tyanna and deliver her to the dungeons.

There the Pentoshi queen made a full confession, even as the king's torturers readied their implements: she had poisoned Jeyne Westerling's child in the womb, just as she had Alys Harroway's. It would be the same with Elinor Costayne's whelp, she promised.

It is said that the king slew her himself, cutting out her heart with Blackfyre and feeding it to his dogs. But even in death, Tyanna of the Tower had her revenge, for it came to pass just as she had promised. The moon turned and turned again, and in the black of night Queen Elinor too was delivered of a malformed and stillborn child, an eyeless boy born with rudimentary wings.

That was in the forty-eighth year After the Conquest, the sixth year of King Maegor's reign and the last year of his life. No man in the Seven Kingdoms could doubt that the king was accursed now. What followers still remained to him began to melt away, evaporating like dew in the morning sun. Word reached King's Landing that Ser Joffrey Doggett had been seen entering Riverrun, not as a captive but as a guest of Lord Tully. Septon Moon appeared once more, leading thousands of the Faithful on a march across the Reach to Oldtown, with the announced intent of bearding the Lickspittle in the Starry Sept to demand that he denounce "the Abomination on the Iron Throne," and lift his ban on the military orders. When Lord Oakheart and Lord Rowan appeared before him with their levies, they came not to attack Moon but to join him. Lord Celtigar resigned as King's Hand and returned to his seat on Claw Isle.

Reports from the Dornish marches suggested that the Dornishmen were gathering in the passes, preparing to invade the realm.

The worst blow came from Storm's End. There on the shores of Shipbreaker Bay, Lord Rogar Baratheon proclaimed young Jaehaerys Targaryen to be the true and lawful king of the Andals, the Rhoynar, and the First Men, and Prince Jaehaerys named Lord Rogar Protector of the Realm and Hand of the King. The prince's mother Queen Alyssa and his sister Alysanne stood beside him as Jaehaerys unsheathed Dark Sister and vowed to end the reign of his usurping uncle. A hundred banner lords and stormland knights cheered the proclamation. Prince Jaehaerys was fourteen years old when he claimed the throne: a handsome youth, skilled with lance and longbow, and a gifted rider. More, he rode a great bronze and tan beast called Vermithor, and his sister Alysanne, a maid of twelve, commanded her own dragon, Silverwing. "Maegor has only one dragon," Lord Rogar told the stormlords. "Our prince has two."

And soon three. When word reached the Red Keep that Jaehaerys was gathering his forces at Storm's End, Rhaena Targaryen mounted Dreamfyre and flew to join him, abandoning the uncle she had been forced to wed. She took her daughter Aerea . . . and Blackfyre, stolen from the king's own scabbard as he slept.

King Maegor's response was sluggish and confused. He commanded the Grand Maester to send forth his ravens, summoning all his leal lords and bannermen to gather at King's Landing, only to find that Benifer had taken ship for Pentos. Finding Princess Aerea gone, he sent a rider to Oldtown to demand the head of her twin sister Rhaella, to punish their mother for her betrayal, but Lord Hightower imprisoned his messenger instead. Two of his Kingsguard vanished one night, to go over to Jaehaerys, and Ser Owen Bush was found dead outside a brothel, his member stuffed into his mouth.

Lord Velaryon of Driftmark was amongst the first to declare for Jaehaerys. As the Velaryons were the realm's traditional admirals, Maegor woke to find he had lost the entire royal fleet. The Tyrells of Highgarden followed, with all the power of the Reach. The Hightowers of Oldtown, the Redwynes of the Arbor, the Lannisters of Casterly Rock, the Arryns of the Eyrie, the Royces of Runestone ... one by one, they came out against the king.

In King's Landing, a score of lesser lords gathered at Maegor's command, amongst them Lord Darklyn of Duskendale, Lord Massey of Stonedance, Lord Towers of Harrenhal, Lord Staunton of Rook's Rest, Lord Bar Emmon of Sharp Point, Lord Buckwell of the Antlers, the Lords Rosby, Stokeworth, Hayford, Harte, Byrch, Rollingford, Bywater, and Mallery. Yet they commanded scarce four thousand men amongst them all, and only one in ten of those were knights.

Maegor brought them together in the Red Keep one night to discuss his plan of battle. When they saw how few they were, and realized that no great lords were coming to join them, many lost heart, and Lord Hayford went so far as to urge His Grace to abdicate and take the black. His Grace ordered Hayford beheaded on the spot and continued the war council with his lordship's head mounted on a lance behind the Iron Throne. All day the lords made plans, and late into the night. It was the hour of the wolf when at last Maegor allowed them to take their leave. The king remained behind, brooding on the Iron Throne as they departed. Lord Towers and Lord Rosby were the last to see His Grace.

Hours later, as dawn was breaking, the last of Maegor's queens came seeking after him. Queen Elinor found him still upon the Iron Throne, pale and dead, his robes soaked through with blood. His arms had been slashed open from wrist to elbow on jagged barbs, and another blade had gone through his neck to emerge beneath his chin.

Many to this day believe it was the Iron Throne itself that killed him. Maegor was alive when Rosby and Towers left the throne room, they argue, and the guards at the doors swore that no one entered afterward, until Queen Elinor made her discovery. Some say it was the queen herself who forced him down onto those barbs and blades, to avenge the murder of her first husband. The Kingsguard might have done the deed, though that would have required them to act in concert, as there were two knights posted at each door. It might also have been a person or persons unknown, entering and leaving the throne room through some secret passage. The Red Keep has its secrets, known only to the dead. It may also be that the king tasted despair in the dark watches of the night and took his own life, twisting the blades as needed and opening his veins to spare himself the defeat and disgrace that surely awaited him.

The reign of King Maegor I Targaryen, known to history and legend as Maegor the Cruel, lasted six years and sixty-six days. Upon his death his corpse was burned in the yard of the Red Keep, his ashes interred afterward on Dragonstone beside those of his mother. He died childless, and left no heir of his body.

Nine days later, three dragons were seen in the sky over King's Landing. Princess Rhaena had returned, and with her came her brother Jaehaerys and her sister Alysanne. Their mother, the Dowager Queen Alyssa, arrived a fortnight later, riding beside the Lord of Storm's End at the head of a great host, their banners streaming. The smallfolk cheered. Ravens were sent forth to every castle in the realm, inviting all lords great and small to come to King's Landing to bear witness at the coronation of a new king, a true king.

And they came.

In the forty-eighth year After the Conquest, before the eyes of gods and men and half the lords of Westeros, the High Septon of Oldtown placed his father's golden crown upon the brow of the young prince, and proclaimed him Jaehaerys of House Targaryen, the First of His Name, King of the Andals, the Rhoynar, and the First Men, and Lord of the Seven Kingdoms. His mother Alyssa would act as his regent during the remaining years of the king's minority, whilst Lord Robar Baratheon was named Protector of the Realm and Hand of the King. (Half a year later, the two of them would wed.)

Fourteen years old at his ascent, Jaehaerys would sit the Iron Throne for five-and-fifty years, and in due course become known as "the Old King" and "the Conciliator."

But that is a tale best told at another time, by another maester.

DANGEROUS WOMEN

PARTS I, II, AND III

IN PAPERBACK - OUT NOW

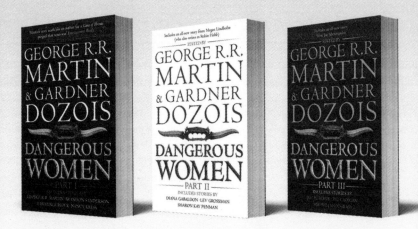